A VOYAGE TO ARCTURUS

David Lindsay (1878–1945) was born the youngest of three children in Blackheath of a Scottish father and an English mother. Brought up in London and with relatives in Jedburgh, Lindsay had to abandon his hopes of taking up a scholarship to university when his father deserted the family. Instead, Lindsay pursued a successful career as an insurance broker for twenty years, though he always nursed hopes of becoming a writer.

During the First World War, Lindsay did his army service with the Grenadier Guards. It was at this time that he married his wife, eighteen years his junior. After the war he resigned his city career and moved to Cornwall to fufill his ambitions as a full-time novelist.

Over the next twenty years Lindsay produced five books and left two unpublished. His first novel *A Voyage to Arcturus* (1920) has become a classic of imaginative fiction. *The Haunted Woman* (1922), like Lindsay's subsequent books, carried a disturbing metaphysical vision into the (apparently) conventional world of middle class society. In the succeeding years he wrote *Sphinx* (1923) and *The Violet Apple*, completed in 1924 and revised two years later, though not published until 1976.

The Lindsays left Cornwall for Ferring, near Worthing in Sussex, where he wrote *Devil's Tor* (1932), the last book to be published in Lindsay's lifetime, and *The Witch* (1976), only part of which has survived. Lindsay became a recluse and died in 1945 from an abscess of the jaw for which he refused medical treatment.

David Lindsay

A VOYAGE TO ARCTURUS

Introduced by
J. B. Pick

CANONGATE
CLASSICS

47

First published in Great Britain 1920 by
Methuen. First published as a Canongate
Classic in 1992 by Canongate Press plc, 14
Frederick Street, Edinburgh EH2 2HB Copy-
right © Victor Gollancz Ltd Introduction ©
1992 J.B. Pick All rights reserved.

British Library Cataloguing-in-Publication Data
A catalogue record for this book is available
on request from the British Library

ISBN 0 86241 377 X

The publishers gratefully acknowledge general
subsidy from the Scottish Arts Council towards
the Canongate Classics series and a specific
grant towards the publication of this title.

Set in 10pt Plantin by Hewer Text Composition
Services Printed and bound in Great Britain by
BPCC Hazells Ltd
Member of BPCC Ltd

Contents

		page
	Introduction	v
I.	The Séance	1
II.	In the Street	15
III.	Starkness	21
IV.	The Voice	26
V.	The Night of Departure	32
VI.	Joiwind	40
VII.	Panawe	57
VIII.	The Lusion Plain	72
IX.	Oceaxe	82
X.	Tydomin	104
XI.	On Disscourn	126
XII.	Spadevil	136
XIII.	The Wombflash Forest	153
XIV.	Polecrab	159
XV.	Swaylone's Island	175
XVI.	Leehallfae	195
XVII.	Corpang	215
XVIII.	Haunte	235
XIX.	Sullenbode	256
XX.	Barey	274
XXI.	Muspel	292

Introduction

A Voyage to Arcturus was first published in 1920, and did not sell. It was not reissued until 1946, a year after its author's death. Since then it has been reprinted several times, and with each appearance has gripped and startled new readers not only for its force as a story but as a ruthless exploration of the meaning of the world.

David Lindsay is unique, yet remains firmly rooted in the Scottish tradition. There is about his work something of the Calvinist extremism which so powerfully dominates Hogg's *Confessions of a Justified Sinner*, and Lindsay himself confessed to the influence of George MacDonald. But what Lindsay and MacDonald have in common is not style, vision, or method, but a passionate concern with the struggle to reach a 'real world' through shadow-worlds of illusion.

Lindsay's books are neither uncontrolled fantasy nor philosophical allegory, but a peculiar embodiment of visionary thought. They were written from a deep layer of the mind which never gained expression in any other way. Although he can tell a story and portray character (as in *The Haunted Woman*, 1922), and show keen social and psychological penetration (as in *Sphinx* 1923), this is peripheral to his intention, which is to convey his burning sense of the nature of reality. Lindsay is reporting on a journey taken outside the normal frames of reference, and to judge him as if he were trying to write science fiction, fantasy, or a tale of adventure, is to miss the point.

The visionary, of course, is not to everyone's taste; it is always possible to characterise any vision as hallucination or delusion, the result of inner conflict. Yet each of us is capable of recognising that although in the past we may have 'thought' this or 'believed' that, there can come a time when we 'see' it alive before us, and 'know it in ourselves'. That is why Lindsay strikes home. *A Voyage to Arcturus* is a profoundly disturbing but authentic view of the world.

The tale is an account of Maskull's pilgrimage through Tormance, a planet of the star Arcturus, guided by mysterious drum-beats to the source of spiritual light. At one moment Maskull says that he voyaged to Tormance because he was 'tired of vulgarity', and at another, 'Every organ tells the same stories; I want to hear different stories.' He is what Lindsay himself would like to have been, a Nietzschean adventurer; but Lindsay's own adventures were entirely in the spirit, his life a catalogue of frustration and disappointment borne with a fierce stoicism.

Although at first reading the style seems disconcertingly dated, and the book grows so wild, uncouth and strange as to prove baffling and difficult, it is best taken not as a problem to be solved, but as a world to be experienced. Maskull remarks, 'I have a simple and unoccupied mind —that may be why I sometimes hear things which up to the present you have not been able to . . .' And indeed a simple and unoccupied mind is the best medium through which an interpretation of the book can be made.

One or two points of guidance may be helpful, nonetheless. Here is Maskull's initial encounter with the drum-beats which lead him to Muspel, the meaning of which destination only grows clear as we stumble on through a wild, dangerous and vivid landscape. The encounter takes place on a cliff-top in Caithness before the Arcturan journey has begun.

> Nothing was to be seen; the gloom had deepened, and the sea was nearly invisible. But, while he was ineffectually gazing, he heard what sounded like the beating of a drum on the narrow strip of shore below. It was very faint, but quite distinct. The beats were in four-time, with the third beat slightly accented. He now continued to hear the noise all the time he was lying there. The beats were in no way drowned by the

far louder sound of the surf, but seemed somehow to
belong to a different world . . .

The relationship between the characters who make the
voyage to Tormance— Maskull, Nightspore, and Krag—is
highly significant. Just before they depart, Maskull hears a
voice, 'a low, sighing whisper', saying, 'Don't you understand, Maskull, that you are only an instrument, to be used
and then broken? Nightspore is asleep now, but when he
wakes you must die . . .' Maskull goes through his adventures passionately involved in their immediacy and power,
and only intermittently conscious of that other 'real' world
to which the drum-beats draw him. Nightspore, on the other
hand, is uninterested in the daily world and concerned only
with his goal. Events prove that Nightspore must be seen
as Maskull's 'second self', who awakens fully at the point
where Maskull encounters for the first time the full force
of Muspel fire.

Muspel, a name from Norse legend used by Lindsay
to designate the source of spiritual light, is contrasted
with the false god of this world, known in the book as
Crystalman. At the end Nightspore sees from the lonely
tower on which he stands the true relationship of Muspel
with Crystalman:

> A flood of fierce light—but it was not light but
> passion—was streaming all the time from Muspel to
> the Shadow, and *through* it. When . . . it emerged on
> the other side . . . it became split, as by a prism . . .
> What had been fiery spirit a moment ago, was now
> a disgusting mass of crawling, wriggling individuals,
> each whirlpool of pleasure-seeking will having as
> nucleus a fragmentary spark of living green fire.

These sparks strive all the time to return to Muspel, but
are whirled and danced from their path by the surrounding
material shape of Crystalman. Crystalman's presence, then,
blinds us all to the Muspel light which is at the very basis
of ourselves, and is indeed our sole reality.

There are strong resemblances here to some of the
doctrines of the medieval Cathars and to those of William

Blake, while the Muspel spark corresponds to the divine principle basic to many traditions from that of the Kabbalah to Tibetan Buddhism; it can be explored through mystical literature to be found in many cultures of our world.

Krag, the third member of the trio of adventurers, is the emissary of Muspel in the world, and brings Maskull and Nightspore to Tormance. It is his function, then, to remind men of their origin.

The characters Maskull meets on Tormance can be seen as representatives of states of being, but they are also embodied adventures. Each in turn captures him temporarily for one delusion after another, and in escaping them he wades through blood. The most powerful of all the delusions, according to Lindsay, is sexual love: Maskull is finally diverted from his pursuit of the drum-beats by his passion for the woman Sullenbode. The result I must leave the reader to find out. In later books sexual love is no longer seen as a delusion but as a form of spiritual awakening, and there is a sense of this in the character of Sullenbode herself.

If that account gives the impression of *A Voyage to Arcturus* as a kind of abstract pilgrim's progress, I can only say that Lindsay himself expressly rejected allegory, and allows his imagination to burn and sport with astonishing power, producing flashing insights as he goes, creating new organs, new plants, even new sexes from page to page. The book is a torrent of vivid incidents, all of a terrifying immediacy.

Let me give just two examples of what is in store. First, here is Lindsay's description of entirely new colours: 'Just as blue is delicate and mysterious, yellow clear and unsubtle, and red sanguine and passionate, so he felt ulfire to be wild and painful, and jale dreamlike, feverish and voluptuous.' And second, here is the creation of a new being: 'When it was directly opposite to Maskull . . . [the cloud's] motion stopped altogether and there was a complete pause . . . Suddenly, like a stab of forked lightning, the great cloud shot together, became small, indented and coloured, and as a plant-animal started walking about on legs and rooting up the ground in search of food.'

Lindsay's key words are 'wildness' and 'grandeur'; his vision is bleak, tonic, and burns with a fierce sincerity. 'Muspel was fighting for its life . . . against all that is most shameful and frightful—against sin masquerading as eternal beauty, against baseness masquerading as nature, against the Devil masquerading as God . . .'

No one who reads this extraordinary book with attention will emerge unscathed. It is the result of many years of pent-up thought and feeling which exploded when Lindsay married, threw up his job in the City of London, and set out to write down all that he had been brooding on. His strength lies in the insistence in all his books that 'the Sublime is not a metaphysical theory, but a terrible fact, which stands above and behind the world . . .' In Lindsay's view, were this not so we would soon cease to bother about novels, poetry, art or music. And indeed recognition of the Sublime as 'a terrible fact' stands at the heart of the Scottish metaphysical tradition in literature, both when it is asserted and when it is denied.

J. B. Pick

CHAPTER ONE

The Séance

On a March evening, at eight o'clock, Backhouse, the medium—a fast-riding star in the psychic world—was ushered into the study at "Prolands," the Hampstead residence of Montague Faull. The room was illuminated only by the light of a blazing fire. The host, eyeing him with indolent curiosity, got up, and the usual conventional greetings were exchanged. Having indicated an easy chair before the fire to his guest, the South-American merchant sank back again into his own. The electric light was switched on. Faull's prominent, clear-cut features, metallic-looking skin, and general air of bored impassiveness, did not seem greatly to impress the medium, who was accustomed to regard men from a special angle. Backhouse, on the contrary, was a novelty to the merchant. As he tranquilly studied him through half-closed lids and the smoke of a cigar, he wondered how this little, thick-set person with the pointed beard contrived to remain so fresh and sane in appearance, in view of the morbid nature of his occupation.

"Do you smoke?" drawled Faull, by way of starting the conversation. "No? Then will you take a drink?"

"Not at present, I thank you."

A pause.

"Everything is satisfactory? The materialisation will take place?"

"I see no reason to doubt it."

"That's good, for I should not like my guests to be disappointed. I have your cheque written out in my pocket."

"Afterwards will do quite well."

"Nine o'clock was the time specified, I believe?"

"I fancy so."

The conversation continued to flag. Faull sprawled in his chair, and remained apathetic.

"Would you care to hear what arrangements I have made?"

"I am unaware that any are necessary, beyond chairs for your guests."

"I mean the decoration of the séance-room, the music, and so forth."

Backhouse stared at his host. "But this is not a theatrical performance."

"That's correct. Perhaps I ought to explain . . . There will be ladies present, and ladies, you know, are aesthetically inclined."

"In that case I have no objection. I only hope they will enjoy the performance to the end."

He spoke rather dryly.

"Well, that's all right, then," said Faull. Flicking his cigar into the fire, he got up and helped himself to whisky.

"Will you come and see the room?"

"Thank you, no. I prefer to have nothing to do with it till the time arrives."

"Then let's go and see my sister, Mrs Jameson, who is in the drawing-room. She sometimes does me the kindness to act as my hostess, as I am unmarried."

"I shall be delighted," said Backhouse coldly.

They found the lady alone, sitting by the open pianoforte, in a pensive attitude. She had been playing Scriabine, and was overcome. The medium took in her small, tight, patrician features and porcelain-like hands, and wondered how Faull came by such a sister. She received him bravely, with just a shade of quiet emotion. He was used to such receptions at the hands of the sex, and knew well how to respond to them.

"What amazes me," she half whispered, after ten minutes of graceful, hollow conversation, "is, if you must know it, not so much the manifestation itself—though that will surely be wonderful—as your assurance that it will take place. Tell me the grounds of your confidence."

"I dream with open eyes," he answered, looking round at the door, "and others see my dreams. That is all."

"But that's beautiful," responded Mrs Jameson. She smiled rather absently, for the first guest had just entered.

It was Kent-Smith, the ex-magistrate, celebrated for his shrewd judicial humour, which, however, he had the good sense not to attempt to carry into private life. Although well on the wrong side of seventy, his eyes were still disconcertingly bright. With the selective skill of an old man, he immediately settled himself in the most comfortable of many comfortable chairs.

"So we are to see wonders tonight?"

"Fresh material for your Autobiography," remarked Faull.

"Ah, you should not have mentioned my unfortunate book. An old public servant is merely amusing himself in his retirement, Mr Backhouse. You have no cause for alarm—I have studied in the school of discretion."

"I am not alarmed. There can be no possible objection to your publishing whatever you please."

"You are most kind," said the old man, with a cunning smile.

"Trent is not coming tonight," remarked Mrs Jameson, throwing a curious little glance at her brother.

"I never thought he would. It's not in his line."

"Mrs Trent, you must understand," she went on, addressing the ex-magistrate, "has placed us all under a debt of gratitude. She has decorated the old lounge-hall upstairs most beautifully, and has secured the services of the sweetest little orchestra."

"But this is Roman magnificence."

"Backhouse thinks the spirits should be treated with more deference," laughed Faull.

"Surely, Mr Backhouse . . . a poetic environment . . ."

"Pardon me. I am a simple man, and always prefer to reduce things to elemental simplicity. I raise no opposition, but I express my opnion. Nature is one thing, and Art is another."

"And I am not sure that I don't agree with you," said the ex-magistrate. "An occasion like this ought to be simple, to guard against the possibility of deception—if you will forgive my bluntness, Mr Backhouse."

"We shall sit in full light," replied Backhouse, "and every opportunity will be given to all to inspect the room. I shall also ask you to submit me to a personal examination."

A rather embarrassed silence followed. It was broken by the arrival of two more guests, who entered together. These were Prior, the prosperous City coffee importer, and Lang, the stock-jobber, well known in his own circle as an amateur prestidigitator. Backhouse was slightly acquainted with the latter. Prior, perfuming the room with the faint odour of wine and tobacco smoke, tried to introduce an atmosphere of joviality into the proceedings. Finding that no one seconded his efforts, however, he shortly subsided and fell to examining the watercolours on the walls. Lang, tall, thin, and growing bald, said little, but stared a good deal at Backhouse.

Coffee, liqueurs, and cigarettes were now brought in. Every one partook, except Lang and the medium. At the same moment, Professor Halbart was announced. He was the eminent psychologist, the author and lecturer on crime, insanity, genius, etc., considered in their mental aspects. His presence at such a gathering somewhat mystified the other guests, but all felt as if the object of their meeting had immediately acquired additional solemnity. He was small, meagre-looking, and mild in manner, but was probably the most stubborn brained of all that mixed company. Completely ignoring the medium, he at once sat down beside Kent-Smith, with whom he began to exchange remarks.

At a few minutes past the appointed hour Mrs Trent entered, unannounced. She was a woman of about eight-and-twenty. She had a white, demure, saint-like face, smooth black hair, and lips so crimson and full that they seemed as if bursting with blood. Her tall, graceful body was most expensively attired. Kisses were exchanged between her and

Mrs Jameson. She bowed to the rest of the assembly, and stole a half-glance and a smile at Faull. The latter gave her a queer look, and Backhouse, who lost nothing, saw the concealed barbarian in the complacent gleam of his eye. She refused the refreshment that was offered her, and Faull proposed that, as every one had now arrived, they should adjourn to the lounge-hall.

Mrs Trent held up a slender palm.

"Did you, or did you not, give me carte blanche, Montague?"

"Of course I did," said Faull, laughing. "But what's the matter?"

"Perhaps I have been rather presumptuous. I don't know. I have invited a couple of friends to join us. No, no one knows them . . . The two most extraordinary individuals you ever saw. And mediums, I am sure."

"It sounds very mysterious. Who are these conspirators?"

"At least tell us their names, you provoking girl," put in Mrs Jameson.

"One rejoices in the name of Maskull, and the other in that of Nightspore. That's nearly all that I know about them, so don't overwhelm me with any more questions."

"But where did you pick them up? You must have picked them up somewhere."

"But this is a cross-examination. Have I sinned against convention? I swear I will tell you not another word about them. They will be here directly, and then I will deliver them to your tender mercy."

"I don't know them," said Faull, "and nobody else seems to, but, of course, we shall all be very pleased to have them . . . Shall we wait, or what?"

"I said nine, and it's past that now. It's quite possible they may not turn up after all . . . Anyway, don't wait."

"I would prefer to start at once," said Backhouse.

The lounge, a lofty apartment, forty feet long by twenty broad, had been divided for the occasion into two equal parts by a heavy brocade curtain drawn across the middle. The far end was thus concealed. The nearer half had been converted into an auditorium by a crescent of armchairs. There was no other furniture. A large fire was burning half-way along the wall, between the chair-backs and the door. The room was brilliantly lighted by electric bracket-lamps. A sumptuous carpet covered the floor.

Having settled his guests in their seats, Faull stepped up to the curtain and flung it aside. A replica, or nearly so, of the Drury Lane presentation of the temple scene in the 'Magic Flute' was then exposed to view. The gloomy, massive architecture of the interior, the glowing sky above it in the background and, silhouetted against the latter, the gigantic seated statue of the Pharaoh. A fantastically-carved wooden couch lay before the pedestal of the statue. Near the curtain, obliquely placed to the auditorium, was a plain oaken armchair, for the use of the medium.

Many of those present privately felt that the setting was quite inappropriate to the occasion and savoured rather unpleasantly of ostentation. Backhouse in particular seemed put out. The usual compliments, however, were showered on Mrs Trent, as the deviser of so remarkable a theatre. Faull invited his friends to step forward and examine the apartment as minutely as they might desire. Prior and Lang were the only ones to accept. The former wandered about among the pasteboard scenery, whistling to himself and occasionally tapping a part of it with his knuckles. Lang, who was in his element, ignored the rest of his party and commenced a patient, systematic search, on his own account, for secret apparatus. Faull and Mrs Trent stood in a corner of the temple, talking together in low tones; while Mrs Jameson, pretending to hold Backhouse in conversation, watched them, as only a deeply-interested woman knows how to watch.

Lang, to his own disgust, having failed to find anything of a suspicious nature, the medium now requested that his own clothing should be searched.

"All these precautions are quite needless and beside the matter in hand, as you will immediately see for yourselves.

My reputation demands, however, that other people who are not present should not be able afterwards to say that trickery has been restored to."

To Lang again fell the ungrateful task of investigating pockets and sleeves. Within a few minutes he expressed himself satisfied that nothing mechanical was in Backhouse's possession. The guests reseated themselves. Faull ordered two more chairs to be brought for Mrs Trent's friends, who, however, had not yet arrived. He then pressed an electric bell, and took his own seat.

The signal was for the hidden orchestra to begin playing. A murmur of surprise passed through the audience as, without previous warning, the beautiful and solemn strains of Mozart's 'Temple' music pulsated through the air. The expectation of everyone was raised, while, beneath her pallor and composure, it could be seen that Mrs Trent was deeply moved. It was evident that aesthetically she was by far the most important person present. Faull watched her, with his face sunk on his chest, sprawling as usual.

Backhouse stood up, with one hand on the back of his chair, and began speaking. The music instantly sank to *pianissimo*, and remained so for as long as he was on his legs.

"Ladies and gentlemen, you are about to witness a materialisation. That means, you will see something appear in space which was not previously there. At first it will appear as a vaporous form, but finally it will be a solid body, which anyone present may feel and handle . . . and, for example, shake hands with. For this body will be in the human shape. It will be a real man or woman—which, I can't say—but a man or woman without known antecedents. If, however, you demand from me an explanation of the origin of this materialised form—where it comes from, whence the atoms and molecules composing its tissues are derived— I am unable to satisfy you. I am about to produce the phenomenon; if anyone can explain it to me afterwards, I shall be very grateful . . . that is all I have to say."

He resumed his seat, half turning his back on the assembly, and paused for a moment before beginning his task.

It was precisely at this minute that the man servant opened the door, and announced in a subdued but distinct voice—"Mr Maskull, Mr Nightspore."

Everyone turned round. Faull rose to welcome the late arrivals. Backhouse also stood up, and stared hard at them.

The two strangers remained standing by the door, which was closed quietly behind them. They seemed to be waiting for the mild sensation caused by their appearance to subside, before advancing into the room. Maskull was a kind of giant, but of broader and robuster physique than most giants. He wore a full beard. His features were thick and heavy, coarsely modelled, like those of a wooden carving; but his eyes, small and black, sparkled with the fires of intelligence and audacity. His hair was short, black, and bristling. Nightspore was of middle height, but so tough-looking that he appeared as if trained out of all human frailties and susceptibilities. His hairless face seemed consumed by an intense spiritual hunger, and his eyes were wild and distant. Both men were dressed in tweeds.

Before any words were spoken, a loud and terrible crash of falling masonry caused the assembled party to start up from their chairs in consternation. It sounded as if the entire upper part of the building had collapsed. Faull sprang to the door, and called to the servant to say what was happening. The man had to be questioned twice before he gathered what was required of him. He said he had heard nothing. In obedience to his master's order, he went upstairs. Nothing, however, was amiss there, neither had the maids heard anything.

In the meantime Backhouse, who almost alone of those assembled had preserved his sang-froid, went straight up to Nightspore, who stood gnawing his nails.

"Perhaps you can explain it, sir?"

"It was supernatural," said Nightspore, in a harsh, muffled voice, turning away from his questioner.

"I guessed so. It is a familiar phenomenon, but I have never heard it so loud."

He then went among the guests, reassuring them. By degrees they settled down, but it was observable that their former easy and good-humoured interest in the proceedings was now changed to strained watchfulness. Maskull and Nightspore took the places allotted to them. Mrs Trent kept stealing uneasy glances at them. Throughout the entire incident, Mozart's Hymn continued to be played. The orchestra also had heard nothing.

Backhouse now entered on his task. It was one that began to be familiar to him, and he had no anxiety about the result. It was not possible to effect the materialisation by mere concentration of will, or the exercise of any faculty; otherwise many people could have done what he had engaged himself to do. His nature was phenomenal—the dividing wall between himself and the spiritual world was broken in many places. Through the gaps in his mind the inhabitants of the invisible, when he summoned them, passed for a moment timidly and awfully into the solid, coloured universe . . . He could not say how it was brought about . . . The experience was a rough one for the body, and many such struggles would lead to insanity and early death. That is why Backhouse was stern and abrupt in his manner. The coarse, clumsy suspicion of some of the witnesses, the frivolous aestheticism of others, were equally obnoxious to his grim, bursting heart; but he was obliged to live and, to pay his way, must put up with these impertinences.

He sat down, facing the wooden couch. His eyes remained open, but seemed to look inwards. His cheeks paled, and he became noticeably thinner. The spectators almost forgot to breathe. The more sensitive among them began to feel, or imagine, strange presences all around them. Maskull's eyes glittered with anticipation, and his brows went up and down, but Nightspore appeared bored.

After a long ten minutes the pedestal of the statue was seen to become slightly blurred, as though an intervening mist were rising from the ground. This slowly developed into a visible cloud, coiling hither and thither, and constantly changing shape. The professor half-rose, and held his glasses with one hand further forward on the bridge of his nose.

By slow stages the cloud acquired the dimensions and approximate outline of an adult human body, although all was still vague and blurred. It hovered slightly in the air, a foot or so above the couch. Backhouse looked haggard and ghastly. Mrs Jameson quietly fainted in her chair, but she was unnoticed, and presently revived. The apparition now settled down upon the couch, and at the moment of doing so seemed suddenly to grow dark, solid, and manlike. Many of the guests were as pale as the medium himself, but Faull preserved his stoical apathy, and glanced once or twice at Mrs Trent. She was staring straight at the couch, and was twisting a little lace handkerchief through the different fingers of her hand. The music went on playing.

The figure was by this time unmistakably that of a man lying down. The face focused itself into distinctness. The body was draped in a sort of shroud, but the features were those of a young man. One smooth hand fell over, nearly touching the floor, white and motionless. The weaker spirits of the company stared at the vision in sick horror, the rest were grave and perplexed. The seeming man was *dead*, but somehow it did not appear like a death succeeding life, but like a death preliminary to life. All felt that he might sit up at any minute.

"Stop that music!" muttered Backhouse, tottering from his chair and facing the party. Faull touched the bell. A few more bars sounded, and then total silence ensued.

"Anyone who wants to may approach the couch," said Backhouse, with difficulty.

Lang at once advanced, and stared awestruck at the supernatural youth.

"You are at liberty to touch," said the medium.

But Lang did not venture, nor did any of the others, who one by one stole up to the couch; until it came to Faull's turn. He looked straight at Mrs Trent, who seemed frightened and disgusted at the spectacle before her, and then not only touched the apparition, but suddenly grasped the drooping hand in his own and gave it a powerful squeeze. Mrs Trent gave a low scream. The ghostly visitor opened his eyes, looked at Faull strangely, and sat up on the couch. A cryptic smile started playing over his mouth. Faull looked at his hand; a feeling of intense pleasure passed through his body.

Maskull caught Mrs Jameson in his arms; she was attacked by another spell of faintness. Mrs Trent ran forward, and led her out of the room. Neither of them returned.

The phantom body now stood upright, looking about him, still with his peculiar smile. Prior suddenly felt sick, and went out. The other men more or less hung together, for the sake of human society, but Nightspore paced up and down, like a man weary and impatient, while Maskull attempted to interrogate the youth. The apparition watched him with a baffling expression, but did not answer. Backhouse was sitting apart, his face buried in his hands.

It was at this moment that the door was burst violently open, and a stranger, unannounced, half leapt, half strode a few yards into the room, and then stopped. None of Faull's friends had ever seen him before. He was a thick, shortish man, with surprising muscular development and a head far too large in proportion to his body. His beardless, yellow face indicated, as a first impression, a mixture of sagacity, brutality, and humour.

"Aha-i, gentlemen!" he called out loudly. His voice was piercing, and oddly disagreeable to the ear. "So we have a little visitor here."

Nightspore turned his back, but everyone else stared at the intruder in astonishment. He took another few paces forward, which brought him to the edge of the theatre.

"May I ask, sir, how I come to have the honour of being your host?" asked Faull suddenly. He thought that the evening was not proceeding as smoothly as he had anticipated.

The newcomer looked at him for a second, and then broke into a great, roaring guffaw. He thumped Faull on the back playfully—but the play was rather rough, for the victim was sent staggering against the wall before he could recover his balance.

"Good evening, my host!"

"And good evening to you too, my lad!" he went on, addressing the supernatural youth, who was now beginning to wander about the room, in apparent unconsciousness of his surroundings. "I have seen someone very like you before, I think."

There was no response.

The intruder thrust his head almost up to the phantom's face. "You have no right here, as you know."

The shape looked back at him, with a smile full of significance, which, however, no one could understand.

"Be careful what you are doing," said Backhouse quickly.

"What's the matter, spirit-usher?"

"I don't know who you are, but if you use physical violence towards *that*, as you seem inclined to do, the consequences may prove very unpleasant."

"And without pleasure our evening would be spoilt, wouldn't it, my little mercenary friend?"

Humour vanished from his face, like sunlight from a landscape, leaving it hard and rocky. Before anyone realised what he was doing, he encircled the soft, white neck of the materialised shape with his hairy hands and, with a double-turn, twisted it completely round. A faint, unearthly shriek sounded, and the body fell in a heap to the floor. Its face was uppermost. The guests were unutterably shocked to observe that its expression had changed from the mysterious but fascinating smile to a vulgar, sordid, bestial grin, which cast a cold shadow of moral nastiness into every heart. The transformation was accompanied by a sickening stench of the graveyard.

The features faded rapidly away, the body lost its consistence, passing from the solid to the shadowy condition, and before two minutes had elapsed the spirit-form had entirely disappeared.

The short stranger turned and confronted the party, with a long, loud laugh, like nothing in nature.

The professor talked excitedly to Kent-Smith, in low tones. Faull beckoned Backhouse behind a wing of scenery, and handed him his cheque without a word. The medium put it in his pocket, buttoned his coat, and walked out of the room. Lang followed him, in order to get a drink.

The stranger poked his face up into Maskull's.

"Well, giant, what do you think of it all? Shouldn't you like to see the land where this sort of fruit grows wild?"

"What sort of fruit?"

"That specimen goblin."

Maskull put him away with his huge hand.

"Who are you, and how did you come here?"

"Call your friend up. Perhaps he may recognise me."

Nightspore had moved a chair to the fire, and was watching the embers with a set, fanatical expression.

"Let Krag come to me, if he wants me," he said, in his strange voice.

"You see, he does know me," uttered Krag, with a humorous look. Walking over to Nightspore, he put a hand on the back of his chair.

"Still the same old gnawing hunger?"

"What is doing in these days?" demanded Nightspore disdainfully, without altering his attitude.

"Surtur has gone, and we are to follow him."

"How do you two come to know each other, and of whom are you speaking?" asked Maskull, looking from one to the other in perplexity.

"Krag has something for us. Let us get outside," replied

Nightspore. He got up, and glanced over his shoulder. Maskull, following the direction of his eye, observed that the few remaining men were watching their little group attentively.

CHAPTER TWO

In the Street

The three men gathered in the road outside the house. The night was slightly frosty, but particularly clear, with an east wind blowing. The multitude of blazing stars caused the sky to appear like a vast scroll of hieroglyphic symbols. Maskull felt oddly excited; he had a sense that something extraordinary was about to happen.

"What brought you to this house tonight, Krag, and what made you do what you did? . . . How are we to understand that apparition?"

"That must have been Crystalman's expression on its face," muttered Nightspore.

"We have discussed that, haven't we, Maskull? Maskull is anxious to behold that rare fruit in its native wilds."

Maskull looked at Krag carefully, trying to analyse his own feelings towards him. He was distinctly repelled by the man's personality, yet side by side with this aversion a savage, living energy seemed to spring up in his heart which in some strange fashion was attributable to Krag.

"Why do you insist on this simile?" he asked.

"Because it is apropos. Nightspore's quite right. That was Crystalman's face, and we are going to Crystalman's country."

"And where is this mysterious country?"

"Tormance."

"That's a quaint name. But where is it?"

Krag grinned, showing his yellow teeth, in the light of the street lamp.

"It is the residential suburb of Arcturus."

"What is he talking about, Nightspore? . . . Do you mean the star of that name?" he went on, to Krag.

"Which you have in front of you at this very minute," said Krag, pointing a thick finger towards the brightest star in the south-eastern sky. "There you see Arcturus, and Tormance is its one inhabited planet."

Maskull looked at the heavy, gleaming star, and again at Krag. Then he pulled out a pipe, and began to fill it.

"You must have cultivated a new form of humour, Krag."

"I am glad if I can amuse you, Maskull, if only for a few days."

"I meant to ask you—how do you know my name?"

"It would be odd if I didn't, seeing that I only came here on your account. As a matter of fact, Nightspore and I are old friends."

Maskull paused with his suspended match.

"You came here on my account?"

"Surely. On your account and Nightspore's. We three are to be fellow-travellers."

Maskull now lit his pipe, and puffed away coolly for a few moments.

"I'm sorry, Krag, but I must assume you are mad."

Krag threw his head back, and gave a scraping laugh.

"Am I mad, Nightspore?"

"Has Surtur gone to Tormance?" ejaculated Nightspore in a strangled voice, fixing his eyes on Krag's face.

"Yes, and he requires us to follow him at once."

Maskull's heart began to beat strangely. It all sounded to him like a dream-conversation.

"And since how long, Krag, have I been *required* to do things by a total stranger . . . besides, who is this individual?"

"Krag's chief," said Nightspore, turning his head away.

"The riddle is too elaborate for me. I give it up."

"You are looking for mysteries," said Krag, "so naturally you are finding them. Try and simplify your ideas, my friend. The affair is plain and serious."

Maskull stared hard at him, and smoked rapidly.

"Where have you come from now?" demanded Nightspore suddenly.

"From the old Observatory at Starkness . . . Have you heard of the famous Starkness Observatory, Maskull?"

"No. Where is it?"

"On the north-east coast of Scotland. Curious discoveries are made there from time to time."

"As for example, how to make voyages to the stars. So this Surtur turns out to be an astronomer. And you too, presumably?"

Krag grinned again. "How long will it take you to wind up your affairs? When can you be ready to start?"

"You are too considerate," said Maskull, laughing outright. "I was beginning to fear that I should be hauled away at once . . . However, I have neither wife, land, nor profession, so there's nothing to wait for . . . What is the itinerary?"

"You are a fortunate man. A bold, daring heart, and no encumbrances." Krag's features became suddenly grave and rigid. "Don't be a fool, and refuse a gift of luck. A gift declined is not offered a second time."

"Krag," replied Maskull simply, returning his pipe to his pocket, "I ask you to put yourself in my place. Even if I were a man sick for adventures, how could I listen seriously to such an insane proposition as this? What do I know about you, or your past record? You may be a practical joker, or you may have come out of a madhouse—I know nothing about it. If you claim to be an exceptional man, and want my co-operation, you must offer me exceptional proofs."

"And what proofs would you consider adequate, Maskull?"

As he spoke he gripped Maskull's arm. A sharp, chilling pain immediately passed through the latter's body . . . and at the same moment his brain caught fire. A light burst in upon him like the rising of the sun. He asked himself for the first time if this fantastic conversation could by any chance refer to real things.

"Listen, Krag," he said slowly, while peculiar images and conceptions started to travel in rich disorder through his mind. "You talk about a certain journey. Well, if that journey were a possible one, and I were given the chance of making it, I would be willing never to come back. For four-and-twenty hours in that Arcturian planet, I would give my life. This is my attitude towards that journey . . . Now prove to me that you're not talking nonsense. Produce your credentials."

Krag stared at him all the time he was speaking, his face gradually resuming its jesting expression.

"Oh, you will get your twenty-four hours, and perhaps longer, but not much longer. You're an audacious fellow, Maskull, but this trip will prove a little strenuous, even for you . . . And so, like the unbelievers of old, you want a sign from heaven?"

Maskull frowned. "But the whole thing is ridiculous. Our brains are overexcited by what took place in *there*. Let us go home, and sleep it off."

Krag detained him with one hand, while groping in his breastpocket with the other. He presently fished out what resembled a small folding-lens. The diameter of the glass did not exceed two inches.

"First take a peep at Arcturus through this, Maskull. It may serve as a provisional sign. It's the best I can do, unfortunately. I am not a travelling magician . . . Be very careful not to drop it. It's somewhat heavy."

Maskull took the lens in his hand, struggled with it for a minute, and then looked at Krag in amazement. The little object weighed at least twenty pounds, though in size not much bigger than a crown piece.

"What stuff can this be, Krag?"

"Look through it, my good friend. That's what I gave it to you for."

Maskull held it up with difficulty, directed it towards the gleaming Arcturus, and snatched as long and as steady a glance at the star as the muscles of his arm would permit. What he saw was this. The star, which to the naked eye appeared as a single yellow point of light, now became clearly split into two bright but minute suns, the larger of which was still yellow, while its smaller companion was a beautiful blue. But this was not all. Apparently circulating round the yellow sun was a comparatively small and hardly distinguishable satellite, which seemed to shine, not by its own, but by reflected light . . . Maskull lowered and raised his arm repeatedly. The same spectacle revealed itself again and again, but he was able to see nothing else. Then he passed back the lens to Krag, without a word, and stood chewing his under-lip.

"You too take a glimpse," scraped Krag, proffering the glass to Nightspore.

Nightspore turned his back, and began to pace up and down. Krag laughed sardonically, and returned the lens to his pocket.

"Well, Maskull, are you satisfied?"

"Arcturus, then, is a double sun. And is that third point the planet Tormance?"

"Our future home, Maskull."

Maskull continued to ponder.

"You inquire if I am satisfied. I don't know, Krag. It's miraculous, and that's all I can say about it . . . But I'm satisfied of one thing. There must be very wonderful astronomers at Starkness, and if you invite me to your Observatory I will surely come."

"I do invite you. It's from there that we set off."

"And you, Nightspore?" demanded Maskull.

"The journey has to be made," answered his friend in indistinct tones, "though I don't see what will come of it."

Krag shot a penetrating glance at him.

"More remarkable adventures than this would need to be arranged before we could excite Nightspore."

"Yet he is coming."

"But not *con amore*. He is coming merely to bear you company."

Maskull again sought the heavy, sombre star, gleaming in solitary might, in the south-eastern heavens, and, as he gazed, his heart swelled with grand and painful longings, for which, however, he was unable to account to his own intellect. He felt that his destiny was in some say bound up with this gigantic, far-distant sun. But still he did not dare to admit to himself Krag's seriousness.

He heard his parting remarks in deep abstraction, and only after the lapse of several minutes, when alone with Nightspore, did he realize that they referred to such mundane matters as travelling routes and times of trains.

"Does Krag travel north with us, Nightspore? I didn't catch."

"No. We go on first, and he joins us at Starkness on the evening of the day after tomorrow."

Maskull remained thoughtful.

"What am I to think of that man?"

"For your information," replied Nightspore wearily, "I have never known him to lie."

CHAPTER THREE

Starkness

A couple of days later, at two o'clock in the afternoon, Maskull and Nightspore arrived at Starkness Observatory, having covered the seven miles from Haillar Station on foot. The road, very wild and lonely, ran for the greater part of the way near the edge of rather lofty cliffs, within sight of the North Sea. The sun shone, but a brisk east wind was blowing and the air was salt and cold. The dark green waves were flecked with white. Throughout the walk, they were accompanied by the plaintive, beautiful crying of the gulls.

The Observatory presented itself to their eyes as a self-contained little community, without neighbours, and perched on the extreme end of the land. There were three buildings: a small, stone-built dwelling house, a low workshop, and, about two hundred yards further north, a square tower of granite masonry, seventy feet in height. The house and the shop were separated by an open yard, littered with waste. A single stone wall surrounded both, except on the side facing the sea, where the house itself formed a continuation of the cliff. No one appeared. The windows were all closed, and Maskull could have sworn that the whole establishment was shut up and deserted.

He passed through the open gate, followed by Nightspore, and knocked vigorously at the front door. The knocker was thick with dust and had obviously not been used for a long time. He put his ear to the door, but could hear no movements inside the house. He then tried the handle; the door was locked.

They walked round the house, looking for another entrance, but there was but the one door.

"This isn't promising," growled Maskull. "There's no one here . . . Now you try the shed, while I go over to that tower."

Nightspore, who had spoken not half a dozen words since leaving the train, complied in silence, and started off across the yard. Maskull passed out of the gate again. When he arrived at the foot of the tower, which stood some way back from the cliff, he found the door heavily padlocked. Gazing up, he saw six windows, one above the other at equal distances, all on the east face—that is, overlooking the sea. Realising that no satisfaction was to be gained here, he came away again, still more irritated than before. When he rejoined his friend, Nightspore reported that the workshop also was locked.

"Did we, or did we not, receive an invitation?" demanded Maskull energetically.

"The house is empty," replied Nightspore, biting his nails. "Better break a window."

"I certainly don't mean to camp out till Krag condescends to come."

He picked up an old iron bolt from the yard and, retreating to a safe distance, hurled it against a sash-window on the ground floor. The lower pane was completely shattered. Carefully avoiding the broken glass, Maskull thrust his hand through the aperture and pushed back the frame-fastening. A minute later they had climbed through and were standing inside the house.

The room, which was a kitchen, was in an indescribably filthy and neglected condition. The furniture scarcely held together, broken utensils and rubbish lay on the floor instead of on the dustheap, everything was covered with a deep deposit of dust. The atmosphere was so foul that Maskull judged that no fresh air had passed into the apartment for several months. Insects were crawling on the walls.

They went into the other rooms on the lower floor—a scullery, a barely-furnished dining-room, and a store place for lumber. The same dirt, mustiness, and neglect met their eyes. Half a year at least must have elapsed since these rooms were last touched, or even entered.

"Does your faith in Krag still hold?" asked Maskull. "I confess mine is at vanishing-point. If this affair isn't one big practical joke, it has every promise of one. Krag never lived here in his life."

"Come upstairs first," said Nightspore.

The upstairs rooms proved to consist of a library and three bedrooms. All the windows were tightly closed, and the air was insufferable. The beds had been slept in, evidently a long time ago, and had never been made up since. The tumbled, discoloured bed linen actually preserved the impressions of the sleepers. There was no doubt that these impressions were ancient, for all sorts of floating dirt had accumulated on the sheets and coverlets.

"Who could have slept here, do you think?" interrogated Maskull. "The Observatory staff?"

"More likely travellers like ourselves. They left suddenly."

Maskull flung the windows wide open in every room he came to, and held his breath until he had done so. Two of the bedrooms faced the sea; the third, and the library, the upward-sloping moorland. This library was now the only apartment left unvisited, and unless they discovered signs of recent occupation here Maskull made up his mind to regard the whole business as a gigantic hoax.

But the library, like all the other rooms, was foul with stale air and dust-laden. Maskull, having thrown the window up and down, fell heavily into an armchair and looked disgustedly at his friend.

"Now what is your opinion of Krag?"

Nightspore sat on the edge of the table which stood before the window.

"He may still have left a message for us."

"What message? Why? Do you mean in this room?—I see no message."

Nightspore's eyes wandered strangely about the room, finally seeming to linger upon a glass-fronted wall-cupboard, which contained a few old bottles on one of the shelves, and nothing else. Maskull glanced at him, and at the cupboard. Then, without a word, he got up to examine the bottles.

There were four altogether, one of which was larger than the rest. The smaller ones were about eight inches long. All were torpedo-shaped, but had flattened bottoms, which enabled them to stand upright. Two of the smaller ones were empty and unstoppered, the others contained a colourless liquid, and possessed queer-looking, nozzle-like stoppers which were connected by a thin metal rod with a catch half-way down the side of the bottle. They were labelled, but the labels were yellow with age and the writing was nearly undecipherable. Maskull carried the filled bottles with him to the table in front of the window, in order to get better light. Nightspore moved away to make room for him.

He now made out on the larger bottle the words 'Solar Back-Rays'; and on the other one, after some doubt, he thought that he could distinguish something like 'Arcturian Back-Rays.'

He looked up, to stare curiously at his friend.

"Have you been here before, Nightspore?"

"I guessed Krag would leave a message."

"Well, I don't know—it may be a message, but it means nothing to us, or at all events to me. What are 'back-rays'?"

"Light which goes back to its source," muttered Nightspore.

"And what kind of light may that be?"

Nightspore seemed unwilling to answer, but finding Maskull's eyes still fixed on him he brought out—"Unless light pulled, as well as pushed, how would flowers contrive to twist their heads round after the sun?"

"I don't know. But the point is, what are these bottles for?"

While he was still talking, with his hand on the smaller bottle, the other, which was lying on its side, accidentally rolled over in such a manner that the metal caught against the table. He made a movement to stop it, his hand was actually descending, when . . . the bottle suddenly disappeared before his eyes. It had not rolled off the table, but had really vanished—it was nowhere at all . . .

Maskull stared at the table. After a minute he raised his brows, and turned to Nightspore with a smile.

"The message grows more intricate."

Nightspore looked bored.

"The valve became unfastened. The contents have escaped through the open window towards the sun, carrying the bottle with them. But the bottle will be burnt up by the earth's atmosphere, and the contents will dissipate, and will not reach the sun."

Maskull listened attentively, and his smile faded.

"Does anything prevent us from experimenting with this other bottle?"

"Replace it in the cupboard," said Nightspore. "Arcturus is still below the horizon, and you would only succeed in wrecking the house."

Maskull remained standing before the window, pensively gazing out at the sunlit moors.

"Krag treats me like a child," he remarked presently. "And perhaps I really am a child . . . My cynicism must seem most amusing to Krag. But why does he leave me to find out all this by myself—for I don't include you, Nightspore . . . But what time will Krag be here?"

"Not before dark, I expect," his friend replied.

CHAPTER FOUR

The Voice

It was by this time past three o'clock. Feeling hungry, for they had eaten nothing since early morning, Maskull went downstairs to forage, but without much hope of finding anything in the shape of food. In a safe in the kitchen he discovered a bag of mouldy oatmeal, which was untouchable, a quantity of quite good tea in an airtight caddy, and an unopened tin of oxtongue. Best of all, in the dining-room cupboard he came across an uncorked bottle of first-class Scotch whisky. He at once made preparations for a scratch meal.

A pump in the yard ran clear after a good deal of hard working at it, and he washed out and filled the antique kettle. For firewood, one of the kitchen chairs was broken up with a chopper. The light, dusty wood made a good blaze in the grate, the kettle was boiled, and cups were procured and washed. Ten minutes later the friends were dining in the library.

Nightspore ate and drank little, but Maskull sat down with good appetite. There being no milk, whisky took the place of it; the nearly black tea was mixed with an equal quantity of the spirit. Of this concoction he drank cup after cup, and long after the tongue had disappeared he was still imbibing. Nightspore looked at him queerly.

"Do you mean to finish the bottle before Krag comes?"

"Krag won't want any, and one must do something. I feel restless."

"Let us take a look at the country."

The cup, which was on its way to Maskull's lips, remained poised in the air.

"Have you anything in view, Nightspore?"

26

"Let us walk out to the Gap of Sorgie."

"What's that, then?"

"A show-place," answered Nightspore, biting his lip.

Maskull drank off the cup, and rose to his feet.

"Walking is better than soaking at any time, and especially on a day like this . . . How far is it?"

"Three or four miles each way."

"You probably mean something," said Maskull, "for I'm beginning to regard you as a second Krag. But if so, so much the better. I am growing nervous, and need incidents."

They quitted the house by the door, which they left ajar, and immediately found themselves again on the moorland road which had brought them from Haillar. This time they continued along it, past the tower. Maskull, as they went by, regarded the erection with puzzled interest.

"What *is* that tower, Nightspore?"

"We sail from the platform on the top."

"Tonight?"—throwing him a quick look.

"Yes."

Maskull smiled, but his eyes were grave.

"Then we are looking at the gateway of Arcturus, and Krag is now travelling north to unlock it."

"You no longer think it impossible, I fancy," mumbled Nightspore.

After a mile or two, the road parted from the sea coast and swerved sharply inland, across the hills. With Nightspore as guide, they quitted it and took to the grass. A faint sheep-path marked the way along the cliff-edge for some distance, but at the end of another mile it vanished. The two men then had some rough walking up and down hillsides and across deep gullies. The sun disappeared behind the hills, and twilight imperceptibly came on. They presently reached a spot where further progress appeared impossible. The buttress of a mountain descended at a steep angle to the very edge of the cliff, forming an impassable slope of slippery grass. Maskull halted, stroked his beard, and wondered what the next step was to be.

"There's a little scrambling here," said Nightspore.

"We are both used to climbing, and there is not much in it."

He indicated a narrow ledge, winding along the face of the precipice a few yards beneath where they were standing. It averaged from fifteen to thirty inches in width. Without waiting for Maskull's consent to the undertaking, he instantly swung himself down and started walking along this ledge at a rapid pace. Maskull, seeing that there was no help for it, followed him. The shelf did not extend for above a quarter of a mile, but its passage was somewhat unnerving; there was a sheer drop to the sea, four hundred feet below. In a few places they were obliged to sidle along without passing one foot before another. The sound of the breakers came up to them in a low, threatening roar.

Upon rounding a corner, the ledge broadened out into a fair-sized platform of rock and came to a sudden end. A narrow inlet of the sea separated them from the continuation of the cliffs beyond.

"As we can't get any further," said Maskull, "I presume this is your Gap of Sorgie?"

"Yes," answered his friend, first dropping on his knees and then lying at full length, face downwards. He drew his head and shoulders over the edge and began to stare straight down at the water.

"What is there interesting down there, Nightspore?"

Receiving no reply, however, he followed his friend's example, and the next minute was watching for himself. Nothing was to be seen; the gloom had deepened, and the sea was nearly invisible. But, while he was ineffectually gazing, he heard what sounded like the beating of a drum on the narrow strip of shore below. It was very faint, but quite distinct. The beats were in four-time, with the third beat slightly accented. He now continued to hear the noise all the time he was lying there. The beats were in no way drowned by the far louder sound of the surf, but seemed somehow to belong to a different world . . .

When they were on their feet again, he questioned Nightspore.

"We came here solely to hear that?"

Nightspore cast one of his odd looks at him.

"It's called locally 'The Drum-Taps of Sorgie'. You will not hear that name again, but perhaps you will hear the sound again."

"And if I do, what will it imply?" demanded Maskull in amazement.

"It bears its own message. Only try always to hear it more and more distinctly. . . Now it's growing dark, and we must get back."

Maskull pulled out his watch automatically, and looked at the time. It was past six . . . But he was thinking of Nightspore's words, and not of the time.

Night had already fallen by the time they regained the tower. The black sea was glorious with liquid stars. Arcturus was a little way above the sea, directly opposite to them, in the east. As they were passing the base of the tower, Maskull observed with a sudden shock that the gate was open. He caught hold of Nightspore's arm violently.

"Look! Krag is back."

"Yes, we must make haste to the house."

"And why not the tower? He's probably in there, since the gate is open. I'm going up to look."

Nightspore grunted, but made no opposition.

All was pitch-black inside the gate. Maskull struck a match, and the flickering light disclosed the lower end of a circular flight of stone steps.

"Are you coming up?" he asked.

"No, I'll wait here."

Maskull immediately began the ascent. Hardly had he mounted half a dozen steps, however, before he was compelled to pause, to gain breath. He seemed to be carrying upstairs not one Maskull, but three. As he proceeded, the sensation of crushing weight, so far from diminishing, grew worse and worse. It was nearly physically impossible to go on; his lungs could not take in enough oxygen, while his heart thumped like a ship's engine. Sweat coursed down his face. At the twentieth step he completed the first revolution of the tower and came face to face with the first window, which was set in a high embrasure.

Realising that he could go no higher, he struck another match, and climbed into the embrasure, in order that he might at all events see something from the tower. The match died, and he stared through the window at the stars. Then, to his astonishment, he discovered that it was not a window at all but a lens . . . The sky was not a wide expanse of space containing a multitude of stars, but a blurred darkness, focused only in one part, where two very bright stars, like small moons in size, appeared in close conjunction; and near them a more minute planetary object, brilliant as Venus and with an observable disc. One of the suns shone with a glaring white light; the other was a weird and awful blue. Their light, though almost solar in intensity, did not illuminate the interior of the tower.

Maskull knew at once that the system of spheres at which he was gazing was what is known to astronomy as the star Arcturus . . . He had seen the sight before, through Krag's glass, but then the scale had been smaller, the colours of the twin suns had not appeared in their naked reality . . . These colours seemed to him most marvellous, as if, in seeing them through earth-eyes, he was not seeing them aright . . . But it was at Tormance that he stared the longest time and most earnestly. On that mysterious and terrible earth, countless millions of miles distant, it had been promised him that he would set foot, even though he might leave his bones there. The strange creatures which he was to behold and touch were already living, at this very moment . . .

A low, sighing whisper sounded in his ear, from not more than a yard away. "Don't you understand, Maskull, that you are only an instrument, to be used and then broken? Nightspore is asleep now, but when he wakes you must die. You will go, but he will return."

Maskull hastily struck another match, with trembling fingers. No one was in sight, and all was quiet as the tomb.

The voice did not sound again. After waiting a few minutes, he redescended to the foot of the tower. On gaining the open air, his sensation of weight was instantly removed, but he continued panting and palpitating, like a man who has lifted a far too heavy load.

Nightspore's dark form came forward.

"Was Krag there?"

"If he was, I didn't see him. But I heard someone speak."

"Was it Krag?"

"It was not Krag—but a voice warned me against you."

"Yes, you will hear these voices too," said Nightspore enigmatically.

CHAPTER FIVE

The Night of Departure

When they returned to the house, the windows were all in darkness and the door was ajar, just as they had left it; Krag presumably was not there. Maskull went all over the house, striking matches in every room—at the end of the examination he was ready to swear that the man they were expecting had not even put his nose inside the premises. Groping their way into the library, they sat down in the total darkness to wait, for nothing else remained to be done. Maskull lit his pipe, and began to drink the remainder of the whisky. Through the open window sounded in their ears the train-like grinding of the sea at the foot of the cliffs.

"Krag must be in the tower after all," remarked Maskull, breaking the silence.

"Yes, he is getting ready."

"I hope he doesn't expect us to join him there. It was beyond my powers—but why, heaven knows. The stairs must have a magnetic pull of some sort."

"It is Tormantic gravity," muttered Nightspore.

"I understand you . . . or, rather, I don't—but it doesn't matter."

He went on smoking in silence, occasionally taking a mouthful of the neat spirit.

"Who is Surtur?" he demanded abruptly.

"We others are gropers and bunglers, but he is a *master*."

Maskull digested this.

"I fancy you are right, for though I know nothing about him his mere name has an exciting effect on me . . . Are you personally acquainted with him?"

"I must be . . . I forget . . ." replied Nightspore, in a

choking voice.

Maskull looked up, surprised, but could make nothing out in the blackness of the room.

"Do you know so many extraordinary men that you can forget some of them? . . . Perhaps you can tell me this—shall we meet him, where we are going?"

"You will meet death, Maskull . . . Ask me no more questions—I can't answer them."

"Then let us go on waiting for Krag," said Maskull coldly.

Ten minutes later the front door slammed, and a light, quick footstep was heard running up the stairs. Maskull got up, with a beating heart.

Krag appeared on the threshold of the door, bearing in his hand a feebly glimmering lantern. A hat was on his head, and he looked stern and forbidding. After scrutinising the two friends for a moment or so, he strode into the room and thrust the lantern on the table. Its light hardly served to illuminate the walls.

"You have got here, then, Maskull?"

"So it seems—but I shan't thank you for your hospitality, for it has been conspicuous by its absence."

Krag ignored the remark.

"Are you ready to start?"

"By all means—when you are. It is not so amusing here."

Krag surveyed him critically. "I heard you stumbling about in the tower. You couldn't get up, it seems."

"It looks like an obstacle, for Nightspore informs me that the start takes place from the top."

"But your other doubts are all removed?"

"So far, Krag, that I now possess an open mind. I am quite willing to see what you can do."

"Nothing more is asked . . . But this tower business. You know that until you are able to climb to the top you are unfit to stand the gravitation of Tormance?"

"Then I repeat, it's an awkward obstacle, for I certainly can't get up."

Krag hunted about in his pockets, and at length produced a clasp-knife.

"Remove your coat, and roll up your shirt-sleeve," he directed.

"Do you propose to make an incision with that?"

"Yes, and don't start difficulties, because the effect is certain, but you can't possibly understand it beforehand."

"Still, a cut with a pocket-knife . . ." began Maskull, laughing.

"It will answer, Maskull," interrupted Nightspore.

"Then bare your arm too, you aristocrat of the universe," said Krag. "Let us see what *your* blood is made of."

Nightspore obeyed.

Krag pulled out the big blade of the knife, and made a careless and almost savage slash at Maskull's upper arm. The wound was deep, and blood flowed freely.

"Do I bind it up?" asked Maskull, scowling with pain.

Krag spat on the wound. "Pull your shirt down. It won't bleed any more."

He then turned his attention to Nightspore, who endured his operation with grim indifference. Krag threw the knife on the floor.

An awful agony, emanating from the wound, started to run through Maskull's body, and he began to doubt whether he should not have to swoon, but it subsided almost immediately, and then he felt nothing but a gnawing ache in the injured arm, just strong enough to make life one long discomfort.

"That's finished," said Krag. "Now you can follow me."

Picking up the lantern, he walked towards the door. The others hastened after him, to take advantage of the light, and a moment later their footsteps, clattering down the uncarpeted stairs, resounded through the deserted house. Krag waited till they were out, and then banged the front door after them with such violence that the windows shook.

While they were walking swiftly across to the tower,

Maskull caught his arm.

"I heard a voice up those stairs."

"What did it say?"

"That I am to go, but Nightspore is to return."

Krag smiled.

"The journey is getting notorious," he remarked, after a pause. "There must be ill-wishers about . . . Well, do you want to return?"

"I don't know what I want. But I thought the thing was curious enough to be mentioned."

"It is not a bad thing to hear voices," said Krag, "but you mustn't for a minute imagine that all is wise that comes to you out of the night-world."

When they had arrived at the open gateway of the tower, he immediately set foot on the bottom step of the spiral staircase and ran nimbly up, bearing the lantern. Maskull followed him with some trepidation, in view of his previous painful experience on these stairs, but when, after the first half-dozen steps, he discovered that he was still breathing freely, his dread changed to relief and astonishment, and he could have chattered like a girl.

At the lowest window Krag went straight ahead without stopping, but Maskull clambered into the embrasure, in order to renew his acquaintance with the miraculous spectacle of the Arcturian group . . . The lens had lost its magic property . . . It had become a common sheet of glass, through which the ordinary sky-field appeared.

The climb continued, and at the second and third windows he again mounted and stared out, but still the common sights presented themselves. After that, he gave it up and looked through no more windows.

Krag and Nightspore meanwhile had got on ahead with the light, so that he had to complete the ascent in darkness. When he was near the top, he saw yellow light shining through the crack of a half-opened door. His companions were standing just inside a small room, shut off from the staircase by rough wooden planking; it was rudely furnished and contained nothing of astronomical interest. The lantern was resting on a table.

Maskull walked in, and looked around him with curiosity.

"Are we at the top?"

"Except for the platform over our heads," replied Krag.

"Why didn't that lowest window magnify, as it did earlier in the evening?"

"Oh, you missed your opportunity," said Krag, grinning. "If you had finished your climb then, you would have seen heart-expanding sights. From the fifth window, for example, you would have seen Tormance like a continent in relief; from the sixth you would have seen it like a landscape . . . But now there's no need."

"Why not—and what has need got to do with it?"

"Things are changed, my friend, since that wound of yours. For the same reason that you have now been able to mount the stairs, there was no necessity to stop and gape at illusions *en route*."

"Very well," said Maskull, not quite understanding what he meant . . . "But is this Surtur's den?"

"He has spent time here."

"I wish you would describe this mysterious individual, Krag. We may not get another chance."

"What I said about the windows also applies to Surtur. There's no need to waste time over visualising him, because you are immediately going on to the reality."

"Then let us go." He pressed his eyeballs wearily.

"Do we strip?" asked Nightspore.

"Naturally," answered Krag, and he began to tear off his clothes, with slow, uncouth movements.

"Why?" demanded Maskull, following, however, the example of the other two men.

Krag thumped his vast chest, which was covered with thick hairs, like an ape's. "Who knows what the Tormance fashions are like? We may sprout limbs—I don't say we shall."

"Aha!" exclaimed Maskull, pausing in the middle of his undressing.

Krag smote him on the back. "New pleasure organs possible, Maskull. You like that?"

The three men stood as nature made them. Maskull's spirits rose fast, as the moment of departure drew near.

"A farewell drink to success!" cried Krag, seizing a bottle, and breaking its head off between his fingers. There were no glasses, but he poured the amber-coloured wine into some cracked cups.

Perceiving that the others drank, Maskull tossed off his cupful . . . It was as if he had swallowed a draught of liquid electricity . . . Krag dropped on to the floor, and rolled about on his back, kicking his legs in the air. He tried to drag Maskull down on top of him, and a little horse-play went on between the two. Nightspore took no part in it, but walked to and fro, like a hungry caged animal.

Suddenly, from out of doors, there came a single prolonged, piercing wail, such as a banshee might be imagined to utter. It ceased abruptly, and was not repeated.

"What's that?" called out Maskull, disengaging himself impatiently from Krag.

Krag rocked with laughter. "A Scottish spirit trying to reproduce the bagpipes of its earth-life—in honour of our departure."

Nightspore turned to Krag.

"Maskull will sleep throughout the journey?"

"And you too, if you wish, my altruistic friend. I am pilot, and you passengers can amuse yourselves as you please."

"Are we off at last?" asked Maskull.

"Yes, you are about to cross your Rubicon, Maskull. But what a Rubicon! . . . Do you know that it takes light a hundred years or so to arrive here from Arcturus? Yet we shall do it in nineteen hours."

"Then you assert that Surtur is already there?"

"Surtur is where he is. He is a great traveller."

"Shall I not see him?"

Krag went up to him, and looked him in the eyes.

"Don't forget that you have asked for it, and wanted it. Few people in Tormance will know more about him than you do, but your memory will be your worst friend."

He led the way up a short iron ladder, mounting through a trap to the flat roof above. When they were up, he switched on a small electric torch.

Maskull beheld with awe the torpedo of crystal which was to convey them through the whole breadth of visible space. It was forty feet long, eight broad, and eight high; the tank containing the Arcturian back-rays was in front, the car behind. The nose of the torpedo was directed towards the south-eastern sky. The whole machine rested upon a flat platform, raised about four feet above the level of the roof, so as to encounter no obstruction on starting its flight.

Krag flashed the light on to the door of the car, to enable them to enter. Before doing so, Maskull gazed sternly once again at the gigantic, far-distant star, which was from now onwards to be their sun. He frowned, shivered slightly, and got in beside Nightspore. Krag clambered past them on to his pilot's seat. He threw the torch through the open door, which was then carefully closed, fastened, and screwed up.

He pulled the starting lever. The torpedo glided gently from its platform, and passed rather slowly away from the tower, seawards. Its speed increased sensibly, though not excessively, until the approximate limits of the earth's atmosphere were reached. Krag then released the speed valve, and the car sped on its way with a velocity more nearly approaching that of thought than of light.

Maskull had no opportunity of examining through the crystal walls the rapidly-changing panorama of the heavens. An extreme drowsiness oppressed him. He opened his eyes violently a dozen times, but on the thirteenth attempt he failed. From that time forward he slept heavily.

The bored, hungry expression never left Nightspore's

face. The alterations in the aspect of the sky seemed to possess not the least interest for him.

Krag sat with his hand on the lever, watching with savage intentness his phosphorescent charts and gauges.

CHAPTER SIX

Joiwind

It was dense night when Maskull awoke from his profound sleep. A wind was blowing against him, gentle but wall-like, such as he had never experienced on earth. He remained sprawling on the ground, as he was unable to lift his body on account of its intense weight. A numbing pain, which he could not identify with any region of his frame, acted from now onwards as a lower, sympathetic note to all his other sensations. It gnawed away at him continuously; sometimes it embittered and irritated him, at other times he forgot it.

He felt something hard on his forehead. Putting his hand up, he discovered there a fleshy protuberance, the size of a small plum, having a cavity in the middle, of which he could not feel the bottom. Then he also became aware of a large knob on each side of his neck, an inch below the ear.

From the region of his heart, a tentacle had budded. It was as long as his arm, but thin, like whipcord, and soft and flexible.

As soon as he thoroughly realised the significance of these new organs, his heart began to pump. Whatever might, or might not, be their use, they proved one thing—that he was in a new world.

One part of the sky began to get lighter than the rest. Maskull cried out to his companions, but received no response. This frightened him. He went on shouting out, at irregular intervals—equally alarmed at the silence and at the sound of his own voice. Finally, as no answering hail came, he thought it wiser not to make too much noise, and after that he lay quiet, waiting in cold blood for what might happen.

In a short while he perceived dim shadows around him, but these were not his friends.

A pale, milky vapour over the ground began to succeed the black night, while in the upper sky rosy tints appeared. On earth, one would have said that day was breaking. The brightness went on imperceptibly increasing for a very long time.

Maskull then discovered that he was lying on sand. The colour of the sand was scarlet. The obscure shadows he had seen were bushes, with black stems and purple leaves. So far, nothing else was visible.

The day surged up. It was too misty for direct sunshine, but before long the brilliance of the light was already greater than that of the midday sun on earth. The heat too was intense, but Maskull welcomed it—it relieved his pain and diminished his sense of crushing weight. The wind had dropped with the rising of the sun.

He now tried to get on to his feet, but only succeeded in kneeling. He was unable to see far. The mists had no more than partially dissolved, and all that he could distinguish was a narrow circle of red sand, dotted with ten or twenty bushes.

He felt a soft, cool touch on the back of his neck. He started forward in nervous fright and, in doing so, tumbled over on to the sand. Looking up over his shoulder quickly, he was astounded to see a woman standing beside him.

She was clothed in a single flowing, pale-green garment, rather classically draped. According to earth-standards she was not beautiful, for, although her face was otherwise human, she was endowed—or afflicted—with the additional disfiguring organs which Maskull had discovered in himself. She also possessed the heart-tentacle. But when he sat up, and their eyes met and remained in sympathetic contact, he seemed to see right into a soul which was the home of love, warmth, kindness, tenderness, and intimacy. Such was the noble familiarity of that gaze, that he thought he *knew* her. After that, he recognised all the loveliness of her person. She was tall and slight. All her movements were graceful as music. Her skin was not of a dead, opaque colour, like that of an earth-beauty, but was opalescent; its hue was continually changing, with every thought and emotion, but none of these tints were vivid—all were delicate, half-toned, and poetic. She had very long, loosely-plaited, flaxen hair. The new organs, as soon as Maskull had familiarised himself with them, imparted something to her face which was unique and striking. He could not quite define it to himself, but subtlety and inwardness seemed added. The organs did not contradict the love of her eyes or the angelic purity of her features, but nevertheless sounded a deeper note—a note which saved her from mere girlishness.

Her gaze was so friendly and unembarrassed that Maskull felt scarcely any humiliation at sitting at her feet, naked and helpless. She realised his plight, and put into his hands a garment which she had been carrying over her arm. It was similar to the one she was wearing, but of a darker, more masculine colour.

"Do you think you can put it on by yourself?"

He was distinctly conscious of these words, yet her voice had not sounded.

He forced himself up to his feet, and she helped him to master the complications of the drapery.

"Poor man—how you are suffering!" she said, in the same inaudible language. This time he discovered that the sense of what she said was received by his brain through the organ on his forehead.

"Where am I?—Is this Tormance?" he asked. As he spoke, he staggered. She caught him, and helped him to sit down.

"Yes. You are with friends."

Then she regarded him with a smile, and began speaking aloud, in English. Her voice somehow reminded him of an April day, it was so fresh, nervous, and girlish.

"I can now understand your language. It was strange at first. In future I'll speak to you with my mouth."

"This is extraordinary! What is this organ?"—touching his forehead.

"It is named the 'breve'. By means of it we read one another's thoughts. Still, speech is better, for then the heart can be read too."

He smiled. "They say that speech is given us to deceive others."

"One can deceive with thought too. But I'm thinking of the best, not the worst."

"Have you seen my friends?"

She scrutinised him quietly, before answering.

"Did you not come alone?"

"I came with two other men, in a machine. I must have lost consciousness on arrival, and I haven't seen them since."

"That's very strange! No, I haven't seen them. They can't be here, or we should have known it. My husband and I—"

"What is your name, and your husband's name?"

"Mine is Joiwind—my husband's is Panawe. We live a very long way from here; still, it came to us both last night that you were lying here insensible. We almost quarrelled about which of us should come to you, but in the end I won."—Here she laughed.—"I won, because I am the stronger-hearted of the two; he is the purer in perception."

"Thanks, Joiwind!" said Maskull simply.

The colours chased each other rapidly beneath her skin.

"Oh, why do you say that? What pleasure is greater than loving-kindness? I rejoiced at the opportunity . . . But now we must exchange blood."

"What is this?" he demanded, rather puzzled.

"It must be so. Your blood is far too thick and heavy for our world. Until you have an infusion of mine, you will never get up."

Maskull flushed.

"I feel a thorough ignoramus here . . . Won't it hurt you?"

"If your blood pains you, I suppose it will pain me. But we will share the pain."

"This is a new kind of hospitality to me," he muttered.

"Wouldn't you do the same for me?" asked Joiwind, half-smiling, half-agitated.

"I can't answer for any of my actions in this world. I scarcely know where I am . . . Why, yes—of course I would, Joiwind."

While they were talking it had become full day. The mists had rolled away from the ground, and only the upper atmosphere remained fog-charged. The desert of scarlet sand stretched in all directions, except one, where there was a sort of little oasis—some low hills, clothed sparsely with little, purple trees from base to summit. It was about a quarter of a mile distant.

Joiwind had brought with her a small flint knife. Without any trace of nervousness, she made a careful, deep incision on her upper arm. Maskull expostulated.

"Really, this part of it is nothing," she said, laughing. "And if it were . . . a sacrifice which is no sacrifice—what merit is there in that? . . . Come, now—your arm!"

The blood was streaming down her arm. But it was not red blood, but a milky, opalescent fluid.

"Not that one!" said Maskull, shrinking. "I have already been cut there." He submitted the other, and his blood poured forth.

Joiwind delicately and skilfully placed the mouths of the two wounds together, and then kept her arm pressed tightly against Maskull's for a long time. He felt a stream of pleasure entering his body through the incision. His old lightness and vigour began to return to him. After about five minutes a duel of kindness started between them; he wanted to remove his arm, and she to continue. At last he had his way, but it was none too soon—she stood there pale and dispirited.

She looked at him with a more serious expression than before, as if strange depths had opened up before her eyes.

"What is your name?"

"Maskull."

'Where have you come from, with this awful blood?"

"From a world called Earth . . . The blood is clearly unsuitable for this world, Joiwind, but after all, that was only to be expected . . . I am sorry I let you have your way."

"Oh, don't say that! There was nothing else to be done. We must all help one another. Yet, somehow—forgive me . . . I feel polluted."

"And well you may, for it's a fearful thing for a girl to accept in her own veins the blood of a strange man from a strange planet. If I had not been so dazed and weak I would never have allowed it."

"But I should have insisted. Are we not all brothers and sisters? Why did you come here, Maskull?"

He was conscious of a slight degree of embarrassment.

"Shall you think it foolish if I say I hardly know?— I came with those two men. Perhaps I was attracted by curiosity, or perhaps it was the love of adventure."

"Perhaps," said Joiwind . . . "I wonder . . . These friends of yours must be terrible men. Why did *they* come?"

"That I can tell you. They came to follow Surtur."

Her face grew troubled.

"I don't understand it. One of them at least must be a bad man, and yet if he is following Surtur—or Shaping, as he is called here—he can't be really bad."

"What do you know of Surtur?" asked Maskull in astonishment.

Joiwind remained silent for a time, studying his face. His brain moved restlessly, as though it were being probed from outside.

"I see . . . and yet I don't see," she said at last. "It is very difficult . . . Your God is a dreadful Being— bodyless, unfriendly, invisible. Here we don't worship a God like that. Tell me, has any man set eyes on your God?"

"What does all this mean, Joiwind? Why speak of God?"

"I wish to know."

"In ancient times, when the earth was young and grand,

a few holy men are reputed to have walked and spoken with God, but those days are past."

"Our world is still young," said Joiwind. "Shaping goes amongst us and converses with us. He is real and active – a friend and lover. Shaping made us, and he loves his work."

"Have *you* met him?" demanded Maskull, hardly believing his ears.

"No. I have done nothing to deserve it yet. Some day I may have an opportunity to sacrifice myself, and then I may be rewarded by meeting and talking with Shaping."

"I have certainly come to another world. But why do you say he is the same as Surtur?"

"Yes, he is the same. We women call him Shaping, and so do most men, but a few name him Surtur."

Maskull bit his nail. "Have you ever heard of Crystalman?"

"That is Shaping once again. You see he has many names—which shows how much he occupies our minds. Crystalman is a name of affection."

"It's odd," said Maskull. "I came here with quite different ideas about Crystalman."

Joiwind shook her hair.

"In that grove of trees yonder stands a desert-shrine of his. Let us go and pray there, and then we'll go one our way to Poolingdred. That is my home. It's a long way off, and we must get there before Blodsombre."

"Now, what is Blodsombre?"

"For about four hours in the middle of the day Branchspell's rays are so hot that no one can endure them. We call it Blodsombre."

"Is Branchspell another name for Arcturus?"

Joiwind threw off her seriousness and laughed. "Naturally we don't take our names from you, Maskull. I don't think our names are very poetic, but they follow nature."

She took his arm affectionately, and directed their walk towards the tree-covered hills. As they went along, the sun broke through the upper mists and a terrible gust of scorching heat, like a blast from a furnace, struck Maskull's head. He involuntarily looked up, but lowered his eyes again like lightning. All that he saw in that instant was a glaring ball of electric white, thrice the apparent diameter of the sun. For a few minutes he was quite blind.

"My God!" he exclaimed. "If it's like this in early morning, you must be right enough about Blodsombre."

When he had somewhat recovered himself he asked, "How long are the days here, Joiwind?"

Again he felt his brain being probed.

"At this time of the year, for every hour's daylight that you have in summer, we have two."

"The heat is terrific—and yet somehow I don't feel so distressed by it as I should have expected."

"I feel it more than usual. It's not difficult to account for it; you have some of my blood, and I have some of yours."

"Yes, every time I realise that, I . . . Tell me, Joiwind, will my blood alter, if I stay here long enough?—I mean, will it lose its redness and thickness, and become pure and thin and light-coloured, like yours?"

"Why not? If you live as we live, you will assuredly grow like us."

"Do you mean food and drink?"

"We eat no food, and drink only water."

"And on that you contrive to sustain life?"

"Well, Maskull, our water is good water," replied Joiwind, smiling.

As soon as he could see again he stared around at the land-scape. The enormous scarlet desert extended everywhere to the horizon, excepting where it was broken by the oasis. It was roofed by a cloudless, deep blue, almost violet sky. The circle of the horizon was far larger than on earth. On the skyline, at a right-angle to the direction in which they were walking, appeared a chain of mountains, apparently about forty miles distant. One, which was higher than the rest, was shaped like a cup. Maskull would have felt inclined to believe he was travelling in dreamland, but for the intensity of the light, which made everything vividly real.

Joiwind pointed to the cup-shaped mountain.

"That's Poolingdred."

"You never came from there!" he exclaimed, quite startled.

"Yes, I did, indeed. And that is where we have to go to now."

"With the single object of finding me?"

"Why, yes."

The colour mounted to his face.

"Then you are the bravest and noblest of all girls," he said quietly, after a pause . . . "Without exception . . . Why, this is a journey for an athlete!"

She pressed his arm, while a score of unpaintable, delicate hues stained her cheeks in rapid transition.

"Please don't say any more about it, Maskull. It makes me feel unpleasant."

"Very well. But can we possibly get there before midday?"

"Oh, yes. And you mustn't be frightened at the distance. We think nothing of long distances here—we have so much to think about and feel. Time goes all too quickly."

During their conversation they had drawn near to the base of the hills. They sloped gently, and were not above fifty feet in height. Maskull now began to see strange specimens of vegetable life. What looked like a small patch of purple grass, about five feet square, was moving across the sand in their direction. When it came near enough he perceived that it was not grass; there were no blades, but only purple roots. The roots were revolving, for each small plant in the whole patch, like the spokes of a rimless wheel. They were alternately plunged in the sand, and withdrawn from it, and by this means the plant proceeded forward. Some uncanny, semi-intelligent instinct was keeping all the plants together, moving at one pace, in one direction, like a flock of migrating birds in flight.

Another remarkable plant was a large, feathery ball, resembling a dandelion-fruit, which they encountered sailing through the air. Joiwind caught it with an exceedingly graceful movement of her arm, and showed it to Maskull. It had roots and presumably lived in the air and fed on the chemical constituents of the atmosphere. But what was peculiar about it was its colour. It was an entirely new colour—not a new shade or combination, but a new primary colour, as vivid as blue, red, or yellow, but quite different. When he inquired, she told him that it was known as *ulfire*. Presently he met with a second new colour. This she designated *jale*. The sense-impressions caused in Maskull by these two additional primary colours can only be vaguely hinted at by analogy. Just as blue is delicate and mysterious, yellow clear and unsubtle, and red sanguine and passionate, so he felt ulfire to be wild and painful, and jale dreamlike, feverish and voluptuous.

The hills were composed of a rich, dark mould. Small trees, of weird shapes, all differing from each other, but all purple coloured, covered the slopes and top. Maskull and Joiwind climbed up and through. Some hard fruit, bright blue in colour, of the size of a large apple, and shaped like an egg, was lying in profusion underneath the trees.

"Is the fruit here poisonous, or why don't you eat it?" asked Maskull.

She looked at him tranquilly. "We don't eat living things. The thought is horrible to us."

"I have nothing to say against that, theoretically. But do you really sustain your bodies on water?"

"Supposing you could find nothing else to live on, Maskull—would you eat other men?"

"I would not."

"Neither will we eat plants and animals, which are our fellow-creatures. So nothing is left to us but water, and as one can really live on anything, water does very well."

Maskull picked up one of the fruits and handled it curiously. As he did so another of his newly-acquired sense-organs came into action. He found that the fleshy knobs beneath his ears were in some novel fashion acquainting him with the inward properties of the fruit. He could not only see, feel and smell it, but could detect its intrinsic nature. This nature was hard, persistent, and melancholy.

Joiwind answered the questions he had not asked.

"Those organs are called 'poigns.' Their use is to enable us to understand and sympathise with all living creatures."

"What advantage do you derive from that, Joiwind?"

"The advantage of not being cruel and selfish, dear Maskull."

He threw the fruit away and flushed again.

Joiwind looked into his swarthy, bearded face without embarrassment and slowly smiled.

"Have I said too much? Have I been too familiar? . . . Do you know why you think so? It's because you are still impure. By-and-by you will listen to all language without shame."

Before he realised what she was about to do, she threw her tentacle round his neck, like another arm. He offered no resistance to its cool pressure. The contact of her soft flesh with his own was so moist and sensitive that it resembled another kind of kiss. He saw who it was that embraced him – a pale, beautiful girl. Yet, oddly enough, he experienced neither voluptuousness nor sexual pride. The love expressed by the caress was rich, glowing, and personal, but there was not the least trace of sex in it—and so he received it.

She removed her tentacle, placed her two arms on his shoulders and penetrated with her eyes right into his very soul.

"Yes, I wish to be pure," he muttered. "Without that what can I ever be but a weak, squirming devil?"

Joiwind released him.

"This we call the 'magn'," she said, indicating her tentacle. "By means of it what we love already we love more, and what we don't love at all we begin to love."

"A god-like organ!"

"It is the one we guard most jealously," said Joiwind.

The shade of the trees afforded a timely screen from the now almost insufferable rays of Branchspell, which was

climbing steadily upwards to the zenith. On descending
the other side of the little hills, Maskull looked anxiously
for traces of Nightspore and Krag, but without result.
After staring about him for a few minutes he shrugged
his shoulders; but suspicions had already begun to gather
in his mind.

A small, natural amphitheatre lay at their feet, completely
circled by the tree-clad heights. The centre was of red sand.
In the very middle shot up a tall, stately tree, with a black
trunk and branches, and transparent, crystal leaves. At the
foot of this tree was a natural, circular well, containing dark
green water.

When they had reached the bottom, Joiwind took him
straight over to the well. Maskull gazed at it intently.

"Is this the shrine you talked about?"

"Yes. It is called Shaping's Well. The man or woman
who wishes to invoke Shaping must take up some of the
gnawl-water, and drink it."

"Pray for me," said Maskull. "Your unspotted prayer
will carry more weight."

"What do you wish for?"

"For purity," answered Maskull, in a troubled voice.

Joiwind made a cup of her hand, and drank a little of
the water. She held it up to Maskull's mouth. "You must
drink too." He obeyed. She then stood erect, closed her
eyes, and, in a voice like the soft murmurings of spring,
prayed aloud.

"Shaping, my father, I am hoping you can hear me.
A strange man has come to us weighed down with heavy
blood. He wishes to be pure. Let him know the meaning
of love, let him live for others. Don't spare him pain, dear
Shaping, but let him seek his own pain. Breathe into him
a noble soul."

Maskull listened, with tears in his heart.

As Joiwind left off speaking, a blurred mist came over his
eyes, and, half-buried in the scarlet sand, appeared a large
circle of dazzlingly white pillars. For some minutes they
flickered to and fro between distinctness and indistinctness,

like an object being focused. Then they faded out of sight again.

"Is that a sign from Shaping?" asked Maskull, in a low, awed tone.

"Perhaps it is. It is a time-mirage."

"What can that be, Joiwind?"

"You see, dear Maskull, the temple does not yet exist, but it will do so, because it must. What you and I are now doing in simplicity, wise men will do hereafter in full knowledge."

"It is right for man to pray," said Maskull. "Good and evil in the world don't originate from nothing. God and Devil must exist. And we should pray to the one, and fight the other."

"Yes, we must fight Krag."

"What name do you say?" asked Maskull in amazement.

"Krag—the author of evil and misery . . . whom you call Devil."

He immediately concealed his thoughts. To prevent Joiwind from learning his relationship to this being, he made his mind a blank.

"Why do you hide your mind from me?" she demanded, looking at him strangely, and changing colour.

"In this bright, pure, radiant world, evil seems so remote . . . One can scarcely grasp its meaning." But he lied.

Joiwind continued gazing at him, straight out of her clean soul.

"The world is good and pure, but many men are corrupt. Panawe, my husband, has travelled, and he has told me things I would almost rather have not heard. One person he met believed the universe to be, from top to bottom, a conjurer's cave."

"I should like to meet your husband."

"Well, we are going home now."

Maskull was on the point of inquiring whether she had any children, but was afraid of offending her, and checked himself.

She read the mental question. "What need is there? Is not the whole world full of lovely children? Why should I want selfish possessions?"

An extraordinary creature flew past, uttering a plaintive cry of five distinct notes. It was not a bird, but had a balloon-shaped body, paddled by five webbed feet. It disappeared among the trees.

Joiwind pointed to it, as it went by. "I love that beast, grotesque as it is—perhaps all the more for its grotesqueness. But if I had children of my own, should I still love it? Which is best—to love two or three, or to love all?"

"Every woman can't be like you, Joiwind, but it is good to have a few like you.

"Wouldn't it be as well," he went on, "as we've got to walk through that sun-baked wilderness, to make turbans for our heads out of some of those long leaves?"

She smiled rather pathetically. "You will think me foolish, but every tearing-off of a leaf would be a wound in my heart . . . We have only to throw our robes over our heads."

"No doubt that will answer the same purpose, but tell me—weren't these very robes once part of a living creature?"

"Oh, no—no, they are the webs of a certain animal, but they have never been in themselves alive."

"You reduce life to extreme simplicity," remarked Maskull meditatively, "but it is very beautiful."

Climbing back over the hills, they now without further ceremony commenced their march across the desert.

They walked side by side. Joiwind directed their course straight towards Poolingdred. From the position of the sun, Maskull judged their way to lie due north. The sand was soft and powdery, very tiring to his naked feet. The red glare dazed his eyes, and made him semi-blind. He was hot, parched, and tormented with the craving to drink; his undertone of pain emerged into full consciousness.

"I see my friends nowhere, and it is very queer."

"Yes, it is queer—if it is accidental," said Joiwind, with a peculiar intonation.

"Exactly!" agreed Maskull. "If they had met with a mishap, their bodies would still be there. It begins to look like a piece of bad work to me. They must have gone on, and left me . . . Well, I am here, and I must make the best of it. I shall trouble no more about them."

"I don't wish to speak ill of anyone," said Joiwind, "but my instinct tells me that you are better away from those men. They did not come here for your sake, but for their own."

They walked on for a long time. Maskull was beginning to feel faint. She twined her magn lovingly around his waist, and a strong current of confidence and well-being instantly coursed through his veins.

"Thanks, Joiwind! . . . But am I not weakening *you*?"

"Yes," she replied, with a quick, thrilling glance. "But not much—and it gives me great happiness."

Presently they met a fantastic little creature, the size of a newborn lamb, waltzing along on three legs. Each leg in turn moved to the front, and so the little monstrosity proceeded by means of a series of complete rotations. It was vividly coloured, as though it had been dipped into pots of bright blue and yellow paint. It looked up with small, shining eyes, as they passed.

Joiwind nodded and smiled to it. "That's a personal friend of mine, Maskull. Whenever I come this way, I see it. It's always waltzing, and always in a hurry, but it never seems to get anywhere."

"It seems to me that life is so self-sufficient here that there is no need for anyone to get anywhere . . . What I don't quite understand is how you manage to pass your days without ennui."

"That's a strange word. It means, does it not, craving for excitement."

"Something of the kind," said Maskull.

"That must be a disease brought on by rich food."

"But are you never dull?"

"How could we be? Our blood is quick and light and free, our flesh is clean and unclogged, inside and out . . . Before long I hope you will understand what sort of question you have asked."

Further on they encountered a strange phenomenon. In the heart of the desert a fountain rose perpendicularly fifty feet into the air, with a cool and pleasant hissing sound. It differed, however, from a fountain in this respect—that the water of which it was composed did not return to the ground, but was absorbed by the atmosphere at the summit. It was in fact a tall, graceful column of dark green fluid, with a capital of coiling and twisting vapours.

When they came closer, Maskull perceived that this water column was the continuation and termination of a flowing brook, which came down from the direction of the mountains. The explanation of the phenomenon was evidently that the water at this spot found chemical affinities in the upper air, and consequently forsook the ground.

"Now let us drink," said Joiwind.

She threw herself unaffectedly at full length on the sand, face downwards, by the side of the brook, and Maskull was not long in following her example. She refused to quench her thirst until she had seen him drink. He found the water heavy, but bubbling with gas. He drank copiously. It affected his palate in a new way . . . with the purity and cleannesss of water was combined the exhilaration of a sparkling wine, raising his spirits . . . but somehow the intoxication brought out his better nature, and not his lower.

"We call it 'gnawl-water'," said Joiwind. "This is not quite pure, as you can see by the colour. At Poolingdred it is crystal clear. But we should be ungrateful if we complained. After this you'll find we shall get along much better."

Maskull now began to realise his environment, as it were for the first time. All his sense-organs started to show him beauties and wonders which he had not hitherto suspected. The uniform glaring scarlet of the sands became separated into a score of clearly-distinguished shades of red. The sky was similarly split up into different blues. The radiant heat of Branchspell he found to affect every part of his body with unequal intensities. His ears awakened; the atmosphere was full of murmurs, the sands hummed, even the sun's rays had a sound of their own—a kind of faint Aeolian harp. Subtle, puzzling perfumes assailed his nostrils. His palate lingered over the memory of the gnawl-water. All the pores of his skin were tickled and soothed by hitherto unperceived currents of air. His poigns explored actively the inward nature of everything in his immediate vicinity. His magn touched Joiwind, and drew from her person a stream of love and joy. And lastly by means of his breve he exchanged thought with her in silence. This mighty sense-symphony stirred him to the depths, and throughout the walk of that endless morning he felt no more fatigue.

When it was drawing near to Blodsombre, they approached the sedgy margin of a dark green lake, which lay underneath Poolingdred.

Panawe was sitting on a dark rock, waiting for them.

CHAPTER SEVEN

Panawe

The husband got up to meet his wife and their guest.
He was clothed in white. He had a beardless face, with
breve and poigns. His skin, on face and body alike, was
so white, fresh, and soft, that it scarcely looked skin
at all—it rather resembled a new kind of pure, snowy
flesh, extending right down to his bones. It had nothing in common with the artificially-whitened skin of an
over-civilised woman. Its whiteness and delicacy aroused
no voluptuous thoughts . . . it was was obviously the
manifestation of a cold, and almost cruel chastity of nature.
His hair, which fell to the nape of his neck, also was
white; but again, from vigour, not decay. His eyes were
black, quiet, and fathomless. He was still a young man,
but so stern were his features that he had the appearance
of a lawgiver, and this in spite of their great beauty and
harmony.

His magn and Joiwind's intertwined for a single moment,
and Maskull saw his face soften with love, while she looked
exultant. She put him in her husband's arms with gentle
force, and stood back, gazing and smiling. Maskull felt
rather embarrassed at being embraced by a man, but
submitted to it; a sense of cool, pleasant languor passed
through him in the act.

"The stranger is red-blooded, then?"

He was startled by Panawe's speaking in English, and the
voice too was extraordinary. It was absolutely tranquil, but
its tranquillity seemed in a curious fashion to be an illusion,
proceeding from a rapidity of thoughts and feelings so great
that their motion could not be detected. How this could be,
he did not know.

"How do you come to speak in a tongue you have never heard before?" demanded Maskull.

"Thought is a rich, complex thing. I can't say if I am really speaking your tongue, by instinct, or if you yourself are translating my thoughts into your tongue, as I utter them."

"Already you see that Panawe is wiser than I am," said Joiwind gaily.

"What is your name?" asked the husband.

"Maskull."

"That name must have a meaning . . . but again, thought is a strange thing. I connect that name with something—but with what?"

"Try to discover," said Joiwind.

"Has there been a man in your world who stole something from the Maker of the universe, in order to ennoble his fellow creatures?"

"There is such a myth. The hero's name was Prometheus."

"Well, you seem to be identified in my mind with that action—but what it all means I can't say, Maskull."

"Accept it as a good omen, for Panawe never lies, and never speaks thoughtlessly."

"There must be some confusion. These are heights beyond me," said Maskull calmly, but looking rather contemplative.

"Where do you come from?"

"From the planet of a distant sun, called Earth."

"What for?"

"I was tired of vulgarity," returned Maskull laconically. He intentionally avoided mentioning his fellow-voyagers, in order that Krag's name should not come to light.

"That's an honourable motive," said Panawe. "And what's more, it may be true, though you spoke it as a prevarication."

"As far as it goes, it's quite true," said Maskull, staring at him with annoyance and surprise.

The swampy lake extended for about half a mile from where they were standing to the lower buttresses of the mountain. Feathery purple reeds showed themselves here and there through the shallows. The water was dark green . . . Maskull did not see how they were going to cross it.

Joiwind caught his arm. "Perhaps you don't know that the lake will bear us?"

Panawe walked on to the water; it was so heavy that it carried his weight. Joiwind followed with Maskull. He instantly started to slip about—nevertheless the motion was amusing, and he learnt so hard, by watching and imitating Panawe, that he was soon able to balance himself without assistance . . . After that he found the sport excellent.

For the same reason that women excel in dancing, Joiwind's half-falls and recoveries were far more graceful and sure than those of either of the men. Her slight, draped form . . . dripping, bending, rising, swaying, twisting upon the surface of the dark water . . . this was a picture Maskull could not keep his eyes away from.

The lake grew deeper. The gnawl-water became green-black. The crags, gullies, and precipices of the shore could now be distinguished in detail. A waterfall was visible, descending several hundred feet. The surface of the lake grew disturbed—so much so that Maskull had difficulty in keeping his balance. He therefore threw himself down and started swimming on the face of the water. Joiwind turned her head, and laughed so joyously that all her teeth flashed in the sunlight.

They landed in a few more minutes on a promontory of black rock. The water on Maskull's garment and body evaporated very quickly. He gazed upwards at the towering mountain, but at that moment some strange movements on the part of Panawe attracted his attention. His face was working convulsively, and he began to stagger about. Then he put his hand to his mouth and took from it what looked like a bright-coloured pebble. He looked at it carefully for some seconds. Joiwind also looked, over his shoulder, with quickly-changing colours. After this inspection, Panawe let the object—whatever it was—fall to the ground, and took no more interest in it.

"May I look?" asked Maskull . . . and without waiting for permission he picked it up. It was a delicately beautiful egg-shaped crystal of pale green.

"Where did this come from?" he asked queerly.

Panawe turned away, but Joiwind answered for him.

"It came out of my husband."

"That's what I thought, but I couldn't believe it. But what is it?"

"I don't know that it has either name or use. It is merely an overflowing of beauty."

"Beauty?"

Joiwind smiled. "If you were to regard nature as the husband, and Panawe as the wife, Maskull, perhaps everything would be explained."

Maskull reflected.

"On Earth," he said after a minute, "men like Panawe are called artists, poets and musicians. Beauty overflows into them too, and out of them again. The only distinction is that *their* productions are more human and intelligible."

"Nothing comes from it but vanity," said Panawe, and, taking the crystal out of Maskull's hand, he threw it into the lake.

The precipice which they now had to climb was several hundred feet in height. Maskull was more anxious for Joiwind than for himself. She was evidently tiring . . . but she refused all help, and was in fact still the nimbler of the two. She made a mocking face at him. Panawe seemed lost in quiet thoughts. The rock was sound, and did not crumble under their weight. The heat of Branchspell, however, was by this time almost killing, the radiance was shocking in its white intensity, and Maskull's pain steadily grew worse.

When they got to the top, a plateau of dark rock appeared, bare of vegetation, stretching in both directions as far as the eye could see. It was of a nearly uniform width of five hundred yards, from the edge of the cliffs to the lower slopes of the chain of hills inland. The hills varied in height. The cup-shaped Poolingdred was approximately a thousand feet above them. The upper part of it was covered with a kind of glittering vegetation which he could not comprehend.

Joiwind put her hand on Maskull's shoulder, and pointed upwards. "Here you have the highest peak in the whole land . . . that is, until you come to the Ifdawn Marest."

On hearing that strange name, he experienced a momentary unaccountable sensation of wild vigour and restlessness —but it passed away.

Without losing time, Panawe led the way up the mountainside. The lower half was of bare rock, not difficult to climb. Half-way up, however, it grew steeper, and they began to meet bushes and small trees. The growth became thicker as they continued to ascend, and when they neared the summit, tall forest trees appeared.

These bushes and trees had pale, glassy trunks and branches, but the small twigs and the leaves were translucent and crystal. They cast no shadows from above, but still the shade was cool. Both leaves and branches were fantastically shaped. What surprised Maskull the most, however, was the fact that, as far as he could see, scarcely any two plants belonged to the same species.

"Won't you help Maskull out of his difficulty?" said Joiwind, pulling her husband's arm.

He smiled. "If he'll forgive me for again trespassing in his brain. But the difficulty is small . . . Life in a new planet, Maskull, is necessarily energetic and lawless, and not sedate and imitative. Nature is still fluid—not yet rigid—and matter is plastic. The will forks and sports incessantly, and thus no two creatures are alike."

"Well, I understand all that," replied Maskull, after listening attentively. "But what I don't grasp is this— if living creatures here sport so energetically, how does it come about that human beings wear much the same shape as in my world?"

"I'll explain that too," said Panawe. "All creatures which resemble Shaping must of necessity resemble one another."

"Then sporting is the blind will to become like Shaping?"

"Exactly."

"It is most wonderful," said Maskull. ". . . Then the brotherhood of man is not a fable invented by idealists, but a solid fact."

Joiwind looked at him, and changed colour. Panawe relapsed into sternness.

Maskull became interested in a new phenomenon. The jale-coloured blossoms of a crystal bush were emitting mental waves, which with his breve he could clearly distinguish. They cried out silently—"To me! To me!" While he looked, a flying worm guided itself through the air to one of these blossoms and began to suck its nectar. The floral cry immediately ceased.

They now gained the crest of the mountain, and looked down beyond. A lake occupied its crater-like cavity. A fringe of trees partly intercepted the view, but Maskull was able to perceive that this mountain lake was nearly circular and perhaps a quarter of a mile across. Its shore stood a hundred feet below them.

Observing that his hosts did not propose to descend, he begged them to wait for him, and scrambled down to the surface. When he got there, he found the water perfectly motionless and of a colourless transparency. He walked on to it, lay down at full length, and peered into the depths. It was weirdly clear . . . he could see down for an indefinite distance, without arriving at any bottom. Some dark, shadowy objects, almost out of reach of his eyes, were moving about. Then a sound, very faint and mysterious, seemed to come up through the gnawl-water from an immense depth. It was like the rhythm of a drum. There were four beats of equal length, but the accent was on the third. It went on for a considerable time, and then ceased.

The sound appeared to him to belong to a different world from that in which he was travelling. The latter was mystical, dream-like, and unbelievable . . . the drumming was like a very dim undertone of reality. It resembled the ticking of a clock in a room full of voices—only occasionally possible to be picked up by the ear.

He rejoined Panawe and Joiwind, but said nothing to them about his experience. They all walked round the rim of the crater, and gazed down on the opposite side. Similar precipices to those which had overlooked the desert here formed the boundary of a vast moorland plain, whose dimensions could not be measured by the eye. It was solid land, yet he could not make out its prevailing colour. It was as if made of transparent glass, but it did not glitter in the sunlight. No objects in it could be distinguished, except a rolling river in the far distance, and, further off still, on the horizon, a line of dark mountains, of strange shapes. Instead of being rounded, conical, or hog-backed, these heights were carved by nature into the semblance of castle battlements, but with extremely deep indentations.

The sky immediately above the mountains was of a vivid, intense blue. It contrasted in a most marvellous way with the blue of the rest of the heavens. It seemed more luminous and radiant, and was in fact like the afterglow of a gorgeous *blue* sunset.

Maskull kept on looking. The more he gazed, the more restless and noble became his feelings.

"What is that light?"

Panawe was sterner than usual, while his wife clung to his arm.

"It is Alppain—our second sun," he replied. "Those hills are the Ifdawn Marest . . . Now let us get to our shelter."

"Is it imagination, or am I really being affected . . . tormented by that light?"

"No, it's not imagination—it's real . . . How can it be otherwise when two suns, of different natures, are drawing you at the same time? Luckily you are not looking at Alppain itself. It's invisible here. You would require to go at least as far as Ifdawn, to set eyes on it."

"Why do you say 'luckily'?"

"Because the agony caused by those opposing forces

would perhaps be more than you could bear . . . But I don't know."

For the short distance which remained of their walk, Maskull was very thoughtful and uneasy. He understood nothing. Whatever object his eye chanced to rest on changed immediately into a puzzle. The silence and stillness of the mountain peak seemed brooding, mysterious, and *waiting*. Panawe gave him a friendly, anxious look, and without further delay led the way down a little track, which traversed the side of the mountain and terminated in the mouth of a cave.

This cave was the home of Panawe and Joiwind. It was dark inside. The host took a shell and, filling it with liquid from a well, carelessly sprinkled the sandy floor of the interior. A greenish, phosphorescent light gradually spread to the furthest limits of the cavern, and continued to illuminate it for the whole time they were there. There was no furniture. Some dried fern-like leaves served for couches.

The moment she got in, Joiwind fell down in exhaustion. Her husband tended her with calm concern. He bathed her face, put drink to her lips, energised her with his magn, and finally laid her down to sleep. At the sight of the noble woman thus suffering on his account, Maskull was distressed. Panawe, however, endeavoured to reassure him. "It's quite true this has been a very long, hard double-journey, but for the future it will lighten all her other journeys for her . . . Such is the nature of sacrifice."

"I can't conceive how I have walked so far in a morning," said Maskull, "and she has been twice the distance."

"Love flows in her veins, instead of blood, and that's why she is so strong."

"You know she gave me some of it?"

"Otherwise you couldn't even have started."

"I shall never forget that."

The languorous heat of the day outside, the bright mouth of the cavern, the cool seclusion of the interior, with its pale green glow, invited Maskull to sleep. But curiosity got the better of his lassitude.

"Will it disturb her if we talk?"

"No."

"But how do you feel disposed?"

"I require little sleep. In any case, it's more important that you should hear something about your new life. It's not all as innocent and idyllic as this . . . If you intend to go through, you ought to be instructed about the dangers."

"Oh, I guessed as much. But how shall we arrange . . . shall I put questions, or will you tell me what you think is most essential?"

Panawe motioned to Maskull to sit down on a pile of ferns, and at the same time reclined himself, leaning on one arm, with outstretched legs.

"I will give some incidents of my life. You will begin to learn from them what sort of place you have come to."

"I shall be grateful," said Maskull, preparing himself to listen.

Panawe paused for a moment or two, and then started his narrative in tranquil, measured, yet sympathetic tones.

PANAWE'S STORY

"My earliest recollection is of being taken, when three years old (that's equivalent to fifteen of your years, but we develop more slowly here), by my father and mother, to see Broodviol, the wisest man in Tormance. He dwelt in the great Wombflash Forest. We walked through trees for three days, sleeping at night. The trees grew taller as we went along, until it ended that the tops were out of sight. The trunks were of a dark red colour and the leaves were of pale ulfire. My father kept stopping to think. If left uninterrupted, he would remain for half a day in deep abstraction. My mother came out of Poolingdred, and was of a different stamp. She was beautiful, generous, and charming . . . but also active. She kept urging him on. This led to many disputes between them, which made me miserable. On the fourth day we passed through a part of the forest which bordered on the Sinking Sea. This sea is full of pouches of water which will not bear a man's weight, and as these light parts don't differ in appearance from the rest, it is dangerous to cross. My father pointed out a dim outline on the horizon, and told me it was Swaylone's Island. Men sometimes go there, but none ever return. In the evening of the same day we found Broodviol, standing in a deep, miry pit in the forest, surrounded on all sides by trees three hundred feet high. He was a big, gnarled, rugged, wrinkled, sturdy old man. His age at that time was a hundred and twenty of our years, or nearly six hundred of yours. His body was trilateral . . . he had three legs, three arms, and six eyes, placed at equal distances all round his head. This gave him an aspect of great watchfulness and sagacity. He was standing in a sort of trance. I afterwards heard this saying of his: 'To lie is to sleep, to sit is to dream, to stand is to think.' My father caught the infection, and fell into meditation, but my mother roused them both thoroughly. Broodviol scowled at her savagely, and demanded what she required. Then I too learnt for the first time the object of our journey. I was a prodigy . . . That is to say, I was without sex. My parents were troubled over this, and wished to consult the wisest of men.

"Old Broodviol smoothed his face, and said: 'This perhaps will not be so difficult. I will explain the marvel. Every man and woman among us is a walking murderer. If a male, he has struggled with and killed the female who was born in the same body with him—if a female, she has killed the male. But in this child the struggle is still continuing.'

"'How shall we end it?' asked my mother.

"'Let the child direct its will to the scene of the combat, and it will be of whichever sex it pleases.'

"'You want, of course, to be a man, don't you?' said my mother to me earnestly.'

"'Then I shall be slaying your daughter, and that would be a crime.'

"Something in my tone attracted Broodviol's notice.

"'That was spoken, not selfishly, but magnanimously. Therefore the male must have spoken it, and you need not trouble further. Before you arrive home, the child will be a boy.'

"My father walked away out of sight. My mother bent very low before Broodviol for about ten minutes, and he remained all that time looking kindly at her.

"I heard that shortly afterwards Alppain came into that land for a few hours daily. Broodviol grew melancholy, and died.

"His prophecy came true . . . before we reached home, I knew the meaning of shame. But I have often pondered over his words since, in later years, when trying to understand my own nature; and I have come to the conclusion that, wisest of men as he was, he still did not see quite straight on this occasion. Between me and my twin sister, enclosed in one body, there never was any struggle, but instinctive reverence for life withheld both of us from fighting for existence. Hers was the stronger temperament, and she sacrificed herself—though not consciously—for me.

"As soon as I comprehended this, I made a vow never to eat or destroy anything which should contain life . . . and I have kept it ever since.

"While I was still hardly a grown man, my father died. My mother's death followed immediately, and I hated the associations of the land. I therefore determined to travel into my mother's country, where, as she had often told me, Nature was most sacred and solitary.

"One hot morning I came to Shaping's Causeway. It is so called either because Shaping once crossed it, or on account of its stupendous character. It is a natural embankment, twenty miles long, which links the mountains bordering my homeland with the Ifdawn Marest. The valley lies below at a depth varying from eight to ten thousand feet —a terrible precipice on either side. The knife-edge of the ridge is generally not much over a foot wide. The Causeway goes due north and south. The valley on my right hand was plunged in shadow—that on my left was sparkling with sunlight and dew. I walked fearfully along this precarious path for some miles. Far to the east the valley was closed by a lofty tableland, connecting the two chains of mountains, but overtopping even the most towering pinnacles. This is called the Sant Levels. I was never there, but I have heard two curious facts concerning the inhabitants. The first is that they have no women; the second, that though they are addicted to travelling in other parts they never acquire the habits of the peoples with whom they reside.

"Presently I turned giddy, and lay at full length for a great while, clutching the two edges of the path with both hands, and staring at the ground I was lying on with wide-open eyes. When that passed I felt a different man and grew conceited and gay. About half-way across I saw someone approaching me a long way off. This put fear into my heart again, for I did not see how we could very well pass. However, I went slowly on, and presently we drew near enough together for me to recognise the walker . . . It was Slofork, the so-called sorcerer. I had never met him before, but I knew him by his peculiarities of person. He was of a bright gamboge colour and possessed a very long, proboscis-like nose, which appeared to be a useful organ, but did not add to his beauty, as I knew beauty. He was dubbed 'sorcerer' from his wondrous skill in budding limbs and organs. The tale is told that one evening he slowly sawed his leg off with a blunt stone and then lay for two days in agony while his new leg was sprouting. He was not reputed a consistently wise man, but he had periodical flashes of penetration and audacity which none could equal.

"We sat down and faced one another, about two yards apart.

"'Which of us walks over the other?' asked Slofork. His manner was as calm as the day itself, but, to my young nature, terrible with hidden terrors. I smiled at him, but did not wish for this humiliation. We continued sitting thus, in friendly wise, for many minutes.

"'What is greater than Pleasure?' he asked suddenly.

"I was at an age when one wishes to be thought equal

to any emergency, so, concealing my surprise, I applied myself to the conversation, as if it were for that purpose we had met.

"'Pain,' I replied, 'for pain drives out pleasure.'

"'What is greater than Pain?'

"I reflected. 'Love. Because we will accept our loved-one's share of pain.'

"'But what is greater than Love?' he persisted.

"'Nothing, Slofork.'

"'And what is Nothing?'

"'That you must tell me.'

"'Tell you I will. This is Shaping's world. He that is a good child here, knows pleasure, pain, and love, and gets his rewards. But there's another world . . . not Shaping's . . . and there all this is unknown, and another order of things reigns. That world we call Nothing . . . but it is not Nothing, but Something.'

"There was a pause.

"'I have heard,' said I, 'that you are good at growing and ungrowing organs?'

"'That's not enough for me. Every organ tells me the same story. I want to hear different stories.'

"'Is it true, what men say, that your wisdom flows and ebbs in pulses?'

"'Quite true,' replied Slofork. 'But those you had it from did not add that they have always mistaken the flow for the ebb.'

"'My experience is,' said I sententiously, 'that wisdom is misery.'

"'Perhaps it is, young man . . . but you have never learnt that, and never will. For you the world will continue to wear a noble, awful face. You will never rise above mysticism . . . But be happy in your own way.'

"Before I realised what he was doing, he jumped tranquilly from the path, down into the empty void . . . He crashed with ever-increasing momentum towards the valley below. I screeched, flung myself down on the ground, and shut my eyes.

"Often have I wondered which of my ill-considered, juvenile remarks it was which caused this sudden resolution on his part to commit suicide. Whichever it might be, since then I have made it a rigid law never to speak for my own pleasure, but only to help others.

"I came eventually to the Marest. I threaded its mazes in terror for four days. I was frightened of death, but still more terrified at the possibility of losing my sacred attitude towards life. When I was nearly through, and was beginning to congratulate myself, I stumbled across the third extraordinary personage of my experience . . . the grim Muremaker. It was under horrible circumstances. On an afternoon, cloudy and stormy, I saw, suspended in the air without visible support, a living man. He was hanging in an upright position in front of a cliff . . . a yawning gulf, a thousand feet deep, lay beneath his feet. I climbed as near as I could, and looked on. He saw me, and made a wry grimace, like one who wishes to turn his humiliation into humour. The spectacle so astounded me that I could not even grasp what had happened.

" 'I am Muremaker,' he cried, in a scraping voice which shocked my ears. 'All my life I have sorbed others . . . now I am sorbed. Nuclamp and I fell out over a woman. Now Nuclamp holds me up like this. While the strength of his will lasts I shall remain suspended; but when he gets tired —and it can't be long now—I drop into those depths.'

"Had it been another man, I would have tried to save him, but this ogre-like being was too well known to me as one who passed his whole existence in tormenting, murdering, and absorbing others, for the sake of his own delight. I hurried away, and did not pause again that day.

"In Poolingdred I met Joiwind. We walked and talked together for a month, and by that time we found that we loved each other too well to part."

Panawe left off speaking.

"That is a fascinating story," remarked Maskull. "Now

I begin to know my way about better. But one thing puzzles me."

"What's that?"

"How it happens that men here are ignorant of tools and arts, and have no civilisation, and yet contrive to be social in their habits and wise in their thoughts."

"Do you imagine, then, that love and wisdom spring from tools? . . . But I see how it arises. In your world you have fewer sense-organs, and to make up for the deficiency you have been obliged to call in the assistance of stones and metals . . . That's by no means a sign of superiority."

"No, I suppose not," said Maskull, "but I see I have a great deal to unlearn."

They talked together a little longer, and then gradually fell asleep. Joiwind opened her eyes, smiled, and slumbered again.

CHAPTER EIGHT

The Lusion Plain

Maskull awoke before the others. He got up, stretched himself, and walked out into the sunlight. Branchspell was already declining. He climbed to the top of the crater-edge and looked away towards Ifdawn. The afterglow of Alppain had by now completely disappeared. The mountains stood up wild and grand.

They impressed him like a simple musical theme, the notes of which are widely separated in the scale . . . a spirit of rashness, daring, and adventure seemed to call to him from them. It was at that moment that the determination flashed into his heart to walk to the Marest, and explore its dangers.

He returned to the cavern to say goodbye to his hosts. Joiwind looked at him with her brave and honest eyes.

"Is this selfishness, Maskull?" she asked, "or are you drawn by something stronger than yourself?"

"We must be reasonable," he answered, smiling. "I can't settle down in Poolingdred before I have found out something about this surprising new planet of yours. Remember what a long way I have come . . . But very likely I shall come back here."

"Will you make me a promise?"

Maskull hesitated. "Ask nothing difficult, for I hardly know my powers yet."

"It is not hard, and I wish it. Promise this—never to raise your hand against a living creature, either to strike, pluck, or eat, without first recollecting its mother, who suffered for it."

"Perhaps I won't promise that," said Maskull slowly, "but I'll undertake something more tangible. I will never lift

72

my hand against a living creature without first recollecting you, Joiwind."

She turned a little pale. "Now if Panawe knew that Panawe existed, he might be jealous."

Panawe put his hand on her gently.

"You would not talk like that in Shaping's presence," he said.

"No. Forgive me! I'm not quite myself . . . Perhaps it is Maskull's blood in my veins . . . Now let us bid him adieu. Let us pray that he will do only honourable deeds, wherever he may be."

"I'll put Maskull on his way," said Panawe.

"There's no need," replied Maskull. "The way is plain."

"But talking shortens the road."

Maskull turned to go. Joiwind pulled him round towards her softly.

"You won't think badly of other women on my account?"

"You are a blessed spirit," answered he.

She trod quietly to the inner extremity of the cave and stood there thinking. Panawe and Maskull emerged into the open air.

Half-way down the cliff-face a little spring was encountered. Its water was colourless, transparent, but gaseous. As soon as Maskull had satisfied his thirst he felt himself different. His surroundings were so real to him in their vividness and colour, so unreal in their phantom-like mystery, that he scrambled downhill like one in a winter's dream.

When they reached the plain he saw in front of them an interminable forest of tall trees, the shapes of which were extraordinarily foreign-looking. The leaves were crystalline and, looking upwards, it was as if he were gazing through a roof of glass. The moment they got underneath the trees the light-rays of the sun continued to come through—white, savage, and blazing—but they were gelded of heat. Then it was not hard to imagine that they were wandering through cool, bright elfin glades.

Through the forest, commencing at their very feet, an

avenue, perfectly straight and not very wide, went forward as far as the eye could see.

Maskull wanted to talk to his travelling companion, but was somehow unable to find words. Panawe glanced at him with an inscrutable smile—stern, yet enchanting and half-feminine. He then broke the silence, but, strangely enough, Maskull could not make out whether he was singing or speaking. From his lips issued a slow musical recitative, exactly like a bewitching adagio from a low-toned stringed instrument . . . but there was a difference. Instead of the repetition and variation of one or two short themes, as in music, Panawe's theme was prolonged—it never came to an end, but rather resembled a conversation in rhythm and melody. And, at the same time, it was no recitative, for it was not declamatory. It was a long, quiet stream of lovely emotion.

Maskull listened entranced, yet agitated. The song, if it might be termed song, seemed to be always just on the point of becoming clear and intelligible—not with the intelligibility of words, but in the way one sympathises with another's moods and feelings; and Maskull felt that something important was about to be uttered, which would explain all that had gone before. But it was invariably postponed, he never understood . . . and yet somehow he did understand.

Late in the afternoon they came to a clearing, and there Panawe ceased his recitative. He slowed his pace and stopped, in the fashion of a man who wishes to convey that he intends to go no further.

"What is the name of this country?" asked Maskull.

"It is the Lusion Plain."

"Was that music in the nature of a temptation . . . do you wish me not to go on?"

"Your work lies before you, and not behind you."

"What was it, then? What work do you allude to?"

"It must have seemed like something to you, Maskull."

"It seemed like Shaping-music to me."

The instant he had absently uttered these words, Maskull

wondered why he had done so, as they now appeared meaningless to him. Panawe, however, showed no surprise.

"Shaping you will find everywhere."

"Am I dreaming, or awake?"

"You are awake."

Maskull fell into deep thought.

"So be it!" he said, rousing himself. "Now I will go on. But where must I sleep tonight?"

"You will reach a broad river. On that you can travel to the foot of the Marest tomorrow; but tonight you had better sleep where the forest and river meet."

"Adieu, then, Panawe! But do you wish to say anything more to me?"

"Only this, Maskull—wherever you go, help to make the world beautiful, and not ugly."

"That's more than any of us can undertake. I am a simple man, and have no ambitions in the way of beautifying life . . . but tell Joiwind I will try to keep myself pure."

They parted rather coldly. Maskull stood erect where they had stopped, and watched Panawe out of sight. He sighed more than once.

He became aware that something was about to happen. The air was breathless. The late afternoon sunshine, unobstructed, wrapped his frame in voluptuous heat. A solitary cloud, immensely high, raced through the sky overhead.

A single trumpet note sounded in the far distance from somewhere behind him. It gave him an impression of being several miles away at first; but then it slowly swelled, and came nearer and nearer at the same time that it increased in volume. Still the same note sounded, but now it was as if blown by a giant-trumpeter immediately over his head. Then it gradually diminished in force, and travelled away in front of him. It ended very faintly and distantly.

He felt himself alone with Nature. A sacred stillness came over his heart. Past and future were forgotten. The forest, the sun, the day, did not exist for him. He was unconscious of himself—he had no thoughts and no feelings. Yet never had Life had such an altitude for him.

A man stood, with crossed arms, right in his path. He was so clothed that his limbs were exposed, while his body was covered. He was young rather than old. Maskull observed that his countenance possessed none of the special organs of Tormance, to which he had not even yet become reconciled. He was smooth-faced. His whole person seemed to radiate an excess of life, like the trembling of air on a hot day. His eyes had such force that Maskull could not meet them.

He addressed Maskull by name, in an extraordinary voice. It had a double tone. The primary one sounded far away; the second was an undertone, like a sympathetic tanging string.

Maskull felt a rising joy, as he continued standing in the presence of this individual. He believed that something good was happening to him.

He found it physically difficult to bring any words out. "Why do you stop me?"

"Maskull, look well at me. Who am I?"

"I think you are Shaping."

"I am Surtur."

Maskull again attempted to meet his eyes, but felt as if he were being stabbed.

"You know that this is my world. Why do you think I have brought you here? I wish you to serve me."

Maskull could no longer speak.

"Those who joke at my world," continued the vision, "those who make a mock of its stern, eternal rhythm, its beauty and sublimity, which are not skin deep, but proceed from fathomless roots . . . they shall not escape."

"I do not mock it."

"Ask me your questions, and I will answer them."

"I have nothing."

"It is necessary for you to serve me, Maskull. Do you not understand? . . . You are my servant and helper."

"I shall not fail."

"This is for my sake, and not for yours."

These last words had no sooner left Surtur's mouth, than Maskull saw him spring suddenly upwards and outwards.

Looking up at the vault of the sky, he saw the whole expanse of vision filled by Surtur's form—not as a concrete man, but as a vast, concave cloud-image, looking down and frowning at him. Then the spectacle vanished, as a light goes out.

Maskull stood inactive, with a thumping heart. Now he again heard the solitary trumpet note. The sound began this time faintly in the far distance in front of him, travelled slowly towards him with regularly-increasing intensity, passed overhead at its loudest, and then grew more and more quiet, wonderful, and solemn, as it fell away in the rear, until the note was merged in the deathlike silence of the forest. It appeared to Maskull like the closing of a marvellous and important chapter.

Simultaneously with the fading away of the sound, the heavens seemed to open up with the rapidity of lightning into a blue vault of immeasurable height. He breathed a great breath, stretched all his limbs, and looked around him with a slow smile.

After awhile he resumed his journey. His brain was all dark and confused, but one idea was already beginning to stand out from the rest—huge, shapeless, and grand, like the growing image in the soul of a creative artist . . . the staggering thought that he was a man of destiny.

The more he reflected upon all that had occurred since his arrival in this new world . . . and even before leaving Earth . . . the clearer and more indisputable it became, that he could not be here for his own purposes, but must be here for an end . . . But what that end was, he could not imagine.

Through the forest he saw Branchspell at last sinking in the west. It looked a stupendous ball of red fire—now he could realise at his ease what a sun it was! The avenue took an abrupt turn to the left and began to descend steeply.

A wide, rolling river of clear and dark water was visible in front of him, no great way off. It flowed from north to south. The forest path led him straight to its banks. Maskull stood there, and regarded the lapping, gurgling waters pensively. On the opposite bank, the forest continued. Miles to the south, Poolingdred could just be distinguished. On the northern skyline the Ifdawn mountains loomed up—high, wild, beautiful, and dangerous. They were not a dozen miles away.

Like the first mutterings of a thunder storm, the first faint breaths of cool wind, Maskull felt the stirrings of passion in his heart. In spite of his bodily fatigue, he wished to test his strength against something. This craving he identified with the crags of the Marest. They seemed to have the same magical attraction for his will as the loadstone for iron. He kept biting his nails, as he turned his eyes in that direction—wondering if it would not be possible to conquer the heights that evening. But when he glanced back again at Poolingdred, he remembered Joiwind and Panawe, and grew more tranquil. He decided to make his bed at this spot, and to set off as soon after daybreak as he should awake.

He drank at the river, washed himself, and lay down on the bank to sleep. By this time, so far had his idea progressed, that he cared nothing for the possible dangers of the night . . . he confided in his star.

Branchspell set, the day faded, night with its terrible weight came on, and through it all Maskull slept. Long before midnight, however, he was awakened by a crimson glow in the sky. He opened his eyes, and wondered where he was. He felt heaviness and pain. The red glow was a terrestrial phenomenon; it came from among the trees. He got up and went towards the source of the light.

Away from the river, not a hundred feet off, he nearly stumbled across the form of a sleeping woman. The object which emitted the crimson rays was lying on the ground, several yards away from her. It was like a small jewel, throwing off sparks of red light. He barely threw a glance at that, however.

The woman was clothed in the large skin of an animal. She had big, smooth, shapely limbs, rather muscular than fat. Her magn was not a thin tentacle, but a third arm, terminating in a hand. Her face, which was upturned, was wild, powerful, and exceedingly handsome. But he saw with surprise that in place of a breve on her forehead, she possessed another eye. All three were closed. The colour of her skin in the crimson glow he could not distinguish.

He touched her gently with his hand. She awoke calmly and looked up at him without stirring a muscle. All three eyes stared at him; but the two lower ones were dull and vacant—mere carriers of vision. The middle, upper one alone expressed her inner nature. Its haughty, unflinching glare had yet something seductive and alluring in it. Maskull felt a challenge in that look of lordly, feminine will, and his manner instinctively stiffened.

She sat up.

"Can you speak my language?" he asked. "I shouldn't put such a question, but others have been able to."

"Why should you imagine that I can't read your mind? Is it so extremely complex?"

She spoke in a rich, lingering, musical voice, which delighted him to listen to.

"No, but you have no breve."

"Well, but haven't I a sorb, which is better?" And she pointed to the eye on her brow.

"What is your name?"

"Oceaxe."

"And where do you come from?"

"Ifdawn."

These contemptuous replies began to irritate him, and yet the mere sound of her voice was fascinating.

"I am going there tomorrow," he remarked.

She laughed; as if against her will, but made no comment.

"My name is Maskull," he went on. "I am a stranger . . . from another world."

"So I should judge, from your absurd appearance."

"Perhaps it would be as well to say at once," said Maskull bluntly, "are we, or are we not, to be friends?"

She yawned and stretched her arms, without rising. "Why

should we be friends? . . . If I thought you were a man,
I might accept you as a lover."

"You must look elsewhere for that."

"So be it, Maskull! Now go away, and leave me in
peace."

She dropped her head again to the ground, but did not
at once close her eyes.

"What are you doing here?" he interrogated.

"Oh, we Ifdawn folk occasionally come here to sleep,
for *there* often enough it is a night for us which has no
next morning."

"Being such a terrible place, and seeing that I am a total
stranger, it would be merely courteous if you were to warn
me what I have to expect in the way of dangers."

"I am perfectly and utterly indifferent what becomes of
you," retorted Oceaxe.

"Are you returning in the morning?" persisted Maskull.

"If I wish."

"Then we will go together."

She got up again on her elbow. "Instead of making plans
for other people, I would do a very necessary thing."

"Pray tell me."

"Well, there's no reason why I should, but I will. I would
try to convert my women's organs into men's organs. It is a
man's country."

"Speak more plainly."

"Oh, it's plain enough. If you attempt to pass through
Ifdawn without a sorb, you are simply committing suicide.
And that magn too is worse than useless."

"You probably know what you are talking about, Oceaxe.
But what do you advise me to do?"

She negligently pointed to the light-emitting stone lying
on the ground.

"There is the solution. If you hold that drude to your
organs for a good while, perhaps it will start the change,
and perhaps nature will do the rest during the night . . .
I promise nothing."

Oceaxe now really turned her back on Maskull.

He considered for a few minutes, and then walked over to where the stone was lying, and took it in his hand. It was a pebble the size of a hen's egg, radiant with crimson light, as though red-hot, and throwing out a continuous shower of small blood-red sparks.

Finally deciding that Oceaxe's advice was good, he applied the drude first to his magn, and then to his breve. He experienced a cauterising sensation—a feeling of healing pain.

CHAPTER NINE

Oceaxe

Maskull's second day on Tormance dawned. Branchspell was already above the horizon when he awoke. He was instantly aware that his organs had changed during the night. His fleshy breve was altered into an eye-like sorb; his magn had swelled and developed into a third arm, springing from the breast. The arm gave him at once a sense of greater physical security, but with the sorb he was obliged to experiment, before he could grasp its function.

As he lay there in the white sunlight, opening and shutting each of his three eyes in turn, he found that the two lower ones served his understanding, the upper one his will. That is to say, with the lower eyes he saw things in clear detail, but without personal interest; with the sorb he saw nothing as self-existent—everything appeared as an object of importance or non-importance to his own needs.

Rather puzzled as to how this would turn out, he got up and looked about him. He had slept out of sight of Oceaxe. He was anxious to learn if she were still on the spot, but before going to ascertain he determined to bathe in the river.

It was a glorious morning. The hot, white sun already began to glare, but its heat was tempered by a strong wind, which whistled through the trees. A host of fantastic clouds filled the sky. They looked like animals, and were always changing shape. The ground, as well as the leaves and branches of the forest trees, still held traces of heavy dew or rain during the night. A poignantly sweet smell of nature entered his nostrils. His pain was quiescent, and his spirits were high.

Before he bathed, he viewed the mountains of the Ifdawn

Marest. In the morning sunlight they stood out pictorially. He guessed that they were from five to six thousand feet high. The lofty, irregular, castellated line seemed like the walls of a magic city. The cliffs fronting him were composed of gaudy rocks—vermilion, emerald, yellow, ulfire, and black. As he gazed at them, his heart began to beat like a slow, heavy drum, and he thrilled all over . . . indescribable hopes, aspirations, and emotions came over him. It was more than the conquest of a new world which he felt—it was something different . . .

He bathed and drank, and as he was reclothing himself, Oceaxe strolled indolently up.

He could now perceive the colour of her skin—it was a vivid, yet delicate mixture of carmine, white, and jale. The effect was startlingly unearthly. With these new colours she looked a genuine representative of a strange planet. Her frame also had something curious about it. The curves were womanly, the bones were characteristically female—yet all seemed somehow to express a daring, masculine underlying will. The commanding eye on her forehead set the same puzzle in plainer language. Its bold, domineering egotism was shot with under-gleams of sex and softness.

She came to the river's edge, and reviewed him from top to toe.

"Now you are built more like a man," she said, in her lovely, lingering voice.

"You see the experiment was successful," he answered, smiling gaily.

Oceaxe continued looking him over. "Did some woman give you that ridiculous robe?"

"A woman did give it to me"—dropping his smile—"but I saw nothing ridiculous in the gift at the time, and I don't now."

"I think I should look better in it."

As she drawled the words, she began stripping off the skin, which suited her form so well, and motioned to him to exchange garments. He obeyed, rather shamefacedly, for he realised that the proposed exchange was in fact more appropriate to his sex. He found the skin a freer dress. Oceaxe in her drapery appeared more dangerously feminine to him.

"I don't want you to receive gifts at all from other women," she remarked slowly.

"Why not? What can I be to you?"

"I have been thinking about you during the night."

Her voice was retarded, scornful, viola-like. She sat down on the trunk of a fallen tree, and looked away.

"In what way?"

She returned no answer to his question, but began to pull off pieces of the bark.

"Last night you were so contemptuous."

"Last night is not today. Do you always walk through the world with your head over your shoulder?"

It was now Maskull's turn to be silent.

"Still, if you have male instincts, as I suppose you have, you can't go on resisting me for ever."

"But this is preposterous!" said Maskull, opening his eyes wide. "Granted that you are a beautiful woman . . . we can't be quite so primaeval."

Oceaxe sighed, and rose to her feet. "It makes no odds. I can wait."

"From that I gather that you intend to make the journey in my society. I have no objection—in fact I shall be glad . . . but only on condition that you drop this language."

"Yet you do think me beautiful?"

"Why shouldn't I think so, if it is the fact? I fail to see what that has to do with my feelings. Bring it to an end, Oceaxe. You will find plenty of men to admire . . . and love you."

At that she blazed up. "Does love pick and choose, you fool? Do you imagine I am so hard put to it that I have to hunt for lovers? . . . Is not Crimtyphon waiting for me at this very moment?"

"Very well. I am sorry to have hurt your feelings. Now carry the temptation no further . . . for it *is* a temptation, where a lovely woman is concerned. I am not my own master."

"I'm not proposing anything so very hateful, am I? Why do you humiliate me so?"

Maskull put his hands behind his back. "I repeat, I am not my own master."

"Then who is your master?"

"Yesterday I saw Surtur, and from today I am serving *him*."

"Did you speak with him?" she asked curiously.

"I did."

"Tell me what he said."

"No, I can't—I won't. But whatever he said, his beauty was more tormenting than yours, Oceaxe, and that's why I can look at you in cool blood."

"Did Surtur forbid you to be a man?"

Maskull frowned. "Is love such a manly sport, then? I should have thought it effeminate."

"It doesn't matter. You won't always be so boyish . . . But don't try my patience too far."

"Let us talk about something else—and, above all, let us get on our road."

She suddenly broke into a laugh, so rich, sweet, and enchanting, that he grew half-inflamed, and half-wished to catch her body in his arms. "Oh, Maskull, Maskull— what a fool you are!"

"In what way am I a fool?" he demanded, scowling— not at her words, but at his own weakness.

"Isn't the whole world the handiwork of innumerable pairs of lovers? . . . and yet you think yourself above all that. You try to fly away from nature, but where will you find a hole to hide yourself in?"

"Besides beauty, I now credit you with a second quality . . . persistence."

"Read me well, and then it is natural law that you'll think twice and thrice before throwing me away . . . And now, before we go, we had better eat."

"Eat?" said Maskull thoughtfully.

"Don't you eat? Is food in the same category as love?"

"What food is it?"

"Fish from the river."

Maskull recollected his promise to Joiwind. At the same time, he felt hungry.

"Is there nothing milder?"

She pulled her mouth scornfully. "You came through Poolingdred, didn't you? All the people there are the same. They think life is to be looked at, and not lived. Now that you are visiting Ifdawn, you will have to change your notions."

"Go catch your fish," he returned, pulling down his brows.

The broad, clear waters flowed past them with swelling undulations, from the direction of the mountains. Oceaxe knelt down on the bank, and peered into the depths. Presently her look became tense and concentrated; she dipped her hand in and pulled out some sort of little monster. It was more like a reptile than a fish, with its scaly plates and teeth. She threw it on the ground, and it started crawling about. Suddenly she darted all her will into her sorb. The creature leapt into the air, and fell down dead.

She picked up a sharp-edged slate, and with it removed the scales and entrails. During this operation, her hands and garment became stained with the light scarlet blood.

"Find the drude, Maskull," she said, with a lazy smile. "You had it last night."

He searched for it. It was hard to locate, for its rays had grown dull and feeble in the sunlight, but at last he found it. Oceaxe placed it in the interior of the monster, and left the body lying on the ground.

"While it's cooking, I'll wash some of this blood away, which frightens you so much. Have you never seen blood before?"

Maskull gazed at her in perplexity. The old paradox came back—the contrasting sexual characteristics in her person. Her bold, masterful, masculine egotism of manner seemed quite incongruous with the fascinating and disturbing femininity of her voice. A startling idea flashed into his mind.

"In your country I'm told there is an act of will called 'absorbing'. What is that?"

She held her red, dripping hands away from her draperies, and uttered a delicious, clashing laugh.

"You think I am half a man?"

"Answer my question."

"I'm a woman through and through, Maskull . . . to the marrow bone. But that's not to say I have never absorbed males."

"And that means . . . ?"

"New strings for my harp, Maskull . . . A wider range of passions, a stormier heart . . ."

"For you, yes . . . but for them . . . ?"

"I don't know. The victims don't describe their experiences. Probably unhappiness of some sort . . . if they still know anything."

"This is a fearful business!" he exclaimed, regarding her gloomily. "One would think Ifdawn a land of devils."

Oceaxe gave a beautiful sneer, as she took a step towards the river. "Better men than you—better in every sense of the word—are walking about with foreign wills inside them. You may be as moral as you like, Maskull, but the fact remains, animals were made to be eaten, and simple natures were made to be absorbed."

"And human rights count for nothing!"

She had bent over the river's edge, to wash her arms and hands, but glanced up over her shoulder to answer his remark. "They do count. But we only regard a man as human for just as long as he's able to hold his own with others."

The flesh was soon cooked, and they breakfasted in silence. Maskull cast heavy, doubtful glances from time to time towards his companion. Whether it was due to the strange quality of the food, or to his long abstention, he did not know, but the meal tasted nauseous, and even cannibalistic. He ate little, and the moment he got up he felt defiled.

"Let me bury this drude, where I can find it some other

time," said Oceaxe. "On the next occasion, though, I shall have no Maskull with me, to shock . . . Now we have to take to the river."

They stepped off the land on to the water. It flowed against them with a sluggish current, but the opposition, instead of hindering them, had the contrary effect—it caused them to exert themselves, and they got on faster. They climbed the river in this way for several miles. The exercise gradually improved the circulation of Maskull's blood, and he began to look at things in a far more cheerful way. The hot sunshine, the diminished wind, the marvellous cloud scenery, the quiet, crystal forests—all was soothing and delightful. They approached nearer and nearer to the gaily-painted heights of Ifdawn.

There was something enigmatic to him in those bright walls. He was attracted by them, yet felt a sort of awe. They looked real, but at the same time very supernatural. If one could see the portrait of a ghost, painted with a hard, firm outline, in substantial colours, the feelings produced by such a sight would be exactly similar to Maskull's impressions as he studied the Ifdawn precipices.

He broke the long silence. "Those mountains have most extraordinary shapes. All the lines are straight and perpendicular . . . no slopes or curves."

She walked backwards on the water, in order to face him. "That's typical of Ifdawn. Nature is all hammer-blows with us. Nothing soft and gradual."

"I hear you, but I don't understand you."

"All over the Marest you'll find patches of ground plunging down or rushing up. Trees grow fast. Women and men don't think twice before acting. One may call Ifdawn a place of quick decisions."

Maskull was impressed. "A fresh, wild, primitive land."

"How is it where you come from?" asked Oceaxe.

"Oh, mine is a decrepit world, where nature takes a hundred years to move a foot of solid land. Men and animals go about in flocks. Originality is a lost habit."

"Are there women there?"

"As with you, and not very differently formed."

"Do they love?"

He laughed—"So much so that it has changed the dress, speech, and thoughts of the whole sex."

"Probably they are more beautiful than I?"

"No, I think not," said Maskull.

There was another rather long silence, as they travelled unsteadily onwards.

"What is your business in Ifdawn?" demanded Oceaxe suddenly.

He hesitated over his answer. "Can you grasp that it's possible to have an aim right in front of one, so big that one can't see it as a whole?"

She stole a long, inquisitive look at him. "What sort of aim?"

"A moral aim."

"Are you proposing to set the world right?"

"I propose nothing . . . I am waiting . . ."

"Don't wait too long, for time doesn't wait—especially in Ifdawn."

"Something will happen," said Maskull.

Oceaxe threw a subtle smile. "So you have no special destination in the Marest?"

"No, and if you'll permit me, I will come home with you."

"Singular man!" she said, with a short, thrilling laugh. "That's what I have been offering all the time. Of course you will come home with me . . . As for Crimtyphon . . ."

"You mentioned that name before. Who is he?"

"Oh! My lover, or as you would say, my husband."

"This doesn't improve matters," said Maskull.

"It leaves them exactly where they were. We merely have to remove him."

"We are certainly misunderstanding each other," said Maskull, quite startled. "Do you by any chance imagine that I am making a compact with you?"

"You will do nothing against your will. But you have promised to come home with me."

"Tell me, how do you remove husbands in Ifdawn?"

"Either you or I must kill him."

He eyed her for a full minute.

"Now we are passing from folly to insanity."

"Not at all," replied Oceaxe. "It is the too-sad truth. And when you have seen Crimtyphon, you will realise it."

"I'm aware I am on a strange planet," said Maskull slowly, "where all sorts of unheard of things may happen, and where the very laws of morality may be different. Still as far as I am concerned, murder is murder, and I'll have no more to do with a woman who wants to make use of me, to get rid of her husband."

"You think me wicked?" demanded Oceaxe steadily.

"Or mad."

"Then you had better leave me, Maskull . . . only . . ."

"Only what?"

"You wish to be consistent, don't you? Leave all other mad and wicked people as well . . . Then you'll find it all the easier to reform the rest."

Maskull frowned, but said nothing.

"Well?" demanded Oceaxe, with a half-smile.

"I'll come with you, and I'll see Crimtyphon—if only to warn him."

Oceaxe broke into a cascade of rich, feminine laughter . . . but whether at the image conjured up by Maskull's last words, or from some other cause, he did not know. The conversation dropped.

At a distance of a couple of miles from the now towering cliffs, the river made a sharp right-angled turn to the west, and was no longer of use to them on their journey. Maskull stared up doubtfully.

"It's a stiff climb for a hot morning."

"Let's rest here a little," said she, indicating a smooth flat island of black rock, standing up just out of the water, in the middle of the river.

They accordingly went to it, and Maskull sat down. Oceaxe, however, standing graceful and erect, turned her face towards the cliffs opposite, and uttered a piercing and peculiar call.

"What is that for?"

She did not answer. After waiting a minute, she repeated the call. Maskull now saw a large bird detach itself from the top of one of the precipices, and sail slowly down towards them. It was followed by two others. The flight of these birds was exceedingly slow and clumsy.

"What are they?" he asked.

She still returned no answer, but smiled rather queerly, and sat down beside him. Before many minutes he was able to distinguish the shapes and colours of the flying monsters. They were not birds, but creatures with long, snake-like bodies, and ten reptilian legs apiece, terminating in fins which acted as wings. The bodies were of bright blue, the legs and fins were yellow. They were flying, without haste, but in a somewhat ominous fashion, straight towards them. He could make out a long, thin spike projecting from each of the heads.

"They are shrowks," explained Oceaxe at last. "If you want to know their intention, I'll tell you. To make a meal of us. First of all their spikes will pierce us, and then their mouths, which are really suckers, will drain us dry of blood . . . pretty thoroughly too; there are no half-measures with shrowks. They are toothless beasts, so don't eat flesh."

"As you show such admirable sang-froid," said Maskull dryly, "I take it there's no particular danger."

Neverthless he instinctively tried to get on to his feet . . . and failed. A new form of paralysis was chaining him to the ground.

"Are you trying to get up?" asked Oceaxe smoothly.

"Well, yes, but those cursed reptiles seem to be nailing me down to the rock with their wills. May I ask if you had any special object in view in waking them up?"

"I assure you the danger is quite real, Maskull. Instead of talking and asking questions, you had much better see what you can do with *your* will."

"I seem to have no will, unfortunately."

Oceaxe was seized with a paroxysm of laughter, but it was still rich and beautiful. "It's obvious you aren't a very heroic protector, Maskull. It seems I must play the man, and you the woman. I expected better things of your big body . . . Why, my husband would send those creatures dancing all round the sky, by way of joke, before disposing of them. Now watch me. Two of the three I'll kill; the third we will ride home on. Which one shall we keep?"

The shrowks continued their slow, wobbling flight towards them. Their bodies were of huge size. They produced in Maskull the same sensation of loathing as insects. He instinctively understood that as they hunted with their wills, there was no necessity for them to possess a swift motion.

"Choose which you please," he said shortly. "They are equally objectionable to me."

"Then I'll choose the leader, as it is presumably the most energetic animal. Watch now."

She stood upright, and her sorb suddenly blazed with fire. Maskull felt something snap inside his brain. His limbs were free once more. The two monsters in the rear staggered and darted head foremost towards the earth, one after the other. He watched them crash on the ground, and then lie motionless. The leader still came towards them, but he fancied that its flight was altered in character; it was no longer menacing, but tame and unwilling.

Oceaxe guided it with her will to the mainland shore opposite their island rock. Its vast bulk lay there extended, awaiting her pleasure. They immediately crossed the water.

Maskull viewed the shrowk at close quarters. It was about thirty feet long. Its bright-coloured skin was shining, slippery, and leathery; a mane of black hair covered its long neck. Its face was awesome and unnatural, with its carnivorous eyes, frightful stiletto, and blood-sucking cavity. There were true fins on its back and tail.

"Have you a good seat?" asked Oceaxe, patting the creature's flank. "As I have to steer, let me jump on first."

She pulled up her gown, then climbed up and sat astride the animal's back, just behind the mane, which she clutched. Between her and the fin there was just room for Maskull. He grasped the two flanks with his outer hands; his third, new arm pressed against Oceaxe's back, and for additional security he was compelled to encircle her waist with it.

Directly he did so, he realised that he had been tricked, and that this ride had been planned for one purpose only —to inflame his desires.

The third arm possessed a function of its own, of which hitherto he had been ignorant. It was a developed magn. But the stream of love which was communicated to it was no longer pure and noble—it was boiling, passionate, and torturing. He gritted his teeth, and kept quiet, but Oceaxe had not plotted the adventure to remain unconscious of his feelings. She looked round, with a golden, triumphant smile . . . "The ride will last some time . . . so hold on well!" Her voice was soft like a flute, but rather malicious.

Maskull grinned, and said nothing. He dared not remove his arm.

The shrowk straddled on to its legs. It jerked itself forward, and rose slowly and uncouthly in the air. They began to paddle upwards towards the painted cliffs. The motion was swaying, rocking, and sickening; the contact of the brute's slimy skin was disgusting. All this, however, was merely background to Maskull, as he sat there with closed eyes, holding on to Oceaxe. In the front and centre of his consciousness was the knowledge that he was gripping a fair woman, and that her flesh was responding to his touch like a lovely harp.

They climbed up and up. He opened his eyes, and ventured to look around him. By this time they were already level with the top of the outer rampart of precipices. There now came in sight a wild archipelago of islands, with jagged outlines, emerging from a sea of air. The islands were mountain summits; or, more accurately speaking, the country was a high table-land, fissured everywhere by narrow and apparently bottomless cracks. These cracks were in some cases like canals, in others like lakes, in others merely holes in the ground, closed in all round. The perpendicular sides of the islands, that is, the upper, visible parts of the innumerable cliff-faces were of bare rock, gaudily coloured; but the level surfaces were a tangle of wild plant life. The taller trees alone were distinguishable from the shrowk's back. They were of different shapes, and did not look ancient; they were slender and swaying but did not appear very graceful . . . they looked tough, wiry, and savage.

As Maskull continued to explore the landscape, he forgot Oceaxe and his passion. Other strange feelings came to the front. The morning was gay and bright, the sun scorched down, quickly-changing clouds sailed across the sky, the earth was vivid, wild, and lonely. Yet he experienced no aesthetic sensations . . . he felt nothing but an intense longing for action and possession. When he looked at anything, he immediately wanted to deal with it. The atmosphere of the land seemed not free, but sticky . . . attraction and repulsion were its constituents. Apart from this wish to play a personal part in what was going on around and beneath him, the scenery had no significance for him.

So preoccupied was he, that his arm partly released its clasp. Oceaxe turned round to gaze at him. Whether or not she were satisfied with what she saw, she uttered a low laugh, like a peculiar chord.

"Cold again so quickly, Maskull?"

"What do you want?" he asked absently, still looking over the side . . . "It's extraordinary how drawn I feel to all this."

"You wish to take a hand?"

"I wish to get down."

"Oh, we have a good way to go yet . . . So you really feel different?"

"Different from what? What are you talking about?" said Maskull, still lost in abstraction.

Oceaxe laughed again. "It would be strange if we couldn't make a man of you, for the material is excellent."

After that, she turned her back once more.

The air-islands differed from water-islands in another way. They were not on a plane surface, but sloped upwards, like a succession of broken terraces, as the journey progressed. The shrowk had hitherto been flying well above the ground; but now, when a new line of towering cliffs confronted them, Oceaxe did not urge the beast upwards, but caused it to enter a narrow canyon, which intersected the mountains like a channel. They were instantly plunged into deep shade. The canal was not above thirty feet wide; the walls stretched upwards on both sides for many hundred feet. It was as cool as an ice-chamber. When Maskull attempted to plumb the chasm with his eyes, he saw nothing but black obscurity.

"What is at the bottom?" he asked.

"Death for you, if you go to look for it."

"We know that . . . I mean, is there any kind of life down there?"

"Not that I have ever heard of," said Oceaxe, "but of course all things are possible."

"I think very likely there is life," he returned thoughtfully.

Her ironical laugh sounded out of the gloom. "Shall we go down and see?"

"You find that amusing?"

"No, not that . . . What I do find amusing is the big stranger with the beard, who is so keenly interested in everything except himself."

Maskull then laughed too. "I happen to be the only thing in Tormance which is not a novelty for me."

"Yes, but I am a novelty for you."

The channel went zigzagging its way through the belly of the mountain, and all the time they were gradually rising.

"At least I have heard nothing like your voice before," said Maskull, who, as he had no longer anything to look at, was at last ready for conversation.

"What's the matter with my voice?"

"It's all that I can distinguish of you now, that's why I mentioned it."

"Isn't it clear . . . don't I speak distinctly?"

"Oh, it's clear enough, but . . . it's inappropriate."

"Inappropriate?"

"I won't explain further," said Maskull, "but whether you are speaking or laughing, your voice is by far the loveliest and strangest instrument I have ever listened to . . . and yet I repeat, it is inappropriate."

"You mean that my nature doesn't correspond?"

He was just considering his reply, when their talk was abruptly broken off by a huge and terrifying, but not very loud sound rising up from the gulf directly underneath them. It was a low, grinding, roaring thunder.

"The ground is rising under us," cried Oceaxe.

"Shall we escape?"

She made no answer, but urged the shrowk's flight upwards, at such a steep gradient that they retained their seats with difficulty. The floor of the canyon, upheaved by some mighty subterranean force, could be heard, and almost felt, coming up after them, like a gigantic landslip in the wrong direction. The cliffs cracked, and fragments began to fall. A hundred awful noises filled the air, growing louder and louder each second . . . splitting, hissing, cracking, grinding, booming, exploding, roaring. When they had still fifty feet or so to go, to reach the top, a sort of dark, indefinite sea of broken rocks and soil appeared under their feet, ascending rapidy, with irresistible might, accompanied by the most horrible noises. The canal was filled up for two hundred yards, before and behind them. Millions of tons of solid matter seemed to be raised. The shrowk in its ascent was caught by the uplifted debris . . . Beast and riders experienced in that moment all the horrors of an earthquake—they were rolled violently over, and thrown amongst the rocks and dirt. All was thunder, instability, motion, confusion.

Before they had time to realise their position, they were in the sunlight. The upheaval still continued. In another minute or two the valley floor had formed a new mountain, a hundred feet or more higher than the old. Then its movement ceased suddenly. Every noise stopped, as if by magic . . . not a rock moved. Oceaxe and Maskull picked themselves up and examined themselves for cuts and bruises. The shrowk lay on its side, panting violently, and sweating with fright.

"That was a nasty affair," said Maskull, flicking the dirt off his person.

Oceaxe stanched a cut on her chin with a corner of her robe.

"It might have been far worse . . . I mean, it's bad enough to come up, but it's death to go down, and that happens just as often."

"Whatever induces you to live in such a country?"

"I don't know, Maskull. Habit, I suppose. I have often thought of moving out of it."

"A good deal must be forgiven you for having to spend your life in a place like this, where one is obviously never safe from one minute to another."

"You will learn by degrees," she answered smiling.

She looked hard at the monster, and it got heavily to its feet.

"Get on again, Maskull!" she directed, climbing back to her perch. "We haven't too much time to waste."

He obeyed. They resumed their interrupted flight, this time over the mountains, and in full sunlight. Maskull settled down again to his thoughts. The peculiar atmosphere of the country continued to soak into his brain. His will became so restless and uneasy that merely to sit there in inactivity was a torture. He could scarcely endure not to be doing something.

"How secretive you are, Maskull!" said Oceaxe quietly, without turning her head.

"What secrets . . . what do you mean?"

"Oh, I know perfectly well what's passing inside you. Now I think it wouldn't be amiss to ask you . . . is friendship still enough?"

"Oh, don't ask me anything," growled Maskull. "I've far too many problems in my head already. I only wish I could answer some of them."

He stared stonily at the landscape. The beast was winging its way towards a distant mountain, of singular shape. It was an enormous natural quadrilateral pyramid, rising in great terraces and terminating in a broad, flat top, on which what looked like green snow still lingered.

"What mountain is that?" he asked.

"Disscourn. The highest point in Ifdawn."

"Are we going there?"

"Why should we go there? But if you were going on further, it might be worth your while to pay a visit to the top. It commands the whole land as far as the Sinking Sea and Swaylone's Island—and beyond. You can also see Alppain from it."

"That's a sight I mean to see before I have finished."

"Do you, Maskull?" she turned round and put her hand on his wrist. "Stay with me, and one day we'll go to Disscourn together."

He grunted unintelligibly.

There were no signs of human existence in the country under their feet. While Maskull was still grimly regarding it, a large tract of forest not far ahead, bearing many trees and rocks, suddenly subsided with an awful roar and crashed down into an invisible gulf. What was solid land one minute became a clean-cut chasm the next. He jumped violently up with the shock. "This is frightful."

Oceaxe remained unmoved.

"Why, life here must be absolutely impossible," he went on, when he had somewhat recovered himself. "A man would need nerves of steel . . . Is there no means at all of foreseeing a catastrophe like this?"

"Oh, I suppose we shouldn't be alive if there weren't," replied Oceaxe, with composure. "We are more or less clever at it—but that doesn't prevent our often getting caught."

"You had better teach me the signs."

"We shall have many things to go over together. And

among them, I expect, will be whether we are to stop in the land at all . . . But first let us go home."

"How far is it now?"

"It is right in front of you," said Oceaxe, pointing with her forefinger. "You can see it."

He followed the direction of the finger and, after a few questions, made out the spot she was indicating. It was a broad peninsula, about two miles distant. Three of its sides rose sheer out of a lake of air, the bottom of which was invisible; its fourth was a bottle-neck, joining it to the mainland. It was overgrown with bright vegetation, distinct in the brilliant atmosphere. A single tall tree, shooting up in the middle of the peninsula, dwarfed everything else; it was wide and shady with sea-green leaves.

"I wonder if Crimtyphon is there," remarked Oceaxe. "Can I see two figures, or am I mistaken?"

"I also see something," said Maskull.

In twenty minutes they were directly above the peninsula, at a height of about fifty feet. The shrowk slackened speed, and came to earth on the mainland, exactly at the gateway of the isthmus. They both descended—Maskull with aching thighs.

"What shall we do with the monster?" asked Oceaxe. Without waiting for a suggestion, she patted its hideous face with her hand. "Fly away home! I may want you some other time."

It gave a stupid grunt, elevated itself on its legs again and, after half-running, half-flying for a few yards, rose awkwardly into the air, and paddled away in the same direction from which they had come. They watched it out of sight, and then Oceaxe started to cross the neck of land, followed by Maskull.

Branchspell's white rays beat down on them with pitiless force. The sky had by degrees become cloudless, and the wind had entirely dropped. The ground was a rich riot of vividly-coloured ferns, shrubs, and grasses. Through these could be seen here and there the golden chalky soil—and occasionally a glittering, white metallic boulder. Everything looked extraordinary and barbaric. Maskull was at last walking in the weird Ifdawn Marest, which had created such strange feelings in him when seen from a distance . . . And now he felt no wonder or curiosity at all, but only desired to meet human beings—so intense had grown his will. He longed to test his powers on his fellow creatures, and nothing else seemed of the least importance to him.

On the peninsula all was coolness and delicate shade. It resembled a large spinney, about two acres in extent. In the heart of the tangle of small trees and undergrowth, was a partially cleared space . . . perhaps the roots of the giant tree growing in the centre had killed off the smaller fry all around it. By the side of the tree sparkled a little, bubbling fountain, whose water was iron-red. The precipices on all sides, overhung with thorns, flowers, and creepers, invested the enclosure with an air of wild and charming seclusion— a mythological mountain god might have dwelt there . . . Maskull's restless eye left everything, to fall on the two men who formed the centre of the picture.

One was reclining, in the ancient Grecian fashion of banqueters on a tall couch of mosses, sprinkled with flowers; he rested on one arm, and was eating a kind of plum, with calm enjoyment. A pile of these plums lay on the couch beside him. The overspreading branches of the tree completely sheltered him from the sun. His small, boyish form was clad in a rough skin, leaving his limbs naked. Maskull could not tell from his face whether he were a young boy or a grown man. The features were smooth, soft, and childish, their expression was seraphically tranquil; but his violet upper eye was sinister and adult. His skin was of the colour of yellow ivory. His long, curling hair matched his sorb—it was violet . . . The second man was standing erect before the other, a few feet away from him. He was short and muscular, his face was broad, bearded, and rather commonplace but there was something terrible about his appearance. The features were distorted by a deep-seated look of pain, despair, and horror.

Oceaxe, without pausing, strolled lightly and lazily up

to the outermost shadows of the tree, some distance from the couch.

"We have met with an uplift," she remarked carelessly, looking towards the youth.

He eyed her, but said nothing.

"How is your plant-man getting on?" Her tone was artificial but extremely beautiful. While waiting for an answer, she sat down on the ground, her legs gracefully thrust under her body, and pulled down the skirt of her robe. Maskull remained standing just behind her, with crossed arms.

There was silence for a minute.

"Why don't you answer your mistress, Sature?" said the boy on the couch, in a calm, treble voice.

The man addressed did not alter his expression, but replied in a strangled tone, "I am getting on very well, Oceaxe. There are already buds on my feet. Tomorrow I hope to take root."

Maskull felt a rising storm inside him. He was perfectly aware that although these words were uttered by Sature, they were being dictated by the boy.

"What he says is quite true," remarked the latter. "Tomorrow roots will reach the ground, and in a few days they ought to be well-established. Then I shall set to work to convert his arms into branches, and his fingers into leaves. It will take longer to transform his head into a crown, but still I hope—in fact I can almost promise—that within a month you and I, Oceaxe, will be plucking and enjoying fruit from this new and remarkable tree."

"I love these natural experiments," he concluded, putting out his hand for another plum. "They thrill me."

"This must be a joke," said Maskull, taking a step forward.

The youth looked at him serenely. He made no reply, but Maskull felt as if he were being thrust backwards by an iron hand on his throat.

"The morning's work is now concluded, Sature. Come here again after Blodsombre. After tonight you will remain here permanently, I expect, so you had better set to work to clear a patch of ground for your roots. Never forget—however fresh and charming these plants appear to you now, in future they will be your deadliest rivals and enemies. Now you may go."

The man limped painfully away, across the isthmus, out of sight. Oceaxe yawned.

Maskull pushed his way forward, as if against a wall. "Are you joking, or are you a devil?"

"I am Crimtyphon. I never joke. For that epithet of yours, I will devise a new punishment for you."

The duels of wills commenced without ceremony. Oceaxe got up, stretched her beautiful limbs, smiled, and prepared herself to witness the struggle between her old lover and her new. Crimtyphon smiled too; he reached out his hand for more fruit, but did not eat it. Maskull's self-control broke down, and he dashed at the boy, choking with red fury—his beard wagged and his face was crimson. When he realised with whom he had to deal, Crimtyphon left off smiling, slipped off the couch, and threw a terrible and malignant glare into his sorb. Maskull staggered. He gathered together all the brute force of his will, and by sheer weight continued his advance. The boy shrieked and ran behind the couch, trying to get away . . . His opposition suddenly collapsed. Maskull stumbled forward, recovered himself, and then vaulted clear over the high pile of mosses, to get at his antagonist. He fell on top of him with all his bulk. Grasping his throat, he pulled his little head completely round, so that the neck was broken. Crimtyphon immediately died.

The corpse lay underneath the tree with its face upturned. Maskull viewed it attentively, and as he did so an expression of awe and wonder came into his own countenance. In the moment of death Crimtyphon's face had undergone a startling and even shocking alteration. Its personal character had wholly vanished, giving place to a vulgar, grinning mask which expressed nothing.

He did not have to search his mind long, to remember where he had seen the brother of that expression. It was identical with that on the face of the apparition at the séance, after Krag had dealt with it.

CHAPTER TEN

Tydomin

Oceaxe sat down carelessly on the couch of mosses, and began eating the plums.

"You see, you had to kill him, Maskull," she said, in a rather quizzical voice.

He came away from the corpse and regarded her—still red, and still breathing hard. "It's no joking matter. You especially ought to keep quiet."

"Why?"

"Because he was your husband."

"You think I ought to show grief . . . when I feel none?"

"Don't pretend, woman!"

Oceaxe smiled. "From your manner one would think you were accusing me of some crime."

Maskull literally snorted at her words. "What, you live with filth—you live in the arms of a morbid monstrosity . . . and then . . ."

"Oh, now I grasp," she said, in a tone of perfect detachment.

"I'm glad."

"Well, Maskull," she proceeded, after a pause, "and who gave you the right to rule my conduct? Am I not mistress of my own person?"

He looked at her with disgust, but said nothing. There was another long interval of silence.

"I never loved him," said Oceaxe at last, looking at the ground.

"That makes it all the worse."

"What does all this mean—what do you want?"

"Nothing from you—absolutely nothing . . . thank

heaven!"

She gave a hard laugh. "You come here with your foreign preconceptions and expect us to all bow down to them."

"What preconceptions?"

"Just because Crymtyphon's sports are strange to you, you murder him . . . and you would like to murder me."

"Sports! That diabolical cruelty."

"Oh, you're sentimental!" said Oceaxe contemptuously. "Why do you need to make such a fuss over that man? Life is life, all the world over, and one form is as good as another . . . He was only to be made a tree, like a million other trees. If they can endure the life, why can't he?"

"And this is Ifdawn morality!"

Oceaxe began to grow angry. "It's you who have peculiar ideas. You rave about the beauty of flowers and trees— you think them divine. But when it's a question of taking on this divine, fresh, pure, enchanting loveliness yourself, in your own person, it immediately becomes a cruel and wicked degradation . . . Here we have a strange riddle, in my opinion."

"Oceaxe, you're a beautiful, heartless wild beast—nothing more . . . If you weren't a woman . . ."

"Well"—curling her lip—"let us hear what would happen if I weren't a woman?"

Maskull bit his nails.

"It doesn't matter. I can't touch you—though there's certainly not the difference of a hair between you and your boy-husband. For this you may thank my 'foreign preconceptions' . . . Farewell!"

He turned to go. Oceaxe's eyes slanted at him through their long lashes.

"Where are you off to, Maskull?"

"That's a matter of no importance, for wherever I go it must be a change for the better . . . You walking whirlpools of crime!"

"Wait a minute. I only want to say this. Blodsombre is

just starting, and you had better stay here till the afternoon. We can quickly put that body out of sight, and, as you seem to detest me so much, the place is big enough . . . we needn't talk, or even see each other."

"I don't wish to breathe the same air."

"Singular man!"

She was sitting erect and motionless, like a beautiful statue.

"And what of your wonderful interview with Surtur, and all the undone things which you set out to do?"

"You aren't the one I shall speak to about that . . . But" —he eyed her meditatively—"while I'm still here you can tell me this. What's the meaning of the expression on that corpse's face?"

"Is that another crime, Maskull? All dead people look like that. Ought they not to?"

"I once heard it called 'Crystalman's face'."

"Why not? We are all daughters and sons of Crystalman. It is doubtless the family resemblance."

"It has also been told me that Surtur and Crystalman are one and the same."

"You have wise and truthful acquaintances."

"Then how could it have been Surtur whom I saw?" said Maskull, more to himself than to her. "That apparition was something quite different."

She dropped her mocking manner and, sliding imperceptibly towards him, gently pulled his arm.

"You see . . . we have got to talk. Sit down beside me, and ask me your questions. I'm not excessively clever, but I'll try to be of assistance."

Maskull permitted himself to be dragged down with soft violence. She bent towards him, as if confidentially, and contrived that her sweet, cool, feminine breath should fan his cheek.

"Aren't you here to alter the evil to the good, Maskull? Then what does it matter who sent you?"

"What can you possibly know of good and evil?"

"Are you only instructing the initiated?"

"Who am I, to instruct anybody? However, you're quite right. I wish to do what I can . . . not because I am qualified, but because I am here . . ."

Oceaxe's voice dropped to a whisper. "You're a giant, both in body and soul. What you want to do, you *can* do."

"Is that your honest opinion, or are you flattering me for your own ends?"

She sighed. "Don't you see how difficult you are making the conversation? Let's talk about your work, not about ourselves."

Maskull suddenly noticed a strange blue light glowing in the northern sky. It was from Alppain, but Alppain itself was behind the hills. While he was observing it, a peculiar wave of self-denial, of a disquieting nature, passed through him. He looked at Oceaxe, and it struck him for the first time that he was being unnecessarily brutal to her. He had forgotten that she was a woman, and defenceless.

"Won't you stay?" she asked of a sudden, quite openly and frankly.

"Yes, I think I'll stay," he replied slowly. "And another thing, Oceaxe . . . if I've misjudged your character, pray forgive me. I'm a hasty, passionate man."

"There are enough easy-going men. Hard knocks are a good medicine for vicious hearts . . . And you didn't misjudge my character, as far as you went—only, every woman has more than one character. Don't you know that?"

During the pause that followed, a snapping of twigs was heard, and both looked round, startled. They saw a woman stepping slowly across the neck which separated them from the mainland.

"Tydomin," muttered Oceaxe, in a vexed, frightened voice. She immediately moved away from Maskull and stood up.

The newcomer was of middle height, very slight and graceful. She was no longer quite young. Her face wore the composure of a woman who knows her way about the

world. It was intensely pale, and under its quiescence there
was just a glimpse of something queer and dangerous. It
was curiously alluring, though not exactly beautiful. Her
hair was clustering and boyish, reaching only to the neck.
It was of a strange indigo colour. She was quaintly attired
in a tunic and breeches, pieced together from the square,
blue-green plates of some reptile. Her small, ivory-white
breasts were exposed. Her sorb was black and sad—rather
contemplative.

Without once glancing up at Oceaxe and Maskull, she
quietly glided straight towards Crimtyphon's corpse. When
she arrived within a few feet of it, she stopped and looked
down, with arms folded.

Oceaxe drew Maskull a little away, and whispered, "It's
Crimtyphon's other wife, who lives under Disscourn. She's
a most dangerous woman. Be careful what you say. If she
asks you to do anything, refuse it outright."

"The poor soul looks harmless enough."

"Yes, she does—but the poor soul is quite capable of
swallowing up Krag himself . . . Now you play the
man."

The murmur of their voices seemed to attract Tydomin's
notice, for she now slowly turned her eyes towards them.

"Who killed him?" she demanded.

Her voice was so soft, low, and refined, that Maskull
hardly was able to catch the words. The sounds, however,
lingered in his ears, and curiously enough seemed to grow
stronger, instead of fainter.

Oceaxe whispered, "Don't say a word, leave it all to
me." Then she swung her body round to face Tydomin
squarely, and said aloud—"I killed him."

Tydomin's words by this time were ringing in Maskull's
head like an actual physical sound. There was no question
of being able to ignore them . . . he had to make an open
confession of his act, whatever the consequences might
be. Quietly taking Oceaxe by the shoulder and putting
her behind him, he said in a low, but perfectly distinct
voice, "It was I that killed Crimtyphon."

Oceaxe looked both haughty and frightened. "Maskull says so to shield me, as he thinks. I require no shield, Maskull. I killed him, Tydomin."

"I believe you, Oceaxe. You did murder him. Not with your own strength, for you brought this man along for the purpose."

Maskull took a couple of steps towards Tydomin. "It's of little consequence who killed him, for he's better dead than alive, in my opinion. Still, I did it. Oceaxe had no hand in the affair."

Tydomin appeared not to hear him—she looked beyond him at Oceaxe musingly. "When you murdered him, didn't it occur to you that I should come here, to find out?"

"I never once thought of you," replied Oceaxe, with an angry laugh. "Do you really imagine that I carry your image with me wherever I go?"

"If someone were to murder your lover here, what would you do?"

"Lying hypocrite!" Oceaxe spat out. "You never were in love with Crimtyphon. You always hated me, and now you think it an excellent opportunity to make it good . . . Now that Crimtyphon's gone . . . For we both know he would have made a footstool of you, if I had asked him. He worshipped me, but he laughed at you. He thought you ugly."

Tydomin flashed a quick, gentle smile at Maskull. "Is it necessary for you to listen to all of this?"

Without question, and feeling it the right thing to do, he walked away out of earshot.

Tydomin approached Oceaxe. "Perhaps because my beauty fades and I'm no longer young, I needed *him* all the more."

Oceaxe gave a kind of snarl. "Well, he's dead, and there's an end of it. What are you going to do now, Tydomin?"

The other woman smiled faintly and rather pathetically. "There's nothing left to do, except mourn the dead. You won't grudge me that last office?"

"Do you want to stop here?" demanded Oceaxe suspiciously.

"Yes, Oceaxe dear, I wish to be alone."

"Then what is to become of us?"

"I thought that you and your lover—what is his name?"

"Maskull."

"I thought that perhaps you two would go to Disscourn, and spend Blodsombre at my home."

Oceaxe called out aloud to Maskull, "Will you come with me now to Disscourn?"

"If you wish," returned Maskull.

"Go first, Oceaxe. I must question your friend about Crimtyphon's death. I won't keep him."

"Why don't you question me, rather?" demanded Oceaxe, looking up sharply.

Tydomin gave the shadow of a smile. "We know each other too well."

"Play no tricks!" said Oceaxe, and she turned to go.

"Surely you must be dreaming," said Tydomin. "That's the way—unless you want to walk over the cliff-side."

The path Oceaxe had chosen led across the isthmus. The direction which Tydomin proposed for her was over the edge of the precipice, into empty space.

"Shaping! I must be mad," cried Oceaxe, with a laugh. And she obediently followed the other's finger.

She walked straight on towards the edge of the abyss, twenty paces away. Maskull pulled his beard about, and wondered what she was doing. Tydomin remained standing with outstretched finger, watching her. Without hesitation, without slackening her step once, Oceaxe strolled on . . . and when she had reached the extreme end of the land she still took one more step.

Maskull saw her limbs wrench as she stumbled over the edge. Her body disappeared, and as it did so an awful shriek sounded. Disillusionment had come to her an instant too late. He tore himself out of his stupor, rushed to the edge of the cliff, threw himself on the ground recklessly, and looked over . . . Oceaxe had vanished.

He continued staring wildly down for several minutes, and then began to sob. Tydomin came up to him, and he got to his feet.

The blood kept rushing to his face and leaving it again. It was some time before he could speak at all. Then he brought out the words with difficulty. "You shall pay for this, Tydomin. But first I want to hear why you did it."

"Hadn't I cause?" she asked, standing with downcast eyes.

"Was it pure fiendishness?"

"It was for Crimtyphon's sake."

"She had nothing to do with that death. I told you so."

"You are loyal to her, and I'm loyal to him."

"Loyal? You've made a terrible blunder. She wasn't my mistress. I killed Crimtyphon for quite another reason. She had absolutely no part in it."

"Wasn't she your lover?" asked Tydomin slowly.

"You've made a terrible mistake," repeated Maskull. "I killed him because he was a wild beast. She was as innocent of his death as you are."

Tydomin's face took on a hard look. "So you are guilty of two deaths."

There was a dreadful silence.

"Why couldn't you believe me?" asked Maskull, who was pale and sweating painfully.

"Who gave you the right to kill him?" demanded Tydomin sternly.

He said nothing, and perhaps did not hear her question.

She sighed two or three times and began to stir restlessly. "Since you murdered him, you must help me bury him."

"What's to be done? . . . This is a most fearful crime."

"You are a most fearful man . . . Why did you come here, to do all this? What are we to you?"

"Unfortunately you are right."

Another pause ensued.

"It's no use standing here," said Tydomin. "Nothing can be done. You must come with me."

"Come with you? Where to?"

"To Disscourn. There's a burning lake on the far side of it. He always wished to be cast there after death. We can do that after Blodsombre . . . in the meantime we must take him home."

"You're a callous, heartless woman. Why should he be buried, when that poor girl must remain unburied?"

"You know that's out of the question," replied Tydomin quietly.

Maskull's eyes roamed about agitatedly, apparently seeing nothing.

"We must do something," she continued. "I shall go. You can't wish to stay here alone?"

"No, I couldn't stop here—and why should I want to? . . . You wish me to carry the corpse?"

"He can't carry himself, and you murdered him . . . Perhaps it will ease your mind to carry it."

"Ease my mind?" said Maskull, rather stupidly.

"There's only one relief for remorse, and that's voluntary pain."

"And have *you* no remorse?" he asked, fixing her with a heavy eye.

"These crimes are yours, Maskull," she said in a low but incisive voice.

They walked over to Crimtyphon's body, and Maskull hoisted it on to his shoulders. It weighed heavier than he had thought. Tydomin did not offer to assist him to adjust the ghastly burden.

She crossed the isthmus, followed by Maskull. Their path lay through sunshine and shadow. Branchspell was blazing in a cloudless sky, the heat was insufferable—streams of sweat coursed down his face, and the corpse seemed to grow heavier and heavier. Tydomin always walked in front of him. His eyes were fastened in an unseeing stare on her white, womanish calves . . . he looked neither to right nor left. His features grew sullen . . . At the end of ten minutes he suddenly allowed his burden to slip off his shoulders on to the ground, where it lay anyhow. He called out to Tydomin.

She quickly looked round.

"Come here. It has just occurred to me"—he laughed—"why should I be carrying this corpse . . . and why should I be following you at all? . . . What surprises me is, why this has never struck me before."

She at once came back to him. "I suppose you're tired, Maskull. Let us sit down. Perhaps you have come a long way this morning?"

"Oh, it's not tiredness, but a sudden gleam of sense. Do you know of any reason why I should be acting as your porter?" He laughed again, but nevertheless sat down on the ground beside her.

Tydomin neither looked at him nor answered. Her head was half-bent, so as to face the northern sky, where the Alppain light was still glowing. Maskull followed her gaze, and also watched the glow for a moment or two in silence.

"Why don't you speak?" he asked at last.

"What does that light suggest to you, Maskull?"

"I'm not speaking of that light."

"Doesn't it suggest anything at all?"

"Perhaps it doesn't. What does it matter?"

"Not sacrifice?"

Maskull grew sullen again. "Sacrifice of what? What do you mean?"

"Hasn't it entered your head yet," said Tydomin, looking straight in front of her, and speaking in her delicate, hard manner, "that this adventure of yours will scarcely come to an end until you have made some sort of sacrifice?"

He returned no answer, and she said nothing more. In a few minutes' time Maskull got up of his own accord, and irreverently, and almost angrily, threw Crimtyphon's corpse over his shoulder again.

"How far have we to go?" he asked in a surly tone.

"An hour's walking."

"Lead on."

"Still, this isn't the sacrifice I mean," said Tydomin quietly, as she went on in front.

Almost immediately they reached more difficult ground. They had to pass from peak to peak, as from island to island. In some cases they were able to stride or jump across, but in others they had to make use of rude bridges of fallen timber. It appeared to be a frequented path. Underneath were the black, impenetrable abysses—on the surface were the glaring sunshine, the gay, painted rocks, the chaotic tangle of strange plants. There were countless reptiles and insects. The latter were thicker-built than those of Earth— consequently still more disgusting, and some of them were of enormous size. One monstrous insect, as large as a horse, stood right in the centre of their path without budging. It was armour-plated, had jaws like scimitars, and underneath its body was a forest of legs. Tydomin gave one malignant look at it, and sent it crashing into the gulf.

"What have I to offer, except my life?" Maskull suddenly broke out. "And what good is that? It won't bring that poor girl back into the world!"

"Sacrifice is not for utility. It's a penalty which we pay."

"I know that."

"The point is whether you can go on enjoying life, after what has happened."

She waited for Maskull to come up with her.

"Perhaps you imagine I'm not man enough . . . you imagine that because I allowed poor Oceaxe to die for me . . ."

"She did die for you," said Tydomin, in a quiet, emphatic voice.

"That would be a second blunder of yours," returned Maskull, just as firmly. "I was not in love with Oceaxe, and I'm not in love with life."

"Your life is not required."

"Then I don't understand what you want, or what you are speaking about."

"It's not for me to ask a sacrifice from you, Maskull. That

would be compliance on your part, but not sacrifice . . . You must wait until you feel there's nothing else for you to do."

"It's all very mysterious."

The conversation was abruptly cut short by a prolonged and frightful crashing, roaring sound, coming from a short distance ahead. It was accompanied by a violent oscillation of the ground on which they stood. They looked up, startled, just in time to witness the final disappearance of a huge mass of forestland, not two hundred yards in front of them. Several acres of trees, plants, rocks, and soil, with all its teeming animal life, vanished before their eyes, like a magic story. The new chasm was cut, as if by a knife. Beyond its farther edge the Alppain glow burned blue just over the horizon.

"Now we shall have to make a detour," said Tydomin, halting.

Maskull caught hold of her with his third hand. "Listen to me, while I try to describe what I'm feeling . . . When I saw that landslip, everything I have heard about the last destruction of the world came into my mind. It seemed to me as if I were actually witnessing it, and that the world were really falling to pieces . . . Then, where the land was, we now have this empty, awful gulf—that's to say, *nothing*—and it seems to me as if our life will come to the same condition, where there was something there will be nothing . . . But that terrible blue glare on the opposite side is exactly like the eye of fate. It accuses us, and demands what we have made of our life, which is no more . . . At the same time, it is grand and joyful. The joy consists in this—that it is in our power to give freely what will later on be taken from us by force . . ."

Tydomin watched him attentively. "Then your feeling is that your life is worthless, and you make a present of it to the first one who asks?"

"No, it goes beyond that. I feel that the only thing worth living for is to be so magnanimous that fate itself will be astonished at us. Understand me. It isn't cynicism, or bitterness, or despair, but heroism . . . It's hard to explain."

"Now you shall hear what sacrifice I offer you, Maskull. It's a heavy one, but that's what you seem to wish."

"That is so. In my present mood it can't be too heavy."

"Then, if you are in earnest, resign your body to me. Now that Crimtyphon's dead, I'm tired of being a woman."

"I fail to comprehend."

"Listen, then. I wish to start a new existence in your body. I wish to be a male. I see it isn't worthwhile being a woman . . . I mean to dedicate my own body to Crimtyphon. I shall tie his body and mine together, and give them a common funeral in the burning lake . . . That's the sacrifice I offer you. As I said, it's a hard one."

"So you do ask me to die. Though how you can make use of my body is difficult to understand."

"No, I don't ask you to die. You will go on living."

"How is it possible without a body?"

Tydomin gazed at him earnestly. "There are many such beings, even in your world. There you call them spirits, apparitions, phantoms. They are in reality living wills, deprived of material bodies . . . always longing to act and enjoy, but quite unable to do so. Are you noble-minded enough to accept such a state, do you think?"

"If it's possible, I accept it," replied Maskull quietly. ". . . Not in spite of its heaviness but because of it. But how is it possible?"

"Undoubtedly there are very many things possible in our world of which you have no conception . . . Now let us wait till we get home. I don't hold you to your word, for unless it's a free sacrifice I will have nothing to do with it."

"I am not a man who speaks lightly. If you can perform this miracle, you have my consent, once and for all."

"Then we'll leave it like that for the present," said Tydomin sadly.

They proceeded on their way. Owing to the subsidence, Tydomin seemed rather doubtful at first as to the right road, but by making a long divergence they eventually got round to the other side of the newly formed chasm. A little later on, in a narrow copse crowning a miniature, insulated peak, they fell in with a man. He was resting himself against a tree, and looked tired, overheated, and despondent. He was young. His beardless expression bore an expression of unusual sincerity, and in other respects he seemed a hardy, hard-working youth, of an intellectual type. His hair was thick, short, and flaxen. He possessed neither a sorb nor a third arm—so presumably was not a native of Ifdawn. His forehead, however, was disfigured by what looked like a haphazard assortment of eyes, eight in number, of different sizes and shapes. They went in pairs, and whenever two were in use, it was indicated by a peculiar shining—the rest remained dull, until their turn came. In addition to the upper eyes he had the two lower ones, but they were vacant and lifeless. This extraordinary battery of eyes, alternatively alive and dead, gave the young man an appearance of almost alarming mental activity. He was wearing nothing but a sort of skin kilt. Maskull seemed somehow to recognise the face, though he had certainly never set eyes on it before.

Tydomin suggested to him to set down the corpse, and both sat down to rest in the shade.

"Question him, Maskull," she said, rather carelessly, jerking her head towards the stranger.

Maskull sighed and asked aloud, from his seat on the ground—"What's your name, and where do you come from?"

The man studied him for a few moments, first with one pair of eyes, then with another, then with a third. He next turned his attention to Tydomin, who occupied him a still longer time. He replied at last, in a dry, manly, nervous voice. "I am Digrung. I have arrived here from Matterplay." His colour kept changing, and Maskull suddenly realised of whom he reminded him. It was of Joiwind.

"Perhaps you're going to Poolingdred, Digrung?" he inquired, interested.

"As a matter of fact I am—if I can find my way out of this accursed country."

"Possibly you are acquainted with Joiwind there?"

"She's my sister. I'm on my way to see her now. Why, do you know her?"

"I met her yesterday."

"What is your name, then?"

"Maskull."

"I shall tell her I met you. This will be our first meeting for four years. Is she well, and happy?"

"Both, as far as I could judge. You know Panawe?"

"Her husband—yes . . . But where do you come from? I've seen nothing like you before."

"From another world. Where is Matterplay?"

"It's the first country one comes to beyond the Sinking Sea."

"What is it like there . . . how do you amuse yourselves? . . . The same old murders and sudden deaths?"

"Are you ill?" asked Digrung. "Who is this woman, and why are you following at her heels like a slave? She looks insane to me . . . What's that corpse . . . why are you dragging it about the country with you?"

Tydomin smiled. "I've already heard it said about Matterplay, that if one sows an answer there, a rich crop of questions immediately springs up. But why do you make this unprovoked attack on me, Digrung?"

"I don't attack you, woman, but I know you . . . I see into you, and I see insanity. That wouldn't matter, but I don't like to see a man of intelligence like Maskull caught in your filthy meshes."

"I suppose even you clever Matterplay people sometimes misjudge character. However, I don't mind. Your opinion's nothing to me, Digrung. You'd better answer his questions, Maskull. Not for his own sake—but your feminine friend is sure to be curious about your having been seen carrying a dead man."

Maskull's under-lip shot out. "Tell your sister nothing, Digrung. Don't mention my name at all. I don't want her to know about this meeting of ours."

"Why not?"

"I don't wish it—isn't that enough?"

Digrung looked impassive.

"Thoughts and words," he said, "which don't correspond with the real events of the world are considered most shameful in Matterplay."

"I'm not asking you to lie, only to keep silent."

"To hide the truth is a special branch of lying. I can't accede to your wish. I must tell Joiwind everything, as far as I know it."

Maskull got up, and Tydomin followed his example.

She touched Digrung on the arm, and gave him a strange look. "The dead man is my husband, and Maskull murdered him. Now you'll understand why he wishes you to hold your tongue."

"I guessed there was some foul play," said Digrung. "It makes no odds—I can't falsify facts. Joiwind must know."

"You refuse to consider her feelings?" said Maskull, turning pale.

"Feelings which flourish on illusions, and sicken and die on realities, aren't worth considering. But Joiwind's are not of that kind."

"If you decline to do what I ask, at least return home without seeing her; your sister will get very little pleasure out of the meeting when she hears your news."

"What are these strange relations between you?" demanded Digrung, eyeing him with suddenly aroused suspicion.

Maskull stared back in a sort of bewilderment. "Good God! You don't doubt your own sister . . . That pure angel!"

Tydomin caught hold of him delicately. "I don't know Joiwind, but, whoever she is and whatever she's like, I know this—she's more fortunate in her friend than in her brother . . . Now, if you really value her happiness, Maskull, you will have to take some firm step or other."

"I mean to. Digrung, I shall stop your journey."

"If you intend a second murder, no doubt you are big enough."

Maskull turned round to Tydomin, and laughed. "I seem to be leaving a wake of corpses behind me on this journey."

"Why a corpse? There's no need to kill him."

"Thanks for that!" said Digrung dryly. "All the same, some crime is about to burst . . . I feel it."

"What must I do then?" asked Maskull.

"It is not my business, and to tell the truth I am little interested . . . If I were in your place, Maskull, I would not hesitate long. Don't you understand how to absorb these creatures, who set their feeble, obstinate wills against yours?"

"That is a worse crime," said Maskull.

"Who knows? . . . He will live, but he will tell no tales."

Digrung laughed, but changed colour. "I was right then. The monster has sprung into the light of day."

Maskull laid a hand on his shoulder. "You have the choice, and we are not joking . . . Do as I ask."

"You have fallen low, Maskull. But you are walking in a dream, and I can't talk to you . . . As for you, woman —sin must be like a pleasant bath to you . . ."

"There are strange ties between Maskull and myself; but you are a passer-by, a foreigner. I care nothing for you."

"Nevertheless, I shall not be frightened out of my plans, which are legitimate and right."

"Do as you please," said Tydomin. "If you come to grief, your thoughts will hardly have corresponded with the real events of the world, which is what you boast about . . . It is no affair of mine."

"I shall go on, and not back," exclaimed Digrung, with angry emphasis.

Tydomin threw a swift, evil smile at Maskull. "Bear witness that I have tried to persuade this young man . . . Now you must come to a quick decision in your own mind, as to which is of the greater importance, Digrung's happiness or Joiwind's. Digrung won't allow you to preserve them both."

"It won't take me long to decide. Digrung, I gave you a last chance to change your mind."

"As long as it's in my power I shall go on, and warn my sister against her criminal friends."

Maskull again clutched at him, but this time with violence. Instructed in his actions by some new and horrible instinct, he pressed the young man tightly to his body with all three arms. A feeling of wild, sweet delight immediately passed through him. Then for the first time he comprehended the triumphant joys of 'absorbing'. It satisfied the hunger of the will, exactly as food satisfies the hunger of the body . . . Digrung proved feeble—he made little opposition. His personality passed slowly and evenly into Maskull's . . . the latter became strong and gorged. The victim gradually became paler and limper, until Maskull held a corpse in his arms. He dropped the body, and stood trembling . . . He had committed his second crime. He felt no immediate difference in his soul, but . . .

Tydomin shed a sad smile on him, like winter sunshine. He half-expected her to speak, but she said nothing. Instead, she made a sign to him to pick up Crimtyphon's corpse. As he obeyed he wondered why Digrung's dead face did not wear the frightful Crystalman mask.

"Why hasn't he altered?" he muttered to himself.

Tydomin heard him. She kicked Digrung lightly with her little foot. "He isn't dead—that's why. The expression you mean is waiting for *your* death."

"Then is that my real character?"

She laughed softly. "You came here to carve a strange world, and now it appears you are carved yourself. Oh, there's no doubt about it, Maskull. You needn't stand there gaping. You belong to Shaping, like the rest of us. You are not a king, or a god."

"Since when have I belonged to him?"

"What does that matter? . . . Perhaps since you first breathed the air of Tormance, or perhaps since five minutes ago."

Without waiting for his response, she set off through the

copse, and strode on to the next island. Maskull followed, physically distressed and looking very grave.

The journey continued for half an hour longer, without incident. The character of the scenery slowly changed. The mountain tops became loftier and more widely separated from one another. The gaps were filled with rolling, white clouds, which bathed the shores of the peaks like a mysterious sea. To pass from island to island was hard work, the intervening spaces were so wide—Tydomin, however, knew the way. The intense light, the violet-blue sky, the patches of vivid landscape, emerging from the white vapour-ocean, made a profound impression on Maskull's mind. The glow of Alppain was hidden by the huge mass of Disscourn, which loomed up straight in front of them.

The green snow on the top of the gigantic pyramid had by now completely melted away. The black, gold, and crimson of its mighty cliffs stood out with terrific brilliance. They were directly beneath the bulk of the mountain, which was not a mile away. It did not appear dangerous to climb, but he was unaware on which side of it their destination lay.

It was split from top to bottom by numerous straight fissures. A few pale-green waterfalls descended here and there, like narrow, motionless threads. The face of the mountain was rugged and bare. It was strewn with detached boulders, and great, jagged rocks projected everywhere like iron teeth. Tydomin pointed to a small black hole near the base, which might be a cave. "That's where I live."

"You live here alone?"

"Yes."

"It's an odd choice for a woman—and you are not unbeautiful, either."

"A woman's life is over at five-and-twenty," she replied, sighing. "And I am far older than that . . . Ten years ago it would have been I who lived yonder, and not Oceaxe. Then all this wouldn't have happened."

A quarter of an hour later they stood within the mouth of the cave. It was ten feet high, and its interior was impenetrably black.

"Put down the body in the entrance, out of the sun," directed Tydomin. He did so.

She cast a keenly scrutinising glance at him. "Does your resolution still hold, Maskull?"

"Why shouldn't it hold? My brains are not feathers."

"Follow me, then."

They both stepped into the cave. At that very moment a sickening crash, like heavy thunder just over their heads, set Maskull's weakened heart thumping violently. An avalanche of boulders, stones, and dust, swept past the cave entrance from above. If their going in had been delayed by a single minute, they must have been killed.

Tydomin did not even look up. She took his hand in hers, and started walking with him into the darkness. The temperature became as cold as ice. At the first bend the light from the outer world disappeared, leaving them in absolute blackness. Maskull kept stumbling over the uneven ground, but she kept tight hold of him, and hurried him along.

The tunnel seemed of interminable length. Presently, however, the atmosphere changed—or such was his impression. He was somehow led to fancy that they had come to a larger chamber. Here Tydomin stopped, and then forced him down with quiet pressure. His groping hand encountered stone and, by feeling it all over, he discovered that it was a sort of stone slab, or couch, raised a foot or eighteen inches from the ground. She told him to lie down.

"Has the time come?" asked Maskull.

"Yes."

He lay there waiting in the darkness, ignorant of what was going to happen. He felt her hand clasping his. Without perceiving any gradation, he lost all consciousness of his body . . . he was no longer able to feel his limbs or internal organs. His mind remained active and alert. Nothing particular appeared to be taking place.

Then the chamber began to grow light, like very early morning. He could see nothing, but the retina of his eye was affected. He fancied that he heard music, but while he was listening for it, it stopped. The light grew stronger, the air grew warmer . . . he heard the confused sound of distant voices.

Suddenly Tydomin gave his hand a powerful squeeze. He heard someone scream faintly, and then the light leapt up, and he saw everything clearly.

He was lying on a wooden couch, in a strangely decorated room, lighted by electricity. His hand was being squeezed, not by Tydomin, but by a man dressed in the garments of civilisation, with whose face he was certainly familiar, but under what circumstances he could not recall. Other people stood in the background—they too were vaguely known to him. He sat up and began to smile, without any especial reason; and then stood upright.

Everybody seemed to be watching him with anxiety and emotion—he wondered why. Yet he felt that they were all acquaintances. Two in particular he knew—the man at the farther end of the room, who paced restlessly backwards and forwards, his face transfigured by stern, holy grandeur; and that other big, bearded man . . . who was *himself*. Yes—he was looking at his own "double" . . . But it was just as if a crime-riddled man of middle-age were suddenly confronted with his own photograph as an earnest, idealistic youth.

His other self spoke to him. He heard the sounds, but did not comprehend the sense. Then the door was abruptly flung open, and a short, brutish-looking individual leapt in. He began to behave in an extraordinary manner to everyone round him; and after that came straight up to him—Maskull. He spoke some words, but they were incomprehensible. A terrible expression came over the newcomer's face, and he grasped his neck with a pair of hairy hands. Maskull felt his bones bending and breaking, excruciating pains passed through all the nerves of his body, and he experienced a sense of impending death. He cried out, and sank helplessly on the floor, in a heap. The chamber and the company vanished—the light went out.

Once more he found himself in the blackness of the cave. He was this time lying on the ground, but Tydomin was still with him, holding his hand. He was in horrible bodily agony, but this was only a setting for the despairing anguish which filled his mind.

Tydomin addressed him in tones of gentle reproach. "Why are you back so soon? I've not had time yet. You must return."

He caught hold of her, and pulled himself up to his feet. She gave a low scream, as though in pain. "What does this mean—what are you doing, Maskull?"

"Krag . . ." began Maskull, but the effort to produce his words choked him, so that he was obliged to stop.

"Krag . . . what of Krag? Tell me quickly what has happened. Free my arm."

He gripped her arm tighter.

"Yes, I've seen Krag. I'm awake."

"Oh! . . . You are awake, awake."

"And you must die," said Maskull, in an awful voice.

"But why? What has happened? . . ."

"You must die, and I must kill you . . . Because I am awake, and for no other reason . . . You blood-stained dancing mistress!"

Tydomin breathed hard for a little time. Then she seemed suddenly to regain her self-possession.

"You won't offer me violence, surely, in this black cave?"

"No, the sun shall look on, for it is not a murder. But rest assured that you must die—you must expiate your fearful crimes."

"You have already said so, and I see you have the power. You have escaped me . . . It is very curious . . . Well, then, Maskull, let us come outside. I am not afraid . . . But kill me courteously, for I have also been courteous to you. I make no other supplication."

CHAPTER ELEVEN

On Disscourn

By the time that they regained the mouth of the cavern, Blodsombre was at its height. In front of them the scenery sloped downwards—a long succession of mountain-islands in a sea of clouds. Behind them the bright, stupendous crags of Disscourn loomed up for a thousand feet or more. Maskull's eyes were red, and his face looked stupid; he was still holding the woman by the arm. She made no attempt to speak, or to get away. She seemed perfectly gentle and composed.

After gazing at the country for a long time in silence, he turned towards her.

"Whereabouts is the fiery lake you spoke of?"

"It lies on the other side of the mountain. But why do you ask?"

"It is just as well if we have some way to walk. I shall grow calmer, and that's what I want. I wish you to understand that what is going to happen is not a murder, but an execution."

"It will taste the same," said Tydomin.

"When I have gone out of this country, I don't wish to feel that I have left a demon behind me, wandering at large. That would not be fair to others . . . So we will go to the lake, which promises an easy death for you."

She shrugged her shoulders. "We must wait till Blodsombre is over."

"Is this a time for luxurious feelings? However hot it is now, we shall both be cool by evening . . . We must start at once."

"Without doubt, you are the master, Maskull . . . May I not carry Crimtyphon?"

Maskull looked at her strangely.

"I grudge no man his funeral."

She painfully hoisted the body on her narrow shoulders, and they stepped out into the sunlight. The heat struck them like a blow on the head. Maskull moved aside, to allow her to precede him, but no compassion entered his heart. He brooded over the wrongs the woman had done him.

The way went along the south side of the great pyramid, near its base. It was a rough road, clogged with boulders and crossed by cracks and water-gullies; they could see the water, but could not get at it. There was no shade. Blisters formed on their skin, while all the water in their blood seemed to dry up . . . Maskull forgot his own tortures in his devil's delight at Tydomin's.

"Sing me a song!" he called out presently. "A characteristic one."

She turned her head and gave him a long, peculiar look; then, without any sort of expostulation, started singing. Her voice was low and weird. The song was so extraordinary that he had to rub his eyes to ascertain whether he were awake or dreaming. The slow surprises of the grotesque melody began to agitate him in a horrible fashion; the words were pure nonsense—or else their significance was too deep for him.

"Where, in the name of all unholy things, did you acquire that stuff, woman?"

Tydomin shed a sickly smile, while the corpse swayed about with ghastly jerks over her left shoulder. She held it in position with her two left arms.

"It's a pity we could not have met as friends, Maskull. I could have shown you a side of Tormance which now perhaps you will never see. The wild, mad side. But now it's too late, and it doesn't matter."

They turned the angle of the mountain, and commenced to traverse the western base.

"Which is the quickest way out of this miserable land?" asked Maskull.

"Is it easiest to go to Sant."

"Shall we see it from anywhere?"

"Yes, though it is a long way off."

"Have you been there?"

"I am a woman, and interdicted."

"True. I have heard something of the sort."

"But don't ask me any more questions," said Tydomin, who was becoming faint.

Maskull stopped at a little spring. He drank himself, and then made a cup of his hand for the woman, so that she might not have to lay down her burden. The gnawl-water acted like magic—it seemed to replenish all the cells of his body as though they had been thirsty sponge-pores, sucking up liquid. Tydomin recovered her self-possession.

About three-quarters of an hour later they worked round the second corner, and entered into full view of the north aspect of Disscourn.

A hundred yards lower down the slope on which they were walking, the mountain ended abruptly in a chasm. The air above it was filled with a sort of green haze, which trembled violently like the atmosphere immediately over a furnace.

"The lake is underneath," said Tydomin.

Maskull looked curiously about him. Beyond the crater the country sloped away in a continuous descent to the skyline. Behind them, a narrow path channelled its way up through the rocks towards the towering summit of the pyramid. Miles away, in the north-east quarter, a long, flat-topped plateau raised its head far above all the surrounding country. It was Sant . . . and there and then he made up his mind that that should be his destination that day.

Tydomin meanwhile had walked straight to the gulf, and set down Crimtyphon's body on the edge. In a minute or two, Maskull joined her; arrived at the brink, he straightway flung himself at full length on his chest, to see what could be seen of the lake of fire. A gust of hot, asphyxiating air smote his face and set him coughing, but he did not get up until he had stared his fill at the huge sea of green, molten lava, tossing and swirling at no great distance below, like a living will.

A faint sound of drumming came up. He listened intently, and as he did so his heart quickened and the black cares rolled away from his soul. All the world and its accidents seemed at that moment *false*, and without meaning . . .

He climbed abstractedly to his feet. Tydomin was talking to her dead husband. She was peering into the hideous face of ivory, and fondling his violet hair. When she perceived Maskull, she hastily kissed the withered lips, and got up from her knees. Lifting the corpse with all three arms, she staggered with it to the extreme edge of the gulf and, after an instant's hesitation, allowed it to drop into the lava. It disappeared immediately without sound; a metallic splash came up . . . That was Crimtyphon's funeral.

"Now I am ready, Maskull."

He did not answer, but stared past her. Another figure was standing, erect and mournful, not far behind her. It was Joiwind. Her face was wan, and there was an accusing look in her eyes . . . Maskull knew that it was a phantasm, and that the real Joiwind was miles away, at Poolingdred.

"Turn round, Tydomin," he said queerly, "and tell me what you see behind you."

"I don't see anything," she answered, looking round.

"But I see Joiwind."

Just as he was speaking the apparition vanished.

"Now I present you with your life, Tydomin. *She* wishes it."

The woman fingered her chin thoughtfully.

"I little expected I should ever be beholden for my life to one of my own sex . . . but so be it . . . What really happened to you in my cavern?"

"I really saw Krag."

"Yes, some miracle must have taken place." She suddenly shivered. "Come let us quit this horrible spot. I shall never come here again."

"Yes," said Maskull, "it stinks of death and dying. But where are we to go—what are we to do? . . .

Take me to Sant . . . I must get away from this hell-
ish land."

Tydomin remained standing, dull and hollow-eyed. Then
she gave an abrupt, bitter little laugh. "We make our journey
together in singular stages. Rather than be alone, I'll come
with you . . . but you know that if I set foot in Sant they
will kill me."

"At least put me on the way. I wish to get there before
night. Is it possible?"

"If you are willing to take risks with Nature. And why
should you not take risks today? Your luck holds . . . But
some day or other it won't hold—your luck."

"Let us start," said Maskull. "The luck I've had so far
is nothing to brag about."

Blodsombre was over when they set off; it was early
afternoon, but the heat seemed more stifling than ever.
They made no more pretence at conversation, both were
buried in their own painful thoughts. The land fell away
from Disscourn in all other directions, but towards Sant
there was a gentle, persistent rise. Its dark, distant plateau
continued to dominate the landscape, and after walking for
an hour they seemed none the nearer to it. The air was stale
and stagnant.

By and by, an upright object, apparently the work of
man, attracted Maskull's notice. It was a slender tree-stem,
with the bark still on, imbedded in the stony ground. From
the upper end three branches sprang out, pointing aloft at
a sharp angle. They were stripped to twigs and leaves and,
getting closer, he saw that they had been artificially fastened
on, at equal distances from each other.

As he stared at the object, a strange, sudden flush of
confident vanity and self-sufficiency seemed to pass through
him, but it was so momentary that he could be sure of
nothing.

"What may that be, Tydomin?"

"It is Hator's Trifork."

"And what is its purpose?"

"It's a guide to Sant."

"But who or what is Hator?"

"Hator was the founder of Sant . . . many thousands of years ago. He laid down the principles they all live by, and that trifork is his symbol. When I was a little child my father told me the legends, but I've forgotten most of them."

Maskull regarded it attentively.

"Does it affect you in any way?"

"And why should it do that?" she said, dropping her lip scornfully. "I am only a woman, and these are masculine mysteries."

"A sort of gladness came over me," said Maskull, "but perhaps I am mistaken."

They passed on. The scenery gradually changed in character. The solid parts of the land grew more continuous, the fissures became narrower and more infrequent. There were now no more subsidences or upheavals. The peculiar nature of the Ifdawn Marest appeared to be giving place to a different order of things.

Later on, they encountered a flock of pale blue jellies floating in the air. They were miniature animals. Tydomin caught one in her hand and began to eat it, just as one eats a luscious pear plucked from a tree. Maskull, who had fasted since early morning, was not slow in following her example. A sort of electric vigour at once entered his limbs and body, his muscles regained their elasticity, his heart began to beat with hard, slow, strong throbs.

"Food and body seem to agree well in this world," he remarked smiling.

She glanced towards him. "Perhaps the explanation is not in the food, but in your body."

"I brought my body with me."

"You brought your soul with you, but that's altering fast, too."

In a copse they came across a short, wide tree, without leaves, but possessing a multitude of thin, flexible branches, like the tentacles of a cuttle fish. Some of these branches were moving rapidly. A furry animal, somewhat resembling a wild cat, leapt about among them in the most extraordinary way . . . But the next minute Maskull was shocked to realise that the beast was not leaping at all, but was being thrown from branch to branch by the volition of the tree, exactly as an imprisoned mouse is thrown by a cat from paw to paw.

He watched the spectacle awhile with morbid interest.

"That's a gruesome reversal of rôles, Tydomin."

"One can see you're disgusted," she replied, stifling a yawn. "But that is because you are a slave to words. If you called that plant an animal, you would find its occupation perfectly natural and pleasing. And why should you not call it an animal?"

"I am quite aware that, as long as I remain in the Ifdawn Marest, I shall go on listening to this sort of language."

They trudged along for an hour or more without talking. The day became overcast. A thin mist began to shroud the landscape, and the sun changed into an immense ruddy disc which could be stared at without flinching. A chill, damp wind blew against them. Presently it grew still darker, the sun disappeared and, glancing first at his companion and then at himself, Maskull noticed that their skin and clothing were coated by a kind of green hoar-frost.

The land was now completely solid. About half a mile in front of them, against a background of dark fog, a moving forest of tall waterspouts gyrated slowly and gracefully hither and thither. They were green and self-luminous, and looked terrifying . . . Tydomin explained that they were not waterspouts at all, but mobile columns of lightning.

"Then they are dangerous?"

"So we think," she answered, watching them closely. "Someone is wandering there who appears to have a different opinion."

Among the spouts, and entirely encompassed by them, a man was walking with a slow, calm, composed gait, his back turned towards Maskull and Tydomin. There was something unusual in his appearance—his form looked extraordinarily distinct, solid, and real.

"If there's danger, he ought to be warned," said Maskull.

"He who is always anxious to teach, will learn nothing," returned the woman coolly. She restrained Maskull by a pressure of the arm, and continued to watch.

The base of one of the columns touched the man. He remained unharmed, but turned sharply round, as if for the first time made aware of the proximity of these deadly waltzers. Then he raised himself to his full height, and stretched both arms aloft above his head, like a diver. He seemed to be addressing the columns.

While they looked on, the electric spouts discharged themselves, with a series of loud explosions. The stranger stood alone, uninjured. He dropped his arms. The next moment he caught sight of the two, and stood still, waiting for them to come up. The pictorial clarity of his person grew more and more noticeable as they approached; his body seemed to be composed of some substance heavier and denser than solid matter.

Tydomin looked perplexed.

"He must be a Sant man. I have seen no one quite like him before . . . This is a day of days for me."

"He must be an individual of great importance," murmured Maskull.

They now came up to him. He was tall, strong, and bearded, and was clothed in a shirt and breeches of skin. Since turning his back to the wind, the green deposit on his face and limbs had changed to streaming moisture, through which his natural colour was visible; it was that of pale iron. There was no third arm. His face was harsh and frowning, and a projecting chin pushed the beard forward. On his forehead there were two flat membranes, like rudimentary eyes, but no sorb. These membranes were expressionless, but in some strange way seemed to add vigour to the stern eyes underneath. When his glance rested on Maskull, the latter felt as though his brain were being thoroughly travelled through. The man was middle-aged.

His physical distinctness transcended nature. By contrast with him, every object in the neighbourhood looked vague and blurred. Tydomin's person suddenly appeared faint, sketch-like, without significance, and Maskull realised that it was no better with himself . . . A queer, quickening fire began running through his veins.

He turned to the woman.

"If this man is going to Sant, I shall bear him company. We can now part. No doubt you will think it high time."

"Let Tydomin come too."

The words were delivered in a rough, foreign tongue, but were as intelligible to Maskull as if spoken in English.

"You who know my name, also know my sex," said Tydomin quietly. "It is death for me to enter Sant."

"That is the old law. I am the bearer of the new law."

"Is it so . . . and will it be accepted?"

"The old skin is cracking, the new skin has been silently forming underneath, the moment of sloughing has arrived."

The storm gathered. The green snow drove against them, as they stood talking, and it grew intensely cold. None noticed it.

"What is your name?" asked Maskull, with a beating heart.

"My name, Maskull, is Spadevil. You, a voyager across the dark ocean of space, shall be my first witness and follower. You, Tydomin, a daughter of the despised sex, shall be my second."

"The new law? But what is it?"

"Until eye sees, of what use is it for ear to hear? . . . Come both of you to me!"

Tydomin went to him unhesitatingly. Spadevil pressed his hand on her sorb and kept it there for a few minutes, while he closed his own eyes. When he removed it, Maskull observed that the sorb was transformed into twin membranes like Spadevil's own.

Tydomin looked dazed. She glanced quietly about for a little while, apparently testing her new faculty. Then the tears started to her eyes and, snatching up Spadevil's hand, she bent over and kissed it hurriedly many times.

"My past has been bad," she said. "Numbers have

received harm from me, and none good. I have killed . . . and worse . . . But now I can throw all that away, and laugh. Nothing can now injure me . . . Oh, Maskull, you and I have been fools together!"

"Don't you repent your crimes?" asked Maskull.

"Leave the past alone," said Spadevil. "It cannot be reshaped. The future alone is ours. It starts fresh and clean from this very minute . . . Why do you hesitate, Maskull . . . are you afraid?"

"What is the name of those organs, and what is their function?"

"They are *probes*, and they are the gates opening into a new world."

Maskull lingered no longer, but permitted Spadevil to cover his sorb.

While the iron hand was still pressing his forehead, the new law quietly flowed into his consciousness, like a smooth-running stream of clean water which had hitherto been dammed by his obstructive will. The law was *duty*.

CHAPTER TWELVE

Spadevil

Maskull found that his new organs had no independent function of their own, but only intensified and altered his other senses. When he used his eyes, ears, or nostrils, the same objects presented themselves to him, but his judgment concerning them was different. Previously all external things had existed for him; now he existed for them. According to whether they served his purpose or were in harmony with his nature, or otherwise, they had been pleasant or painful. Now these words "pleasure" and "pain" simply had no meaning.

The other two watched him, while he was making himself acquainted with his new mental outlook. He smiled at them.

"You were quite right, Tydomin," he said, in a bold, cheerful voice. "We have been fools. So near the light all the time, and we never guessed it. Always buried in the past or future—systematically ignoring the present . . . and now it turns out that apart from the present we have no life at all."

"Thank Spadevil for it," she answered, more loudly than usual.

Maskull looked at the man's dark, concrete form. "Spadevil, now I mean to follow you to the end. I can do nothing less."

The severe face showed no sign of gratification—not a muscle relaxed.

"Watch that you don't lose your gift," he said gruffly.

Tydomin spoke. "You promised that I should enter Sant with you."

"Attach yourself to the truth, not to me. For I may die

before you, but the truth will accompany you to your death. However, now let us journey together, all three of us."

The words had not left his mouth before he put his face against the fine, driving snow, and pressed onward towards his destination. He walked with a long stride; Tydomin was obliged to half-run, in order to keep up with him. The three travelled abreast; Spadevil in the middle. The fog was so dense that it was impossible to see a hundred yards ahead. The ground was covered by the green snow. The wind blew in gusts from the Sant highlands, and was piercingly cold.

"Spadevil, are you a man, or more than a man?" asked Maskull.

"He that is not more than a man is nothing."

"Where have you now come from?"

"From brooding, Maskull. Out of no other mother can truth be born. I have brooded, and rejected; and I have brooded again. Now, after many months' absence from Sant, the truth at last shines forth for me in its simple splendour, like an upturned diamond."

"I see its shining," said Maskull. "But how much does it owe to ancient Hator?"

"Knowledge has its seasons. The blossom was to Hator, the fruit is to me. Hator also was a brooder—but now his followers do not brood. In Sant all is icy selfishness, a living death. They hate pleasure, and this hatred is the greatest pleasure to them."

"But in what way have they fallen off from Hator's doctrines?"

"For him, in his sullen purity of nature, all the world was a snare, a limed twig. Knowing that pleasure was everywhere, a fierce, mocking enemy, crouching and waiting at every corner of the road of life, in order to kill with its sweet sting the naked grandeur of the soul, he shielded himself behind *pain*. This also his followers do, but they do not do it for the sake of the soul, but for the sake of vanity and pride."

"What is the Trifork?"

"The stem, Maskull, is hatred of pleasure. The first fork is disentanglement from the sweetness of the world. The second fork is power over those who still writhe in the nets of illusion. The third fork is the healthy glow of one who steps into ice-cold water."

"From what land did Hator come?"

"Is it not said. He lived in Ifdawn for awhile. There are many legends told of him while there."

"We have a long way to go," said Tydomin. "Relate some of these legends, Spadevil."

The snow had ceased, the day brightened, Branchspell reappeared like a phantom sun, but bitter blasts of wind still swept over the plain.

"In those days," said Spadevil, "there existed in Ifdawn a mountain-island separated by wide spaces from the land around it. A handsome girl, who knew sorcery, caused a bridge to be constructed across which men and women might pass to it. Having by a false tale drawn Hator on to this rock, she pushed at the bridge with her foot until it tumbled into the depths below. 'You and I, Hator, are now together, and there is no means of separating. I wish to see how long the famous frost-man can withstand the breath, smiles, and perfume of a girl.' Hator said no word, either then or all that day. He stood till sunset like a tree-trunk, and thought of other things. Then the girl grew passionate, and shook her curls. She rose from where she was sitting, she looked at him, and touched his arm; but he did not see her. She looked at him, so that all the soul was in her eyes; and then she fell down dead. Hator awoke from his thoughts, and saw her lying, still warm, at his feet, a corpse. He passed to the mainland; but how, it is not related."

Tydomin shuddered. "You too have met your wicked woman, Spadevil; but your method is a nobler one."

"Don't pity other women," said Spadevil, "but love the *right*. Hator also once conversed with Shaping."

"With the Maker of the World?" said Maskull thoughtfully.

"With the Maker of Pleasure. It is told how Shaping

defended his world, and tried to force Hator to acknowledge loveliness and joy. But Hator, answering all his marvellous speeches in a few concise, iron words, showed how this joy and beauty was but another name for the bestiality of souls wallowing in luxury and sloth. Shaping smiled, and said, 'How comes it that your wisdom is greater than that of the Master of wisdom?' Hator said, 'My wisdom does not come from you, nor from your world, but from that other world, which you, Shaping, have vainly tried to imitate.' Shaping replied, 'What, then, do you do in my world?' Hator said, 'I am here falsely, and therefore I am subject to your false pleasures. But I wrap myself in *pain*—not because it is good, but because I wish to keep myself as far from you as possible. For pain is not yours, neither does it belong to the other world, but it is the shadow cast by your false pleasures.' Shaping then said, 'What is this far away other world, of which you say "This is so —this is not so?" How happens it that you alone of all my creatures have knowledge of it?' But Hator spat at his feet, and said, 'You lie, Shaping. All have knowledge of it. You, with your pretty toys, alone obscure it from our view.' Shaping asked, 'What, then, am I?' Hator answered, 'You are the dreamer of impossible dreams.' And then the story goes that Shaping departed, ill-pleased with what had been said."

"What other world did Hator refer to?" asked Maskull.

"One where grandeur reigns, Maskull, just as pleasure reigns here."

"Whether grandeur or pleasure, it makes no difference," said Maskull. "The individual spirit which lives and wishes to live is mean and corrupt-natured."

"Guard you your pride!" returned Spadevil. "Do not make law for the universe and for all time, but for yourself and for this small, false life of yours."

"In what shape did death come to that hard, unconquerable man?" asked Tydomin.

"He lived to be old, but went upright and free-limbed to his last hour. When he saw that death could not be staved off longer he determined to destroy himself. He gathered his friends around him; not from vanity, but that they might see to what lengths this human soul can go in its perpetual warfare with the voluptuous body. Standing erect, without support, he died by withholding his breath."

A silence followed, which lasted for perhaps an hour. Their minds refused to acknowledge the icy winds, but the current of their thoughts became frozen.

When Branchspell, however, shone out again, though with subdued power, Maskull's curiosity rose once more.

"Your fellow countrymen, then, Spadevil, are sick with self-love?"

"The men of other countries," said Spadevil, "are the slaves of pleasure and desire, knowing it. But the men of my country are the slaves of pleasure and desire, not knowing it."

"And yet that proud pleasure, which rejoices in self-torture, has something noble in it."

"He who studies himself at all, is ignoble. Only by despising soul, as well as body, can a man enter into true life."

"On what grounds do they reject women?"

"Inasmuch as a woman has ideal love, and cannot live for herself. Love for another is pleasure for the loved-one, and therefore injurious to him."

"A forest of false ideas is waiting for your axe," said Maskull. "But will they allow it?"

"Spadevil knows, Maskull," said Tydomin, "that be it today or be it tomorrow, love can't be kept out of a land, even by the disciples of Hator."

"Beware of love—beware of emotion!" exclaimed Spadevil. "Love is but pleasure once removed. Think not of pleasing others, but of serving them."

'Forgive me, Spadevil, if I am still feminine."

"*Right* has no sex. So long, Tydomin, as you remember that you are a woman, so long you will not enter into divine apathy of soul."

"But where there are no women, there are no children," said Maskull. "How came there to be all these generations of Hator men?"

"Life breeds passion, passion breeds suffering, suffering breeds the yearning for relief from suffering. Men throng to Sant from all parts, in order to have the scars of their souls healed."

"In place of hatred of pleasure, which all can understand, what simple formula do you offer?"

"Iron obedience to duty," answered Spadevil.

"And if they ask 'How far is this consistent with hatred of pleasure?' what will your pronouncement be?"

"I do not answer them, but I answer you, Maskull, who ask the question. Hatred is passion, and all passion springs from the dark fires of Self. Do not hate pleasure at all, but pass it by on one side, calm and undisturbed."

"What is the criterion of pleasure? How can we always recognise it, in order to avoid it?"

"Rigidly follow duty, and such questions will not arise."

Later in the afternoon, Tydomin timidly placed her fingers on Spadevil's arm.

"Fearful doubts are in my mind," she said. "This expedition to Sant may turn out badly. I have seen a vision of you, Spadevil, and myself lying dead and covered in blood, but Maskull was not there."

"We may drop the torch, but it will not be extinguished, and others will raise it."

"Show me a sign that you are not as other men—so that I may know that our blood will not be wasted."

Spadevil regarded her sternly. "I am not a magician. I don't persuade the senses, but the soul. Does your duty call you to Sant, Tydomin? Then go there. Does it not call you to Sant? Then go no further. Is not this simple? What signs are necessary?"

"Did I not see you dispel those spouts of lightning? No common man could have done that."

"Who knows what any man can do? This man can do

one thing, that man can do another. But what all men can do, is their duty; and to open their eyes to this, I must go to Sant, and if necessary lay down my life. Will you not still accompany me?"

"Yes," said Tydomin, "I will follow you to the end. It is all the more essential, because I keep on displeasing you with my remarks, and that means I have not yet learnt my lesson properly."

"Do not be humble, for humility is only self-judgment, and while we are thinking of self, we must be neglecting some action which we could be planning or shaping in our mind."

Tydomin continued to be uneasy and preoccupied.

"Why was Maskull not in the picture?" she asked.

"You dwell on this foreboding because you imagine it is tragical. There is nothing tragical in death, Tydomin, nor in life. There is only right and wrong. What arises from right or wrong action does not matter. We are not gods, constructing a world, but simple men and women, doing our immediate duty. We may die in Sant—so you have seen it; but the truth will go on living."

"Spadevil, why do you choose Sant to start your work in?" asked Maskull. "These men with fixed ideas seem to me the least likely of any to follow a new light."

"Where a bad tree thrives, a good tree will flourish. But where no tree at all can be found, nothing will grow."

"I understand you," said Maskull. "Here perhaps we are going to martyrdom, but elsewhere we should resemble men preaching to cattle."

Shortly before sunset they arrived at the extremity of the upland plain, above which towered the black cliffs of the Sant Levels. A dizzy, artificially constructed staircase, of more than a thousand steps of varying depth, twisting and forking in order to conform to the angles of the precipices, led to the world overhead. In the place where they stood they were sheltered from the cutting winds. Branchspell, radiantly shining at last, but on the point of sinking, filled the cloudy sky with violent, lurid colours, some of the combinations of which were new to Maskull. The circle of the horizon was so gigantic, that had he been suddenly carried back to Earth, he would by comparison have fancied himself to be moving beneath the dome of some little closed-in cathedral. He realised that he was on a foreign planet. But he was not stirred or uplifted by the knowledge; he was conscious only of moral ideas. Looking backwards, he saw the plain, which for several miles past had been without vegetation, stretching back away to Disscourn. So regular had been the ascent, and so great was the distance, that the huge pyramid looked nothing more than a slight swelling on the face of the earth.

Spadevil stopped, and gazed over the landscape in silence. In the evening sunlight his form looked more dense, dark, and real than ever before. His features were set hard in grimness. He turned round to his companions.

"What is the greatest wonder in all this wonderful scene?" he demanded.

"Acquaint us," said Maskull.

"All that you see is born from pleasure, and moves on from pleasure to pleasure. Nowhere is *right* to be found. It is Shaping's world."

"There is another wonder," said Tydomin, and she pointed her finger towards the sky overhead.

A small cloud, so low down that it was perhaps not more than five hundred feet above them, was sailing along in front of the dark wall of cliff. It was in the exact shape of an open human hand, with downward-pointing fingers. It was stained crimson by the sun; and one or two tiny cloudlets beneath the fingers looked like falling drops of blood.

"Who can doubt now that our death is close at hand?" said Tydomin. "I have been close to death twice today. The first time I was ready, but now I am more ready, for I shall die side-by-side with the man who has given me my first happiness."

"Do not think of death, but of right persistence," replied

Spadevil. "I am not here to tremble before Shaping's portents; but to snatch men from him."

He at once proceeded to lead the way up the staircase. Tydomin gazed upwards after him for a moment, with an odd, worshipping light in her eyes. Then she followed him, the second of the party. Maskull climbed last. He was travel-stained, unkempt, and very tired; but his soul was at peace. As they steadily ascended the almost perpendicular stairs, the sun got higher in the sky. Its light dyed their bodies a ruddy gold.

They gained the top. There they found rolling in front of them, as far as the eye could see, a barren desert of white sand, broken here and there by large, jagged masses of black rock. Tracts of the sand were reddened by the sinking sun. The vast expanse of the sky was filled by evil-shaped clouds and wild colours. The freezing wind, flurrying across the desert, drove the fine particles of sand painfully against their faces.

"Where now do you take us?" asked Maskull.

"He who guards the old wisdom of Sant must give up that wisdom to me, that I may change it. What he says, others will say. I go to find Maulger."

"And where will you seek him, in this bare country?"

Spadevil struck off towards the north unhesitatingly.

"It is not so far," he said. "It is his custom to be in that part where Sant overhangs the Wombflash Forest. Perhaps he will be there, but I cannot say."

Maskull glanced towards Tydomin. Her sunken cheeks, and the dark circles beneath her eyes, told of her extreme weariness.

"The woman is tired, Spadevil," he said.

She smiled. "It's but another step into the land of death. I can manage it. Give me your arm, Maskull."

He put his arm around her waist, and supported her along that way.

"The sun is now sinking," said Maskull. "Shall we get there before dark?"

"Fear nothing, Maskull and Tydomin; this pain is eating

up the evil in your nature. The road you are walking cannot remain unwalked. We shall arrive before dark."

The sun then disappeared behind the far-distant ridges which formed the western boundary of the Ifdawn Marest. The sky blazed up into more vivid colours. The wind grew colder.

They passed some pools of colourless gnawl-water, round the banks of which were planted fruit trees. Maskull ate some of the fruit. It was hard, bitter, and astringent; he could not get rid of the taste, but he felt braced and invigorated by the downward-flowing juices. No other trees or shrubs were to be seen anywhere. No animals appeared, no birds or insects. It was a desolate land.

A mile or two passed, when they again approached the edge of the plateau. Far down, beneath their feet, the great Wombflash Forest began. But daylight had vanished there; Maskull's eyes rested only on a vague darkness. He faintly heard what sounded like the distant sighing of innumerable tree-tops.

In the rapidly darkening twilight, they came abruptly on a man. He was standing in a pool, on one leg. A pile of boulders had hidden him from their view. The water came as far up as his calf. A trifork, similar to the one Maskull had seen on Disscourn, but smaller, had been stuck in the mud close by his hand.

They stopped by the side of the pond, and waited. Immediately he became aware of their presence, the man set down his other leg, and waded out of the water towards them, picking up his trifork in doing so.

"This is not Maulger, but Catice," said Spadevil.

"Maulger is dead," said Catice, speaking the same tongue as Spadevil, but with an even harsher accent, so that the tympanum of Maskull's ear was affected painfully.

The latter saw before him a bowed, powerful individual, advanced in years. He wore nothing but a scanty loin-cloth. His trunk was long and heavy, but his legs were rather short. His face was beardless, lemon-coloured, and anxious-looking. It was disfigured by a number of longitudinal ruts, a quarter of an inch deep, the cavities of which seemed clogged with ancient dirt. The hair of his head was black and sparse. Instead of the twin membraneous organs of Spadevil, he possessed but one; and this was in the centre of his brow.

Spadevil's dark, solid person stood out from the rest like a reality among dreams.

"Has the trifork passed to you?" he demanded.

"Yes. Why have you brought this woman to Sant?"

"I have brought another thing to Sant. I have brought the new faith."

Catice stood motionless, and looked troubled. "State it."

"Shall I speak with many words, or few words?"

"If you wish to say what is *not*, many words will not suffice. If you wish to say what *is*, a few words will be enough."

Spadevil frowned.

"To hate pleasure brings pride with it. Pride is a pleasure. To kill pleasure, we much attach ourselves to *duty*. While the mind is planning right action, it has no time to think of pleasure."

"Is that the whole?" asked Catice.

"The truth is simple, even for the simplest man."

"Do you destroy Hator, and all his generations, with a single word?"

"I destroy nature, and set up law."

A long silence followed.

"My probe is double," said Spadevil. "Suffer me to double yours, and you will see as I see."

"Come you here, you big man!" said Catice to Maskull. Maskull advanced a step closer.

"Do you follow Spadevil in his new faith?"

"As far as death," exclaimed Maskull.

Catice picked up a flint. "With this stone I strike out one of your two probes. When you have but one, you will see with me, and you will recollect with Spadevil. Choose you then the superior faith, and I shall obey your choice."

"Endure this little pain, Maskull, for the sake of future men," said Spadevil.

"The pain is nothing," replied Maskull, "but I fear the result."

"Permit me, although I am only a woman, to take his place, Catice," said Tydomin, stretching out her hand.

He struck at it violently with the flint, and gashed it from wrist to thumb; the pale carmine blood spouted up. "What brings this kiss-lover to Sant?" he said. "How does she presume to make the rules of life for the sons of Hator?"

She bit her lip, and stepped back. "Well then, Maskull, accept! I certainly should not have played false to Spadevil; but you hardly can."

"If he bids me, I must do it," said Maskull. "But who knows what will come of it?"

Spadevil spoke. "Of all the descendants of Hator, Catice is the most wholehearted and sincere. He will trample my truth under foot, thinking me a demon sent by Shaping, to destroy the work of this land. But a seed will escape, and my blood and yours, Tydomin, will wash it. Then men will know that my destroying evil is their greatest good. But none here will live to see that."

Maskull now went quite close to Catice, and offered his head. Catice raised his hand, and after holding the flint poised for a moment, brought it down with adroitness and force upon the left-hand probe. Maskull cried out with the pain. The blood streamed down, and the function of the organ was destroyed.

There was a pause, while he walked to and fro, trying to stanch the blood.

"What now do you feel, Maskull? What do you see?" inquired Tydomin anxiously.

He stopped, and stared hard at her. "I now see straight," he said slowly.

"What does that mean?"

He continued to wipe the blood from his forehead. He looked troubled. "Henceforward, as long as I live, I shall fight with my nature, and refuse to feel pleasure. And I advise you to do the same."

Spadevil gazed at him sternly. "Do you renounce my teaching?"

Maskull, however, returned the gaze without dismay. Spadevil's image-like clearness of form had departed for him; his frowning face he knew to be the deceptive portico of a weak and confused intellect.

"It is false."

"Is it false to sacrifice oneself for another?" demanded Tydomin.

"I can't argue as yet," said Maskull. "At this moment the world with its sweetness seems to me a sort of charnel-house. I feel a loathing for everything in it, including myself. I know no more."

"Is there no duty?" asked Spadevil, in a harsh tone.

"It appears to me but a cloak under which we share the pleasure of other people."

Tydomin pulled at Spadevil's arm. "Maskull has betrayed you, as he has so many others.—Let us go."

He stood fast. "You have changed quickly, Maskull."

Maskull, without answering him, turned to Catice. "Why do men go on living in this soft, shameful world, when they can kill themselves?"

"Pain is the native air of Surtur's children. To what other air do you wish to escape?"

"Surtur's children? Is not Surtur Shaping?"

"It is the greatest of lies. It is Shaping's masterpiece."

"Answer, Maskull!" said Spadevil. "Do you repudiate right-action?"

"Leave me alone. Go back! I am not thinking of you, and your ideas. I wish you no harm."

The darkness came on fast. There was another prolonged silence.

Catice threw away the flint, and picked up his staff.

"The woman must return home," he said. "She was persuaded here, and did not come freely. You, Spadevil, must die—backslider as you are!"

Tydomin said quietly, "He has no power to enforce this. Are you going to allow the truth to fall to the ground, Spadevil?"

"It will not perish by my death, but by my efforts to escape from death. Catice, I accept your judgment."

Tydomin smiled. "For my part, I am too tired to walk farther today, so I shall die with him."

Catice said to Maskull, "Prove your sincerity. Kill this man and his mistress, according to the laws of Hator."

"I can't do that. I have travelled in friendship with them."

"You denied duty; and now you must do your duty," said Spadevil, calmly stroking his beard. "Whatever law you accept, you must obey, without turning to right or left. Your law commands that we must be stoned; and it will soon be dark."

"Have you not even this amount of manhood?" exclaimed Tydomin.

Maskull moved heavily. "Be my witness, Catice, that the thing was forced on me."

"Hator is looking on, and approving," replied Catice.

Maskull then went apart to the pile of boulders scattered by the side of the pool. He glanced about him, and selected two large fragments of rock, the heaviest that he thought he could carry. With these in his arms, he staggered back.

He dropped them on the ground, and stood, recovering his breath. When he could speak again, he said, "I have a bad heart for the business. Is there no alternative? Sleep here tonight, Spadevil, and in the morning go back to where you have come from. No one shall harm you."

Spadevil's ironic smile was lost in the gloom.

"Shall I brood again, Maskull, for still another year, and after that come back to Sant with other truths? Come, waste no time, but choose the heavier stone for me, for I am stronger than Tydomin."

Maskull lifted one of the rocks, and stepped out four full paces. Spadevil confronted him, erect, and waited tranquilly.

The huge stone hurtled through the air. Its flight looked like a dark shadow. It struck Spadevil full in the face, crushing his features, and breaking his neck. He died instantaneously.

Tydomin looked away from the fallen man.

"Be very quick, Maskull, and don't let me keep him waiting."

He panted, and raised the second stone. She placed herself in front of Spadevil's body, and stood there, unsmiling and cold.

The blow caught her between breast and chin, and she fell. Maskull went to her, and, kneeling on the ground, half-raised her in his arms. There she breathed out her last sighs.

After that, he laid her down again, and rested heavily on his hands, while he peered into the dead face. The transition from its heroic, spiritual expression to the vulgar and grinning mask of Crystalman came like a flash; but he saw it.

He stood up in the darkness, and pulled Catice towards him.

"Is that the true likeness of Shaping?"

"It is Shaping stripped of illusion."

"How comes this horrible world to exist?"

Catice did not answer.

"Who is Surtur?"

"You will get nearer to him tomorrow; but not here."

"I am wading through too much blood," said Maskull. "Nothing good can come of it."

"Do not fear change and destruction; but laughter and joy."

Maskull meditated.

"Tell me, Catice. If I had elected to follow Spadevil, would you really have accepted his faith?"

"He was a great-souled man," replied Catice. "I see that the pride of our men is only another sprouting-out of pleasure. Tomorrow I too shall leave Sant, to reflect on all this."

Maskull shuddered. "Then these two deaths were not a necessity, but a crime!"

"His part was played, and henceforward the woman would have dragged down his ideas, with her soft love and loyalty. Regret nothing, stranger, but go away at once out of the land."

"Tonight? Where shall I go?"

"To Wombflash, where you will meet the deepest minds. I will put you on the way."

He linked his arm in Maskull's, and they walked away into the night. For a mile or more they skirted the edge of the precipice. The wind was searching, and drove grit into their faces. Through the rifts of the clouds, stars, faint and brilliant, appeared. Maskull saw no familiar constellations. He wondered if the Sun of earth were visible, and if so which one it was.

They came to the head of a rough staircase, leading down the cliff-side. It resembled the one by which he had come up; but this descended to the Wombflash Forest.

"That is your path," said Catice, "and I shall not come any further."

Maskull detained him. "Say just this, before we part company—why does pleasure appear so shameful to us?"

"Because in feeling pleasure, we forget our *home*."

"And that is—?"

"Muspel," answered Catice.

Having made this reply, he disengaged himself, and, turning his back, disappeared into the darkness.

Maskull stumbled down the staircase as best he could. He was tired, but contemptuous of his pains. His uninjured probe began to discharge matter. He lowered himself from step to step during what seemed an interminable time. The rustling and sighing of the trees grew louder as he approached the bottom; the air became still and warm. Inky blackness was all around him.

He at last reached level ground. Still attempting to proceed, he began to trip over roots, and to collide with tree-trunks. After this had happened a few times, he determined to go no further that night. He heaped together some dry leaves for a pillow, and straightway flung himself down to sleep. Deep and heavy unconsciousness seized him almost instantly.

CHAPTER THIRTEEN

The Wombflash Forest

He awoke to his third day on Tormance. His limbs ached.
He lay on his side, looking stupidly at his surroundings.
The forest was like night, but that period of the night
when the grey dawn is about to break and objects begin
to be guessed at, rather than seen. Two or three amazing
shadowy shapes, as broad as houses, loomed up out of the
twilight. He did not realise that they were trees, until he
turned over on his back and followed their course upwards.
Far overhead, so high up that he dared not calculate the
height, he saw their tops glittering in the sunlight, against
a tiny patch of blue sky.

Clouds of mist, rolling over the floor of the forest, kept
interrupting his view. In their silent passage they were like
phantoms flitting among the trees. The leaves underneath
him were sodden, and heavy drops of moisture splashed
on to his head from time to time.

He continued lying there, trying to reconstruct the events
of the preceding day. His brain was lethargic and confused.
Something terrible had happened, but what it was he could
not for a long time recollect . . . Then suddenly there came
before his eyes that ghastly closing scene at dusk on the
Sant plateau—Spadevil's crushed and bloody features and
Tydomin's dying sighs . . . He shuddered convulsively,
and felt sick.

The peculiar moral outlook which had dictated these
brutal murders had departed from him during the night,
and now he recognised what he had done! . . . During the
whole of the previous day he seemed to have been labouring
under a series of heavy enchantments. First Oceaxe had
enslaved him, then Tydomin, then Spadevil, and lastly

Catice. They had forced him to murder and violate . . . he had guessed nothing, but had imagined that he was travelling as a free and enlightened stranger . . . What was this nightmare-journey for . . . and would it continue in the same way? . . .

The silence of the forest was so intense that he heard no sound except the pumping of blood through his arteries.

Putting his hand to his face, he found that his remaining probe had disappeared and that he was in possession of three eyes. The third eye was on his forehead, where the old sorb had been. He could not guess its use. He still had his third arm, but it was nerveless.

Now he puzzled his head for a long time, trying unsuccessfully to recall that name which had been the last word spoken by Catice.

He got up, with the intention of resuming his journey. He had no toilet to make, and no meal to prepare. The forest was tremendous. The nearest tree appeared to him to have a circumference of at least a hundred feet. Other dim boles looked equally large. But what gave the scene its aspect of immensity was the vast spaces separating tree from tree. It was like some gigantic, supernatural hall in a life after death. The lowest branches were fifty yards or more from the ground. There was no underbrush; the soil was carpeted only by the dead, wet leaves. He looked all around him, to find his direction, but the cliffs of Sant, which he had descended, were invisible—every way was like every other way, he had no idea which quarter to attack. He grew frightened, and muttered to himself. Craning his neck back, he stared upwards and tried to discover the points of the compass from the direction of the sunlight, but it was impossible.

While he was standing there, anxious and hesitating, he heard the drum-taps. The rhythmical beats proceeded from some distance off. The unseen drummer seemed to be marching through the forest, away from him.

"Surtur!" he said, under his breath. The next moment he marvelled at himself for uttering the name. That mysterious

being had not been in his thoughts, nor was there any
ostensible connection between him and the drumming.

He began to reflect . . . but in the meantime the sounds
were travelling away. Automatically he started walking in
the same direction. The drum-beats had this peculiarity—
though odd and mystical, there was nothing awe-inspiring
in them, but on the contrary they reminded him of some
place and some life with which he was perfectly familiar.
Once again they caused all his other sense-impressions to
appear false.

The sounds were intermittent. They would go on for a
minute, or for five minutes, and then cease for perhaps
a quarter of an hour. Maskull followed them as well
as he could. He walked hard among the huge, indistinct trees, in the attempt to come up with the origin
of the noise, but the same distance always seemed to
separate them. The forest from now onwards descended.
The gradient was mostly gentle—about one foot in ten
—but in some places it was much steeper, and in other
parts again it was practically level ground for quite long
stretches. There were great swampy marshes, through
which Maskull was obliged to splash . . . It was a matter of indifference to him how wet he became—if only
he could catch sight of that individual with the drum.
Mile after mile was covered, and still he was no nearer
to doing so.

The gloom of the forest settled down upon his spirits.
He felt despondent, tired, and savage. He had not heard
the drumbeats for some while, and was half-inclined to
discontinue the pursuit.

Passing round a great, columnar tree-trunk, he almost
stumbled against a man who was standing on the farther
side. He was leaning against the trunk with one hand, in
an attitude of repose. His other hand was resting on a staff.
Maskull stopped short and stared at him.

He was nearly naked, and of gigantic build. He over-
topped Maskull by a head. His face and body were faintly
phosphorescent. His eyes—three in number—were pale

green and luminous, shining like lamps. His skin was hairless, but the hair of his head was piled up in thick, black coils, and fastened like a woman's. His features were absolutely tranquil, but a terrible, quiet energy seemed to lie just underneath the surface.

Maskull addressed him. "Did the drumming come from you?"

The man shook his head.

"What is your name?"

He replied in a queer, strained, twisted voice. Maskull gathered that the name he gave was "Dreamsinter".

"What is that drumming?"

"Surtur," said Dreamsinter.

"Is it advisable for me to follow it?"

"Why?"

"Perhaps he intends me to. He brought me here from Earth."

Dreamsinter caught hold of him, bent down, and peered into his face. "Not you, but Nightspore."

This was the first time that Maskull had heard Nightspore's name since his arrival on the planet. He was so astonished that he could frame no more questions.

"Eat this," said Dreamsinter. "Then we will chase the sound together." He picked something up from the ground and handed it to Maskull. He could not see distinctly, but it felt like a hard, round nut, of the size of a fist.

"I can't crack it."

Dreamsinter took it between his hands, and broke it into pieces. Maskull then ate some of the pulpy interior, which was intensely disagreeable.

"What am I doing in Tormance, then?" he asked.

"You came to steal Muspel-fire, to give a deeper life to men—never doubting if your soul could endure that burning."

Maskull could hardly decipher the strangled words.

"Muspel . . . That's the name I've been trying to remember ever since I awoke."

Dreamsinter suddenly turned his head sideways, and

appeared to listen for something. He motioned with his
hand to Maskull to keep quiet.

"Is it the drumming?"

"Hush! They come."

He was looking towards the upper forest. The now
familiar drum rhythm was heard—this time accompanied
by the tramp of marching feet.

Maskull saw, marching through the trees and heading
towards them, three men in single file, separated from one
another by only a yard or so. They were travelling downhill
at a swift pace, and looked neither to left nor right. They
were naked. Their figures were shining against the black
background of the forest with a pale, supernatural light—
green and ghostly. When they were abreast of him, about
twenty feet off, he perceived who they were. The first man
was himself—Maskull. The second was Krag. The third
man was Nightspore. Their faces were grim and set.

The source of the drumming was out of sight. The sound
appeared to come from some point in front of them. Maskull
and Dreamsinter put themselves in motion, to keep up with
the swiftly moving marchers. At the same time a low, faint
music began.

Its rhythm stepped with the drum-beats, but, unlike the
latter, it did not seem to proceed from any particular quarter
of the forest. It resembled the subjective music heard in
dreams, which accompanies the dreamer everywhere, as a
sort of natural atmosphere, rendering all his experiences
emotional. It seemed to issue from an unearthly orchestra,
and was strongly troubled, pathetic, and tragic. Maskull
marched, and listened; and as he listened, it grew louder
and stormier. But the pulse of the drum interpenetrated
all the other sounds, like the quiet beating of reality.

His emotion deepened. He could not have said if minutes
or hours were passing. The spectral procession marched on,
a little way ahead, on a path parallel with his own and
Dreamsinter's. The music pulsated violently. Krag lifted
his arm, and displayed a long, murderous-looking knife. He
sprang forward and, raising it over the phantom-Maskull's

back, stabbed him twice, leaving the knife in the wound
the second time. Maskull threw up his arms, and fell down
dead. Krag leapt into the forest and vanished from sight.
Nightspore marched on alone, stern and unmoved.

The music rose to crescendo. The whole dim, gigantic
forest was roaring with sound. The tones came from all
sides, from above, from the ground under their feet. It was
so grandly passionate that Maskull felt his soul loosening
from its bodily envelope.

He continued to follow Nightspore. A strange brightness
began to glow in front of them. It was not daylight, but a
radiance such as he had never seen before, and such as he
could not have imagined to be possible. Nightspore moved
straight towards it. Maskull felt his chest bursting. The
light flashed higher. The awful harmonies of the music
followed hard one upon another, like the waves of a wild,
magic ocean . . . His body was incapable of enduring such
shocks, and of a sudden he tumbled over in a swoon which
resembled death.

CHAPTER FOURTEEN

Polecrab

The morning slowly passed. Maskull made some convulsive movements, and opened his eyes. He sat up, blinking. All was night-like and silent in the forest. The strange light had gone, the music had ceased, Dreamsinter had vanished. He fingered his beard, clotted with Tydomin's blood, and fell into a deep muse.

"According to Panawe and Catice, this forest contains wise men. Perhaps Dreamsinter was one. Perhaps that vision I have just seen was a specimen of his wisdom. It looked almost like an answer to my question . . . I ought not to have asked about myself, but about Surtur. Then I should have got a different answer. I might have learnt something . . . I might have seen *him*."

He remained quiet and apathetic for a bit.

"But I couldn't face that awful glare," he proceeded. "It was bursting my body. He warned me, too . . . And so Surtur does really exist, and my journey stands for something . . . But why am I here, and what can I do? Who *is* Surtur? Where is he to be found?"

Something wild came into his eyes.

"What did Dreamsinter mean by his 'not you, but Nightspore'? Am I a secondary character . . . is he regarded as important, and I as unimportant? Where is Nightspore, and what is he doing? Am I to wait for his time and pleasure . . . can I originate nothing?"

He continued sitting up, with straight-extended legs.

"I must make up my mind that this is a strange journey, and that the strangest things will happen in it. It's no use making plans, for I can't see two steps ahead—everything is unknown. But one thing's evident . . . nothing but the wildest audacity will carry me through, and I must sacrifice everything else to that . . . And therefore if Surtur shows himself again, I shall go forward to meet him, even if it means death."

Through the black, quiet aisles of the forest the drumbeats came again. The sound was a long way off and very faint. It was like the last mutterings of thunder after a heavy storm. Maskull listened, without getting up. The drumming faded into silence, and did not return.

He smiled queerly, and said aloud, "Thanks, Surtur! I accept the omen."

When he was about to get up, he found that the shrivelled skin which had been his third arm was flapping disconcertingly with every movement of his body. He made perforations in it all round, as close to his chest as possible, with the fingernails of both hands; then he carefully twisted it off. In that world of rapid growth and ungrowth he judged that the stump would soon disappear. After that, he rose and peered into the darkness.

The forest at that point sloped rather steeply and, without thinking twice about it, he took the downhill direction, never doubting it would bring him somewhere. As soon as he started walking, his temper became gloomy and morose—he was shaken, tired, dirty, and languid with hunger; moreover, he realised that the walk was not going to be a short one. Be that as it might, he determined to sit down no more until the whole dismal forest was at his back.

One after another the shadowy, house-like trees were observed, avoided, and passed. Far overhead the little patch of glowing sky was still always visible; otherwise he had no clue to the time of day. He continued tramping sullenly down the slope for many damp, slippery miles—in some places through bogs. When presently the twilight seemed to thin, he guessed that the open world was not far away. The forest grew more palpable and grey, and now he saw its majesty better. The tree-trunks were like round towers, and so wide were the intervals that they resembled natural amphitheatres. He could not make out the colour of the bark. Everything he saw amazed him, but his admiration was of the growling, grudging kind . . . The difference in light between the forest behind him and the forest ahead became so marked that he could no longer doubt that he was on the point of coming out.

Real light was in front of him; looking back, he found he had a shadow. The trunks acquired a reddish tint. He quickened his pace. As the minutes went by, the bright patch ahead grew luminous and vivid; it had a tinge of blue. He also imagined that he heard the sound of surf.

All that part of the forest towards which he was moving became rich with colour. The boles of the trees were of a deep, dark red; their leaves, high above his head, were ulfire-hued; the dead leaves on the ground were of a colour which he could not name. At the same time he discovered the use of his third eye. By adding a third angle to his sight, every object he looked at stood out in greater relief. The world looked less *flat*—more realistic and significant. He had a stronger attraction towards his surroundings . . . he seemed somehow to lose his egotism, and to become free and thoughtful.

Now through the last trees he saw full daylight. Less than half a mile separated him from the border of the forest, and, keen to discover what lay beyond, he broke into a run. He heard the surf louder. It was a peculiar hissing sound which could only proceed from water, yet was unlike the sea. Almost immediately he came within sight of an enormous horizon of dancing waves, which he knew must be the Sinking Sea. He fell back into a quick walk, continuing to stare hard. The wind which met him was hot, fresh, and sweet.

When he arrived at the final fringe of forest, which joined the wide sands of the shore without any change of level, he leant with his back to a great tree and gazed his fill, motionless, at what lay in front of him. The sands continued east and west in a straight line, broken only here and there by a few creeks. They were of a brilliant orange colour, but there were patches of violet. The forest appeared to stand sentinel over the shore for its entire length. Everything else was sea and sky—he had never seen so much water. The semicircle of the skyline was so vast that he might have imagined himself on a flat world, with a range of vision determined only by the power of his eye. The sea was unlike any sea on Earth. It resembled an immense liquid opal. On a body-colour of rich, magnificent emerald-green, bright flashes of red, yellow, and blue, were everywhere shooting up and vanishing. The wave motion was extraordinary. Pinnacles of water were slowly formed until they attained a height of perhaps ten or twenty feet, when they would suddenly sink downwards and outwards, creating in their descent a series of concentric rings for long distances around them. Quickly moving currents, like rivers in the sea, could be seen, racing away from land; they were of a darker green and bore no pinnacles. Where the sea met the shore, the waves rushed over the sands far in, with almost sinister rapidity—accompanied by a weird, hissing, spitting sound, which was what Maskull had heard. The green tongues rolled in without foam.

About twenty miles distant, as he judged, directly opposite to him, a long, low island stood up from the sea, black and not distinguished in outline. It was Swaylone's Island. Maskull was less interested in that than in the blue sunset which glowed behind its back. Alppain had set, but the whole northern sky was plunged into the minor key by its afterlight. Branchspell in the zenith was white and overpowering, the day was cloudless and terrifically hot; but where the blue sun had sunk, a sombre shadow seemed to overhang the world. Maskull had a feeling of disintegration—just as if two chemically-distinct forces were simultaneously acting upon the cells of his body. Since the afterglow of Alppain affected him like this, he thought it more than likely that he should never be able to face that sun itself, and go on living . . . Still, some modification might happen to him which would make it possible.

The sea tempted him. He made up his mind to bathe, and at once walked towards the shore. The instant he stepped outside the shadow-line of the forest trees, the blinding rays of the sun beat down on him so savagely that for a few minutes he felt sick and his head swam. He trod quickly across the sands. The orange-coloured parts were nearly hot enough to roast food, he judged, but the violet parts were like fire itself. He stepped on a patch in ignorance, and immediately jumped high into the air with a startled yell.

The sea was voluptuously warm. It would not bear his weight, so he determined to try swimming. First of all he stripped off his skin-garment, washed it thoroughly with sand and water, and laid it in the sun to dry. Then he scrubbed himself as well as he could and washed out his beard and hair. After that, he waded in a long way, until the water reached his breast, and took to swimming—avoiding the spouts as far as possible . . . He found it no pastime. The water was everywhere of unequal density. In some places he could swim, in others he could barely save himself from drowning, in others again he could not force himself beneath the surface at all. There were no outward signs to show what the water ahead held in store for him . . . The whole business was most dangerous.

He came out, feeling clean and invigorated. For a time he walked up and down the sands, drying himself in the hot sunshine and looking around him. He was a naked stranger in a huge, foreign, mystical world, and whichever way he turned unknown and threatening forces were glaring at him. The gigantic, white, withering Branchspell, the awful, body-changing Alppain, the beautiful, deadly, treacherous sea, the dark and eerie Swaylone's Island, the spirit-crushing forest out of which he had just escaped—to all these mighty powers, surrounding him on every side, what resources had he, a feeble, ignorant traveller from a tiny planet on the other side of space, to oppose, to avoid being utterly destroyed? . . . Then he smiled to himself. "I've already been here two days, and still I survive. I have luck—and with that one can balance the universe . . . But what is luck—a verbal expression, or a thing?"

As he was putting on his skin, which was now dry, the answer came to him, and this time he was grave. "Surtur brought me here, and Surtur is watching over me. That is my 'luck' . . . But what is Surtur in this world? . . . How is he able to protect me against the blind and ungovernable forces of Nature? Is he stronger than Nature? . . ."

Hungry as he was for food, he was hungrier still for human society, for he wished to inquire about all these things. He asked himself which way he should turn his steps. There were only two ways; along the shore, either east or west. The nearest creek lay to the east, cutting the sands about a mile away. He walked towards it.

The forest-face was forbidding and enormously high. It was so squarely turned to the sea that it looked as though it had been planed by tools. Maskull strode along in the shade of the trees, but kept his head constantly turned away from them, towards the sea—there it was more cheerful. The creek, when he reached it, proved to be broad and flat-banked. It was not a river, but an arm of the sea. Its still, dark green water curved round a bend out of sight, into the forest. The trees on both banks overhung the water, so that it was completely in shadow.

He went as far as the bend, beyond which another short reach appeared. A man was sitting on a narrow shelf of bank, with his feet in the water. He was clothed in a coarse, rough hide, which left his limbs bare. He was short, thick, and sturdy, with short legs and long, powerful arms, terminating in hands of an extraordinary size. He was oldish. His face was plain, slab-like and expressionless; it was full of wrinkles, and walnut-coloured. Both face and head were bald, and his skin was tough and leathery. He seemed to be some sort of peasant, or fisherman; there was no trace in his face of thought for others, or delicacy of feeling. He possessed three eyes, of different colours—jade-green, blue, and ulfire.

In front of him, riding on the water, moored to the bank,

was an elementary raft, consisting of the branches of trees, clumsily corded together.

Maskull addressed him. "Are you another of the wise men of the Wombflash Forest?"

The man answered him in a gruff, husky voice, looking up as he did so. "I'm a fisherman. I know nothing about wisdom."

"What name do you go by?"

"Polecrab. What's yours?"

"Maskull. If you're a fisherman, you ought to have fish. I'm famishing."

Polecrab grunted, and paused a minute before answering.

"There's fish enough. My dinner is cooking in the sands now. It's easy enough to get you some more."

Maskull found this a pleasant speech.

"But how long will it take?" he asked.

The man slid the palms of his hands together, producing a shrill, screeching noise. He lifted his feet from the water, and clambered on to the bank. In a minute or two a curious little beast came crawling up to his feet, turning its face and eyes up affectionately, like a dog. It was about two feet long, and somewhat resembled a small seal, but had six legs, ending in strong claws.

"Arg, go fish!" said Polecrab hoarsely.

The animal immediately tumbled off the bank into the water. It swam gracefully to the middle of the creek and made a pivotal dive beneath the surface, where it remained a great while.

"Simple fishing," remarked Maskull. "But what's the raft for?"

"To go to sea with. The best fish are out at sea. These are eatable."

"That arg seems a highly intelligent creature."

Polecrab grunted again. "I've trained close on a hundred of them. The big-heads learn best, but they're slow swimmers. The narrow-heads swim like eels, but can't be taught. Now I've started inter-breeding them—*he's* one of them."

"Do you live here alone?"

"No, I've got a wife and three boys. My wife's sleeping somewhere, but where the lads are, Shaping knows."

Maskull began to feel very much at home with this unsophisticated being.

"The raft's all crazy," he remarked, staring at it. "If you go far out in that, you've got more pluck than I have."

"I've been to Matterplay on it," said Polecrab.

The arg reappeared and started swimming to shore, but this time clumsily, as if it were bearing a heavy weight under the surface. When it landed at its master's feet, they saw that each set of claws was clutching a fish—six in all. Polecrab took them from it. He proceeded to cut off the heads and tails with a sharp-edged stone which he picked up; these he threw to the arg, which devoured them without any fuss.

Polecrab beckoned to Maskull to follow him and, carrying the fish, walked towards the open shore, by the same way that he had come. When they reached the sands, he sliced the fish, removed the entrails, and digging a shallow hole in a patch of violet sand, placed the remainder of the carcasses in it, and covered them over again. Then he dug up his own dinner. Maskull's nostrils quivered at the savoury smell, but he was not yet to dine.

Polecrab, turning to go with the cooked fish in his hands, said, "These are mine, not yours. When yours are done, you can come back and join me, supposing you want company."

"How soon will that be?"

"About twenty minutes," replied the fisherman, over his shoulder.

Maskull sheltered himself in the shadows of the forest, and waited. When the time had approximately elapsed, he disinterred his meal, scorching his fingers in the operation, although it was only the surface of the sand which was so intensely hot. Then he returned to Polecrab.

In the warm, still air and cheerful shade of the inlet, they munched in silence, looking from their food to the sluggish water, and back again. With every mouthful Maskull felt his strength returning. He finished before Polecrab, who ate like a man for whom time has no value. When he had done, he stood up.

"Come and drink," he said, in his husky voice.

Maskull looked at him inquiringly.

The man led him a little way into the forest, and walked straight up to a certain tree. At a convenient height in its trunk a hole had been tapped and plugged. Polecrab removed the plug and put his mouth to the aperture, sucking for quite a long time, like a child at its mother's breast. Maskull, watching him, fancied that he saw his eyes growing brighter.

When his own turn came to drink, he found the juice of the tree somewhat like coconut milk in flavour, but intoxicating. It was a new sort of intoxication, however, for neither his will nor his emotions were excited, but only his intellect—and that only in a certain way. His thoughts and images were not freed and loosened, but on the contrary kept labouring and swelling painfully, until they reached the full beauty of an *aperçu*, which would then flame up in his consciousness, burst, and vanish. After that, the whole process started over again. But there was never a moment when he was not perfectly cool, and master of his senses. When each had drunk twice, Polecrab replugged the hole, and they returned to their bank.

"Is it Blodsombre yet?" asked Maskull, sprawling on the ground, well content.

Polecrab resumed his old upright sitting posture, with his feet in the water.

"Just beginning," was his hoarse response.

"Then I must stop here till it's over . . . Shall we talk?"

"We can," said the other, without enthusiasm.

Maskull glanced at him through half-closed lids, wondering if he were exactly what he seemed to be. In his eyes he thought he detected a wise light.

"Have you travelled much, Polecrab?"

"Not what *you* would call travelling."

"You tell me you've been to Matterplay—what kind of country is that?"

"I don't know. I went there to pick up flints."

"What countries lie beyond it?"

"Threal comes next, as you go north. They say it's a land of mystics . . . I don't know."

"Mystics?"

"So I'm told . . . Still further north there's Lichstorm."

"Now we're going far afield."

"There are mountains there . . . and altogether it must be a very dangerous place, especially for a full-blooded man like you . . . Take care of yourself."

"This is rather premature, Polecrab. How do you know I'm going there?"

"As you've come from the south, I suppose you'll go north."

"Well, that's right enough," said Maskull, staring hard at him. "But how do you know I've come from the south?"

"Well, then, perhaps you haven't . . . but there's a look of Ifdawn about you."

"What kind of look?"

"A tragical look," said Polecrab. He never even glanced at Maskull, but was gazing at a fixed spot on the water with unblinking eyes.

"What lies beyond Lichstorm?" asked Maskull, after a minute or two.

"Barey, where you have two suns instead of one—but beyond that fact I know nothing about it . . . Then comes the ocean . . ."

"And what's on the other side of the ocean?"

"That you must find out for yourself, for I doubt if anybody has ever crossed it and come back."

Maskull was silent for a little while.

"How is it that your people are so unadventurous? I seem to be the only one travelling from curiosity."

"What do you mean by 'your people'?"

"True—you don't know that I don't belong to your planet at all. I've come from another world, Polecrab."

"What to find?"

"I came here with Krag and Nightspore . . . to follow Surtur. I must have fainted the moment I arrived. When I sat up, it was night and the others had vanished. Since then I've been travelling at random."

Polecrab scratched his nose. "You haven't found Surtur yet?"

"I've heard his drum-taps frequently. In the forest this morning I came quite close to him . . . Then two days ago, in the Lusion Plain, I saw a vision—a being in man's shape, who called himself Surtur."

"Well, maybe it was Surtur."

"No, that's impossible," replied Maskull reflectively. "It was Crystalman . . . And it isn't a question of my suspecting it—I *know* it."

"How?"

"Because this is Crystalman's world, and Surtur's world is something quite different."

"That's queer, then," said Polecrab.

"Since I've come out of that forest," proceeded Maskull, talking half to himself, "a change has come over me, and I see things differently. Everything here looks much more solid and real in my eyes than in other places . . . so much so that I can't entertain the least doubt of its existence. It not only *looks* real, it *is* real—and on that I would stake my life . . . But at the same time that it's real, it is *false* . . ."

"Like a dream?"

"No—not at all like a dream, and that's just what I want to explain. This world of yours—and perhaps of mine too, for that matter—doesn't give me the slightest impression of a dream, or an illusion, or anything of that sort. I know it's really here at this moment, and it's exactly as we're seeing it, you and I. Yet it's false. It's false in this sense, Polecrab. Side by side with it another world exists, and that other world is the true one, and this one is all false and deceitful, to the very core . . . And so it occurs to me that reality and falseness are two words for the same thing."

"Perhaps there is such another world," said Polecrab huskily. "But did that vision also seem real and false to you?"

"Very real, but not false then, for then I didn't understand all this. But just because it was real, it couldn't have been Surtur, who has no connection with reality."

"Didn't those drum-taps sound real to you?"

"I had to hear them with my ears, and so they sounded real to me . . . Still, they were somehow different, and they certainly came from Surtur. If I didn't hear them aright, that was my fault and not his."

Polecrab growled a little. "If Surtur chooses to speak to you in that fashion, it appears he's trying to say something."

"What else can I think? But, Polecrab, what's your opinion—is he calling me to the life after death?"

The old man stirred uneasily.

"I'm a fisherman," he said, after a minute or two. "I live by killing, and so does everybody. This life seems to me all wrong. So maybe life of any kind is wrong, and Surtur's world is not life at all, but something else."

"Yes, but will death lead me to it, whatever it is?"

"Ask the dead," said Polecrab, "and not a living man."

Maskull continued. "In the forest I heard music and saw a light, which could not have belonged to this world. They were too strong for my senses, and I must have swooned for a long time. There was a vision as well, in which I saw myself killed, while Nightspore walked on towards the light, alone."

Polecrab uttered his grunt. "You have enough to think over."

A short silence ensued, which was broken by Maskull.

"So strong is my sense of the untruth of this present life, that it may come to my putting an end to myself." The fisherman remained quiet and immobile.

Maskull lay on his stomach, propped his face on his hands and stared at him.

"What do you think, Polecrab? Is it possible for any man,

while in the body, to gain a closer view of that other world than I have done?"

"I am an ignorant man, stranger, so I can't say. Perhaps there are many others like you who would gladly know."

"Where? I should like to meet them."

"Do you think you were made of one stuff, and the rest of mankind of another stuff?"

"I can't be so presumptuous . . . Possibly all men are reaching out towards Muspel, in most cases without being aware of it."

"In the wrong direction," said Polecrab.

Maskull gave him a strange look. "How so?"

"I don't speak from my own wisdom," said Polecrab, "for I have none; but I have just now recalled what Broodviol once told me, when I was a young man, and he was an old one. He said that Crystalman tries to turn all things into *one*, and that whichever way his shapes march, in order to escape from him, they find themselves again face to face with Crystalman, and are changed into new crystals. But that this marching of shapes (which we call 'forking') springs from the unconscious desire to find Surtur, but is in the opposite direction to the right one. For Surtur's world does not lie on this side of the *one*, which was the beginning of life, but on the other side; and to get to it we must repass through the *one*. But this can only be by renouncing our self-life, and reuniting ourselves to the whole of Crystalman's world. And when this has been done, it is only the first stage of the journey; though many good men imagine it to be the whole journey . . . As far as I can remember, that is what Broodviol said, but perhaps, as I was then a young and ignorant man, I may have left out words which would explain his meaning better."

Maskull, who had listened attentively to all this, remained thoughtful at the end.

"It's plain enough," he said. "But what did he mean by our reuniting ourselves to Crystalman's world? If it is false, are we to make ourselves false as well?"

"I didn't ask him that question, and you are as well qualified to answer it as I am."

"He must have meant that, as it is, we are each of us living in a false private world of our own, a world of dreams and appetites and distorted perceptions . . . By embracing the great world we certainly lose nothing in truth and reality."

Polecrab withdrew his feet from the water, stood up, yawned, and stretched his limbs.

"I have told you all I know," he said in a surly voice. "Now let me go to sleep."

Maskull kept his eyes fixed on him, but made no reply. The old man let himself down stiffly on to the ground, and prepared to rest.

While he was still arranging his position to his liking, a footfall sounded behind the two men, coming from the direction of the forest. Maskull twisted his neck, and saw a woman approaching them. He at once guessed that it was Polecrab's wife. He sat up, but the fisherman did not stir. The woman came and stood in front of them, looking down from what appeared a great height.

Her dress was similar to her husband's, but covered her limbs more. She was young, tall, slender, and strikingly erect. Her skin was lightly tanned, and she looked strong, but not at all peasant-like. Refinement was stamped all over her. Her face had too much energy of expression for a woman, and she was not beautiful. Her three great eyes kept flashing and glowing. She had great masses of fine, yellow hair, coiled up and fastened, but so carelessly that some of the strands were flowing down her back.

When she spoke, it was in a rather weak voice, but full of lights and shades, and somehow intense passionateness never seemed to be far away from it.

"Forgiveness is asked for listening to your conversation," she said, addressing Maskull. "I was resting behind that tree, and heard it all."

He got up slowly. "Are you Polecrab's wife?"

"She is my wife," said Polecrab, "and her name is

Gleameil. Sit down again, stranger—and you too, wife, since you are here."

They both obeyed.

"I heard everything," repeated Gleameil. "But what I did not hear was where you are going to, Maskull, after you have left us."

"I know no more than you do."

"Listen, then. There's only one place for you to go to, and that is Swaylone's Island. I will ferry you across myself before sunset."

"What shall I find there?"

"He may go, wife," put in the old man hoarsely, "but I won't allow you to go. I will take him over myself."

"No, you have always put me off," said Gleameil, with some emotion. "This time I mean to go. When Teargeld shines at night, and I sit on the shore here, listening to Earthrid's music travelling faintly across the sea, I am tortured—I can't endure it . . . I have long since made up my mind to go to the Island, and see what this music is. If it's bad, if it kills me—well . . ."

"What have I to do with the man and his music, Gleameil?" demanded Maskull.

"I think the music will answer all your questions better than Polecrab has done . . . And possibly in a way which will surprise you."

"What kind of music can it be to travel all those miles across the sea?"

"A peculiar kind, so we are told. Not pleasant, but painful. And the man that can play the instrument of Earthrid would be able to conjure up the most astonishing forms, which are not phantasms, but realities."

"That may be so," growled Polecrab. "But I have been to the Island by daylight, and what did I find there? Human bones, new and ancient. Those are Earthrid's victims . . . And you, wife, shall not go."

"But will that music play tonight?" asked Maskull.

"Yes," replied Gleameil, gazing at him intently. "When Teargeld rises, which is our moon."

"If Earthrid plays men to death, it appears to me that his own death is due. In any case I should like to hear those sounds for myself. But as for taking you with me, Gleameil . . . women die too easily in Tormance. I have only just now washed myself clean of the death-blood of another woman."

Gleameil laughed, but said nothing.

"Now go to sleep," said Polecrab. "When the time comes, I will take you across myself."

He lay down again, and closed his eyes. Maskull followed his example; but Gleameil remained sitting erect, with her legs under her.

"Who was that other woman, Maskull?" she asked presently.

He did not answer, but pretended to sleep.

CHAPTER FIFTEEN

Swaylone's Island

When he awoke, the day was not so bright, and he guessed it was late afternoon. Polecrab and his wife were both on their feet, and another meal of fish had been cooked and was waiting for him.

"Is it decided who is to go with me?" he asked, before sitting down.

"I go," said Gleameil.

"Do you agree, Polecrab?"

The fisherman growled a little in his throat and motioned to the others to take their seats. He took a mouthful before answering.

"Something strong is attracting her, and I can't hold her back. I don't think I shall see you again, wife, but the lads are now nearly old enough to fend for themselves."

"Don't take dejected views," replied Gleameil sternly. She was not eating. "I shall come back, and make amends to you. It's only for a night."

Maskull gazed from one to the other in perplexity. "Let me go alone. I should be sorry if anything happened."

Gleameil shook her head.

"Don't regard this as a woman's caprice," she said. "Even if you hadn't passed this way, I must have heard that music soon. I have a hunger for it."

"Haven't you any such feeling, Polecrab?"

"No. A woman is a noble and sensitive creature, and there are attractions in nature too subtle for males. Take her with you, since she is set on it. Maybe she's right. Perhaps Earthrid's music will answer your questions, and hers too."

"What are your questions, Gleameil?"

The woman shed a strange smile. "You may be sure that a question which requires music for an answer, can't be put into words."

"If you are not back by the morning," remarked her husband, "I shall know you are dead."

The meal was finished in a constrained silence. Polecrab wiped his mouth, and produced a seashell from a kind of pocket.

"Will you say goodbye to the boys? Shall I call them?"

She considered a moment.

"Yes. . . . Yes, I must see them."

He put the shell to his mouth, and blew; a loud, mournful noise passed through the air.

A few minutes later there was a sound of scurrying footsteps and the boys were seen emerging from the forest. Maskull looked with curiosity at the first children he had seen on Tormance. The eldest boy was carrying the youngest on his back, while the third trotted some distance behind. The child was let down, and all the three formed a semicircle in front of Maskull, standing staring up at him with wide-open eyes. Polecrab looked on stolidly, but Gleameil glanced away from them, with proudly-raised head, and a baffling expression.

Maskull put the ages of the boys at about nine, seven, and five years respectively; but he was calculating according to Earth-time. The eldest was tall, slim, but strongly built. He, like his brothers, was naked, and his skin from top to toe was ulfire-coloured. His facial muscles indicated a wild and daring nature, and his eyes were like green fires. The second showed promise of being a broad, powerful man. His head was large and heavy, and drooped. His face and skin were reddish. His eyes were almost too sombre and penetrating for a child's.

"That one," said Polecrab, pinching the boy's ear, "may perhaps grow up to be a second Broodviol."

"Who was that?" demanded the boy, bending his head forward, to hear the answer.

"A big, old man, of marvellous wisdom. He became wise

by making up his mind never to ask questions, but to find things out for himself."

"If I had not asked this question, I should not have known about him."

"That would not have mattered," replied the father.

The youngest child was paler and slighter than his brothers. His face was mostly tranquil and expressionless, but it had this peculiarity about it, that every few minutes, without any apparent cause, it would wrinkle up and look perplexed. At these times his eyes, which were of a tawny-gold, seemed to contain secrets difficult to associate with one of his age.

"He puzzles me," said Polecrab. "He has a soul like sap, and he's interested in nothing. He may turn out to be the most remarkable of the bunch."

Maskull took the child in one hand, and lifted him as high as his head. He took a good look at him, and set him down again. The boy never changed countenance.

"What do you make of him?" asked the fisherman.

"It's on the tip of my tongue to say, but it just escapes me. Let me drink again, and then I shall have it."

"Go and drink, then."

Maskull strode over to the tree, drank, and returned.

"In ages to come," he said, speaking deliberately, "he will be a grand and awful tradition . . . A seer possibly, or even a divinity . . . Watch over him well."

The eldest boy looked scornful. "I want to be none of those things. I would like to be like that big fellow." And he pointed his finger at Maskull.

He laughed, and showed his white teeth, through his beard.

"Thanks for the compliment, old warrior!" he said.

"He's great and brawny," continued the boy, "and can hold his own with other men . . . Can you hold me up with one arm, as you did that child?"

Maskull complied.

"That is being a man!" exclaimed the boy.

"Enough!" said Polecrab impatiently. "I called you lads

here to say goodbye to your mother. She is going away with this man. I think she may not return, but we don't know."

The second boy's face became suddenly inflamed.

"Is she going of her own choice?" he inquired.

"Yes," replied the father.

"Then she is bad." He brought the words out with such force and emphasis that they sounded like the crack of a whip.

The old man cuffed him twice. "Is it your mother you are speaking of?"

The boy stood his ground, without change of expression, but said nothing.

The youngest child spoke, for the first time. "My mother will not come back, but she will die, dancing."

Polecrab and his wife looked at one another.

"Where are you going to, mother?" asked the eldest lad.

Gleameil bent down, and kissed him.

"To the Island."

"Well then, if you don't come back by tomorrow morning, I shall go and look for you."

Maskull grew more and more uneasy in his mind.

"This seems to me to be a man's journey," he said. "I think it would be better for you not to come, Gleameil."

"I am not to be dissuaded," she replied.

He stroked his beard in perplexity.

"Is it time to start?"

"It wants four hours to sunset, and we shall need all that."

Maskull sighed. "I'll go to the mouth of the creek, and wait there for you and the raft. You will wish to make your farewells, Gleameil."

He then clasped Polecrab by the hand. "Adieu, fisherman!"

"You have repaid me well for my answers," said the old man gruffly. "But it's not your fault, and in Shaping's world the worst things happen."

The eldest boy came close to Maskull, and frowned at him.

"Farewell, big man!" he said. "But guard my mother well, as you are well able to, or I shall follow you, and kill you."

Maskull walked slowly along the creek-bank till he came to the bend. The glorious sunshine, and the sparkling, brilliant sea then met his eyes again; and all melancholy was swept out of his mind. He continued as far as the seashore, and issuing out of the shadows of the forest, strolled on to the sands, and sat down in the full sunlight. The radiance of Alppain had long since disappeared. He drank in the hot, invigorating wind, listened to the hissing waves, and stared over the coloured sea, with its pinnacles and currents, at Swaylone's Island.

"What music can that be, which tears a wife and mother away from all she loves the most?" he meditated. "It sounds unholy. Will it tell me what I want to know? Can it?"

In a little while he became aware of a movement behind him, and turning his head he saw the raft floating along the creek, towards the open sea. Polecrab was standing upright, propelling it with a rude pole. He passed by Maskull without looking at him, or making any salutation, and proceeded out to sea.

While he was wondering at this strange behaviour, Gleameil and the boys came in sight, walking along the bank of the inlet. The eldest-born was holding her hand, and talking; and the other two were behind. She was calm and smiling, but seemed abstracted.

"What is your husband doing with the raft?" asked Maskull.

"He's putting it in position, and we shall wade out and join it," she answered in her low-toned voice.

"But how shall we make the Island, without oars or sails?"

"Don't you see that current running away from land? See, he is approaching it. That will take us straight there."

"But how can you get back?"

"There is a way; but we need not think of that today."

"Why should not I come too?" demanded the eldest boy.

"Because the raft won't carry three. Maskull is a heavy man."

"It doesn't matter," said the boy. "I know where there is wood for another raft. As soon as you have gone, I shall set to work."

Polecrab had by this time manoeuvred his flimsy craft to the position he desired, within a few yards of the current, which at that point made a sharp bend from the east. He shouted out some words to his wife and Maskull. Gleameil kissed her children convulsively, and broke down a little. The eldest boy bit his lip, till it bled, and tears glistened in his eyes; but the younger children stared wide-eyed, and displayed no emotion.

Gleameil now walked into the sea, followed by Maskull. The water covered first their ankles, then their knees, but when it came as high as their waists, they were close on the raft. Polecrab let himself down into the water, and assisted his wife to climb over the side. When she was up, she bent down and kissed him. No words were exchanged. Maskull scrambled up on to the front part of the raft. The woman sat cross-legged in the stern, and seized the pole.

Polecrab shoved them off towards the current, while she worked her pole until they had got within its power. The raft immediately began to travel swiftly away from land, with a smooth, swaying motion.

The boys waved from the shore. Gleameil responded; but Maskull turned his back squarely to land, and gazed ahead. Polecrab was wading back to the shore.

For upwards of an hour Maskull did not change his position by an inch. No sound was heard but the splashing of the strange waves all around them, and the stream-like gurgle of the current, which threaded its way smoothly through the tossing, tumultuous sea. From their pathway of safety, the beautiful dangers surrounding them were an exhilarating experience. The air was fresh and clean, and the heat from Branchspell, now low in the west, was at last endurable. The riot of sea-colours had long since banished all sadness and anxiety from his heart. Yet he felt such a grudge against the woman for selfishly forsaking those who should have been dear to her, that he could not bring himself to begin a conversation.

But when, over the now enlarged shape of the dark island, he caught sight of a long chain of lofty, distant mountains, glowing salmon-pink in the evening sunlight, he felt constrained to break the silence by inquiring what they were.

"It is Lichstorm," said Gleameil.

Maskull asked no questions about it; but in turning to address her, his eyes had rested on the rapidly receding Wombflash Forest, and he continued to stare at that. They had travelled about eight miles, and now he could better estimate the enormous height of the trees. Overtopping them, far away, he saw Sant; and he fancied, but was not quite sure, that he could distinguish Disscourn as well.

"Now that we are alone in a strange place," said Gleameil, averting her head, and looking down over the side of the raft into the water, "tell me how you found Polecrab?"

Maskull paused before answering.

"He seemed to me like a mountain wrapped in cloud. You see the lower buttresses, and think that is all. But then, high up, far above the clouds, you suddenly catch sight of more mountain—and even then it is not the top."

"You read character well, and have a great perception," remarked Gleameil quietly. "Now say what I am."

"In place of a human heart, you have a wild harp, and that's all I know about you."

"What was that you said to my husband about two worlds?"

"You heard."

"Yes, I heard. And I also am conscious of two worlds. My husband and boys are real to me, and I love them fondly. But there is another world for me, as there is for you, Maskull, and it makes my real world appear all false and vulgar."

"Perhaps we are seeking the same thing. But can it be right to satisfy our self-nature at the expense of other people?"

"No, it's not right. It is wrong and base . . . But in that other world these words have no meaning."

There was a silence.

"It's useless to discuss such topics," said Maskull. "The choice is now out of our hands, and we must go where we are taken. What I would rather speak about is what awaits us on the Island."

"I am ignorant—except that we shall find Earthrid there."

"Who is Earthrid, and why is it called Swaylone's Island?"

"They say Earthrid came from Threal, but I know nothing else about him. As for Swaylone, if you like I will tell you his legend."

"If you please," said Maskull.

"In a far-back age," began Gleameil, "when the seas were hot, and clouds hung heavily over the earth, and life was rich with transformations, Swaylone came to this island, on which men had never before set foot, and began to play his music—the first music in Tormance. Nightly, when the moon shone, people used to gather on this shore behind us, and listen to the faint, sweet strains floating from over the sea. One night, Shaping (whom you call Crystalman) was passing this way in company with Krag. They listened awhile to the music, and Shaping said 'Have you heard more beautiful sounds? This is my world and my music.' Krag stamped with his foot, and laughed. 'You must do better than that, if I am to admire it. Let us pass over, and see this bungler at work.' Shaping consented, and they passed over to the island. Swaylone was not able to see their presence. Shaping stood behind him, and breathed thoughts into his soul, so that his music became ten times lovelier, and people listening on that shore went mad with sick delight. 'Can any strains be nobler?' demanded Shaping. Krag grinned, and said 'You are naturally effeminate. Now let me try.' Then he stood behind Swaylone, and shot ugly discords fast into his head. His instrument was so cracked, that never since has it played right. From that time forth Swaylone could only utter distorted music; yet it called to folk more than the other sort. Many men crossed over to the island during his lifetime, to listen to the amazing tones, but none could endure them; all died. After Swaylone's death, another musician took up the tale; and so the light has passed down from torch to torch, till now Earthrid bears it."

"An interesting legend," commented Maskull. "But who is Krag?"

"They say that when the world was born, Krag was born with it—a spirit compounded of those vestiges of Muspel which Shaping did not know how to transform. Thereafter nothing has gone right with the world, for he dogs Shaping's footsteps everywhere, and whatever the latter does, he undoes. To love he joins death; to sex, shame; to intellect, madness; to virtue, cruelty; and to fair exteriors, bloody entrails. These are Krag's actions, so the lovers of the world call him 'devil'. They don't understand, Maskull, that without him the world would lose its beauty."

"Krag and beauty!" exclaimed he, with a cynical smile.

"Even so. That same beauty which you and I are now voyaging to discover. That beauty for whose sake I am renouncing husband, children, and happiness . . . Did you imagine beauty to be pleasant?"

"Surely."

"That pleasant beauty is an insipid compound of Shaping. To see beauty in its terrible purity, you must tear away the pleasure from it."

"Do you say I am going to seek beauty, Gleameil? Such an idea is far away from my mind."

She did not respond to his remark. After waiting for a few minutes, to hear if she would speak again, he turned his back on her once more. There was no more talk, until they reached the Island.

The air had grown chill and damp by the time that

they approached its shores. Branchspell was on the point of touching the sea. The Island appeared to be some three or four miles in length. There were first of all broad sands, then low, dark cliffs, and behind these a wilderness of insignificant, swelling hills, entirely devoid of vegetation. The current bore them to within a hundred yards of the coast, when it made a sharp angle, and proceeded to skirt the length of the land.

Gleameil jumped overboard, and began swimming to shore. Maskull followed her example, and the raft, abandoned, was rapidly borne away by the current. They soon touched ground, and were able to wade the rest of the way. By the time they reached dry land, the sun had set.

Gleameil made straight for the hills; and Maskull, after casting a single glance at the low, dim outline of the Wombflash Forest, followed her. The cliffs were soon scrambled up. Then the ascent was gentle and easy, while the rich, dry, brown mould was good to walk upon.

A little way off, on their left, something white was shining.

"You need not go to it," said the woman, "It can be nothing else than one of those skeletons Polecrab talked about . . . And look—there is another one over there!"

"This brings it home!" remarked Maskull, smiling.

"There is nothing comical in having died for beauty," said Gleameil, bending her brows at him.

And when in the course of their walk he saw the innumerable human bones, from gleaming white to dirty yellow, lying scattered about, as if it were a naked graveyard among the hills, he agreed with her, and fell into a sombre mood.

It was still light when they reached the highest point, and could set eyes on the other side. The sea to the north of the Island was in no way different from that which they had crossed, but its lively colours were fast becoming invisible.

"That is Matterplay," said the woman, pointing her finger towards some low land on the horizon, which seemed to be even further off than Wombflash.

"I wonder how Digrung passed over," meditated Maskull.

Not far away, in a hollow enclosed by a circle of little hills, they saw a small, circular lake, not more than half a mile in diameter. The sunset colours of the sky were reflected in its waters.

"That must be Irontick." remarked Gleameil.

"What is that?"

"I have heard that it's the instrument Earthrid plays on."

"We are getting close," responded he. "Let us go and investigate."

When they drew nearer, they observed that a man was reclining on the further side, in an attitude of sleep.

"If that's not the man himself, who can it be?" said Maskull. "Let's get across the water, if it will bear us; it will save time."

He now assumed the lead, and took running strides down the slope which bounded the lake on that side. Gleameil followed him with greater dignity, keeping her eyes fixed on the recumbent man, as if fascinated. When Maskull reached the water's edge, he tried it with one foot, to discover if it would carry his weight. Something unusual in its appearance led him to have doubts. It was a tranquil, dark, and beautifully reflecting sheet of water; it resembled a mirror of liquid metal. Finding that it would bear him, and that nothing happened, he placed his second foot on its surface. Instantly he sustained a violent shock throughout his body, as from a powerful electric current; and he was hurled in a tumbled heap back on to the bank.

He picked himself up, brushed the dirt off his person, and started walking round the lake. Gleameil joined him, and they completed the half-circuit together. They came to the man, and Maskull prodded him with his foot. He woke up, and blinked at them.

His face was pale, weak, and vacant-looking, and had a disagreeable expression. There were thin sprouts of black hair on his chin and head. On his forehead, in place of a third eye, he possessed a perfectly circular organ, with elaborate convolutions, like an ear. He had an unpleasant smell. He appeared to be of young middle-age.

"Wake up, man," said Maskull sharply, "and tell us if you are Earthrid."

"What time is it?" counter-questioned the man. "Does it want long to moonrise?"

Without appearing to care about an answer, he sat up, and turning away from them, began to scoop up the loose soil with his hand, and to eat it half-heartedly.

"Now, how can you eat that filth!" demanded Maskull, in disgust.

"Don't be angry, Maskull," said Gleameil, laying hold of his arm, and flushing a little. "It is Earthrid—the man who is to help us."

"He has not said so."

"I am Earthrid," said the other, in his weak and muffled voice, which, however, suddenly struck Maskull as being autocratic. "What do you want here? . . . Or rather, you had better get away as quickly as you can, for it will be too late when Teargeld rises."

"You need not explain," exclaimed Maskull. "We know your reputation, and we have come to hear your music. But what's that organ for on your forehead?"

Earthrid glared, and smiled, and glared again.

"That is for rhythm, which is what changes noise into music . . . Don't stand and argue, but go away. It is no pleasure to me to people the island with corpses. They corrupt the air, and do nothing else."

Darkness now crept swiftly on over the landscape.

"You are rather big-mouthed," said Maskull coolly. "But after we have heard you play, perhaps I shall adventure a tune myself."

"You? Are you a musician, then? Do you even know what music is?"

A flame danced in Gleameil's eyes.

"Maskull thinks music reposes in the instrument," she said in her intense way. "But it is in the soul of the Master."

"Yes," said Earthrid, "but that is not all. I will tell you what it is. In Threal, where I was born and brought up, we learn the mystery of the Three in nature. This world, which lies extended before us, has three directions. Length is the line which shuts off what is, from what is not. Breadth is the surface which shows us in what manner one thing of what-is, lives with another thing. Depth is the path which leads from what-is, to our own body. In music it is not otherwise. Tone is existence, without which nothing at all can be. Symmetry and Numbers are the manner in which tones exist, one with another. Emotion is the movement of our soul towards the wonderful world which is being created. Now, men when they make music are accustomed to build beautiful tones, on account of the delight they cause. Therefore their music-world is based on pleasure; its symmetry is regular and charming, its emotion is sweet and lovely . . . But my music is founded on painful tones; and thus its symmetry is wild, and difficult to discover; its emotion is bitter and terrible."

"If I had not anticipated its being original, I would not have come here," said Maskull. "Still, explain—why can't harsh tones have simple symmetry of form? And why must they necessarily cause more profound emotions in us who listen?"

"Pleasures may harmonise. Pains must clash; and in the order of their clashing lies the symmetry. The emotions follow the music, which is rough and earnest."

"You may call it music," remarked Maskull thoughtfully, "but to me it bears a closer resemblance to actual life."

"If Shaping's plans had gone straight, life would have been like that other sort of music. He who seeks can find traces of that intention in the world of nature. But as it has turned out, real life resembles my music and mine is the true music."

"Shall we see living shapes?"

"I don't know what my mood will be," returned Earthrid. "But when I have finished, you shall adventure your tune, and produce whatever shapes you please—unless, indeed, the tune is out of your own big body."

"The shocks you are preparing may kill us," said Gleameil, in a low, taut voice, "but we shall die, seeing *beauty*."

Earthrid looked at her with a dignified expression.

"Neither you, nor any other person, can endure the thoughts which I put into my music. Still, you must have it your own way . . . It needed a woman to call it 'beauty'. But if this is beauty, what is ugliness?"

"That I can tell you, Master," replied Gleameil, smiling at him. "Ugliness is old, stale life, while yours every night issues fresh from the womb of nature."

Earthrid stared at her, without response.

"Teargeld is rising," he said at last. "And now you shall see—though not for long."

As the words left his mouth, the full moon peeped over the hills in the dark eastern sky. They watched it in silence, and soon it was wholly up. It was larger than the moon of Earth, and seemed nearer. Its shadowy parts stood out in just as strong relief, but somehow it did not give Maksull the impression of being a dead world. Branchspell shone on the whole of it, but Alppain only on a part. The broad crescent which reflected Branchspell's rays alone was white and brilliant; but the part that was illuminated by both suns, shone with a greenish radiance which had almost solar power, and yet was cold and cheerless. On gazing at that combined light, he felt the same sense of disintegration that the afterglow of Alppain had always caused in him; but now the feeling was not physical, but merely aesthetic. The moon did not appear romantic to him, but disturbing and mystical.

Earthrid rose, and stood quietly for a minute. In the bright moonlight, his face seemed to have undergone a change. It lost its loose, weak, disagreeable look, and acquired a sort of crafty grandeur. He clapped his hands together meditatively two or three times, and walked up and down. The others stood together, watching him.

Then he sat down by the side of the lake, and leaning on his side, placed his right hand, open palm downwards, on the ground, at the same time stretching out his right leg, so that the foot was in contact with the water.

While Maskull was in the act of staring at him and at the lake, he felt a stabbing sensation right through his heart, as though he had been pierced by a rapier. He barely recovered himself from falling, and as he did so he saw that a spout had formed on the water, and was now subsiding again. The next moment he was knocked down by a violent blow in the mouth, delivered by an invisible hand. He picked himself up; and observed that a second spout had formed. No sooner was he on his legs, than a hideous pain hammered away inside his brain, as if caused by a malignant tumour. In his agony, he stumbled and fell again; this time on the arm which Krag had wounded. All his other mishaps were forgotten in this one, which half-stunned him. It lasted but a moment, and then sudden relief came, and he found that Earthrid's rough music had lost its power over him.

He saw him still stretched in the same position. Spouts were coming thick and fast on the lake, which was full of lively motion. But Gleameil was not on her legs. She was lying on the ground, in a heap, without moving. Her attitude was ugly, and he guessed she was dead. When he reached her, he discovered that she *was* dead. In what state of mind she had died, he did not know, for her face wore the vulgar Crystalman grin. The whole tragedy had not lasted five minutes.

He went over to Earthrid, and dragged him forcibly away from his playing.

"You have been as good as your word, musician," he said. "Gleameil is dead."

Earthrid tried to collect his scattered senses.

"I warned her," he replied, sitting up. "Did I not beg her to go away? . . . But she died very easily. She did not wait for the beauty she spoke about. She heard nothing of the passion, nor even of the rhythm. Neither have you."

Maskull looked down at him in indignation, but said nothing.

"You should not have interrupted me," went on Earthrid. "When I am playing, nothing else is of importance. I might have lost the thread of my ideas. Fortunately, I never forget . . . I shall start over again."

"If music is to continue, in presence of the dead, I play next."

The man glanced up quickly.

"That can't be."

"It must be," said Maskull decisively. "I prefer playing to listening. Another reason is that you will have every night, but I have only tonight."

Earthrid clenched and unclenched his fist, and began to turn pale.

"With your recklessness, you are likely to kill us both . . . Irontick belongs to me, and until you have learnt how to play, you would only break the instrument."

"Well, then, I will break it; but I am going to try."

The musician jumped to his feet, and confronted him. "Do you intend to take it from me by violence?"

"Keep calm! You will have the same choice that you offered us. I shall give you time to go away somewhere."

"How will that serve me, if you spoil my lake?—You don't understand what you are doing."

"Go, or stay!" responded Maskull. "I give you till the water gets smooth again. After that, I begin playing."

Earthrid kept swallowing. He glanced at the lake and back to Maskull.

"Do you swear it?"

"How long that will take, you know better than I; but till then you are safe."

Earthrid cast him a look of malice, hesitated for an instant, and then moved away, and started to climb the nearest hill. Half-way up he glanced over his shoulder apprehensively, as if to see what was happening. In another minute or so, he had disappeared over the crest, travelling in the direction of the shore which faced Matterplay.

Later, when the water was once more tranquil, Maskull sat down by its edge, in imitation of Earthrid's attitude.

He knew neither how to set about producing his music, nor what would come of it. But audacious projects entered his brain, and he willed to create physical shapes—and, above all, one shape, that of Surtur.

Before putting his foot to the water, he turned things over a little in his mind.

He said, "What *themes* are in common music, *shapes* are in this music. The composer does not find his theme by picking out single notes; but the whole theme flashes into his mind by inspiration. So it must be with shapes. When I start playing, if I am worth anything, the undivided ideas will pass from my unconscious mind to this lake, and then, reflected back in the dimensions of reality, I shall for the first time be made acquainted with them. So it must be."

The instant his foot touched the water, he felt his thoughts flowing from him. He did not know what they were, but the mere act of flowing created a sensation of joyful mastery. With this was curiosity to learn what they would prove to be. Spouts formed on the lake, in increasing numbers; but he experienced no pain. His thoughts, which he knew to be music, did not issue from him in a steady, unbroken stream, but in great, rough gushes, succeeding intervals of quiescence. When these gushes came, the whole lake broke out into an eruption of spouts.

He realized that the ideas passing from him did not arise in his intellect, but had their source in the fathomless depths of his will. He could not decide what character they should have, but he was able to force them out, or retard them, by the exercise of his volition.

At first nothing changed around him. Then the moon

grew dimmer, and a strange, new radiance began to illuminate the landscape. It increased so imperceptibly, that it was some time before he recognised it as the Muspel-light which he had seen in the Wombflash Forest. He could not give it a colour, or a name, but it filled him with a sort of stern and sacred awe. He called up the resources of his powerful will. The spouts thickened like a forest, and many of them were twenty feet high. Teargeld looked faint and pale; the radiance became intense; but it cast no shadows. The wind got up, but where Maskull was sitting, it was calm. Shortly afterwards it began to shriek and whistle, like a full gale. He saw no shapes, and redoubled his efforts.

His ideas were now rushing out on to the lake so furiously, that his whole soul was possessed by exhilaration and defiance. But still he did not know their nature. A huge spout shot up, and at the same moment the hills began to crack and break. Great masses of loose soil were erupted from their bowels, and in the next period of quietness, he saw that the landscape had altered. Still the mysterious light intensified. The moon disappeared entirely. The noise of the unseen tempest was terrifying, but Maskull played heroically on, trying to urge out ideas which would take shape. The hillsides were cleft with chasms. The water escaping from the tops of the spouts swamped the land; but where he was, it was dry.

The radiance grew terrible. It was everywhere, but Maskull fancied that it was far brighter in one particular quarter. He thought that it was becoming localised, preparatory to contracting into a solid form. He strained and strained . . .

Immediately afterwards, the bottom of the lake subsided. Its waters fell through, and his instrument was broken.

The Muspel-light vanished. The moon shone out again, but Maskull could not see it. After that unearthly shining, he seemed to himself to be in total blackness. The screaming wind ceased; there was a dead silence. His thoughts finished flowing towards the lake, and his foot no longer touched water, but hung in space.

He was too stunned by the suddenness of the change, to either think or feel. While he was still lying dazed, a vast explosion occurred in the newly opened depths beneath the lake bed. The water in its descent had met fire. Maskull was lifted bodily in the air, many yards high, and came down heavily. He lost consciousness . . .

When he came to his senses again, he saw everything. Teargeld was gleaming brilliantly. He was lying by the side of the old lake, but it was now a crater, to the bottom of which his eyes could not penetrate. The hills encircling it were torn, as if by heavy gunfire. A few thunder clouds were floating in the air at no great height, from which branched lightning descended to the earth incessantly, accompanied by alarming and singular crashes.

He got on his legs, and tested his actions. Finding that he was uninjured, he first of all viewed the crater at closer quarters, and then started to walk painfully towards the northern shore.

When he had attained the crest above the lake, the landscape sloped gently down for two miles to the sea. Everywhere he passed through traces of his rough work. The country was carved into scarps, grooves, channels, and craters. He arrived at the line of low cliffs overlooking the beach, and found that these also were partly broken down by landslips. He got down on to the sands, and stood looking over the moonlit, agitated sea, wondering how he should contrive to escape from this island of failure.

Then he saw Earthrid's body, lying quite close to him. It was on its back. Both legs had been violently torn off, and he could not see them anywhere. His teeth were buried in the flesh of his right forearm, indicating that the man had died in unreasoning physical agony. The skin gleamed green in the moonlight, but it was stained by darker discolorations, which were wounds. The sand about him was dyed by the pool of blood which had long since filtered through.

Maskull quitted the corpse in dismay, and walked a long way along the sweet-smelling shore. Sitting down on a rock, he waited for daybreak.

CHAPTER SIXTEEN

Leehallfae

At midnight, when Teargeld was in the south, throwing his shadow straight towards the sea and making everything nearly as bright as day, he saw a great tree floating in the water, not far out. It was thirty feet out of the water, upright, and alive, and its roots must have been enormously deep and wide. It was drifting along the coast, through the heavy seas. Maskull eyed it incuriously for a few minutes. Then it dawned on him that it might be a good thing to investigate its nature. Without stopping to weigh the danger, he immediately swam out, caught hold of the lowest branch, and swung himself up.

He looked aloft and saw that the main stem was thick to the very top, terminating in a knob which somewhat resembled a human head. He made his way towards this knob, through the multitude of boughs, which were covered with tough, slippery, marine leaves, like seaweed. Arriving at the crown, he found that it actually was a sort of head for there were membranes like rudimentary eyes all the way round it, denoting some form of low intelligence.

At that moment the tree touched bottom, though some way from the shore, and began to bump heavily. To steady himself, he put his hand out and, in doing so, accidentally covered some of the membranes. The tree sheered off the land, as if by an act of will. When it was steady again, Maskull removed his hand . . . they at once drifted back to shore. He thought a bit, and then started experimenting with the eye-like membranes . . . It was as he had guessed—these eyes were stimulated by the light of the moon, and whichever way the light came from, the tree would travel.

A rather defiant smile crossed his face as it struck him that it might be possible to navigate this huge plant-animal as far as Matterplay. He lost no time in putting the conception into execution. Tearing off some of the long, tough leaves, he bound up all the membranes except the ones which faced the north. The tree instantly left the island, and definitely put out to sea. It travelled due north . . . It was not moving at more than a mile an hour, however, while Matterplay was possibly forty miles distant.

The great spout-waves fell against the trunk with mighty thuds, the breaking seas hissed through the lower branches —Maskull rested high and dry, but was more than a little apprehensive about their slow rate of progress. Presently he sighted a current racing along towards the north-west, and that put another idea into his head. He began to juggle with the membranes again, and before long had succeeded in piloting his tree into the fast-running stream. As soon as they were fairly in its rapids, he blinded the crown entirely, and thenceforward the current acted in the double capacity of road and steed. Maskull made himself secure among the branches, and slept for the remainder of the night.

When his eyes opened again, the island was out of sight. Teargeld was setting in the western sky. The sky in the east was bright with the colours of the approaching day. The air was cool and fresh; the light over the sea was beautiful, gleaming and mysterious. Land—probably Matterplay—lay ahead, a long, dark line of low cliffs, perhaps a mile away. The current no longer ran towards the shore, but began to skirt the coast without drawing any closer to it. As soon as Maskull realised the fact, he manoeuvred the tree out of its channel and started drifting it inshore. The eastern sky blazed up suddenly with violent dyes, and the outer rim of Branchspell lifted itself above the sea. The moon had already sunk.

The shore loomed nearer and nearer. In physical character it was like Swaylone's Island—the same wide sands, small cliffs, and rounded, insignificant hills inland, without vegetation. In the early morning sunlight, however, it looked romantic. Maskull, hollow-eyed and morose, cared nothing for all that, but the moment the tree grounded, clambered swiftly down through the branches and dropped into the sea. By the time he had swum ashore, the white, stupendous sun was high above the horizon.

He walked along the sands towards the east for a considerable distance, without having any special intention in his mind. He thought he would go on until he came to some creek or valley, and then turn up it. The sun's rays were cheering, and began to relieve him of his oppressive night-weight. After strolling along the beach for about a mile, he was stopped by a broad stream which flowed into the sea out of a kind of natural gateway in the line of cliffs. Its water was of a beautiful, limpid green, all filled with bubbles. So ice-cool, aerated, and enticing did it look that he flung himself face-downwards on the ground, and took a prolonged draught. When he got up again his eyes started to play pranks—they became alternately blurred and clear . . . It may have been pure imagination, but he fancied that Digrung was moving inside him . . .

He followed the bank of the stream through the gap in the cliffs, and then for the first time saw the real Matterplay . . . A valley appeared, like a jewel enveloped by naked rock. All the hill country was bare and lifeless, but this valley lying in the heart of it was so fertile that he had never seen such fertility. It wound up among the hills, and all that he was looking at was its broad lower end. The floor of the valley was about half a mile wide; the stream which ran down its middle was nearly a hundred feet across, but was exceedingly shallow—in most places not more than a few inches deep. The sides of the valley were about seventy feet high, but very sloping; they were clothed from top to bottom with little, bright-leaved trees—not of varied tints of one colour, like Earth-trees, but of widely diverse colours, most of which were brilliant and positive. The floor itself was like a magician's garden. Densely interwoven trees, shrubs, and parasitical climbers fought everywhere for possession of it. The forms were strange and grotesque, and each one seemed different; the colours of leaf, flower, sexual organs, and stem were equally peculiar—all the different combinations of the five primary colours of Tormance seemed to be represented, and the result for Maskull was a sort of eye-chaos. So rank was the vegetation that he could not fight his way through it; he was obliged to take to the river-bed. The contact of the water created an odd tingling sensation throughout his body, like a mild electric shock. There were no birds, but a few extraordinary-looking winged reptiles of small size kept crossing the valley from hill to hill. Swarms of flying insects clustered round him, threatening mischief, but in the end it turned out that his blood was disagreeable to them, for he was not once bitten. Repulsive crawling creatures, resembling centipedes, scorpions, snakes, and so forth, were in myriads on the banks of the stream, but they also made no attempt to use their weapons on his bare legs and feet, as he passed through them into the water . . . Presently, however, he was confronted in mid-stream by a hideous monster, of the size of a pony, but resembling in shape—if it resembled anything—a sea-crustacean; and then he came to a halt. They stared at one another, the beast with wicked eyes, Maskull with cool and wary ones. While he was staring, a singular thing happened to him.

His eyes blurred again. But when in a minute or two this blurring passed away and he saw clearly once more, his vision had changed in character. He was looking right through the animal's body and could distinguish all its interior parts. The outer crust, however, and all the hard tissues were misty and semi-transparent; through them a luminous network of blood-red veins and arteries stood out in startling distinctness. The hard parts faded away to nothingness, and the blood-system was left alone. Not even the fleshy ducts remained. The naked blood was alone visible, flowing this way and that like a fiery, liquid skeleton, in the shape of the monster. Then this blood began to change too. Instead of a continuous liquid stream, he perceived that it was composed of a million individual points. The red colour had been an illusion caused by the rapid motion of the points; he now saw clearly that they resembled minute suns in their scintillating brightness. They seemed like a double-drift of stars, streaming through space. One drift was travelling towards a fixed point in the centre, while the other was moving away from it. He recognised the former as the veins of the beast, the latter as the arteries, and the fixed point as the heart.

While he was still looking, lost in amazement, the starry network went out suddenly, like an extinguished flame. Where the crustacean had stood, there was nothing. Yet through this "nothing" he could not see the land-scape. Something was standing there which intercepted the light, though it possessed neither shape, colour, nor substance . . . And now the object, which could no longer be perceived by vision, began to be felt by emotion. A delightful, springlike sense of rising sap, of quickening pulses—of love, adventure, mystery, beauty, feminin-ity—took possession of his being, and strangely enough he identified it with the monster. Why that invisible brute should cause him to feel young, sexual, and audacious, he did not ask himself, for he was fully occupied with the effect . . . But it was as if flesh, bones, and blood had been discarded, and he were face to face with naked Life itself, which slowly passed into his own body.

The sensations died away, there was a brief interval, and then the streaming, star-like skeleton rose up again out of space. It changed to the red blood-system. The hard parts of the body reappeared with more and more distinctness, and at the same time the network of blood grew fainter. Presently the interior parts were entirely concealed by the crust—the creature stood opposite to Maskull in its old formidable ugliness, hard, painted and concrete.

Disliking something about him, the crustacean turned aside and stumbled awkwardly away on its six legs, with laborious and repulsive movements, towards the other bank of the stream.

Maskull's apathy left him after this adventure. He became uneasy and thoughtful. He imagined that he was beginning to see things through Digrung's eyes, and that there were strange troubles immediately ahead . . . The next time his eyes started to blur, he fought it down with his will, and nothing happened.

The valley ascended with many windings towards the hills. It narrowed considerably, and the wooded slopes on either side grew steeper and higher. The stream shrunk to about twenty feet across, but it was deeper—it was alive with motion, music, and bubbles. The electric sensations caused by its water became more pronounced, almost disagreeably so; but there was nowhere else to walk. With its deafening confusion of sounds from the multitude of living creatures, the little valley resembled a vast conversation hall of Nature. The life was still more prolific than before; every square foot of space was a tangle of struggling wills, both animal and vegetable. For a naturalist it would have been paradise, for no two shapes were alike, and all were fantastic with individual character.

It looked as if life-forms were being coined so fast by Nature, that there was not physical room for all. Nevertheless it was not as on Earth, where a hundred seeds are scattered in order that one may be sown. Here the young forms seemed to survive, while, to find accommodation for them, the old ones perished; everywhere he looked they were withering and dying; without any ostensible cause—they were simply being killed by new life.

Other creatures sported so wildly, in front of his very eyes, that they became of different 'kingdoms' altogether. As an example—a fruit was lying on the ground, of the size and shape of a lemon, but with a tougher skin. He picked it up, intending to eat the contained pulp; but inside it was a fully-formed young tree, just on the point of bursting its shell. Maskull threw it away upstream. It floated back towards him . . . by the time that he was up with it, its downward motion had stopped and it was swimming against the current. He fished it out, and discovered that it had sprouted six rudimentary legs.

Maskull sang no paeans of praise in honour of the

gloriously overcrowded valley. On the contrary, he felt deeply cynical and depressed. He thought that the unseen Power—whether it were called Nature, Life, Will, or God—which was so frantic to rush forward and occupy this small, vulgar, contemptible world, could not possess very high aims and was not worth much. How this sordid struggle for an hour or two of physical existence could ever be regarded as a deeply earnest and important business was beyond his comprehension . . . The atmosphere choked him, he longed for air and space. Thrusting his way through to the side of the ravine, he began to climb the overhanging cliff, swinging his way up from tree to tree.

When he arrived at the top, Branchspell beat down on him with such brutal, white intensity that he saw that there was no stopping there. He looked round, to ascertain what part of the country he had come to. He had travelled about ten miles from the sea, as the crow flies. The bare, undulating wolds sloped straight down towards it; the water glittered in the distance, and on the horizon he was just able to make out Swaylone's Island. Looking north, the land continued sloping upwards as far as he could see. Over the crest—that is to say, some miles away, a line of black, fantastic-shaped rocks of quite another character showed themselves; this was probably Threal. Behind these again, against the sky, perhaps fifty or even a hundred miles off, were the peaks of Lichstorm, most of them covered with greenish snow which glittered in the sunlight. They were stupendously high and of weird contours. Most of them were conical to the top, but from the top great masses of mountain balanced themselves at what looked like impossible angles—overhanging without apparent support. A land like that promised something new, he thought . . . extraordinary inhabitants. The idea took shape in his mind to go there, and to travel as swiftly as possible. It might even be feasible to get there before sunset. It was less the mountains themselves which attracted him, than the country which lay beyond—the prospect of setting eyes on the blue sun, which he judged to be the wonder of wonders in Tormance.

The direct route was over the hills, but that was out of the question, on account of the killing heat and the absence of shade. He guessed, however, that the valley would not take him far out of his road, and decided to keep to that for the time being, much as he hated and feared it. Into the hotbed of life, therefore, he once more swung himself.

Once down, he continued to follow the windings of the valley for several miles, through sunlight and shadow. The path became increasingly difficult. The cliffs closed in on either side until they were not a hundred yards apart, while the bed of the ravine was blocked by boulders, great and small, so that the little stream, which was now diminished to the proportions of a brook, had to come down where and how it could. The forms of life grew queerer. Pure plants and pure animals by degrees disappeared, and their place was filled by singular creatures which seemed to partake of both characters. They had limbs, faces, will, and intelligence, but they remained for the greater part of their time rooted in the ground by preference, and they fed only on soil and air. Maskull saw no sexual organs and failed to understand how the young came into existence.

Then he witnessed an astonishing sight. A large and fully developed plant-animal appeared suddenly in front of him, out of empty space. He could not believe his eyes, but stared at the creature for a long time in amazement. It went on calmly moving and burrowing before him, as though it had been there all its life. Giving up the puzzle, he resumed his striding from rock to rock up the gorge, and then, quietly and without warning, the same phenomenon occurred again. No longer could he doubt that he was seeing miracles—that Nature was precipitating its shapes into the world, without making use of the medium of parentage . . . No solution of the problem presented itself.

The brook too had altered in character. A trembling radiance came up from its green water, like some imprisoned force escaping into the air. He had not walked in it for some time; now he did so, to test its quality. He felt new life entering his body, from his feet upwards; it resembled a slowly moving cordial, rather than mere heat. The sensation was quite new in his experience, yet he knew by instinct what it was. The energy emitted by the brook was ascending his body neither as friend nor foe, but simply because it happened to be the direct road to its objective elsewhere. But, although it had no hostile intentions, it was likely to prove a rough traveller . . . he was clearly conscious that its passage through his body threatened to bring about some physical transformation, unless he could do something to prevent it. Leaping quickly out of the water, he leant against a rock, tightened his muscles, and braced himself against the impending change. At that very moment the blurring again attacked his sight, and while he was guarding against that his forehead sprouted out into a galaxy of new eyes. He put his hand up, and counted six, in addition to his old ones.

The danger was past and Maskull laughed, congratulating himself on having got off so easily. Then he wondered what the new organs were for—whether they were a good or a bad thing. He had not taken a dozen steps up the ravine before he found out. Just as he was in the act of jumping down from the top of a boulder, his vision altered and he came to an automatic standstill. He was perceiving two worlds simultaneously. With his own eyes he saw the gorge as before, with its rocks, brook, plant-animals, sunshine, and shadows. But with his acquired eyes he saw differently. All the details of the valley were visible, but the light seemed turned down and everything appeared faint, hard, and uncoloured. The sun was obscured by masses of cloud which filled the whole sky. This vapour was in violent and almost living motion. It was thick in extension, but thin in texture; some parts, however, were far denser than others, as the particles were crushed together or swept apart by the motion. The green sparks from the brook, when closely watched, could be distinguished individually, each one wavering up towards the clouds, but the moment they got within them a fearful struggle seemed to commence. The spark endeavoured to escape through to the upper air, while the clouds concentrated around it, whichever way it darted, trying to create so dense a prison that further movement would be impossible. So far as Maskull could detect, most of the sparks succeeded in eventually finding their way out after frantic efforts; but one that he was looking at was caught, and what happened was this. A complete ring of cloud surrounded it and, in spite of its furious leaps and flashes in all directions—as if it were a live, savage creature taken in a net—nowhere could it find an opening, but it dragged the enveloping cloud-stuff with it, wherever it went. The vapours continued to thicken round it, until they resembled the black, heavy, compressed sky-masses seen before a bad thunder storm. Then the green spark, which was still visible in the interior, ceased its efforts, and remained for a time quite quiescent. The cloud-shape went on consolidating itself, and became nearly spherical; as it grew heavier and stiller, it started to slowly descend towards the valley floor. When it was directly opposite to Maskull, with its lower end but a few feet off the ground, its motion stopped altogether and there was a complete pause for at least two minutes. Suddenly, like a stab of forked lightning, the great cloud shot together, became small, indented, and coloured, and as a plant-animal started walking about on legs and rooting up the ground in search of food. The concluding stage of the phenomenon he witnessed with his normal eyesight. It showed him the creature appearing miraculously out of nowhere.

Maskull was shaken. His cynicism dropped from him, and gave place to curiosity and awe. "That was exactly like the birth of a *thought*," he said to himself, "but who was the thinker? . . . Some great Living Mind is at work in this spot. He has intelligence, for all his shapes are different, and he has character, for all belong to the same general type . . . If I'm not wrong, and if it's the force called Shaping or Crystalman, I've seen enough to make me want to find out something more about him . . . It would be ridiculous to go on to other riddles before I have solved these."

A voice hallooed to him from behind and, turning round,

he saw a human figure hastening towards him from some distance down the ravine. It looked more like a man than a woman. He was rather tall, but nimble, and was clothed in a dark, frock-like garment which reached from the neck to below the knees. Round his head was rolled a turban. Maskull waited for him, and when he was nearer went a little way to meet him.

Then he experienced another surprise, for this person, though clearly a human being, was neither man nor woman, nor anything between the two, but was unmistakably of a third positive sex, which was remarkable to behold and difficult to understand. In order to translate into words the sexual impression produced in Maskull's mind by the stranger's physical aspect, it is necessary to coin a new pronoun, for none in earthly use would be applicable. Instead of 'he,' 'she,' or 'it,' therefore, 'ae' will be used.

He found himself incapable of grasping at first why the bodily peculiarities of this being should strike him as springing from sex, and not from race, and yet there was no doubt about the fact itself. Body, face, and eyes were absolutely neither male nor female, but something quite different. Just as one can distinguish a man from a woman at the first glance by some indefinable difference of expression and atmosphere, apart altogether from the contour of the figure, so the stranger was separated in appearance from both. As with men and women, the whole person expressed a latent sensuality, which gave body and face alike their peculiar character . . . Maskull decided that it was *love* . . . but what love . . . love for whom? It was neither the shame-carrying passion of a male, nor the deep-rooted instinct of a female to obey her destiny. It was as real and irresistible as these, but quite different . . . As he continued staring into those strange, archaic eyes, he had an intuitive feeling that aer lover was no other than Shaping himself. It came to him that the design of this love was not the continuance of the race, but the immortality on earth of the individual. No children were produced by the act; the lover aerself was the eternal child. Further, ae sought like a

man, but received like a woman. All these things were dimly
and confusedly expressed by this extraordinary being, who
seemed to have dropped out of another age, when creation
was different . . . Of all the weird personalities he had so far
met in Tormance, this one struck him as infinitely the most
foreign—that is, the farthest removed from him in spiritual
structure. If they were to live together for a hundred years,
they could never be companions.

Maskull pulled himself out of his trance-like meditations
and, viewing the newcomer in greater detail, tried with
his understanding to account for the marvellous things
told him by his intuitions. Ae possessed broad shoulders
and big bones, and was without female breasts, and so
far ae resembled a man. But the bones were so flat and
angular that aer flesh presented something of the character
of a crystal, having plane surfaces in place of curves. The
body looked as if it had not been ground down by the
sea of ages into smooth and rounded regularity, but had
sprung together in angles and facets as the result of a single,
sudden *idea*. The face too was broken and irregular. With
his racial prejudices, he found little beauty in it, yet beauty
there was, though neither of a masculine nor of a feminine
type, for it had the three essentials of beauty—character,
intelligence, and repose. The skin was copper-coloured and
strangely luminous, as if lighted from within. The face was
beardless, but the hair of the head was as long as a woman's
and, dressed in a single plait, fell down behind as far as the
ankles. Ae possessed only two eyes. That part of the turban
which went across the forehead protruded so far in front
that it evidently concealed some organ.

Maskull found it impossible to compute aer age. The
frame appeared active, vigorous, and healthy, the skin was
clear and glowing, the eyes were powerful and alert—ae
might well be in early youth. Nevertheless, the longer he
gazed the more an impression of unbelievable ancientness
came upon him—aer real youth seemed as far away as the
view observed through a reversed telescope.

At last he addressed the stranger, though it was just as

if he were conversing with a dream. "To what sex do you belong?" he asked.

The voice in which the reply came was neither manly nor womanly, but was oddly suggestive of a mythical forest horn, heard from a great distance.

"Nowadays there are men and women, but in the olden times the world was peopled by *phaens*. I think I am the only survivor of all those beings who were then passing through Faceny's mind."

"Faceny?"

"Who is now miscalled Shaping or Crystalman. The superficial names invented by a race of superficial creatures."

"What's your own name?"

"Leehallfae."

"What?"

"Leehallfae. And yours is Maskull. I read in your mind that you have just come through some wonderful adventures. You seem to possess singular luck. If it lasts long enough, perhaps I can make use of it."

"Do you think that my luck exists for your benefit? . . . But never mind that now. It is your *sex* that interests me. How do you satisfy your desires?"

Leehallfae pointed to the concealed organ on aer brow.

"With that I gather life from the streams which flow in all the hundred Matterplay valleys. The streams spring direct from Faceny. My whole life has been spent in trying to find Faceny himself. I've hunted so long that if I were to state the number of years you would believe I lied."

Maskull looked at the phaen slowly.

"In Ifdawn I met someone else from Matterplay—a young man, called Digrung . . . I absorbed him."

"You can't be telling me this out of vanity."

"It was a fearful crime. What will come of it?"

Leehallfae gave a curious wrinkled smile. "In Matterplay he will stir inside you, for he smells the air. Already you have his eyes . . . I knew him . . . Take care of yourself, or something more startling may happen. Keep out of the water."

"This seems to me a terrible valley, in which anything may occur."

"Don't torment yourself about Digrung. The valleys belong by right to the phaens—the men here are interlopers. It is a good work to remove them."

Maskull continued thoughtful.

"I say no more, but I see I shall have to be cautious . . . What did you mean about my helping you with my luck?"

"Your luck is fast weakening, but it may still be strong enough to serve me. Together we will search for Threal."

"*Search* for Threal . . . why, is it so hard to find?"

"I have told you that my whole life has been spent in the quest."

"You said Faceny, Leehallfae."

The phaen gazed at him with queer, ancient eyes, and smiled again.

"This stream, Maskull, like every other life-stream in Matterplay, has its source in Faceny. But as all these streams issue out from Threal, it is in Threal that we must look for Faceny."

"But what's to prevent your finding Threal? Surely it's a well-known country?"

"It lies underground. Its communications with the upperworld are few, and where they are, none know that I have ever spoken to. I have scoured the valleys and the hills . . . I have been to the very gates of Lichstorm. I am old, so that your aged men would appear newborn infants beside me, but I am as far from Threal as when I was a green youth, dwelling among a throng of fellow-phaens."

"Then, if my luck is good, yours is very bad . . . But when you have found Faceny, what do you gain?"

Leehallfae looked at him in silence. The smile faded from aer face, and its place was taken by such a look of unearthly pain and sorrow that Maskull had no need to press his question. Ae was consumed by the grief and yearning of a lover eternally separated from the loved-one, the scents and traces of whose person were always present. This passion stamped aer features at that moment with a wild, stern, spiritual beauty, far transcending any beauty of woman or man.

But the expression vanished suddenly, and then the abrupt contrast showed Maskull the real Leehallfae . . . Aer sensuality was solitary, but vulgar—it was like the heroism of a lonely nature, pursuing animal aims with untiring persistence . . . He regarded the phaen askance, and drummed his fingers against his thigh.

"Well, we will go together. We may find something, and in any case I shan't be sorry to converse with such a singular individual as yourself."

"But I should warn you, Maskull. You and I are of different creations. A phaen's body contains the whole of life, a man's body contains only the half of life—the other half is in woman. Faceny may be too strong a draught for your body to endure . . . Do you not feel this?"

"I am dull with my different feelings. I must take what precautions I can and chance the rest."

He bent down and, taking hold of the phaen's thin and ragged robe, tore off a broad strip, which he proceeded to swathe in folds round his forehead.

"I'm not forgetting your advice, Leehallfae. I should not like to start the walk as Maskull, and finish it as Digrung."

The phaen gave a twisted grin, and they began to move upstream. The road was difficult; they had to stride from boulder to boulder, and found it warm work. Occasionally a worse obstacle presented itself, which they could only surmount by climbing. There was no more conversation for a long time. Maskull as far as possible adopted his companion's counsel to avoid the water, but here and there he was forced to set foot in it. On the second or third occasion of doing so, he felt a sudden agony in his arm, where it had been wounded by Krag . . . His eyes grew joyful, his fears vanished, and he began deliberately to tread the stream.

Leehallfae stroked aer chin and watched him with screwed-up eyes, trying to comprehend what had happened.

"Is your luck speaking to you, Maskull, or what is the matter?"

"Listen. You are a being of antique experience, and ought to know, if anyone does. What is Muspel?"

The phaen's face was blank. "I don't know the name."

"It is another world of some sort."

"That cannot be. There is only this one world—Faceny's."

Maskull came up to aer, linked arms, and began to talk.

"I'm glad I fell in with you, Leehallfae, for this valley and everything connected with it need a lot of explaining. For example, in this spot there are hardly any organic forms left—why have they all disappeared? You call this brook a 'life-stream,' yet the nearer its source we get the less life it produces. A mile or two lower down we had those spontaneous plant-animals appearing out of nowhere, while right down by the sea, plants and animals were tumbling over one another. Now, if all this is connected in some mysterious way or other with your Faceny, it seems to me he must have a most paradoxical nature. His essence doesn't start creating shapes until it has become thoroughly weakened and watered. . . . But perhaps both of us are talking nonsense."

Leehallfae shook aer head. "Everything hangs together. The stream is life, and it is all the time throwing off sparks of life. When these sparks are caught and imprisoned by matter, they become living shapes. The nearer the stream is to its source, the more terrible and vigorous is its life. You'll see for yourself when we reach the head of the valley that there are no living shapes there at all. That means that there is no kind of matter tough enough to capture and hold the terrible sparks which are to be found there. Lower down the stream, most of the sparks are vigorous enough to escape to the upper air, but some are held when they are a little way up, and these ones burst suddenly into shapes.

I myself am of this nature. Lower down still, towards the sea, the stream has lost a great part of its vital power and the sparks are lazy and sluggish. They spread out, rather than rise into the air. There is hardly any kind of matter, however delicate, which is incapable of capturing these feeble sparks, and they *are* captured in multitudes—that accounts for the innumerable living shapes you see there. But not only that—the sparks are passed from one body to another by way of generation, and can never hope to cease being so until they are worn out by decay. Lowest of all, you have the Sinking Sea itself. There the degenerate and enfeebled life of the Matterplay streams has for its body the whole sea. So weak is its power that it can't succeed in creating any shapes at all, but you can see its ceaseless futile attempts to do so, in those spouts."

"So the slow development of men and women is due to the feebleness of the life-germ in their case?"

"Exactly. It can't attain all its desires at once. And now you can see how immeasurably superior are the phaens, who spring spontaneously from the more electric and vigorous sparks."

"But where does the matter come from which imprisons these sparks?"

"When life dies, it becomes matter. Matter itself dies, but its place is constantly taken by new matter."

"But if life comes from Faceny, how can it die at all?"

"Life is the thoughts of Faceny, and once these thoughts have left his brain they are nothing—mere dying embers."

"This is a cheerless philosophy," said Maskull. "But who is Faceny himself, then, and why does he think at all?"

Leehallfae gave another wrinkled smile. "That I'll explain too. Faceny is of this nature. He faces Nothingness in all directions. He has no back and no sides, but is all face; and this face is his shape. It must necessarily be so, for nothing else can exist between him and Nothingness. His face is all eyes, for he eternally contemplates Nothingness. He draws his inspirations from it; in no other way could he feel himself. . . . For the same reason, phaens and even men love to be in empty places and vast solitudes, for each one is a little Faceny . . ."

"That rings true," said Maskull.

"Thoughts flow perpetually from Faceny's face backwards. As his face is on all sides, however, they flow into his interior. A draught of thought thus continuously flows from Nothingness to the inside of Faceny, which is the world. The thoughts become shapes, and people the world. This outer world, therefore, which is lying all around us, is not outside at all, as it happens, but inside. The visible universe is like a gigantic stomach, and the real outside of the world we shall never see."

Maskull pondered deeply for a while.

"Leehallfae, I fail to see what you personally have to hope for, since you are nothing more than a discarded, dying thought."

"Have you never loved a woman?" asked the phaen, regarding him fixedly.

"Perhaps I have."

"When you loved, did you have no high moments?"

"That's asking the same question in other words."

"In those moments you were approaching Faceny. If you could have drawn nearer still, would you not have done so?"

"I would, regardless of the consequences."

"Even if you personally had nothing to hope for?"

"But I should have *that* to hope for."

Leehallfae walked on in silence.

"A man is the half of life," ae broke out suddenly, "a woman is the other half of life, but a phaen is the whole of life. Moreover, when life becomes split into halves, something else has dropped out of it—something which belongs only to the whole . . . Between your love and mine there is no comparison. If even your sluggish blood is drawn to Faceny, without stopping to ask what will come of it, how do you suppose it is with *me*?"

"I don't question the genuineness of your passion,"

replied Maskull, "but it's a pity you can't see your way to carry it forward into the next world."

Leehallfae gave a distorted grin, expressing heaven knows what emotion. "Men think what they like, but phaens are so made that they can only see the world as it really is."

That ended the conversation.

The sun was high in the sky, and they appeared to be approaching the head of the ravine. Its walls had still further closed in and, except at those moments when Branchspell was directly behind them, they strode along all the time in deep shade; but still it was disagreeably hot and relaxing. All life had ceased. A beautiful, fantastic spectacle was presented by the cliff-faces, the rocky ground, and the boulders which choked the entire width of the gorge. They were of a snow-white, crystalline limestone, heavily scored by veins of bright, gleaming blue. The rivulet was green no longer, but a clear, transparent crystal. Its noise was musical, and altogether it looked most romantic and charming, but Leehallfae seemed to find something else in it—aer features grew more and more set and tortured.

About half an hour after all the other life-forms had vanished, another plant-animal was precipitated out of space, in front of their eyes. It was as tall as Maskull himself, and had a brilliant and vigorous appearance, as befitted a creature just out of Nature's mint. It started to walk about; but hardly had it done so, when it burst silently asunder. Nothing remained of it—the whole body disappeared instantaneously into the same invisible mist from which it had sprung.

"That bears out what you said," commented Maskull, turning rather pale.

"Yes," answered Leehallfae, "we have now come to the region of terrible life."

"Then, as you're right in this, I must believe all that you've been telling me."

As he uttered the words, they were just turning a bend of the ravine. There now loomed up straight ahead a perpendicular cliff about three hundred feet in height, composed of white, marbled rock. It was the head of the valley, and beyond it they could not proceed.

"In return for my wisdom," said the phaen, "you will now lend me your luck."

They walked up to the base of the cliff, and Maskull looked at it reflectively. It was possible to climb it, but the ascent would be difficult. The now tiny brook issued from a hole in the rock, only a few feet up. Apart from its musical running, not a sound was to be heard. The floor of the gorge was in shadow, but about halfway up the precipice the sun was shining.

"What do you want me to do?" demanded Maskull.

"Everything is now in your hands, and I have no suggestions to make. It's now your luck which must help us."

He continued gazing up a little while longer.

"We had better wait till the afternoon, Leehallfae. I shall probably have to climb to the top, but it's too hot at present—and besides, I'm tired. I shall snatch a few hours' sleep. After that we'll see."

Leehallfae seemed annoyed, but raised no opposition.

CHAPTER SEVENTEEN

Corpang

Maskull did not awake till long after Blodsombre. Leehallfae was standing by his side, looking down at him. It was doubtful whether ae had slept at all.

"What time is it?" he asked, rubbing his eyes and sitting up.

"The day is passing," was the vague reply.

Maskull got on to his feet, and gazed up at the cliff.

"Now I'm going to climb *that*. No need for both of us to risk our necks, so you wait here, and if I find anything on top I'll call you."

The phaen glanced at him queerly. "There's nothing up there except a bare hillside. I've been there often. Have you anything special in your mind?"

"Heights often bring me inspiration. Sit you down, and wait."

Refreshed by his sleep, he immediately attacked the face of the cliff, and took the first twenty feet at a single rush. Then it grew precipitous, and the ascent demanded greater circumspection and intelligence. There were few hand or footholds; he had to reflect before every step. On the other hand it was sound rock, and he was no novice at the sport. Branchspell glared full on the wall, so that it half-blinded him with its glittering whiteness.

After many doubts and pauses he drew near to the top. He was hot, sweating copiously, and rather dizzy. To reach a ledge he caught hold of two projecting rocks, one with each hand, at the same time scrambling upwards with his legs between them. The left-hand rock, which was the larger of the two, became dislodged by his weight and, flying like a huge, dark shadow past his head, crashed down with a terrifying sound to the foot of the precipice, followed by an avalanche of smaller stones. Maskull steadied himself as well as he could, but it was some moments before he dared to look down behind him.

At first he could not distinguish Leehallfae. Then he caught sight of legs and hindquarters a few feet up the cliff from the bottom. He perceived that the phaen had aer head in a cavity and was scrutinising something, and waited for aer to reappear.

Ae emerged, looked up to Maskull, and called out in aer hornlike voice, "The entrance is here."

"I'm coming down," roared Maskull. "Wait for me!"

He descended swiftly—without taking too much care, for he thought he recognised his 'luck' in this discovery—and within twenty minutes was standing beside the phaen.

"What's happened?"

"The rock you dislodged struck the other rock just above the spring. It tore it out of its bed. See—there's now room for us to get in!'

"Don't get excited!" said Maskull. "It's a remarkable accident, but we have plenty of time . . . Let me look."

He peered into the hole, which was large enough to admit a big man without stooping. Contrasted with the daylight outside it was dark, yet a peculiar glow pervaded the place, and he could see well enough. A rock tunnel went straight forward into the bowels of the hill, out of sight. The valley-brook did not flow along the floor of this tunnel, as he had expected to find, but came up as a spring just inside the entrance.

"Well, Leehallfae, not much need to deliberate, eh? Still, observe that your stream parts company with us here."

As he turned round for an answer, he noticed that his companion was trembling from head to foot.

"Why, what's the matter?"

Leehallfae pressed a hand to aer heart.

"The stream leaves us, but what makes the stream what it is continues with us. Faceny is there."

"But surely you don't expect me to see him in person?
. . . Why are you shaking?"

"Perhaps after all it will be too much for me."

"Why? How is it affecting you?"

The phaen took him by the shoulder and held him at
arm's length, endeavouring to study him with aer unsteady
eyes.

"Faceny's thoughts are obscure. I am his lover, you are
a lover of women, yet he grants to you what he denies
to me."

"What does he grant to me?"

"To see him, and go on living. I shall die. But it's
immaterial. Tomorrow both of us will be dead."

Maskull impatiently shook himself free. "Your sensations
may be reliable in your own case, but how do you know I
shall die?"

"Life is flaming up inside you," replied Leehallfae, shaking aer head. "But after it has reached its climax—perhaps
tonight—it will sink rapidly and you'll die tomorrow. As
for me, if I enter Threal I shan't come out again. A smell
of death is being wafted to me out of this hole."

"You talk like a frightened man. I smell nothing."

"I am not frightened," said Leehallfae quietly—ae had
been gradually recovering aer tranquillity—"but when one
has lived as long as I have done, it is a serious matter to
die. Every year on earth one puts out new roots."

"Decide what you're going to do," said Maskull, with a
touch of contempt, "for I'm going in at once."

The phaen gave an odd, meditative stare down the ravine,
and after that walked into the cavern without another word.
Maskull, scratching his head, followed close at aer heels.

The moment they stepped across the bubbling spring, the
atmosphere altered. Without becoming stale or unpleasant,
it grew cold, clear, and refined, and somehow suggested
austere and tomb-like thoughts. The daylight disappeared
at the first bend in the tunnel. After that, Maskull could not
say where the light came from. The air itself must have been
luminous, for though it was as light as full moon on Earth,

neither he nor Leehallfae cast a shadow. Another peculiarity of the light was that both the walls of the tunnel and their own bodies appeared colourless. Everything was black and white, like a lunar landscape. This intensified the solemn, funereal feelings created by the atmosphere.

After they had proceeded for about ten minutes, the tunnel began to widen out. The roof was high above their heads, and six men could have walked side by side. Leehallfae was visibly weakening. Ae dragged aerself along slowly and painfully, with sunken head. Maskull caught hold of aer.

"You can't go on like that. Better let me take you back."

The phaen smiled, and staggered. "I'm dying."

"Don't talk like that. It's only a passing indisposition. Let me take you back to the daylight."

"No, help me forward. I wish to see Faceny."

"The sick must have their way," said Maskull. Lifting aer bodily in his arms, he walked quickly along for another hundred yards or so. They then emerged from the tunnel and faced a world the parallel of which he had never set eyes upon before.

"Set me down!" directed Leehallfae feebly. "Here I'll die."

He obeyed, and laid aer down at full length on the rocky ground. The phaen raised aerself with difficulty on one arm, and stared with fast-glazing eyes at the mystic landscape.

Maskull looked too, and what he saw was a vast, undulating plain, lighted as if by the moon—but there was of course no moon, and there were no shadows. He made out running streams in the distance. Beside them were trees of a peculiar kind; they were rooted in the ground, but the branches also were aerial roots, and there were no leaves. No other plants could be seen. The soil was soft, porous rock, resembling pumice. Beyond a mile or two in any direction the light merged into obscurity. At their back a great rocky wall extended on either hand; but it was not square like a wall, but full of bays and promontories like an indented line of sea-cliffs. The roof of this huge underworld was out of sight. Here and there a mighty shaft of naked rock, fantastically weathered, towered aloft into the gloom, doubtless serving to support the roof. There were no colours—every detail of the landscape was black, white, or grey. The scene appeared so still, so solemn and religious, that all his feelings quieted down to absolute tranquillity.

Leehallfae fell back suddenly. Maskull dropped on his knees, and helplessly watched the last flickerings of aer spirit, going out like a candle in foul air. Death came . . . He closed the eyes. The awful grin of Crystalman immediately fastened upon the phaen's dead features.

While he was still kneeling, he became conscious of someone standing beside him. He looked up quickly and saw a man, but did not at once rise.

"Another phaen dead," said the newcomer, in a grave, toneless, and intellectual voice.

Maskull got up.

The man was short and thickset, but emaciated. His forehead was not disfigured by any organs. He was middle-aged. The features were energetic and rather coarse—yet it seemed to Maskull as though a pure, hard life had done something towards refining them. His sanguine eyes carried a twisted, puzzled look; some unanswerable problem was apparently in the forefront of his brain. His face was hairless, the hair of his head was short and manly, his brow was wide. He was clothed in a black, sleeveless robe, and bore a long staff in his hand. There was an air of cleanness and austerity about the whole man that was attractive.

He went on speaking dispassionately to Maskull and, while doing so, kept passing his hand reflectively over his cheeks and chin.

"They all find their way here to die. They come from Matterplay. There they live to an incredible age. Partly on that account and partly because of their spontaneous origin, they regard themselves as the favoured children of Faceny. But when they come here to find him, they die at once."

"I think this one is the last of the race. But whom do I speak to?"

"I am Corpang. Who are you, where do you come from, and what are you doing here?"

"My name is Maskull. My home is on the other side of the universe. As for what I am doing here—I accompanied Leehallfae, that phaen, from Matterplay."

"But a man doesn't accompany a phaen out of friendship. What do you want in Threal?"

"Then this *is* Threal?"

"Yes."

Maskull remained silent. Corpang studied his face with rough, curious eyes.

"Are you ignorant, or merely reticent, Maskull?"

"I came here to ask questions, and not to answer them."

The stillness of the place was almost oppressive. Not a breeze stirred, and not a sound came through the air. Their voices had been lowered, as though they were in a cathedral.

"Then do you want my society, or not?" asked Corpang.

"Yes, if you can fit in with my humour, which is—not to talk about myself."

"But you must at least tell me where you want to go to."

"I want to see what is to be seen here, and then go on to Lichstorm."

"I can guide you through, if that's all you want. Come, let us start."

"First let's do our duty and bury the dead, if possible."

"Turn round," directed Corpang.

Maskull looked round quickly. Leehallfae's body had disappeared.

"What does this mean . . . what has happened?"

"The body has returned whence it came. There was nowhere here for it to be, so it has vanished. No burial will be required."

"Was the phaen an illusion, then?"

"In no sense."

"Well, explain quickly, then, what has taken place. I seem to be going mad."

"There's nothing unintelligible in it, if you'll only listen calmly. The phaen belonged, body and soul, to the outside visible world—to Faceny. This underworld is not Faceny's world, but Thire's, and Faceny's creatures cannot breathe its atmosphere. As this applies not only to whole bodies, but even to the last particles of bodies, the phaen has dissolved into nothingness."

"But don't you and I belong to the outside world too?"

"We belong to all three worlds."

"What three worlds . . . how do you mean?"

"There are three worlds," said Corpang composedly. "The first is Faceny's, the second is Amfuse's, the third is Thire's. From him Threal gets its name."

"But this is mere nomenclature. In what sense are there three worlds?"

Corpang passed his hand over his forehead. "All this we can discuss as we go along. It's a torment to me to be standing still."

Maskull stared again at the spot where Leehallfae's body had lain, quite bewildered at the extraordinary disappearance. He could scarcely tear himself away from the place, so mysterious was it. Not until Corpang called to him a second time did he make up his mind to follow him.

They set off from the rock wall straight across the airlit plain, directing their course towards the nearest trees. The subdued light, the absence of shadows, the massive shafts, springing grey-white out of the jet-like ground, the fantastic trees, the absence of a sky, the deathly silence, the knowledge that he was underground—the combination of all these things predisposed Maskull's mind to mysticism, and he prepared himself with some anxiety to hear Corpang's explanation of the land and its wonders. He already began to grasp that the reality of the outside world and the reality of this world were two quite different things.

"In what sense are there three worlds?" he demanded, repeating his former question.

Corpang smote the end of his staff on the ground.

"First of all, Maskull, what is your motive for asking? If it's mere intellectual curiosity, tell me, for we mustn't play with awful matters."

"No, it isn't that," said Maskull slowly. "I'm not a student. My journey is no holiday tour."

"Isn't there blood on your soul?" asked Corpang, eyeing him intensely.

The blood rose steadily to Maskull's face, but in that light it caused it to appear black.

"Unfortunately there is, and not a little."

The other's face was all wrinkles, but he made no comment.

"And so you see," went on Maskull, with a short laugh, "I'm in the very best condition for receiving your instruction."

Corpang still paused.

"Underneath your crimes I see a man," he said, after a few minutes. "On that account, and because we are commanded to help one another, I won't leave you at present, though I little thought to be walking with a murderer . . . Now to your question . . . Whatever a man sees with his eyes, Maskull, he sees in three ways—length, breadth, depth. Length is existence, breadth is relation, depth is feeling."

"Something of the sort was told me by Earthrid, the musician, who came from Threal."

"I don't know him. What else did he tell you?"

"He went on to apply it to music. Continue, and pardon the interruption."

"These three states of perception are the three worlds. Existence is Faceny's world, relation is Amfuse's world, feeling is Thire's world."

"Can't we come down to hard facts?" said Maskull, frowning. "I understand no more than I did before what you mean by three worlds."

"There are no harder facts than the ones I am giving you. The first world is visible, tangible Nature. It was created by Faceny out of nothingness, and therefore we call it Existence."

"That I understand."

"The second world is Love—by which I don't mean lust. Without love, every individual would be entirely self-centred and unable deliberately to act on others. Without love, there would be no sympathy—not even hatred, anger, or revenge would be possible. These are all imperfect and distorted forms of pure love. Interpenetrating Faceny's world of nature, therefore, we have Amfuse's world of love, or Relation."

"What grounds have you for assuming that this so-called second world is not contained in the first?"

"They are contradictory. A natural man lives for himself; a lover lives for others."

"It may be so. It's rather mystical. But go on—who is Thire?"

"Length and breadth together without depth give flatness. Life and love together without feeling produce shallow, superficial natures. Feeling is the need of men to stretch out towards their creator."

"You mean prayer and worship?"

"I mean intimacy with Thire. This feeling is not to be found in either the first or second world, therefore it is a third world. Just as depth is the line between object and subject, feeling is the line between Thire and man."

"But what is Thire himself?"

"Thire is the afterworld."

"I still don't understand," said Maskull. "Do you believe in three separate gods, or are these merely three ways of regarding one God?"

"There are three gods, for they are mutually antagonistic . . . Yet they are somehow united."

Maskull reflected awhile.

"How have you arrived at these conclusions?"

"None other are possible in Threal, Maskull."

"Why in Threal . . . what is there peculiar here?"

"I will show you presently."

They walked on for above a mile in silence, while Maskull digested what had been said. When they came to the first trees, which grew along the banks of a small stream of transparent water, Corpang halted.

"That bandage round your forehead has long been unnecessary," he remarked.

Maskull removed it. He found that the line of his brow was smooth and uninterrupted, as it had never yet been since his arrival in Tormance.

"How has this come about . . . and how did you know it?"

"They were Faceny's organs. They have vanished, just as the phaen's body vanished."

Maskull kept rubbing his forehead. "I feel more human without them. But why isn't the rest of my body affected?"

"Because its living will contains the element of Thire."

"Why are we stopping here?"

Corpang broke off the tip of one of the aerial roots of a tree, and proffered it to him. "Eat this, Maskull."

"For food, or something else?"

"Food for body and soul."

Maskull bit into the root. It was white and hard; its white sap was bleeding. It had no taste, but after eating it he experienced a change of perception. The landscape, without alteration of light or outline, became several degrees more stern and sacred. When he looked at Corpang he was impressed by his aspect of Gothic awfulness, but the perplexed expression was still in his eyes.

"Do you spend all your time here, Corpang?"

"Occasionally I go above, but not often."

"What fastens you to this gloomy world?"

"The search for Thire."

"Then it's still a search?"

"Let us walk on."

As they resumed their journey across the dim, gradually rising plain, the conversation became even more earnest in character than before.

"Although I was not born here," proceeded Corpang, "I've lived here for five-and-twenty years, and during all that time I have been drawing nearer to Thire, as I hope. But there is this peculiarity about it—the first stages are richer in fruit and more promising than the later ones. The longer a man seeks Thire, the more he seems to absent himself. In the beginning he is felt and known, sometimes as a shape, sometimes as a voice, sometimes as an overpowering emotion. Later on all is dry, dark, and harsh in the soul. Then you would think that Thire is a million miles off . . ."

"How do you explain that?"

"When everything is darkest, he may be nearest, Maskull."

"But this is troubling you?"

"My days are spent in torture."

"You still persist, though? This dry darkness can't be the ultimate state?"

"My questions will be answered."

A silence succeeded.

"What do you propose to show me?" asked Maskull.

"The land is about to grow wilder. I am taking you to the Three Figures, which were carved and erected by an earlier race of men. There we will pray."

"And what then?"

"If you are true-hearted, you will see things which you will not easily forget."

They had been walking slightly uphill in a sort of trough between two parallel, gently sloping downs. The trough now deepened, while the hills on either side grew steeper. They were in an ascending valley and, as it curved this way and that, the landscape was shut out from view. They came to a little spring, bubbling up from the ground. It formed a trickling brook, which was unlike all other brooks in the circumstance that it was flowing *up* the valley, instead of *down*. Before long it was joined by other miniature rivulets, so that in the end it became a fair-sized stream. Maskull kept looking at it, and puckering his forehead.

"Nature has other laws here, it seems?"

"Nothing can exist here which is not a compound of the three worlds."

"Yet the water is flowing somewhere."

"I can't explain it, but there are three wills in it."

"Is there no such thing as pure Thire-matter?"

"Thire cannot exist without Amfuse, and Amfuse cannot exist without Faceny."

Maskull thought over this for some minutes.

"That must be so," he said at last. "Without life there can be no love, and without love there can be no religious feeling."

In the half-light of the land the tops of the hills containing the valley presently attained such a height that they could not be seen. The sides were steep and craggy, while the bed of the valley grew narrower at every step. Not a living organism was visible. All was unnatural and sepulchral.

Maskull said, "I feel as if I were dead and walking in another world."

"I still do not know what you are doing here," answered Corpang.

"Why should I go on making a mystery of it? . . . I came to find Surtur."

"That name I've heard—but under what circumstances?"

"You forget?"

Corpang walked along, his eyes fixed on the ground, obviously troubled.

"Who *is* Surtur?"

Maskull shook his head, and said nothing.

The valley shortly afterwards narrowed, so that the two men, touching fingertips in the middle, could have placed their free hands on the rock walls on either side. It threatened to terminate in a cul-de-sac, but just when the road seemed least promising and they were shut in by cliffs on all sides, a hitherto unperceived bend brought them suddenly into the open. They emerged through a mere crack in the line of precipices.

A sort of huge, natural corridor was running along at right angles to the way they had come; both ends faded into obscurity after a few hundred yards. Right down the centre of this corridor ran a chasm with perpendicular sides; its width varied from thirty to a hundred feet, but its bottom could not be seen. On both sides of the chasm, facing one another, were platforms of rock, twenty feet or so in width; they too proceeded in both directions out of sight. Maskull and Corpang emerged on to one of these platforms. The shelf opposite was a few feet higher than that on which they stood. The platforms were backed by a double line of lofty and unclimbable cliffs, whose tops were invisible.

The stream, which had accompanied them through the gap, went straight forward, but instead of descending the wall of the chasm as a waterfall, it crossed from side to side like a liquid bridge. It then disappeared through a cleft in the cliffs on the opposite side.

To Maskull's mind, however, even more wonderful than this unnatural phenomenon was the absence of shadows, which was more noticeable here than on the open plain. It made the place look like a hall of phantoms.

Corpang, without delaying, led the way along the shelf to the left. When they had walked about a mile, the gulf widened to two hundred feet. Three large rocks loomed up on the ledge opposite; they resembled three upright giants, standing motionless side by side on the extreme edge of the chasm. They drew nearer, and then Maskull saw that they were statues. Each was about thirty feet high, and the workmanship was of the rudest. They represented naked men, but the limbs and trunks had been barely chipped into shape—the faces alone had more care bestowed on them, and even these faces were merely generalised. It was obviously the work of primitive artists. The statues stood erect, with knees closed and arms hanging straight down their sides. All three were exactly alike.

As soon as they were directly opposite, Corpang halted. "Is this a representation of your three Beings?" asked Maskull, awed by the spectacle in spite of his constitutional audacity.

"Ask no questions, but kneel," replied Corpang. He

dropped on to his own knees, but Maskull remained standing.

Corpang covered his eyes with one hand, and prayed silently. After a few minutes the light sensibly faded. Then Maskull knelt as well, but he continued looking.

It grew darker and darker, until all was like the blackest night. Sight and sound no longer existed . . . he was alone with his own spirit.

Then one of the three Colossi came slowly into sight again. But it had ceased to be a statue—it was a living person. Out of the blackness of space a gigantic head and chest emerged, illuminated by a mystic, rosy glow, like a mountain peak bathed by the rising sun. As the light grew stronger he saw that the flesh was translucent and that the glow came from within. The limbs of the apparition were wreathed in mist.

Before long the features of the face stood out distinctly. It was that of a beardless youth of twenty years. It possessed the beauty of a girl and the daring force of a man; it bore a mocking, cryptic smile. Maskull felt the fresh, mysterious thrill of mingled pain and rapture of one who awakes from a deep sleep in mid-winter and sees the gleaming, dark, delicate colours of the half-dawn. The vision smiled, kept still, and looked beyond him. He began to shudder, with delight . . . and many emotions . . . As he gazed, his poetic sensibility acquired such a nervous and indefinable character that he could endure it no more . . . he burst into tears.

When he looked up again the image had nearly disappeared, and in a few moments more he was plunged back into total darkness.

Shortly afterwards a second statue reappeared. It too was transfigured to a living form, but Maskull was unable to see the details of its face and body, on account of the brightness of the light which radiated from them. This light, which started as pale gold, ended as flaming golden fire. It illumined the whole underground landscape. The rock ledges, the cliffs, himself and Corpang on their knees, the two unlighted statues—all appeared as if in sunlight, and the shadows were black and strongly defined. The light carried heat with it, but a singular heat. Maskull was unaware of any rise in temperature, but he felt his heart melting to womanish softness. His male arrogance and egotism faded imperceptibly away; his personality seemed to disappear. What was left behind was not freedom of spirit or lightheartedness, but a passionate and nearly savage mental state of pity and distress. He felt a tormenting desire to *serve*. All this came from the heat of the statue, and was without an object. He glanced anxiously around him, and fastened his eyes on Corpang. He put a hand on his shoulder and aroused him from his praying.

"You must know what I am feeling, Corpang."

Corpang smiled sweetly, but said nothing.

"I care nothing for my own affairs any more. How can I help you?"

"So much the better for you, Maskull, if you respond so quickly to the invisible worlds."

As soon as he had spoken the figure began to vanish, and the light to die away from the landscape. Maskull's emotion slowly subsided, but it was not until he was once more in complete darkness that he became master of himself again. Then he felt ashamed of his boyish exhibition of enthusiasm, and thought ruefully that there must be something wanting in his character. He got up on to his feet.

The very moment that he arose, a man's voice sounded, not a yard from his ear. It was hardly raised above a whisper, but he could distinguish that it was not Corpang's. As he listened he was unable to prevent himself from physically trembling.

"Maskull, you are to die," said the unseen speaker.

"Who is speaking?"

"You have only a few hours of life left. Don't trifle the time away."

Maskull could bring nothing out.

"You have despised life," went on the low-toned voice. "Do you really imagine that this mighty world has no meaning, and that life is a joke?"

"What must I do?"

"Repent your murders, commit no fresh ones, pay honour to . . ."

The voice died away. Maskull waited in silence for it to speak again. All remained still, however, and the speaker appeared to have taken his departure. Supernatural horror seized him; he fell into a sort of catalepsy.

At that moment he saw one of the statues *fading away*, from a pale, white glow to darkness. He had not previously seen it shining.

In a few minutes more the normal light of the land returned. Corpang got up, and shook him out of his trance. He looked round, but saw no third person.

"Whose statue was the last?" he demanded.

"Thire's."

"Did you hear me speaking?"

"I heard your voice, but no one else's."

"I've just had my death foretold, so I suppose I have not long to live. Leehallfae prophesied the same thing."

Corpang shook his head. "What value do you set on life?" he asked.

"Very little. But it's a fearful thing all the same."

"Your death is?"

"No, but this warning."

They stopped talking. A profound silence reigned. Neither of the two men seemed to know what to do next, or where to go. Then both of them heard the sound of drumming. It was slow, emphatic, and impressive, a long way off and not loud, but against the background of quietness, very marked. It appeared to come from some point out of sight, to the left of where they were standing, but on the same rock shelf. Maskull's heart beat quickly.

"What can that sound be?" asked Corpang, peering into the obscurity.

"It is Surtur."

"Once again, who is Surtur?"

Maskull clutched his arm and pressed him to silence. A strange radiance was in the air, in the direction of the drumming. It increased in intensity and gradually occupied the whole scene. Things were no longer seen by Thire's light, but by this new light. It cast no shadows.

Corpang's nostrils swelled, and he held himself more proudly.

"What fire is that?"

"It is Muspel-light."

They both glanced instinctively at the three statues. In the strange glow they had undergone a change. The face of each figure was clothed in the sordid and horrible Crystalman mask.

Corpang cried out, and put his hand over his eyes.

"What can this mean?" he asked, a minute later.

"It must mean that life is wrong, and the creator of life too, whether he is one person or three."

Corpang looked again, like a man trying to accustom himself to a shocking sight.

"Dare we believe this?"

"You must," replied Maskull. "You have always served the highest, and you must continue to do so . . . It has simply turned out that Thire is not the highest."

Corpang's face became swollen with a kind of coarse anger. "Life is clearly false . . . I have been seeking Thire for a lifetime, and now I find—this."

"You have nothing to reproach yourself with. Crystalman has had eternity to practise his cunning in, so it's no wonder if a man can't see straight, even with the best intentions. What have you decided to do?"

"The drumming seems to be moving away. Shall you follow it, Maskull?"

"Yes."

"But where will it take us?"

"Perhaps out of Threal altogether."

"It sounds to me more real than reality," said Corpang. "Tell me, who is Surtur?"

"Surtur's world, or Muspel, we are told, is the original of which this world is a distorted copy. Crystalman is life, but Surtur is other than life."

"How do you know this?"

"It has sprung together somehow . . . from inspiration, from experience, from conversation with the wise men of your planet. Every hour it grows truer for me and takes a more definite shape."

Corpang stood squarely up, facing the three Figures with a harsh, energetic countenance, stamped all over with resolution.

"I believe you, Maskull. No better proof is required than *that*. Thire is not the highest . . . he is even in a certain sense the *lowest*. Nothing but the thoroughly false and base could stoop to such deceits . . . I am coming with you—but don't play the traitor. These signs may be for you, and not for me at all, and if you leave me . . ."

"I make no promises. I don't ask you to come with me. If you prefer to stay in your little world, or if you have any doubts about it, you had better not come."

"Don't talk like that. I shall never forget your service to me . . . Let us make haste, or we shall lose the sound."

Corpang started off more eagerly than Maskull. They walked fast in the direction of the drumming. For upwards of two miles the path went along the ledge without any change of level. The mysterious radiance gradually departed, and was replaced by the normal light of Threal. The rhythmical beats continued, but a very long way ahead—they were never able to diminish the distance.

"What kind of man are you?" Corpang suddenly broke out.

"In what respect?"

"How do you come to be on such terms with the Invisible? How is it that I've never had this experience before I met you, in spite of my never-ending prayers and mortifications? In what way are you superior to me?"

"To hear voices perhaps can't be made a profession," replied Maskull. "I have a simple and unoccupied mind—that may be why I sometimes hear things which up to the present you have not been able to."

Corpang darkened, and kept silent; and then Maskull saw through to his pride.

The ledge presently began to rise. They were high above the platform on the opposite side of the gulf. The road then curved sharply to the right, and they passed over the abyss and the other ledge as by a bridge, coming out upon the top of the opposite cliffs. A new line of precipices immediately confronted them. They followed the drumming along the base of these heights, but as they were passing the mouth of a large cavern the sound came from its recesses, and they turned their steps inwards.

"This leads to the outer world," remarked Corpang. "I've occasionally been there by this passage."

"Then that's where it is taking us, no doubt. I confess I shan't be sorry to see sunlight once more."

"Can you find time to think of sunlight?" asked Corpang, with a rough smile.

"I love the sun, and perhaps I'm rather lacking in the spirit of a zealot."

"Yet, for all that, you may get *there* before me."

"Don't be bitter," said Maskull. "I'll tell you another thing. Muspel can't be willed, for the simple reason that Muspel does not concern the will. To will is a property of this world."

"Then what is your journey for?"

"It's one thing to walk to a destination, and to linger over the walk, and quite another thing to run there at top speed."

"Perhaps I'm not so easily deceived as you think," said Corpang, with another smile.

The light persisted in the cave. The path narrowed and became a steep ascent. Then the angle became one of forty-five degrees, and they had to climb. The tunnel grew so confined that Maskull was reminded of the evil dreams of his childhood.

Not long afterwards daylight appeared. They hastened to complete the last stage. Maskull rushed out first into the world of colours and, all dirty and bleeding from numerous scratches, stood blinking on a hillside, bathed in the brilliant late-afternoon sunshine. Corpang followed closely at his heels. He was obliged to shield his eyes with his hands for a few minutes, so unaccustomed was he to Branchspell's blinding rays.

"The drum-beats have stopped," he exclaimed suddenly.

"You can't expect music all the time," answered Maskull drily. "We mustn't be luxurious."

"But now we have no guide. We're no better off than before."

"Well, Tormance is a big place. But I have an infallible rule, Corpang. As I have come from the south, I always go due north."

"That will take us to Lichstorm."

Maskull gazed at the fantastically piled rocks all around them.

"I saw these rocks from Matterplay. The mountains look as far off now as they did then, and there's not much of the day left. How far is Lichstorm from here?"

Corpang looked away to the distant range. "I don't know, but unless a miracle happens we shan't get there tonight."

"I've a feeling," said Maskull, "that we shall not only get there tonight, but that tonight will be the most important in my life."

And he sat down passively to rest.

CHAPTER EIGHTEEN

Haunte

While Maskull sat, Corpang walked restlessly to and fro, swinging his arms. He had lost his staff. His face was inflamed with suppressed impatience, which accentuated its natural coarseness. At last he stopped short in front of Maskull, and looked down at him.

"What do you mean to do?"

Maskull glanced up, and idly waved his hand towards the distant mountains. "As we can't talk, we must wait."

"For what?"

"I don't know . . . How's this, though? Those peaks have changed colour, from red to green."

"Yes, the lich-wind is travelling this way."

"The lich-wind?"

"It's the atmosphere of Lichstorm. It always clings to the mountains, but when the wind blows from the north it comes as far as Threal."

"It's a sort of fog, then?"

"A peculiar sort, for they say it excites the sexual passions."

"So we are to have love-making," said Maskull, laughing.

"Perhaps you won't find it so joyous," replied Corpang, a little grimly.

"But tell me—these peaks, how do they preserve their balance?"

Corpang gazed at the distant overhanging summits, which were fast fading into obscurity.

"Passion keeps them from falling."

Maskull laughed again; he was feeling a strange disturbance of spirit. "What, the love of rock for rock?"

"It is comical, but true."

"We'll take a closer peep at them presently. Beyond the mountains is Barey, is it not?"

"Yes."

"And then the Ocean. But what is the name of that Ocean?"

"That is told only to those who die beside it."

"Is the secret so precious, Corpang?"

Branchspell was nearing the horizon in the west; there were not above two hours of daylight remaining. The air all around them became murky. It was a thin mist, neither damp nor cold. The Lichstorm range now appeared only as a blur on the sky. The air was electric and tingling, and was exciting in its effect. Maskull felt a sort of emotional inflammation, as though a very slight external cause would serve to overturn his self-control. Corpang stood silent, with a mouth like iron.

Maskull kept looking towards a high pile of rocks in the vicinity.

"That seems to me a good watchtower. Perhaps we shall see something from the top."

Without waiting for his companion's opinion, he began to scramble up the tor, and in a few minutes was standing on the summit. Corpang joined him.

From their viewpoint they saw the whole countryside sloping down to the sea, which appeared as a mere flash of far-off, glittering water. Leaving all that, however, Maskull's eyes immediately fastened themselves on a small, boat-shaped object, about two miles away, which was travelling rapidly towards them, suspended only a few feet in the air.

"What do you make of that?" he asked, in a tone of astonishment.

Corpang shook his head, and said nothing.

Within two minutes the flying object, whatever it was, had diminished the distance between them by one half. It resembled a boat more and more, but its flight was erratic, rather than smooth; its nose was continually jerking upwards

and downwards, and from side to side. Maskull now made
out a man sitting in the stern, and what looked like a large
dead animal lying amidships. As the aerial craft drew nearer,
he observed a thick, blue haze underneath it, and a similar
haze behind, but the front, facing them, was clear.

"Here must be what we are waiting for, Corpang. But
what on earth carries it?"

He stroked his beard contemplatively and then, fearing
that they had not been seen, stepped on to the highest rock,
bellowed loudly, and made wild motions with his arm. The
flying-boat, which was but a few hundred yards distant,
slightly altered its course, now heading towards them in a
way which left no doubt that the steersman had detected
their presence.

The boat slackened speed until it was travelling no faster
than a walking man, but the irregularity of its movements
continued. It was shaped rather queerly. About twenty feet
long, its straight sides tapered off from a flat bow, four
feet broad, to a sharp-angled stern. The flat bottom was
not above ten feet from the ground. It was undecked, and
carried only one living occupant; the other object they had
distinguished was really the carcass of an animal, of about
the size of a large sheep. The blue haze trailing behind
the boat appeared to emanate from the glittering point of
a short upright pole fastened in the stern. When the craft
was within a few feet of them, and they were looking down
at it in wonder from above, the man removed this pole and
covered the brightly shining tip with a cap. The forward
motion then ceased altogether, and the boat began to drift
hither and thither, but still it remained suspended in the air,
while the underneath haze persisted. Finally the broad side
came gently up against the pile of rocks on which they were
standing. The steersman jumped ashore, and immediately
clambered up to meet them.

Maskull offered him a hand, but he refused it disdainfully. He was a young man, of middle height. He wore a
close-fitting fur garment. His limbs were quite ordinary,
but his trunk was disproportionately long, and he had the

biggest and deepest chest that Maskull had ever seen in a man. His hairless face was sharp, pointed, and ugly, with protruding teeth, and a spiteful, grinning expression. His eyes and brows sloped upwards. On his forehead was an organ which looked as though it had been mutilated—it was a mere disagreeable stump of flesh. His hair was short and thin. Maskull could not name the colour of his skin, but it seemed to stand in the same relation to jale, as green to red.

Once up, the stranger stood for a minute or two, scrutinising the two companions through half-closed lids, all the time smiling insolently. Maskull was all eagerness to exchange words, but did not care to be the first to speak. Corpang stood moodily, a little in the background.

"What men are you?" demanded the aerial navigator at last. His voice was extremely loud, and possessed a most unpleasant timbre. It sounded to Maskull like a large volume of air trying to force its way through a narrow orifice.

"I am Maskull, my friend is Corpang. He comes from Threal, but where I come from, don't ask."

"I am Haunte, from Sarclash."

"Where may that be?"

"Half an hour ago I could have shown it to you, but now it has got too murky. It is a mountain in Lichstorm."

"Are you returning there now?"

"Yes."

"And how long will it take to get there in that boat?"

"Two—three hours."

"Will it accommodate us too?"

"What, are you for Lichstorm as well? What can you want there?"

"To see the sights," responded Maskull, with twinkling eyes. "But first of all to dine. I can't remember having eaten all day. You seem to have been hunting to some purpose, so we shan't lack for food."

Haunte eyed him quizzically. "You certainly don't lack impudence. However, I'm a man of that sort myself, and it is the sort I prefer. Your friend, now, would probably rather starve than ask a meal of a stranger. He looks to me just like a bewildered toad dragged up out of a dark hole."

Maskull took Corpang's arm, and constrained him to silence.

"Where have you been hunting, Haunte?"

"Matterplay. I had the worst luck—I speared one wold-horse, and there it lies."

"What is Lichstorm like?"

"There are men there, and there are women there, but there are no men-women, as with you."

"What do you call men-women?"

"Persons of mixed sex, like yourself. In Lichstorm the sexes are pure."

"I have always regarded myself as a man."

"Very likely you have; but the test is, do you hate and fear women?"

"Why, do you?"

Haunte grinned and showed his teeth. "Things are different in Lichstorm . . . So you want to see the sights?"

"I confess I am curious to see your women, for example, after what you say."

"Then I'll introduce you to Sullenbode."

He paused a moment after making this remark, and then suddenly uttered a great, bass laugh, so that his chest shook.

"Let us share the joke," said Maskull.

"Oh, you'll understand it later."

"If you play pranks with me, I shan't stand on ceremony with you."

Haunte laughed again. "I shan't be the one to play pranks . . . Sullenbode will be deeply obliged to me. If I don't visit her myself as often as she would like, I'm always glad to serve her in other ways . . . Well, you shall have your boat-ride."

Maskull rubbed his nose doubtfully.

"If the sexes hate one another in your land, is it because passion is weaker, or stronger?"

"In other parts of the world there is soft passion, but in Lichstorm there is hard passion."

"But what do you call hard passion?"

"Where men are called to women by pain, and not pleasure."

"I mean to understand, before I've finished."

"Yes," answered Haunte, with a taunting look, "it would be a pity to let the chance slip, since you're going to Lichstorm."

It was now Corpang's turn to take Maskull by the arm. "This journey will end badly."

"Why so?"

"Your goal was Muspel a short while ago; now it is women."

"Let me alone," said Maskull. "Give luck a slack rein. What brought this boat here?"

"What is this chat about Muspel?" demanded Haunte.

Corpang caught his shoulder roughly, and stared straight into his eyes. "What do you know?"

"Not much, but something, perhaps. Ask me at supper. Now it is high time to start. Navigating the mountains by night is no child's sport, let me tell you."

"I shall not forget," said Corpang.

Maskull gazed down at the boat.

"Are we to get in?"

"Gently, my friend. It's only canework and skin."

"First of all, you might enlighten me as to how you have contrived to dispense with the laws of gravitation."

Haunte smiled sarcastically. "A secret in your ear, Maskull. All laws are female. A true male is an outlaw . . . outside the law."

"I don't understand."

"The great body of the earth is continually giving out female particles, and the male parts of rocks and living bodies are equally continually trying to reach them. That's gravitation."

"Then how do you manage with your boat?"

"My two male-stones do the work. The one underneath

the boat prevents it from falling to the ground; the one in the stern shuts it off from solid objects in the rear. The only part of the boat attracted by any part of the earth is the bow, for that's the only part the light of the male-stones does not fall on. So in that direction the boat travels."

"And what are these wondrous male-stones?"

"They really are male-stones. There is nothing female in them, they are showering out male sparks all the time. These sparks devour all the female particles rising from the earth. No female particles are left over to attract the male parts of the boat, and so they are not in the least attracted in that direction."

Maskull ruminated for a minute.

"With your hunting, and boat building, and science, you seem a very handy, skilful fellow, Haunte . . . But the sun's sinking, and we'd better start."

"Get down first, then, and shift that carcass further forward. Then you and your gloomy friend can sit amidships."

Maskull immediately climbed down, and dropped himself into the boat; but then he received a surprise. The moment he stood on the frail bottom, still clinging to the rock, not only did his weight entirely disappear, as though he were floating in some heavy medium, like salt water, but the rock he held on to drew him, as by a mild current of electricity, and he was only able to withdraw his hands with difficulty.

After the first moment's shock, he quietly accepted the new order of things, and set about shifting the carcass. Since there was no weight in the boat, this was effected without any great labour. Corpang then descended. The astonishing physical change had no power to disturb his settled composure, which was founded on moral ideas. Haunte came last; grasping the staff which held the upper male-stone, he proceeded to erect it, after removing the cap. Maskull then obtained his first near view of the mysterious light, which, by counteracting the forces of nature, acted indirectly not only as elevator but as motive force. In the last ruddy gleams of the great sun, its rays were obscured, and it looked little more impressive than an extremely brilliant scintillating, blue-white jewel, but its power could be gauged by the visible, coloured mist which it threw out for many yards around.

The steering was effected by means of a shutter attached by a cord to the top of the staff, which could be so manipulated that any segment of the male-stone's rays, or all the rays, or none at all, could be shut off at will. No sooner was the staff raised than the aerial vessel quietly detached itself from the rock to which it had been drawn, and passed slowly forward in the direction of the mountains. Branchspell sank below the horizon. The gathering mist blotted out everything outside a radius of a few miles. The air grew cool and fresh.

Soon the rock masses ceased on the great, rising plain. Haunte withdrew the shutter entirely, and the boat gathered full speed.

"You say that navigation among the mountains is difficult at night," exclaimed Maskull. "I should have thought it impossible."

Haunte grunted. "You will have to take risks, and think yourself fortunate if you come off with nothing worse than a cracked skull. But one thing I can tell you—if you go on disturbing me with your chit-chat we shan't get as far as the mountains."

Thereafter Maskull was silent.

The twilight deepened, the murk grew denser. There was little to look at, but much to feel. The motion of the boat, which was due to the never-ending struggle between the male-stones and the force of gravitation, resembled in an exaggerated fashion the violent tossing of a small craft on a choppy sea. The two passengers became unhappy. Haunte, from his seat in the stern, gazed at them sardonically with one eye. The darkness now came on rapidly.

About ninety minutes after the commencement of the voyage, they arrived at the foothills of Lichstorm. They began to mount. There was no daylight left to see by.

Beneath them, however, on both sides of them, and in the rear, the landscape was lighted up for a considerable distance by the now vivid blue rays of the twin male-stones. Ahead, where these rays did not shine, Haunte was guided by the self-luminous nature of the rocks, grass, and trees. These were faintly phosphorescent; the vegetation shone out more strongly than the soil.

The moon was not shining and there were no stars; Maskull therefore inferred that the upper atmosphere was dense with mist. Once or twice, from his sensations of choking, he thought that they were entering a fogbank, but it was a strange kind of fog, for it had the effect of doubling the intensity of every light in front of them. Whenever this happened, nightmare feelings attacked him; he experienced transitory, unreasoning fright and horror.

Now they passed high above the valley which separated the foothills from the mountains themselves. The boat began an ascent of many thousand feet and, as the cliffs were near, Haunte had to manoeuvre carefully with the rear light in order to keep clear of them. Maskull watched the delicacy of his movements, not without admiration. A long time went by. It grew much colder; the air was damp and draughty. The fog began to deposit something like snow on their persons. Maskull kept sweating with terror, not on account of the danger they were in, but because of the cloudbanks which continued to envelop them.

They cleared the first line of precipices. Still mounting, but this time with a forward motion, as could be seen by the vapours illuminated by the male-stones through which they passed, they were soon altogether out of sight of solid ground. Suddenly and quite unexpectedly the moon broke through. In the upper atmosphere thick masses of fog were seen crawling hither and thither, broken in many places by thin rifts of sky, through one of which Teargeld was shining. Below them, to their left, a gigantic peak, glittering with green ice, showed itself for a few seconds, and was then swallowed up again. All the rest of the world was hidden by the mist. The moon went in again . . . Maskull had

seen quite enough to make him long for the aerial voyage
to end.

The light from the male-stones presently illuminated the
face of a new cliff. It was grand, rugged, and perpendicular. Upwards, downwards, and on both sides, it faded
imperceptibly into the night. After coasting it a little way,
they observed a shelf of rock jutting out. It was square,
measuring about a dozen feet each way. Green snow covered
it to a depth of some inches. Immediately behind it was
a dark slit in the rock, which promised to be the mouth
of a cave.

Haunte skilfully landed the boat on this platform. Standing up, he raised the staff bearing the keel-light and
lowered the other; then removed both male-stones, which
he continued to hold in his hand. His face was thrown
into strong relief by the vivid, sparkling blue-white rays.
It looked rather surly.

"Do we get out?" inquired Maskull.

"Yes. I live here."

"Thanks for the successful end of a dangerous journey."

"Yes, it has been touch-and-go."

Corpang jumped on to the platform. He was smiling
coarsely.

"There has been no danger, for our destinies lie elsewhere. You are merely a ferryman, Haunte."

"Is it so?" returned Haunte, with a most unpleasant
laugh. "I thought I was carrying men, not gods."

"Where are we?" asked Maskull

As he spoke, he got out, but Haunte remained a minute
standing in the boat.

"This is Sarclash—the second highest mountain in the
land."

"Which is the highest, then?"

"Adage. Between Sarclash and Adage there is a long
ridge—very difficult in places. About half-way along the
ridge, at the lowest point, lies the top of the Mornstab
Pass, which goes through to Barey. Now you know the lie
of the land."

"Does the woman Sullenbode live near here?"

"Near enough," grinned Haunte.

He leapt out of the boat and, pushing past the others without ceremony, walked straight into the cave.

Maskull followed, with Corpang at his heels. A few stone steps led to a doorway, curtained by the skin of some large beast. Their host pushed his way in, never offering to hold the skin aside for them. Maskull made no comment, but grabbed it with his fist and tugged it away from its fastenings to the ground. Haunte looked at the skin, and then stared hard at Maskull with his disagreeable smile, but neither said anything.

The place in which they found themselves was a large oblong cavern, with walls, floor, and ceiling of natural rock. There were two doorways; that by which they had entered, and another of smaller size directly opposite. The cave was cold and cheerless; a damp draught passed from door to door. Many skins of wild animals lay scattered on the ground. A number of lumps of sun-dried flesh were hanging on a string along a wall, and a few bulging liquor-skins reposed in a corner. There were tusks, horns, and bones everywhere. Resting against the wall were two short hunting spears, having beautiful crystal heads.

Haunte set down the two male-stones on the ground, near the farther door; their light illuminated the whole cavern. He then walked over to the meat and, snatching a large piece, began to gnaw it ravenously.

"Are we invited to the feast?" asked Maskull.

Haunte pointed to the hanging flesh and to the liquor-skins, but did not pause in his chewing.

"Where's a cup?" inquired Maskull, lifting one of the skins.

Haunte indicated a clay goblet lying on the floor. Maskull picked it up, undid the neck of the skin and, resting it under his arm, filled the cup. Tasting the liquor, he discovered it to be raw spirit. He tossed off the draught, and then felt much better.

The second cupful he proffered to Corpang. The latter

took a single sip, swallowed it, and then passed the cup back without a word. He refused to drink again, as long as they were in the cave. Maskull finished the cup, and began to throw off care.

Going to the meat-line, he took down a large double handful, and sat down on a pile of skins, to eat at his ease. The flesh was tough and coarse, but he had never tasted anything sweeter. He could not understand the flavour, which was not surprising in a world of strange animals. The meal proceeded in silence. Corpang ate sparingly, standing up, and afterwards lay down on a bundle of furs. His bold eyes watched all the movements of the other two. Haunte had not drunk as yet.

At last Maskull concluded his meal. He emptied another cup, sighed pleasantly, and prepared to talk.

"Now explain further about your women, Haunte."

Haunte fetched another skin of liquor and a second cup. He tore off the string with his teeth, and poured out and drank cup after cup in quick succession. Then he sat down, crossed his legs, and turned to Maskull.

"Well?"

"So they are objectionable?"

"They are deadly."

"Deadly? In what way can they possibly be deadly?"

"You will learn. I was watching you in the boat, Maskull. You had some bad feelings, eh?"

"I don't conceal it. There were times when I felt as if I were struggling with a nightmare. What caused it?"

"The female atmosphere of Lichstorm. Sexual passion."

"I had no passion."

"That *was* passion—the first stage. Nature tickles your people into marriage, but it tortures us. Wait till you get outside. You'll have a return of those sensations—only ten times worse. The drink you've had will see to that . . . How do you suppose it will all end?"

"If I knew, I should not be asking you questions."

Haunte laughed loudly.

"Sullenbode."

"You mean it will end in my seeking Sullenbode?"

"But what will come of it, Maskull? What will she give you? Sweet, fainting, white-armed, feminine voluptuousness . . ?"

Maskull coolly drank another cup. "And why should she give all that to a passer-by?"

"Well, as a matter of fact, she hasn't it to give. No, what she will give you, and what you'll accept from her, because you can't help it, is . . . anguish, insanity, possibly death."

"You may be talking sense, but it sounds like raving to me. Why should I accept insanity and death?"

"Because your passion will force you to."

"What about yourself?" Maskull asked, biting his nails.

"Oh, I have my male-stones. I am immune."

"Is that all that prevents your being like other men?"

"Yes, but don't attempt any tricks, Maskull."

Maskull went on drinking steadily, and said nothing for a time.

"So men and women here are hostile to each other, and love is unknown?" he proceeded at last.

"That magic word . . . Shall I tell you what love is, Maskull? Love between male and female is impossible. When Maskull loves a woman, it is Maskull's female ancestors who are loving her. But here in this land the men are pure males. They have drawn nothing from the female side."

"Where do the male-stones come from?"

"Oh, they are not freaks. There must be whole beds of the stuff somewhere. It is all that prevents the world from being a pure female world. It would be one big mass of heavy sweetness, without individual shapes."

"Yet this same sweetness is torturing to men?"

"The life of an absolute male is fierce. An excess of life is dangerous to the body. How can it be anything else than torturing?"

Corpang now sat up suddenly, and addressed Haunte. "I remind you of your promise to tell about Muspel."

Haunte regarded him with a malevolent smile.

"Ha! The underground man has come to life."

"Yes, tell us," put in Maskull carelessly.

Haunte drank, and laughed a little.

"Well, the tale's short, and hardly worth telling, but since you're interested . . . A stranger came here five years ago, inquiring after Muspel-light. His name was Lodd. He came from the east. He came up to me one bright morning in summer, outside this very cave. If you ask me to describe him—I can't imagine a second man like him. He looked so proud, noble, superior, that I felt my own blood to be dirt by comparison . . . You can guess I don't have this feeling for everyone . . . Now I am recalling him, he was not so much superior as *different*. I was so impressed that I rose and talked to him standing. He inquired the direction of the mountain Adage. He went on to say, 'They say Muspel-light is sometimes seen there. What do you know of such a thing?' I told him the truth—that I knew nothing about it, and then he went on, 'Well, I am going to Adage. And tell those who come after me on the same errand that they had better do the same thing.' That was the whole conversation. He started on his way, and I've never seen him or heard of him since."

"So you didn't have the curiosity to follow him?"

"No, because the moment he had turned his back all my interest in the man somehow seemed to vanish."

"Probably because he was useless to you."

Corpang glanced at Maskull. "Our road is marked out for us."

"So it would appear," said Maskull indifferently.

The talk flagged for a time. Maskull felt the silence oppressive, and grew restless.

"What do you call the colour of your skin, Haunte, as I saw it in daylight? It struck me as strange."

"Dolm," said Haunte.

"A compound of ulfire and blue," explained Corpang.

"Now I know. These colours are puzzling for a stranger."

"What colours have you in your world?" asked Corpang.

"Only three primary ones, but here you seem to have five, though how it comes about I can't imagine."

"There are two sets of three primary colours here," said Corpang, "but as one of the colours—blue—is identical in both sets, altogether there are five primary colours."

"Why two sets?"

"Produced by the two suns. Branchspell produces blue, yellow, and red; Alppain, ulfire, blue, and jale."

"It's remarkable that explanation has never occurred to me before."

"So here you have another illustration of the necessary trinity of nature. Blue is existence. It is darkness seen through light; a contrasting of existence and nothingness. Yellow is relation. In yellow light we see the relation of objects in the clearest way. Red is feeling. When we see red, we are thrown back on our personal feelings . . . As regards the Alppain colours, blue stands in the middle and is therefore not existence, but relation. Ulfire is existence; so it must be a different sort of existence."

Haunte yawned. "There are marvellous philosophers in your underground hole."

Maskull got up, and looked about him.

"Where does that other door lead to?"

"Better explore," said Haunte.

Maskull took him at his word, and strolled across the cave, flinging the curtain aside and disappearing into the night. Haunte rose abruptly and hurried after him.

Corpang too got to his feet. He went over to the untouched spirit-skins, untied the necks, and allowed the contents to gush out on to the floor. Next he took the hunting spears, and snapped off the points between his hands. Before he had time to resume his seat, Haunte and Maskull reappeared. The host's quick, shifty eyes at once took in what had happened. He smiled, and turned pale.

"You haven't been idle, friend."

Corpang fixed Haunte with his bold, heavy gaze. "I thought it well to draw your teeth."

Maskull burst out laughing.

"The toad's come into the light to some purpose, Haunte. Who would have expected it?"

Haunte, after staring hard at Corpang for two or three minutes, suddenly uttered a strange cry, like an evil spirit, and flung himself upon him. The two men began to wrestle like wild cats. They were as often on the floor as on their legs, and Maskull could not see who was getting the better of it. He made no attempt to separate them. A thought came into his head and, snatching up the two male-stones, he ran with them, laughing, through the upper doorway, into the open night air.

The door overlooked an abyss on another face of the mountain. A narrow ledge, sprinkled with green snow, wound along the cliff to the right; it was the only available path. He pitched the pebbles over the edge of the chasm. Although hard and heavy in his hand, they sank more like feathers than stones, and left a long trail of vapour behind. While Maskull was still watching them disappear, Haunte came rushing out of the cavern, followed by Corpang. He gripped Maskull's arm excitedly.

"What in Krag's name have you done?"

"Overboard they have gone," replied Maskull, renewing his laughter.

"You accursed madman!"

Haunte's luminous colour came and went, just as though his internal lights were breathing. Then he grew suddenly calm, by a supreme exertion of his will.

"You know this kills me?"

"Haven't you been doing your best this last hour to make me ripe for Sullenbode? Well then, cheer up, and join the pleasure party!"

"You say it as a joke, but it is the miserable truth."

Haunte's jeering malevolence had completely vanished. He looked a sick man . . . yet somehow his face had become nobler.

"I would be very sorry for you, Haunte, if it did not entail my being also very sorry for myself. We are now all three together on the same errand—which doesn't appear to have struck you yet."

"But why this errand at all?" asked Corpang quietly. "Can't you men exercise self-control till you have arrived out of danger?"

Haunte fixed him with wild eyes. "No. The phantoms come trooping in on me already."

He sat down moodily, but the next minute was up again. "And I cannot wait . . . The game is started . . ."

Soon afterwards, by silent consent, they began to walk the ledge, Haunte in front. It was narrow, ascending, and slippery, so that extreme caution was demanded. The way was lighted by the self-luminous snows and rocks.

When they had covered about half a mile, Maskull, who went second of the party, staggered, caught the cliff, and finally sat down.

"The drink works. My old sensations are returning, but worse."

Haunte turned back. "Then you are a doomed man."

Maskull, though fully conscious of his companions and situation, imagined that he was being oppressed by a black, shapeless, supernatural being, who was trying to clasp him. He was filled with horror, trembled violently, yet could not move a limb. Sweat tumbled off his face in great drops. The waking nightmare lasted a long time, but during that space it kept coming and going. At one moment the vision seemed on the point of departing; the next it almost took shape—which he knew would be his death. Suddenly it vanished altogether . . . he was free. A fresh spring breeze fanned his face, he heard the slow, solitary singing of a sweet bird, and it seemed to him as if a poem had shot together in his soul. Such flashing, heart-breaking joy he had never experienced before in all his life . . . Almost immediately that too vanished.

Sitting up, he passed his hand across his eyes, and swayed quietly, like one who has been visited by an angel.

"Your colour changed to white," said Corpang. "What happened?"

"I passed through torture to love," replied Maskull simply.

He stood up. Haunte gazed at him sombrely. "Will you not describe that passage?"

Maskull answered slowly and thoughtfully. "When I was in Matterplay, I saw heavy clouds discharge themselves and change to coloured, living animals. In the same way, my black, chaotic pangs just now seemed to consolidate themselves and spring together as a new sort of joy. The joy would not have been possible without the preliminary nightmare. It is not accidental; Nature intends it so. The truth has just flashed through my brain . . . You men of Lichstorm don't go far enough. You stop at the pangs, without realising that they are birth-pangs."

"If this is true, you're a great pioneer," muttered Haunte.

"How does this sensation differ from common love?" interrogated Corpang.

"This was all that love is, multiplied by wildness."

Corpang fingered his chin awhile. "The Lichstorm men, however, will never reach this stage, for they are too masculine."

Haunte turned pale. "Why should we alone suffer?"

"Nature is freakish and cruel, and doesn't act according to justice . . . Follow us, Haunte, and escape from it all."

"I'll see," muttered Haunte. "Perhaps I will."

"Have we far to go, to Sullenbode?" inquired Maskull.

"No, her home's under the hanging cap of Sarclash."

"What is to happen tonight?" Maskull spoke to himself, but Haunte answered him.

"Don't expect anything pleasant, in spite of what has just occurred. She is not a woman, but a mass of pure sex. Your passion will draw her out into human shape, but only for a moment. If the change were permanent you would have endowed her with a soul."

"Perhaps the change might be made permanent."

"To do that, it is not enough to desire her; she must desire you as well. But why should she desire you?"

"Nothing falls out as one expects," said Maskull, shaking his head. "We had better get on again."

They resumed the journey. The ledge still rose, but, on turning a corner of the cliff, Haunte quitted it and began to climb a steep gully, which mounted directly to the upper heights. Here they were compelled to use both hands and feet. Maskull all the while thought of nothing but the overwhelming sweetness which he had just experienced.

The flat ground on top was dry and springy. There was no more snow, and bright plants appeared. Haunte turned sharp to the left.

"This must be under the cap," said Maskull.

"It is; and within five minutes you will see Sullenbode."

When he spoke his words, Maskull's lips surprised him by their tender sensitiveness. Their action against each other sent thrills throughout his body.

The grass shone dimly. A huge tree, with glowing branches, came into sight. It bore a multitude of red fruit, like hanging lanterns, but no leaves. Underneath this tree Sullenbode was sitting. Her beautiful light—a mingling of jale and white—gleamed softly through the darkness. She sat erect, on crossed legs, asleep. She was clothed in a singular skin garment, which started as a cloak thrown over one shoulder, and ended as loose breeches, terminating above the knees. Her forearms were lightly folded, and in one hand she held a half-eaten fruit.

Maskull stood over her and looked down, deeply interested. He thought he had never seen anything half so feminine. Her flesh was almost melting in its softness. So undeveloped were the facial organs, that they looked scarcely human; only the lips were full, pouting, and expressive. In their richness, these lips seemed like a splash of vivid will on a background of slumbering protoplasm. Her hair was undressed. Its colour could not be distinguished. It was long and tangled, and had been tucked into her garment behind, for convenience.

Corpang looked calm and sullen, but both the others were visibly agitated. Maskull's heart was hammering away under his chest. Haunte pulled him, and said, "My head feels as if it were being torn from my shoulders."

"What can that mean?"

"Yet there's a horrible joy in it," added Haunte, with a sickly smile.

He put his hand on the woman's shoulder. She awoke softly, glanced up at them, smiled, and then resumed the eating of her fruit. Maskull did not imagine that she had intelligence enough to speak. Haunte suddenly dropped on his knees, and kissed her lips.

She did not repulse him. During the continuance of the kiss, Maskull noticed with a shock that her face was altering. The features emerged from their indistinctness and became human, and almost powerful. The smile faded, a scowl took its place. She thrust Haunte away, rose to her feet, and stared beneath bent brows at the three men, each one in turn. Maskull came last; his face she studied for quite a long time, but nothing indicated what she thought.

Meanwhile Haunte again approached her, staggering and grinning. She suffered him quietly; but the instant lips met lips the second time, he fell backwards with a startled cry, as though he had come in contact with an electric wire. The back of his head struck the ground, and he lay there motionless.

Corpang sprang forward to his assistance. But, when he saw what had happened, he left him where he was.

"Maskull, come here quickly!"

The light was perceptibly fading from Haunte's skin, as Maskull bent over. The man was dead. His face was unrecognisable. The head had been split from the top downwards into two halves, streaming with strange-coloured blood, as though it had received a terrible blow from an axe.

"This couldn't be from the fall," said Maskull.

"No, Sullenbode did it."

Maskull turned quickly to look at the woman. She had resumed her former attitude on the ground. The momentary intelligence had vanished from her face, and she was again smiling.

CHAPTER NINETEEN

Sullenbode

Sullenbode's naked skin glowed softly through the darkness, but the clothed part of her person was invisible. Maskull watched her senseless, smiling face, and shivered. Strange feelings ran through his body.

Corpang spoke out of the night. "She looks like an evil spirit filled with deadliness."

"It was like deliberately kissing lightning."

"Haunte was insane with passion."

"So am I," said Maskull quietly. "My body seems full of rocks, all grinding against one another."

"This is what I was afraid of."

"It appears I shall have to kiss her too."

Corpang pulled his arm. "Have you lost all manliness?"

But Maskull impatiently shook himself free. He plucked nervously at his beard, and stared at Sullenbode. His lips kept twitching. After this had gone on for a few minutes, he stepped forward, bent over the woman, and lifted her bodily in his arms. Setting her upright against the rugged tree-trunk, he kissed her.

A cold, knife-like shock passed down his frame. He thought that it was death, and lost consciousness.

When his sense returned, Sullenbode was holding him by the shoulder with one hand at arm's length, searching his face with gloomy eyes. At first he failed to recognise her; it was not the woman he had kissed, but another. Then he gradually realised that her face was identical with that which Haunte's action had called into existence. A great calmness came upon him; his bad sensations had disappeared.

Sullenbode was transformed into a living soul. Her skin was firm, her features were strong, her eyes gleamed with the consciousness of power. She was tall and slight, but slow in all her gestures and movements. Her face was not beautiful. It was long, and palely lighted, while the mouth crossed the lower half like a gash of fire. The lips were as voluptuous as before. Her brows were heavy. There was nothing vulgar in her—she looked the *kingliest* of all women. She appeared not more than five-and-twenty.

Growing tired, apparently, of his scrutiny, she pushed him a little way and allowed her arm to drop, at the same time curving her mouth into a long, bow-like smile.

"Whom have I to thank for this gift of life?"

Her voice was rich, slow, and odd. Maskull felt himself in a dream.

"My name is Maskull."

She motioned to him to come a step nearer.

"Listen, Maskull. Man after man has drawn me into the world, but they could not keep me there, for I did not wish it. But now you have drawn me into it for all time, for good or evil."

Maskull stretched a hand towards the now invisible corpse, and said quietly, "What have you to say about *him*?"

"Who was it?"

"Haunte."

"So that was Haunte. The news will travel far and wide. He was a famous man."

"It's a horrible affair. I can't think that you killed him deliberately."

"We women are endowed with terrible power, but it is our only protection. We do not want these visits; we loathe them."

"I might have died, too."

"You came together?"

"There were three of us. Corpang still stands over there."

"I see a faintly glimmering form. What do you want of me, Corpang?"

"Nothing."

"Then go away, and leave me with Maskull."

"No need, Corpang. I am coming with you."

"This is not that pleasure, then?" demanded the low, earnest voice, out of the darkness.

"No, that pleasure has not returned."

Sullenbode gripped his arm hard. "What pleasure are you speaking of?"

"A presentiment of love, which I felt not long ago."

"But what do you feel now?"

"Calm and free."

Sullenbode's face seemed like a pallid mask, hiding a slow, swelling sea of elemental passions.

"I do not know how it will end, Maskull, but we will still keep together a little. Where are you going?"

"To Adage," said Corpang, stepping forward.

"But why?"

"We are following the steps of Lodd, who went there years ago to find Muspel-light."

"What light is that?"

"It's the light of another world."

"The quest is grand. But cannot women see that light?"

"On one condition," said Corpang. "They must forget their sex. Womanhood and love belong to life, while Muspel is above life."

"I give you all other men," said Sullenbode. "Maskull is mine."

"No. I am not here to help Maskull to a lover but to remind him of the existence of nobler things."

"You are a good man. But you two alone will never strike the road to Adage."

"Are you acquainted with it?"

Again the woman gripped Maskull's arm. "What is love . . . which Corpang despises?"

Maskull looked at her attentively. Sullenbode went on, "Love is that which is perfectly willing to disappear and become nothing, for the sake of the beloved."

Corpang wrinkled his forehead. "A magnanimous female lover is new in my experience."

Maskull put him aside with his hand, and said to Sullenbode, "Are you contemplating a sacrifice?"

She gazed at her feet, and smiled.

"What does it matter what my thoughts are? . . . Tell me, are you starting at once, or do you mean to rest first? It's a rough road to Adage."

"What's in your mind?" demanded Maskull.

"I will guide you a little. When we reach the ridge between Sarclash and Adage, perhaps I shall turn back."

"And then?"

"Then if the moon shines perhaps you will arrive before daybreak, but if it is dark it's hardly likely."

"That's not what I meant. What will become of you after we have parted company?"

"I shall return somewhere . . . perhaps here."

Maskull went close up to her, in order to study her face better.

"Shall you sink back into . . . the old state?"

"No, Maskull, thank heaven."

"Then how will you live?"

Sullenbode calmly removed the hand which he had placed on her arm. There was a sort of swirling flame in her eyes.

"And who said I should go on living?"

Maskull blinked at her in bewilderment. A few moments passed before he spoke again.

"You women are a sacrificing lot. You know I can't leave you like this."

Their eyes met. Neither withdrew them, and neither felt embarrassed.

"You will always be the most generous of men, Maskull. Now let us go . . . Corpang is a single-minded personage, and the least we others—who aren't so single-minded—can do is to help him to his destination. We mustn't inquire whether the destination of single-minded men is as a rule worth arriving at."

"If it is good for Maskull, it will be good for me."

"Well, no vessel can hold more than its appointed measure."

Corpang gave a wry smile. "During your long sleep you appear to have picked up wisdom."

"Yes, Corpang, I have met many men, and explored many minds."

As they moved off, Maskull remembered Haunte.

"Can we not bury that poor fellow?"

"By this time tomorrow we shall need burial ourselves. But I do not include Corpang."

"We have no tools, so you must have your way. You killed him, but I am the real murderer. I stole his protecting light."

"Surely that death is balanced by the life you have given me." They quitted the spot in the direction opposite to that by which the three men had arrived. After a few steps, they came to green snow again. At the same time the flat ground ended, and they started to traverse a steep, pathless mountain slope. The snow and rocks glimmered, their own bodies shone; otherwise everything was dark. The mists swirled around them, but Maskull had no more nightmares. The breeze was cold, pure, and steady. They walked in file, Sullenbode leading; her movements were slow and fascinating. Corpang came last. His stern eyes saw nothing ahead but an alluring girl and a half-infatuated man.

For a long time they continued crossing the rough and rocky slope, maintaining a slightly upward course. The angle was so steep that a false step must have been fatal. The high ground was on their left. After awhile, the hillside on the left hand changed to level ground, and they seemed to have joined another spur of the mountain. The ascending slope on the right hand persisted for a few hundred yards more. Then Sullenbode bore sharply to the left, and they found level ground all around them.

"We are on the ridge," announced the woman, halting.

The others came up to her, and at the same instant the moon burst through the clouds, illuminating the whole scene.

Maskull uttered a cry. The wild, noble, lonely beauty of the view was quite unexpected. Teargeld was high in the sky to their left, shining down on them from behind. Straight in front, like an enormously wide, smoothly descending road, lay the great ridge which went on to Adage, though Adage itself was out of sight. It was never less than two hundred yards wide. It was covered with green snow, in some places entirely, but in other places the naked rocks showed through like black teeth. From where they stood they were unable to see the sides of the ridge, or what lay underneath. On the right hand, which was north, the landscape was blurred and indistinct. There were no peaks there; it was the distant, low-lying land of Barey. But on the left hand appeared a whole forest of mighty pinnacles, near and far, as far as the eye could see in moonlight. All glittered green, and all possessed the extraordinary hanging caps which characterised the Lichstorm range. These caps were of fantastic shapes, and each one was different. The valley directly opposite to them was filled with rolling mist.

Sarclash was a mighty mountain-mass in the shape of a horseshoe. Its two ends pointed west, and were separated from each other by a mile or more of empty space. The northern end became the ridge on which they stood. The southern end was the long line of cliffs on that part of the mountain where Haunte's cave was situated. The connecting curve was the steep slope they had just traversed. The peak of Sarclash was invisible.

In the south-west many mountains raised their heads. In addition, a few summits, which must have been of extraordinary height, appeared over the south side of the horseshoe.

Maskull turned round to put a question to Sullenbode, but when he saw her for the first time in moonlight the words he had framed died on his lips. The gash-like mouth no longer dominated her other features, and the face, pale as ivory and most femininely shaped, suddenly became almost beautiful. The lips were a long, womanish curve of rose-red. Her hair was a dark maroon. Maskull was greatly disturbed; he thought that she resembled a spirit, rather than a woman.

"What puzzles you?" she asked, smiling.

"Nothing. But I should like to see you by sunlight."

"Perhaps you never will."

"Your life must be most solitary."

She explored his features with her black, slow-gleaming eyes.

"Why do you fear to speak your feelings, Maskull?"

"Things seem to open up before me like a sunrise, but what it means I can't say."

Sullenbode laughed outright. "It assuredly does not mean the approach of night."

Corpang, who had been staring steadily along the ridge, here abruptly broke in.

"The road is plain now, Maskull. If you wish it, I'll go on alone."

"No, we'll go on together. Sullenbode will accompany us."

"A little way," said the woman, "but not to Adage, to pit my strength against unseen Powers. That light is not for me. I know how to renounce love, but I will never be a traitor to it."

"Who knows what we shall find on Adage, or what will happen? Corpang is as ignorant as myself."

Corpang looked him full in the face. "Maskull, you are quite well aware that you never dare approach that awful fire in the society of a beautiful woman."

Maskull gave an uneasy laugh.

"What Corpang doesn't tell you, Sullenbode, is that I am far better acquainted with Muspel-light than he, and that, but for a chance meeting with me, he would still be saying his prayers in Threal."

"Still, what he says must be true," she replied, looking from one to the other.

"And so I am not to be allowed to . . ."

"So long as I am with you, I shall urge you onwards, and not backwards, Maskull."

"We need not quarrel yet," he remarked, with a forced smile. "No doubt things will straighten themselves out."

Sullenbode began kicking the snow about with her foot.

"I picked up another piece of wisdom in my sleep, Corpang."

"Tell it me, then."

"Men who live by laws and rules are parasites. Others shed their strength to bring these laws out of nothing into the light of day, but the law-abiders live at their ease—they have conquered nothing for themselves."

"It is given to some to discover, and to others to preserve and perfect. You cannot condemn me for wishing Maskull well."

"No, but a child cannot lead a thunderstorm."

They started walking again along the centre of the ridge. All three were abreast; Sullenbode in the middle. The road descended by an easy gradient, and was for a long distance comparatively smooth. The freezing-point seemed higher than on Earth, for the few inches of snow through which they trudged felt almost warm to their naked feet. Maskull's soles were by now like tough hides. The moonlit snow was green and dazzling. Their slanting, abbreviated shadows were sharply defined, and red-black in colour. Maskull, who walked on Sullenbode's right-hand, looked constantly to the left, towards the galaxy of glorious, distant peaks.

"You cannot belong to this world," said the woman. "Men of your stamp are not to be looked for here."

"No, I have come here from Earth."

"Is that larger than our world?"

"Smaller, I think. Small, and overcrowded with men and women. With all those people, confusion would result but for orderly laws, and therefore the laws are of iron. As adventure would be impossible without encroaching on these laws, there is no longer any spirit of adventure amongst the Earthmen. Everything is safe, vulgar, and completed."

"Do men hate women there, and women men?"

"No, the meeting of the sexes is sweet, though shameful. So poignant is the sweetness that the accompanying shame is ignored, with open eyes. There is no hatred, or only among a few eccentric persons."

"That shame surely must be the rudiment of our Lichstorm passion. But now say—why did you come here?"

"To meet with new experiences, perhaps. The old ones no longer interested me."

"How long have you been in this world?"

"This is the end of my fourth day."

"Then tell me what you have seen and done during those four days. You cannot have been inactive."

"Great misfortunes have happened to me."

He proceeded briefly to relate everything that had taken place from the moment of his first awakening in the scarlet desert. Sullenbode listened, with half-closed eyes, nodding her head from time to time. Only twice did she interrupt him. After his description of Tydomin's death, she said, speaking in a low voice—"None of us women ought by right of nature to fall short of Tydomin in sacrifice. For that one act of hers, I almost love her, although she brought evil to your door." Again, speaking of Gleameil, she remarked, "That grand-souled girl I admire the most of all. She listened to her inner voice, and to nothing else besides. Which of us others is strong enough for that?"

When his tale was quite over, Sullenbode said, "Does it not strike you, Maskull, that these women you have met have been far nobler than the men?"

"I recognise that. We men often sacrifice ourselves, but only for a substantial cause. For you women almost any cause will serve. You love the sacrifice for its own sake, and that is because you are naturally noble."

Turning her head a little, she threw him a smile so proud, yet so sweet, that he was struck into silence.

They tramped on quietly for some distance, and then he said, "Now you understand the sort of man I am. Much brutality, more weakness, scant pity for anyone . . . Oh, it has been a bloody journey!"

She laid her hand on his arm.

"I, for one, would not have it less rugged."

"Nothing good can be said of my crimes."

"To me you seem like a lonely giant, searching for—you

know not what . . . The grandest that life holds . . . You at least have no cause to look up to women."

"Thanks, Sullenbode!" he responded, with a troubled smile.

"When Maskull passes, let people watch. Everyone is thrown out of your road. You go on, looking neither to right nor left."

"Take care that you are not thrown as well," said Corpang gravely.

"Maskull shall do with me whatever he pleases, old skull! And for whatever he does, I will thank him . . . In place of a heart you have a bag of loose dust. Someone has described love to you. You have had it described to you. You have heard that it is a small, fearful, selfish joy. It is not that . . . It is wild, and scornful, and sportive, and bloody . . . How should you know!"

"Selfishness has far too many disguises."

"If a woman wills to give up all, what can there be selfish in that?"

"Only do not deceive yourself. Act decisively, or fate will be too swift for you both."

Sullenbode studied him through her lashes.

"Do you mean death . . . his death as well as mine?"

"You go too far, Corpang," said Maskull, turning a shade darker. "I don't accept you as the arbiter of our fortunes."

"If honest counsel is disagreeable to you, let me go on ahead."

The woman detained him with her slow, light fingers.

"I wish you to stay with us."

"Why?"

"I think you may know what you are talking about. I don't wish to bring harm to Maskull . . . Presently I'll leave you."

"That will be best," said Corpang.

Maskull looked angry.

"I shall decide . . . Sullenbode, whether you go on, or back, I stop with you. My mind is made up."

An expression of joyousness overspread her face, in spite of her efforts to conceal it.

"Why do you scowl at me, Maskull?"

He returned no answer, but continued walking onward with puckered brows. After a dozen paces, or so, he halted abruptly.

"Wait, Sullenbode!"

The others came to a standstill. Corpang looked puzzled, but the woman smiled. Maskull, without a word, bent over and kissed her lips. Then he relinquished her body, and turned round to Corpang.

"How do you, in your great wisdom, interpret that kiss?"

"It requires no great wisdom to interpret kisses, Maskull."

"Hereafter, never dare to come between us. Sullenbode belongs to me."

"Then I say no more; but you are a fated man."

From that time forward he spoke not another word to either of the others.

A heavy gleam appeared in the woman's eyes.

"Now things are changed, Maskull. Where are you taking me?"

"Choose, you."

"The man I love must complete his journey. I won't have it otherwise. You shall not stand lower than Corpang."

"Where you go, I will go."

"And I—as long as your love endures, I will accompany you—even to Adage."

"Do you doubt its lasting?"

"I wish not to . . . Now I will tell you what I refused to tell you before. The term of your love is the term of my life. When you love me no longer, I must die."

"And why?" asked Maskull slowly.

"Yes, that's the responsibility you incurred when you kissed me for the first time. I never meant to tell you."

"Do you mean that if I had gone on alone, you would have died?"

"I have no other life but what you give me."

He gazed at her mournfully, without attempting to reply, and then slowly placed his arms around her body. During this embrace he turned very pale, but Sullenbode grew as white as chalk.

A few minutes later the journey towards Adage was resumed.

They had been walking for two hours. Teargeld was higher in the sky and nearer the south. They had descended many hundred feet, and the character of the ridge began to alter for the worse. The thin snow disappeared, and gave way to moist, boggy ground. It was all little grassy hillocks and marshes. They began to slip about and become draggled with mud. Conversation ceased; Sullenbode led the way, and the men followed in her track. The southern half of the landscape grew grander. The greenish light of the brilliant moon, shining on the multitude of snow-green peaks, caused it to appear like a spectral world. Their nearest neighbour towered high above them on the other side of the valley, due south, some five miles distant. It was a slender, inaccessible, dizzy spire of black rock, the angles of which were too steep to retain snow. A great upward-curving horn of rock sprang out from its topmost pinnacle. For a long time it constituted their chief landmark.

The whole ridge gradually became saturated with moisture. The surface soil was spongy, and rested on impermeable rock; it breathed in the damp mists by night, and breathed them out again by day, under Branchspell's rays. The walking grew first unpleasant, then difficult, and finally dangerous. None of the party could distinguish firm ground from bog. Sullenbode sank up to her waist in a pit of slime; Maskull rescued her, but after this incident took the lead himself. Corpang was the next to meet with trouble. Exploring a new path for himself, he tumbled into liquid mud up to his shoulders, and narrowly escaped a filthy death. After Maskull had got him out, at great personal risk, they proceeded once more; but now the scramble changed from bad to worse. Each step had to be thoroughly tested before weight was put upon it, and even so the test frequently failed. All of them went in so often, that in the end they no longer resembled human beings, but walking pillars plastered from top to toe with black filth. The hardest work fell to Maskull. He not only had the exhausting task of beating the way, but was continually called upon to help his companions out of their difficulties. Without him they could not have got through.

After a peculiarly evil patch, they paused to recruit their strength. Corpang's breathing was difficult, Sullenbode was quiet, listless, and depressed. Maskull gazed at them doubtfully.

"Does this continue?" he inquired.

"No, I think," replied the woman. "We can't be far from the Mornstab Pass. After that we shall begin to climb again, and then the road will improve perhaps."

"Can you have been here before?"

"Once I have been to the Pass, but it was not so bad then."

"You are tired out, Sullenbode."

"What of it?" she replied, smiling faintly. "When one has a terrible lover, one must pay the price."

"We cannot get there tonight, so let us stop at the first shelter we come to."

"I leave it to you."

He paced up and down, while the others sat.

"Do you regret anything?" he demanded suddenly.

"No, Maskull, nothing. I regret nothing."

"Your feelings are unchanged?"

"Love can't go back—it can only go on."

"Yes, eternally on. It is so."

"No, I don't mean that. There is a climax, but when the climax has been reached, love if it still wants to ascend must turn to sacrifice."

"That's a dreadful creed," he said in a low voice, turning pale beneath his coating of mud.

"Perhaps my nature is discordant . . . I am tired. I don't know what I feel."

In a few minutes they were on their feet again, and

the journey recommenced. Within half an hour they had reached the Mornstab Pass.

The ground here was drier; the broken land to the north served to drain off the moisture of the soil. Sullenbode led them to the northern edge of the ridge, to show them the nature of the country. The pass was nothing but a gigantic landslip on both sides of the ridge, where it was the lowest above the underlying land. A series of huge broken terraces of earth and rock descended towards Barey. They were overgrown with stunted vegetation. It was quite possible to get down to the lowlands that way, but rather difficult. On either side of the landslip, to east and west, the ridge came down in a long line of sheer, terrific cliffs. A low haze concealed Barey from view. Complete stillness was in the air, broken only by the distant thundering of an invisible waterfall.

Maskull and Sullenbode sat down on a boulder facing the open country. The moon was directly behind them, high up. It was almost as light as an Earth day.

"Tonight is like life," said Sullenbode.

"How so?"

"So lovely above and around us, so foul underfoot."

Maskull sighed. "Poor girl, you are unhappy?"

"And you—are you happy?"

He thought awhile, and then replied—"No. No, I'm not happy. Love is not happiness."

"What is it, Maskull?"

"Restlessness . . . unshed tears . . . thoughts too grand for our soul to think . . ."

"Yes," said Sullenbode.

After a time she asked—"Why were we created, just to live for a few years and then disappear?"

"We are told that we shall live again."

"Yes, Maskull?"

"Perhaps in Muspel," he added thoughtfully.

"What kind of life will that be?"

"Surely we shall meet again. Love is too wonderful and mysterious a thing to remain uncompleted."

She gave a slight shiver, and turned away from him. "This dream is untrue. Love is completed here."

"How can that be, when sooner or later it is brutally interrupted by Fate?"

"It is completed by anguish . . . Oh, why must it always be enjoyment for us? Can't we suffer—can't we go on suffering, for ever and ever? Maskull, until love crushes our spirit, finally and without remedy, we don't begin to feel ourselves."

Maskull gazed at her with a troubled expression.

"Can the memory of love be worth more than its presence and reality?"

"You don't understand . . . Those pangs are more precious than all the rest beside." She caught at him. "Oh, if you could only see inside my mind, Maskull! You would see strange things . . . I can't explain. It is all confused, even to myself . . . This love is quite different from what I thought."

He sighed again. "Love is a strong drink. Perhaps it is too strong for human beings. And I think that it overturns our reason in different ways."

They remained sitting side by side, staring straight before them with unseeing eyes.

"It doesn't matter," said Sullenbode at last, with a smile, getting up. "Soon it will be ended, one way or another. Come, let us be off!"

Maskull too got up.

"Where's Corpang?" he asked listlessly.

They both looked across the ridge in the direction of Adage. At the point where they stood it was nearly a mile wide. It sloped perceptibly towards the southern edge, giving all the earth the appearance of a heavy list. Towards the west the ground continued level for a thousand yards, but then a high, sloping, grassy hill went right across the ridge from side to side, like a vast billow on the verge of breaking. It shut out all further view beyond. The whole crest of this hill, from one end to the other, was crowned by a long row of enormous stone posts, shining brightly in the moonlight against a background of dark sky. There were about thirty in all, and they were placed at such regular intervals that there was little doubt that they had been set there by human hands. Some were perpendicular, but others dipped so much that an aspect of extreme antiquity was given to the entire colonnade. Corpang was seen climbing the hill, not far from the top.

"He wishes to arrive," said Maskull, watching the energetic ascent with a rather cynical smile.

"The heavens won't open for Corpang," returned Sullenbode. "He need not be in such a hurry . . . What do these pillars seem like to you?"

"They might be the entrance to some mighty temple. Who can have planted them there?"

She did not answer. They watched Corpang gain the summit of the hill, and disappear through the line of posts. Maskull turned again to Sullenbode.

"Now we two are alone in a lonely world."

She regarded him steadily. "Our last night on this earth must be a grand one. I am ready to go on."

"I don't think you are fit to go on. It will be better to go down the Pass a little, and find shelter."

She half-smiled. "We won't study our poor bodies tonight. I mean you to go to Adage, Maskull."

"Then at all events let us rest first, for it must be a long, terrible climb, and who knows what hardships we shall meet?"

She walked a step or two forward, half-turned, and held out her hand to him. "Come, Maskull!"

When they had covered half the distance which separated them from the foot of the hill, Maskull heard the drum-taps. They came from behind the hill, and were loud, sharp, almost explosive. He glanced at Sullenbode, but she appeared to hear nothing. A minute later the whole sky behind and above the long chain of stone posts on the crest of the hill began to be illuminated by a strange radiance. The moonlight in that quarter faded; the posts stood out black on a background of fire. It was the light of Muspel. As the moments passed, it grew more and more vivid, peculiar, and awful. It was of no colour, and resembled nothing—it was supernatural and indescribable. Maskull's spirit swelled. He stood fast, with expanded nostrils and terrible eyes.

Sullenbode touched him lightly.

"What do you see, Maskull?"

"Muspel-light."

"I see nothing."

The light shot up, until Maskull scarcely knew where he stood. It burned with a fiercer and stranger glare than ever before. He forgot the existence of Sullenbode. The drum-beats grew deafeningly loud. Each beat was like a rip of startling thunder, crashing through the sky and making the air tremble. Presently the crashes coalesced, and one continuous roar of thunder rocked the world. But the rhythm persisted—the four beats, with the third accented, still came pulsing through the atmosphere, only now against a background of thunder, and not of silence . . . Maskull's heart beat wildly. His body was like a prison. He longed to throw it off, to spring up and become incorporated with the sublime universe which was beginning to unveil itself . . .

Sullenbode suddenly enfolded him in her arms, and kissed him passionately, again and again. He made no response . . . he was unaware of what she was doing. She unclasped him and, with bent head and streaming eyes, went noiselessly away. She started to go back towards the Mornstab Pass.

A few minutes afterwards the radiance began to fade. The thunder died down. The moonlight reappeared, the stone posts and the hillside were again bright . . . In a short time the supernatural light had entirely vanished, but the drum-taps still sounded faintly, a muffled rhythm, from behind the hill. Maskull started violently, and stared around him like a suddenly-awakened sleeper.

He saw Sullenbode walking slowly away from him, a few hundred yards off. At that sight, death entered his heart.

He ran after her, calling out . . . She did not look round. When he had lessened the distance between them by a half, he saw her suddenly stumble and fall. She did not get up again, but lay motionless where she fell.

He flew towards her, and bent over her body . . . His worst fears were realized. Life had departed.

Beneath its coating of mud, her face bore the vulgar, ghastly Crystalman grin, but Maskull saw nothing of it. She had never appeared so beautiful to him as at that moment.

He remained beside her for a long time, on his knees. He wept . . . but, between his fits of weeping, he raised his head from time to time, and listened to the distant drum-beats.

An hour passed—two hours. Teargeld was now in the south-west. Maskull lifted Sullenbode's dead body on to his shoulders, and started to walk towards the Pass. He cared no more for Muspel. He intended to look for water in which to wash the corpse of his beloved and earth in which to bury her.

When he had reached the boulder overlooking the landslip, on which they had sat together, he lowered his burden, and placing the dead girl on the stone, seated himself beside her for a time, gazing over towards Barey.

After that, he commenced his descent of the Mornstab Pass.

CHAPTER TWENTY

Barey

The day had already dawned, but it was not yet sunrise when Maskull awoke from his miserable sleep. He sat up, and yawned feebly. The air was cool and sweet. Far away down the landslip a bird was singing; the song consisted of only two notes, but it was so plaintive and heartbreaking that he scarcely knew how to endure it.

The eastern sky was a delicate green, crossed by a long, thin band of chocolate-coloured cloud near the horizon. The atmosphere was blue-tinted, mysterious, and hazy. Neither Sarclash nor Adage was visible.

The saddle of the pass was five hundred feet above him; he had descended that distance overnight. The landslip continued downwards, like a huge flying staircase, to the upper slopes of Barey, which lay perhaps fifteen hundred feet beneath. The surface of the pass was rough, and the angle was excessively steep, though not precipitous. It was above a mile across. On each side of it, east and west, the dark walls of the ridge descended sheer. At the point where the pass sprang outwards they were two thousand feet from top to bottom, but as the ridge went upwards, on the one hand towards Adage, on the other towards Sarclash, they attained almost unbelievable heights. Despite the great breadth and solidity of the pass, Maskull felt as though he were suspended in mid-air.

The patch of broken, rich, brown soil observable not far away marked Sullenbode's grave. He had interred her by the light of the moon, with a long, flat stone for spade. A little lower down, the white steam of a hot spring was curling about in the twilight. From where he sat he was unable to see the pool into which the spring ultimately flowed, but it was in that pool that he had last night washed first of all the dead girl's body, and then his own.

He got up, yawned again, stretched himself and looked around him dully. For a long time he eyed the grave. The half-darkness changed by imperceptible degrees to full day; the sun was about to appear. The sky was nearly cloudless. The whole wonderful extent of the mighty ridge behind him began to emerge from the morning mist . . . there was a part of Sarclash, and the ice-green crest of gigantic Adage itself, which he could only take in by throwing his head right back . . . He gazed at everything in weary apathy, like a lost soul. All his desires were gone for ever . . . he wished to go nowhere, and to do nothing. He thought he would go to Barey.

He went to the warm pool, to wash the sleep out of his eyes . . . Sitting beside it, watching the bubbles, was Krag.

Maskull thought that he was dreaming. The man was clothed in a skin shirt and breeches. His face was stern, yellow, and ugly. He eyed Maskull without smiling or getting up.

"Where in the devil's name have you come from, Krag?"

"The great point is, I am here."

"Where's Nightspore?"

"Not far away."

"It seems a hundred years since I saw you. Why did you two leave me in such a damnable fashion?"

"You were strong enough to get through alone."

"So it turned out, but how were you to know? . . . Anyway, you've timed it well. It seems I am to die today."

Krag scowled. "You will die this morning."

"If I am to, I shall. But where have you heard it from?"

"You are ripe for it. You have run through the gamut. What else is there to live for?"

"Nothing," said Maskull, uttering a short laugh. "I am quite ready. I have failed in everything. I only wondered how you knew . . . So now you've come to rejoin me. Where are we going?"

"Through Barey."

"And what about Nightspore?"

Krag jumped to his feet with clumsy agility.

"We won't wait for him. He'll be there as soon as we shall."

"Where?"

"At our destination . . . Come! The sun's rising."

As they started clambering down the pass side by side, Branchspell, huge and white, leapt fiercely into the sky. All the delicacy of the dawn vanished, and another vulgar day began. They passed some trees and plants, the leaves of which were all curled up, as if in sleep.

Maskull pointed them out to his companion. "How is it the sunshine doesn't open them?"

"Branchspell is a second night to them. Their day is Alppain."

"How long will it be before that sun rises?"

"Some time yet."

"Shall I live to see it, do you think?"

"Do you want to?"

"At one time I did, but now I'm indifferent."

"Keep in that humour, and you'll do well. Once for all, there's nothing worth seeing on Tormance."

After a few minutes Maskull said, "Why did we come here, then?"

"To follow Surtur."

"True.—But where is he?"

"Closer at hand than you think, perhaps."

"Do you know that he is regarded as a god here, Krag? . . . There is supernatural fire, too, which I have been led to believe is somehow connected with him . . . Why do you keep up the mystery? Who and what is Surtur?"

"Don't disturb yourself about that. You will never know."

"Do *you* know?"

"I know," snarled Krag.

"The devil here is called Krag," went on Maskull, peering into his face.

"As long as pleasure is worshipped, Krag will always be the devil."

"Here we are, talking face-to-face, two men together . . . What am I to believe of you?"

"Believe your senses. The real devil is Crystalman."

They continued descending the landslip. The sun's rays had grown insufferably hot. In front of them, down below in the far distance, Maskull saw water and land intermingled. It appeared that they were travelling towards a lake district.

"What have you and Nightspore been doing during the last four days, Krag? What happened to the torpedo?"

"You're just about on the same mental level as a man who sees a brand-new palace, and asks what has become of the scaffolding."

"What palace have you been building, then?"

"We have not been idle," said Krag. "While you have been murdering and love-making, we have had our work."

"And how have you been made acquainted with my actions?"

"Oh, you're an open book. Now you've got a mortal heart-wound on account of a woman you knew for six hours."

Maskull turned pale.

"Sneer away, Krag! If you lived with a woman for six hundred years and saw her die, that would never touch your leather heart. You haven't even the feelings of an insect."

"Behold the child defending its toys!" said Krag, grinning faintly.

Maskull stopped short. "What do you want with me, and why did you bring me here?"

"It's no use stopping—even for the sake of theatrical effect," said Krag, pulling him into motion again. "The distance has got to be covered, however often we pull up."

When he touched him, Maskull felt a terrible shooting pain through his heart.

"I can't go on regarding you as a man, Krag. You're something more than a man . . . Whether good or evil, I can't say."

Krag looked yellow and formidable. He did not reply to Maskull's remark, but after a pause said, "So you've been trying to find Surtur on your own account, during the intervals between killing and fondling?"

"What was that drumming?" demanded Maskull.

"You needn't look so important. We know you had your ear to the keyhole. But you couldn't join the assembly . . . the music was not playing for you, my friend."

Maskull smiled rather bitterly. "At all events, I listen through no more keyholes. I have finished with life. I belong to nobody and nothing any more, from this time forward."

"Brave words, brave words! We shall see. Perhaps Crystalman will make one more attempt on you. There is still time for one more."

"Now I don't understand you."

"You think you are thoroughly disillusioned, don't you? Well, that may prove to be the last and strongest illusion of all."

The conversation ceased. They reached the foot of the landslip an hour later. Branchspell was steadily mounting the cloudless sky. It was approaching Sarclash, and it was an open question whether or not it would clear its peak. The heat was sweltering. The long, massive, saucer-shaped ridge behind them, with its terrific precipices, was glowing with bright morning colours. Adage, towering up many thousands of feet higher still, guarded the end of it like a lonely colossus. In front of them, starting from where they stood, was a cool and enchanting wilderness of little lakes and forests. The water of the lakes was dark green; the forests were asleep, waiting for the rising of Alppain.

"Are we now in Barey?" asked Maskull.

"Yes . . . and there is one of the natives."

There was an ugly glint in his eye as he spoke the words, but Maskull did not see it.

A man was leaning in the shade against one of the first trees, apparently waiting for them to come up. He was small, dark, and beardless, and was still in early manhood. He was clothed in a dark blue, loosely flowing robe, and wore a broad-brimmed slouch-hat. His face, which was not disfigured by any special organs, was pale, earnest, and grave, yet somehow remarkably pleasing.

Before a word was spoken, he warmly grasped Maskull's hand, but even while he was in the act of doing so he threw a queer frown at Krag. The latter responded with a scowling grin.

When he opened his mouth to speak, his voice was a vibrating baritone, but it was at the same time strangely womanish in its modulations and variety of tone.

"I've been waiting for you here since sunrise," he said. "Welcome to Barey, Maskull! . . . Let's hope you'll forget your sorrows here, you overtested man."

Maskull stared at him, not without friendliness.

"What made you expect me, and how do you know my name?"

The stranger smiled, which made his face very handsome. "I'm Gangnet. I know most things."

"Haven't you a greeting for me too . . . Gangnet?" asked Krag, thrusting his forbidding features almost into the other's face.

"I know you, Krag. There are few places where you are welcome."

"And I know you, Gangnet—you man-woman . . . Well, we are here together, and you must make what you can of it. We are going down to the Ocean."

The smile faded from Gangnet's face. "I can't drive you away, Krag—but I can make you the unwelcome third."

Krag threw back his head, and gave a loud, grating laugh. "That bargain suits me all right. As long as I have the substance, you may have the shadow, and much good may it do you."

"Now that it's all arranged so satisfactorily," said Maskull, with a hard smile, "permit me to say that I don't desire any society at all at present . . . You take too much for granted, Krag. You have played the false friend once already. . . . I presume I'm a free agent?"

"To be a free man, one must have a universe of one's own," said Krag with a jeering look. "What do you say, Gangnet . . . is this a free world?"

"Freedom from pain and ugliness should be every man's privilege," returned Gangnet tranquilly. "Maskull is quite within his rights, and if you'll engage to leave him I'll do the same."

"Maskull can change face as often as he likes, but he won't get rid of me so easily. Be easy on that point, Maskull."

"It doesn't matter," muttered Maskull. "Let everyone join in the procession. In a few hours I shall be finally free, anyhow, if what they say is true."

"I'll lead the way," said Gangnet. "You don't know this country, of course, Maskull. When we get to the flat lands some miles further down, we shall be able to travel by water, but at present we must walk, I fear."

"Yes, you fear—you fear!" broke out Krag, in a high-pitched, scraping voice. "You eternal loller!"

Maskull kept looking from one to the other in amazement. There seemed to be a determined hostility between the two, which indicated an intimate previous acquaintance.

They set off through a wood, keeping close to its border, so that for a mile or more they were within sight of the long, narrow lake which flowed beside it. The trees were low and thin; their dolm-coloured leaves were all folded. There was no underbrush—they walked on clean, brown earth. A distant waterfall sounded. They were in shade, but the air was pleasantly warm. There were no insects, to irritate them. The bright lake outside looked cool and poetic.

Gangnet pressed Maskull's arm affectionately.

"If the bringing of you from your world had fallen to me, Maskull, it is here I would have brought you, and not to the scarlet desert. Then you would have escaped the dark spots, and Tormance would have appeared beautiful to you."

"And what then, Gangnet? The dark spots would have existed all the same."

"You could have seen them afterwards. It makes all the difference whether one sees darkness through the light, or brightness through the shadows."

"A clear eye is the best. Tormance is an ugly world, and I greatly prefer to know it as it really is."

"The devil made it ugly, not Crystalman. These are Crystalman's thoughts, which you see around you. He is nothing but Beauty and Pleasantness . . . Even Krag won't have the effrontery to deny that."

"It's very nice here," said Krag, looking around him malignantly. "One only wants a cushion and half a dozen houris, to complete it."

Maskull disengaged himself from Gangnet.

"Last night, when I was struggling through the mud in the ghastly moonlight . . . then I thought the world beautiful . . ."

"Poor Sullenbode!" said Gangnet, sighing.

"What! You knew her?"

"I know her through you . . . By mourning for a noble woman, you show your own nobility . . . I think all women are noble."

"There may be millions of noble women, but there's only one Sullenbode."

"If Sullenbode can exist," said Gangnet, "the world cannot be a bad place."

"Change the subject . . . The world's hard and cruel, and I am thankful to be leaving it."

"On one point, though, you both agree," said Krag, smiling evilly. "Pleasure is good, and the cessation of pleasure is bad."

Gangnet glanced at him coldly. "We know your peculiar theories, Krag. You are very fond of them, but they are unworkable. The world could not go on being, without pleasure."

"So Gangnet thinks!" jeered Krag.

They came to the end of the wood, and found themselves

overlooking a little cliff. At the foot of it, about fifty feet below, a fresh series of lakes and forests commenced. Barey appeared to be one big mountain slope, built by nature into terraces. The lake along whose border they had been travelling was not banked at the end, but overflowed to the lower level in half a dozen beautiful, thread-like falls, white and throwing-off spray. The cliff was not perpendicular, and the men found it easy to negotiate.

At the base they entered another world. Here it was much denser, and they had nothing but trees all round them. A clear brook rippled through the heart of it; they followed its bank.

"It has occurred to me," said Maskull, addressing Gangnet, "that Alppain may be my death. Is that so?"

"These trees don't fear Alppain, so why should you? Alppain is a wonderful, life-bringing sun."

"The reason I ask is . . . I've seen its afterglow, and it produced such violent sensations that a little more would have proved too much."

"Because the forces were evenly balanced. When you see Alppain itself, it will reign supreme, and there will be no more struggling of wills inside you."

"And that, I may tell you beforehand, Maskull," said Krag, grinning, "is Crystalman's trump-card."

"How do you mean?"

"You'll see. You'll renounce the world so eagerly, that you'll want to stop in the world merely to enjoy your sensations."

Gangnet smiled. "Krag, you see, is hard to please. You must neither enjoy, nor renounce . . . what *are* you to do?"

Maskull turned towards Krag. "It's very odd, but I don't understand your creed even yet . . . Are you recommending suicide?"

Krag seemed to grow sallower and more repulsive every minute.

"What, because they have left off stroking you?" he exclaimed, laughing and showing his discoloured teeth.

"Whoever you are, and whatever you want," said Maskull, "you seem very certain of yourself."

"Yes, you would like me to blush and stammer like a booby, wouldn't you! That would be an excellent way of destroying lies."

Gangnet glanced towards the foot of one of the trees. He stooped and picked up two or three objects which resembled eggs.

"To eat?" asked Maskull, accepting the offered gift.

"Yes, eat them . . . you must be hungry. I want none myself and one mustn't insult Krag by offering him a pleasure—especially such a low pleasure."

Maskull knocked the ends off two of the eggs, and swallowed the liquid contents. They tasted rather alcoholic. Krag snatched the remaining egg out of his hand and flung it against a tree-trunk, where it broke and stuck, a splash of slime.

"I don't wait to be asked, Gangnet . . . Say, is there a filthier sight than a smashed pleasure?"

Gangnet did not reply, but took Maskull's arm.

After they had alternately walked through forests and descended cliffs and slopes for upwards of two hours, the landscape altered. A steep mountain side commenced and continued for at least a couple of miles, during which space the land must have dropped nearly four thousand feet, at a practically uniform gradient. Maskull had seen nothing like this immense slide of country anywhere. The hill slope carried an enormous forest on its back. This forest, however, was different from those they had hitherto passed through. The leaves of the trees were curled in sleep, but the boughs were so close and numerous that, but for the fact that they were translucent, the rays of the sun would have been completely intercepted. As it was, the whole forest was flooded with light, and this light, being tinged with the colour of the branches, was a soft and lovely rose. So gay, feminine, and dawn-like was the illumination, that Maskull's spirits immediately started to rise, although he did not wish it.

He checked himself, sighed and grew pensive.

"What a place for languishing eyes and necks of ivory, Maskull!" rasped Krag mockingly. "Why isn't Sullenbode here?"

Maskull gripped him roughly and flung him against the nearest tree. Krag recovered himself, and burst into a roaring laugh, seeming not a whit discomposed.

"Still what I said . . . was it true or untrue?"

Maskull gazed at him sternly. "You seem to regard yourself as a necessary evil. I'm under no obligation to go on with you any further. I think we had better part."

Krag turned to Gangnet with an air of grotesque mock-earnestness.

"What do *you* say . . . do we part when Maskull pleases, or when I please?"

"Keep your temper, Maskull," said Gangnet, showing Krag his back. "I know the man better than you do. Now that he has fastened on to you there's only one way of making him lose his hold . . . by ignoring him. Despise him . . . say nothing to him, don't answer his questions. If you refuse to recognise his existence, he is as good as not here."

"I'm beginning to be tired of it all," said Maskull. "It seems as if I shall add one more to my murders, before I have finished."

"I smell murder in the air," exclaimed Krag, pretending to sniff. "But whose?"

"Do as I say, Maskull. To bandy words with him is to throw oil on fire."

"I'll say no more to anyone . . . When shall we get out of this accursed forest?"

"It's some way yet, but when we're once out we can take to the water, and you will be able to rest, and think."

"And brood comfortably over your sufferings," added Krag.

None of the three men said anything more until they emerged into the open day. The slope of the forest was so steep that they were forced to run, rather than walk, and this would have prevented any conversation, even if they had otherwise felt inclined towards it. In less than half an hour they were through. A flat, open landscape lay stretched in front of them as far as they could see.

Three parts of this country consisted of smooth water. It was a succession of large, low-shored lakes, divided by narrow strips of tree-covered land. The lake immediately before them had its small end to the forest. It was there about a third of a mile wide. The water at the sides and end was shallow, and choked with dolm-coloured rushes; but in the middle, beginning a few yards from the shore, there was a perceptible current away from them. In view of this current, it was difficult to decide whether it were a lake or a river. Some little floating islands were in the shallows.

"Is it here that we take to the water?" inquired Maskull.

"Yes, here," answered Gangnet.

"But how?"

"One of those islands will serve. It only needs to move it into the stream."

Maskull frowned. "Where will it carry us to?"

"Come, get on, get on!" said Krag, laughing uncouthly. "The morning's wearing away, and you have to die before noon. We are going to the Ocean."

"If you are omniscient, Krag . . . what is my death to be?"

"Gangnet will murder you."

"You lie!" said Gangnet. "I wish Maskull nothing but good."

"At all events, he will be the cause of your death . . . But what does it matter? The great point is you are quitting this futile world . . . Well, Gangnet, I see you're as slack as ever. I suppose I must do the work."

He jumped into the lake and began to run through the shallow water, splashing it about. When he came to the nearest island, the water was up to his thighs. The island was lozenge-shaped, and about fifteen feet from end to end. It was composed of a sort of light, brown peat; there was no form of living vegetation on its surface. Krag went behind it, and started shoving it towards the current, apparently without having unduly to exert himself. When it was within the influence of the stream the others waded out to him, and all three climbed on.

The voyage began. The current was not travelling at more than two miles an hour. The sun glared down on their heads mercilessly, and there was no shade, or prospect of shade. Maskull sat down near the edge, and periodically splashed water over his head. Gangnet sat on his haunches next to him. Krag paced up and down with short, quick steps, like an animal in a cage. The lake widened out more and more, and the width of the stream increased in proportion until they seemed to themselves to be floating in the bosom of some broad, flowing estuary.

Krag suddenly bent over and snatched off Gangnet's hat, crushing it together in his hairy fist and throwing it far out into the stream.

"Why should you disguise yourself like a woman?" he asked, with a harsh guffaw. "Show Maskull your face. Perhaps he has seen it somewhere."

Gangnet did remind Maskull of someone, but he could not say of whom. His dark hair curled down to his neck, his brow was wide, lofty, and noble, and there was an air of serious sweetness about the whole man which was strangely appealing to the feelings.

"Let Maskull judge," he said, with proud composure, "whether I have anything to be ashamed of."

"There can be nothing but magnificent thoughts in that head," muttered Maskull, staring hard at him.

"A capital valuation. Gangnet is the king of poets . . . But what happens when poets try to carry through practical enterprises?"

"What enterprises?" asked Maskull in astonishment.

"What have you got on hand, Gangnet? . . . Tell Maskull."

"There are two forms of practical activity," replied Gangnet calmly. "One may either build up, or destroy."

"No, there's a third species. One may steal . . . and not even know one is stealing. One may take the purse and leave the money."

Maskull raised his eyebrows. "Where have you two met before?"

"I'm paying Gangnet a visit today, Maskull, but once upon a time Gangnet paid me a visit."

"Where?"

"In my home—wherever that is. Gangnet is a common thief."

"You are speaking in riddles, and I don't understand you. I don't know either of you, but it's clear that if Gangnet is a poet, you're a buffoon . . . Must you go on talking? I want to be quiet."

Krag laughed, but said no more. Presently he lay down at full length, with his face to the sun, and in a few minutes was fast asleep, and snoring disagreeably. Maskull kept glancing over at his yellow, repulsive face, with strong disfavour.

Two hours passed. The land on either side was more than a mile distant. In front of them there was no land at all. Behind them, the Lichstorm Mountains were blotted out from view by a haze which had gathered together. The sky ahead, just above the horizon, began to be of a strange colour. It was an intense jale-blue. The whole northern atmosphere was stained with ulfire.

Maskull's mind grew disturbed.

"Alppain is rising, Gangnet."

Gangnet smiled wistfully. "It begins to trouble you?"

"It is so solemn . . . tragical, almost . . . yet it recalls me to Earth. Life was no longer important, but this is important."

"Daylight is night to this other daylight. Within half an hour you will be like a man who has stepped from a dark forest into the open day. Then you will ask yourself how you could have been blind."

The two men went on watching the blue sunrise. The entire sky in the north, half-way up to the zenith, was streaked with extraordinary colours, among which jale and dolm predominated. Just as the principal character of an ordinary dawn is *mystery*, the outstanding character of this dawn was *wildness*. It did not baffle the understanding, but the heart. Maskull felt no inarticulate craving to seize and perpetuate the sunrise, and make it his own. Instead of that, it agitated and tormented him, like the opening bars of a supernatural symphony.

When he looked back to the south, Branchspell's day had lost its glare, and he could gaze at the immense white sun without flinching . . . He instinctively turned to the north again, as one turns from darkness to light.

"If those were Crystalman's thoughts that you showed me before, Gangnet, these must be his feelings . . . I mean it literally. What I am feeling now, he must have felt before me."

"He is all *feeling*, Maskull . . . don't you understand that?"

Maskull was feeding greedily on the spectacle before him; he did not reply. His face was set like a rock, but his eyes were dim with the beginning of tears. The sky blazed deeper and deeper . . . it was obvious that Alppain was about to lift itself above the sea. The island had by this time floated past the mouth of the estuary. On three sides they were surrounded by water. The haze crept up behind them and shut out all sight of land. Krag was still sleeping—an ugly, wrinkled monstrosity.

Maskull looked over the side at the flowing water. It had lost its dark green colour, and was now of a perfect crystal transparency.

"Are we already on the Ocean, Gangnet?"

"Yes."

"Then nothing remains except my death."

"Don't think of death, but life."

"It's growing brighter . . . at the same time, more sombre . . . Krag seems to be fading away . . ."

"There is Alppain!" said Gangnet, touching his arm.

The deep, glowing disc of the blue sun peeped above the sea. Maskull was struck to silence. He was hardly so much looking, as feeling . . . His emotions were unutterable. His soul seemed too strong for his body . . . The great blue orb rose rapidly out of the water, like an awful eye . . . watching him . . .

It shot above the sea with a bound, and Alppain's day commenced.

"What do you feel?" Gangnet still held his arm.

"I have set myself against the Infinite," muttered Maskull.

Suddenly his chaos of passions sprang together, and a wonderful idea swept through his whole being, accompanied by the intensest joy.

"Why, Gangnet . . . I am *nothing*!"

"No, you are nothing."

The mist closed in all around them. Nothing was visible except the two suns, and a few feet of sea. The shadows of the three men cast by Alppain were not black, but were composed of white daylight.

"Then nothing can hurt me," said Maskull, with a peculiar smile.

Gangnet smiled too. "How could it?"

"I have lost my will . . . I feel as if some foul tumour had been scraped away, leaving me clean and free."

"Do you now understand life, Maskull?"

Gangnet's face was transfigured with an extraordinary spiritual beauty . . . he looked as if he had descended from heaven.

"I understand nothing, except that I have no self any more . . . But this *is* life."

"Is Gangnet expatiating on his famous blue sun?" said a jeering voice above them. Looking up, they saw that Krag had got to his feet.

They both rose. At the same moment the gathering mist began to obscure Alppain's disc, changing it from blue to a vivid jale.

"What do you want with us, Krag?" asked Maskull, with simple composure.

Krag looked at him strangely for a few seconds. The water lapped around them.

"Don't you comprehend, Maskull, that your death has arrived?"

Maskull made no response. Krag rested an arm lightly on his shoulder, and suddenly he felt sick and faint. He sank to the ground, near the edge of the island-raft. His heart was thumping heavily and queerly . . . its beating reminded him of the drum-taps. He gazed languidly at the rippling water, and it seemed to him as if he could see right through it . . . away, away down . . . to a strange fire . . .

The water disappeared. The two suns were extinguished. The island was transformed into a cloud, and Maskull—alone on it—was floating through the atmosphere . . . Down below, it was all fire . . . the fire of Muspel. The light mounted higher and higher, until it filled the whole world . . .

He floated towards an immense perpendicular cliff of black rock, without top or bottom. Half-way up it Krag, suspended in mid-air, was dealing terrific blows at a blood-red spot with a huge hammer. The rhythmical, clanging sounds were hideous . . . Presently Maskull made out that these sounds were the familiar drum-beats.

"What are you doing, Krag?" he asked.

Krag suspended his work, and turned round.

"Beating on your heart, Maskull," was his grinning response.

The cliff and Krag vanished. Maskull saw Gangnet struggling in the air . . . but it was not Gangnet—it was Crystalman. He seemed to be trying to escape from the Muspel-fire, which kept surrounding and licking him, whichever way he turned. He was screaming . . . The fire caught him. He shrieked horribly. Maskull caught one glimpse of a vulgar, slobbering face . . . and then that too disappeared.

He opened his eyes. The floating-island was still faintly illuminated by Alppain. Krag was standing by his side, but Gangnet was no longer there.

"What is this Ocean called?" asked Maskull, bringing out the words with difficulty.

"Surtur's Ocean."

Maskull nodded, and kept quiet for some time. He rested his face on his arm.

"Where's Nightspore?" he asked suddenly.

Krag bent over him, with a grave expression.

"You are Nightspore."

The dying man closed his eyes, and smiled.

Opening them again, a few moments later, with an effort, he murmured, "Who are you?"

Krag maintained a gloomy silence.

Shortly afterwards a frightful pang passed through Maskull's heart, and he died immediately.

Krag turned his head round. "The night is really past at last, Nightspore . . . The day is here."

Nightspore gazed long and earnestly at Maskull's body.

"Why was all this necessary?"

"Ask Crystalman," replied Krag sternly. "His world is no joke. He has a strong clutch . . . but I have a stronger . . . Maskull was his, but Nightspore is mine."

CHAPTER TWENTY ONE

Muspel

The fog thickened so, that the two suns wholly disappeared, and all grew as black as night. Nightspore could no longer see his companion. The water lapped gently against the side of the island-raft.

"You say the night is past," said Nightspore. "But the night is still here. Am I dead, or alive?"

"You are still in Crystalman's world, but you belong to it no more. We are approaching Muspel."

Nightspore felt a strong, silent throbbing of the air . . . a rhythmical pulsation, in four-time.

"There is the drumming," he exclaimed.

"Do you understand it, or have you forgotten?"

"I half-understand it, but I'm all confused."

"It's evident Crystalman has dug his claws into you pretty deeply," said Krag. "The sound comes from Muspel, but the rhythm is caused by its travelling through Crystalman's atmosphere. His nature is rhythm as he loves to call it . . . or dull, deadly repetition, as I name it.

"I remember," said Nightspore, biting his nails in the dark.

The throbbing became audible; it now sounded like a distant drum. A small patch of strange light in the far distance, straight ahead of them, began faintly to illuminate the floating island and the glassy sea around it.

"Do all men escape from that ghastly world . . . or only I, and a few like me?" asked Nightspore.

"If all escaped, I shouldn't sweat, my friend . . . There's hard work, and anguish, and the risk of total death, waiting for us *yonder*."

Nightspore's heart sank. "Have I not yet finished, then?"

"If you wish it. You have got through. But will you wish it?"

The drumming grew loud and painful. The light resolved itself into a tiny oblong of mysterious brightness in a huge wall of night. Krag's grim and rock-like features were revealed.

"I can't face rebirth," said Nightspore. "The horror of death is nothing to it."

"You will choose."

"I can do nothing. Crystalman is too powerful. I barely escaped with my own soul."

"You are still stupid with earth-fumes, and see nothing straight," said Krag.

Nightspore made no reply, but seemed to be trying to recall something. The water around them was so still, colourless, and transparent, that they scarcely seemed to be borne up by liquid matter at all. Maskull's corpse had disappeared.

The drumming was now like the clanging of iron. The oblong patch of light grew much bigger; it burned, fierce and wild. The darkness above, below, and on either side of it, began to shape itself into the semblance of a huge, black wall, without bounds.

"Is that really a wall we are coming to?"

"You will soon find out. What you see is Muspel, and that light is the gate you have to enter."

Nightspore's heart beat wildly.

"Shall I remember?" he muttered.

"Yes, you'll remember."

"Accompany me, Krag, or I shall be lost."

"There is nothing for me to do in there. I shall wait outside for you."

"You are returning to the struggle?" demanded Nightspore, gnawing his fingertips.

"Yes."

"I dare not."

The thunderous clangour of the rhythmical beats struck on his head like actual blows. The light glared so vividly that he was no longer able to look at it. It had the startling irregularity of continuous lightning, but it possessed this further peculiarity—that it seemed somehow to give out not actual light, but *emotion*, seen as light. They continued to approach the wall of darkness, straight towards the door. The glass-like water flowed right against it, its surface reaching up almost to the threshold.

They could not speak any more; the noise was too deafening.

In a few minutes they were before the gateway. Nightspore turned his back and hid his eyes in his two hands, but even then he was blinded by the light. So passionate were his feelings, that his body seemed to enlarge itself. At every frightful beat of sound, he quivered violently.

The entrance was doorless. Krag jumped on to the rocky platform, and pulled Nightspore after him.

Once through the gateway, the light vanished. The rhythmical sound-blows totally ceased. Nightspore dropped his hands . . . All was dark and quiet as an opened tomb. But the air was filled with grim, burning *passion*, which was to light and sound what light itself is to opaque colour.

Nightspore pressed his hand to his heart.

"I don't know if I can endure it," he said, looking towards Krag. He *felt* his person far more vividly and distinctly than if he had been able to see them.

"Go in, and lose no time, Nightspore . . . Time here is more precious than on Earth. We can't squander the minutes. There are terrible and tragic affairs to attend to, which won't wait for us . . . Go in at once. Stop for nothing."

"Where shall I go to?" muttered Nightspore. "I have forgotten everything."

"Enter, enter! There is only one way. You can't mistake it."

"Why do you bid me go in, if I am to come out again?"

"To have your wounds healed."

Almost before the words had left his mouth, Krag sprang back on to the island-raft. Nightspore involuntarily started after him, but at once recovered himself and remained standing where he was. Krag was completely invisible; everything outside was black night.

The moment he had gone, a feeling shot up in Nightspore's heart like a thousand trumpets.

Straight in front of him, almost at his feet, was the lower end of a steep, narrow, circular flight of stone steps. There was no other way forward.

He put his foot on the bottom stair, at the same time peering aloft. He saw nothing, yet as he proceeded upwards every inch of the way was perceptible to his inner feelings. The staircase was cold, dismal, and deserted, but it seemed to him, in his exaltation of soul, like a ladder to heaven.

After he had mounted a dozen steps or so, he paused to take breath. Each step was increasingly difficult to ascend; he felt as though he were carrying a heavy man on his shoulders. It struck a familiar chord in his mind. He went on and, ten stairs higher up, came to a window set in a high embrasure.

On to this he clambered, and looked through. The window was of a sort of glass, but he could see nothing. Coming to him, however, from the world outside, a disturbance of the atmosphere struck his senses, causing his blood to run cold. At one moment it resembled a low, mocking, vulgar laugh, travelling from the ends of the earth; at the next it was like a rhythmical vibration of the air—the silent, continuous throbbing of some mighty engine. The two sensations were identical, yet different. They seemed to be related in the same manner as soul and body. After feeling them for a long time, Nightspore got down from the embrasure, and continued his ascent, having meanwhile grown very serious.

The climbing became still more laborious, and he was forced to stop at every third or fourth step, to rest his muscles and regain breath. When he had mounted another twenty stairs in this way, he came to a second window. Again he saw nothing. The laughing disturbance of the air, too, had ceased; but the atmospheric throb was now twice as distinct as before, and its rhythm had become *double*. There were two separate pulses: one was in the time of a march, the other in the time of a waltz. The first was bitter and petrifying to feel, but the second was gay, enervating, and horrible.

Nightspore spent little time at that window, for he felt that he was on the eve of a great discovery, and that something far more important awaited him higher up. He proceeded aloft. The ascent grew more and more exhausting, so much so that he had frequently to sit down, utterly crushed by his own dead-weight. Still, he got to the third window.

He climbed into the embrasure. His feelings translated themselves into vision, and he saw a sight which caused him to turn pale. A gigantic, self-luminous sphere was hanging in the sky, occupying nearly the whole of it. This sphere was composed entirely of two kinds of active beings. There were a myriad of tiny green corpuscles, varying in size from the very small to the almost indiscernible. They were not green, but he somehow saw them so. They were all striving in one direction—towards himself, towards Muspel, but were too feeble and miniature to make any headway. Their action produced the marching rhythm which he had previously felt, but this rhythm was not intrinsic in the corpuscles themselves, but was a consequence of the obstruction they met with. And, surrounding these atoms of life and light, were far larger whirls of white light which gyrated hither and thither, carrying the green corpuscles with them wherever they desired. Their whirling motion was accompanied by the waltzing rhythm. It seemed to Nightspore that the green atoms were not only being danced about against their will, but were suffering excruciating shame and degradation in consequence. The larger ones were steadier than the extremely small, a few were even almost stationary, and one was advancing in the direction it wished to go.

He turned his back to the window, buried his face in his hands, and searched in the dim recesses of his memory for an explanation of what he had just seen. Nothing came straight, but horror and wrath began to take possession of him.

On his way upwards to the next window, invisible fingers seemed to him to be squeezing his heart and twisting it about here and there; but he never dreamt of turning back. His mood was so grim that he did not once permit himself to pause. Such was his physical distress by the time that he had clambered into the recess that for several minutes he could see nothing at all . . . the world seemed to be spinning round him rapidly.

When at last he looked, he saw the same sphere as before, but now all was changed on it. It was a world of rocks, minerals, water, plants, animals, and men. He saw the whole world at one view, yet everything was so magnified that he could distinguish the smallest details of life. In the interior of every individual, of every aggregate of individuals, of every chemical atom, he clearly perceived the presence of the green corpuscles. But, according to the degree of dignity of the life-form, they were fragmentary or comparatively large. In the crystal, for instance, the green, imprisoned life was so minute as to be scarcely visible; in some men it was hardly bigger; but in other men and women it was twenty or a hundred times greater. But, great or small, it played an important part in every individual. It appeared as if the whirls of white light, which *were* the individuals, and plainly showed themselves beneath the enveloping bodies, were delighted with existence and wished only to enjoy it, but the green corpuscles were in a condition of eternal discontent, yet, blind and not knowing which way to turn for liberation, kept changing form, as though breaking a new path, by way of experiment. Whenever the old grotesque became metamorphosed into the new grotesque, it was in every case the direct work of the green atoms, trying to escape towards Muspel, but encountering immediate opposition. These subdivided sparks of living, fiery spirit were hopelessly imprisoned in a ghastly mush of soft pleasure . . . They were being effeminated and corrupted—that is to say, *absorbed* in the foul, sickly enveloping forms . . . Nightspore felt a sickening shame in his soul as he looked on at that spectacle.

His exaltation had long since vanished. He bit his nails, and understood why Krag was waiting for him below.

He mounted slowly to the fifth window. The pressure of air against him was as strong as a full gale, divested of violence and irregularity, so that he was not for an instant suffered to relax his efforts. Nevertheless, not a breath stirred.

Looking through the window, he was startled by a new sight. The sphere was still there, but between it and the Muspel world in which he was standing he perceived a dim, vast shadow, without any distinguishable shape, but somehow throwing out a scent of disgusting sweetness. Nightspore knew that it was Crystalman. A flood of fierce light—but it was not light, but passion—was streaming all the time from Muspel to the Shadow, and *through* it. When, however, it emerged on the other side, which was the sphere, the light was altered in character. It became split, as by a prism, into the two forms of life which he had previously seen—the green corpuscles and the whirls. What had been fiery spirit but a moment ago, was now a disgusting mass of crawling, wriggling individuals, each whirl of pleasure-seeking will having, as nucleus, a fragmentary spark of living green fire . . . Nightspore recollected the back-rays of Starkness, and it flashed across him with the certainty of truth that the green sparks were the back-rays, and the whirls the forward-rays, of Muspel. The former were trying desperately to return to their place of origin, but were overpowered by the brute force of the latter, which wished only to remain where they were.

The individual whirls were jostling and fighting with, and even devouring, each other. This created pain, but, whatever pain they felt, it was always pleasure that they sought. Sometimes the green sparks were strong enough for a moment to move a little way in the direction of Muspel; the whirls would then accept the movement, not only without demur, but with pride and pleasure, as if it were their own handiwork—but they never saw beyond the Shadow, they thought that they were travelling towards *it*. The instant the direct movement wearied them, as contrary to their whirling nature, they fell again to killing, dancing, and loving.

Nightspore had a foreknowledge that the sixth window would prove to be the last. Nothing would have kept him from ascending to it, for he guessed that the nature of Crystalman himself would there become manifest. Every step upwards was like a bloody life-and-death struggle. The stairs nailed him to the ground, the air pressure caused blood to gush from his nose and ears, his head clanged like an iron bell. When he had fought his way up a dozen steps, he found himself suddenly at the top; the staircase terminated in a small, bare chamber of cold stone, possessing a single window. On the other side of the apartment another short flight of stairs mounted through a trap, apparently to the roof of the building. Before ascending these stairs, Nightspore hastened to the window and stared out.

The shadow-form of Crystalman had drawn much closer to him, and filled the whole sky, but it was not a shadow of darkness, but a bright shadow. It had neither shape, nor colour, yet it in some way suggested the delicate tints of early morning. It was so nebulous that the sphere could be clearly distinguished through it; in extension, however, it was thick. The sweet smell emanating from it was strong, loathsome, and terrible . . . it seemed to spring from a sort of loose, mocking slime, inexpressibly vulgar and ignorant.

The spirit-stream from Muspel flashed with complexity

and variety. It was not below individuality, but above it. It was not the One, or the Many, but something else far beyond either. It approached Crystalman, and entered his body—if that bright mist could be called a body. It passed right through him, and the passage caused him the most exquisite pleasure. *The Muspel-stream was Crystalman's food* . . . The stream emerged from the other side on to the sphere, in a double condition. Part of it reappeared intrinsically unaltered, but shivered into a million fragments. These were the green corpuscles. In passing through Crystalman they had escaped absorption by reason of their extreme minuteness. The other part of the stream had not escaped. Its fire had been abstracted, its cement was withdrawn and, after being fouled and softened by the horrible sweetness of the host, it broke into individuals, which were the whirls of living will.

Nightspore shuddered . . . He comprehended at last how the whole world of will was doomed to eternal anguish in order that one Being might feel joy.

Presently he set foot on the final flight leading to the roof . . . for he remembered vaguely that now only that remained.

Half-way up, he fainted . . . but when he recovered consciousness he persisted, as though nothing had happened to him. As soon as his head was above the trap, breathing the free air, he had the same physical sensation as a man stepping out of water. He pulled his body up, and stood expectantly on the stone-floored roof, looking round for his first glimpse of Muspel.

There was nothing.

He was standing upon the top of a tower, measuring not above fifteen feet each way. Darkness was all around him. He sat down on the stone parapet, with a sinking heart . . . a heavy foreboding possessed him.

Suddenly, without seeing or hearing anything, he had the distinct impression that the darkness around him, on all four sides, was *grinning* . . . As soon as that happened, he understood that he was wholly surrounded by Crystalman's world, and that Muspel consisted of himself and the stone tower on which he was sitting . . .

Fire flashed in his heart . . . Millions upon millions of grotesque, vulgar, ridiculous, sweetened individuals—once *Spirit*—were calling out from their degradation and agony for salvation from Muspel . . . To answer that cry there was only himself . . . and Krag waiting below . . . and Surtur . . . but where was Surtur?

The truth forced itself upon him in all its cold, brutal reality. Muspel was no all-powerful Universe, tolerating from pure indifference the existence side by side with it of another false world, which had no right to be . . . Muspel was fighting for its life . . . against all that is most shameful and frightful—against sin masquerading as eternal beauty, against baseness masquerading as nature, against the Devil masquerading as God . . . Now he understood everything. The moral combat was no mock one, no Valhalla, where warriors are cut to pieces by day and feast by night; but a grim death-struggle in which what is worse than death—namely, spiritual death—inevitably awaited the vanquished of Muspel . . . By what means could he hold back from this horrible war!

During those moments of anguish, all thoughts of Self—the corruption of his life on Earth—were scorched out of Nightspore's soul . . . perhaps not for the first time.

After sitting a long time, he prepared to descend. Without warning, a strange, wailing cry swept over the face of the world. Starting in awful mystery, it ended with such a note of low and sordid mockery that he could not doubt for a moment whence it originated. It was the voice of Crystalman.

Krag was waiting for him on the island-raft. He threw a stern glance at Nightspore.

"Have you seen everything?"

"The struggle is hopeless," muttered Nightspore.

"Did I not say I am the stronger?"

"You may be the stronger, but he is the mightier."

"I am the stronger and the mightier. Crystalman's Empire is but a shadow on the face of Muspel. But nothing will be done without the bloodiest blows . . . What do you mean to do?"

Nightspore looked at him strangely.

"Are you not Surtur, Krag?"

"Yes."

"Yes," said Nightspore in a slow voice, without surprise. "But what is your name on Earth?"

"It is Pain."

"That, too, I must have known."

He was silent for a few minutes; then he stepped quietly on to the raft. Krag pushed off, and they proceeded into the darkness.

CANONGATE CLASSICS
TITLES IN PRINT

1. Imagined Corners by Willa Muir
   ISBN 0 86241 140 8   £3.95
2. Consider the Lilies by Iain Crichton Smith
   ISBN 0 86241 415 6   £3.95
3. Island Landfalls: Reflections from the South Seas
   by Robert Louis Stevenson
   ISBN 0 86241 144 0   £3.95
4. The Quarry Wood by Nan Shepherd
   ISBN 0 86241 141 6   £3.95
5. The Story of My Boyhood and Youth by John Muir
   ISBN 0 86241 153 X   £2.95
6. The Land of the Leal by James Barke
   ISBN 0 86241 142 4   £4.95
7. Two Worlds by David Daiches
   ISBN 0 86241 148 3   £2.95
8. Mr Alfred M.A. by George Friel
   ISBN 0 86241 163 7   £3.95
9. The Haunted Woman by David Lindsay
   ISBN 0 86241 162 9   £3.95
   Memoirs of a Highland Lady vols.I&II (complete)
   by Elizabeth Grant of Rothiemurchus
   ISBN 0 86241 396 6   £7.95
12. Sunset Song by Lewis Grassic Gibbon
    ISBN 0 86241 179 3   £3.50
13. Homeward Journey by John MacNair Reid
    ISBN 0 86241 178 5   £3.95
14. The Blood of the Martyrs by Naomi Mitchison
    ISBN 0 86241 192 0   £4.95
15. My First Summer in the Sierra by John Muir
    ISBN 0 86241 193 9   £2.95
16. The Weatherhouse by Nan Shepherd
    ISBN 0 86241 194 7   £3.95
17. Witch Wood by John Buchan
    ISBN 0 86241 202 1   £3.95
18. Ane Satyre of the Thrie Estatis by Sir David Lindsay
    ISBN 0 86241 191 2   £3.95

19. Cloud Howe by Lewis Grassic Gibbon
    ISBN 0 86241 227 7   £3.50
20. The Gowk Storm by Nancy Brysson Morrison
    ISBN 0 86241 222 6   £3.95
21. Tunes of Glory by James Kennaway
    ISBN 0 86241 223 4   £3.50
22. The Changeling by Robin Jenkins
    ISBN 0 86241 228 5   £3.95
23. A Childhood in Scotland by Christian Miller
    ISBN 0 86241 230 7   £2.95
24. The Silver Bough by F. Marian McNeill
    ISBN 0 86241 231 5   £3.95
25. Kidnapped by Robert Louis Stevenson
    ISBN 0 86241 232 2   £2.95
26. Catriona by Robert Louis Stevenson
    ISBN 0 86241 233 1   £2.95
27. Wild Harbour by Ian Macpherson
    ISBN 0 86241 234 X   £3.95
28. Linmill Stories by Robert McLellen
    ISBN 0 86241 282 X   £4.95
29. The Corn King and the Spring Queen
    by Naomi Mitchison
    ISBN 0 86241 287 0   £6.95
30. The Life of Robert Burns by Catherine Carswell
    ISBN 0 86241 292 7   £5.95
31. Dance of the Apprentices by Edward Gaitens
    ISBN 0 86241 297 8   £4.95
32. Fergus Lamont by Robin Jenkins
    ISBN 0 86241 310 9   £4.95
33. End of an Old Song by J.D. Scott
    ISBN 0 86241 311 7   £4.95
34. Grey Granite by Lewis Grassic Gibbon
    ISBN 0 86241 312 5   £3.50
35. Magnus Merriman by Eric Linklater
    ISBN 0 86241 313 3   £4.95
36. Diaries of a Dying Man by William Soutar
    ISBN 0 86241 347 8   £4.95

37. Highland River by Neil M. Gunn
    ISBN 0 86241 358 3   £4.95
38. The Exploits of Brigadier Gerard
    by Sir Arthur Conan Doyle
    ISBN 0 86241 341 9   £4.95
39. The Private Memoirs and Confessions of a Justified
    Sinner by James Hogg
    ISBN o 86241 340 0   £3.95
40. The Devil and the Giro:
    Two Centuries of Scottish Stories
    ISBN 0 86241 359 1   £7.95
41. The Highland Lady in Ireland
    by Elizabeth Grant of Rothiemurchus
    ISBN 0 86241 361 3   £6.95
42. Island on the Edge of the World:
    The Story of St Kilda by Charles Maclean
    ISBN 0 86241 388 5   £5.95
43. Divided Loyalties: A Scotswoman in Occupied France
    by Janet Teissier du Cros
    ISBN 0 86241 375 3   £6.95
44. Private Angelo by Eric Linklater
    ISBN 0 86241 376 1   £5.95
45. Three Scottish Poets: MacCaig, Morgan, Lochhead
    ISBN 0 86241 400 8   £4.95
46. The Master of Ballantrae by Robert Louis Stevenson
    ISBN 0 86241 405 9   £5.95
47. A Voyage to Arcturus by David Lindsay
    ISBN 0 86241 377 X   £5.95